THE LAST VICTORY

'I am proud of you all,' Mohandas K. Gandhi said softly. 'You have left your villages, your people, your fields and families, to come here to fight for the British Empire. Three years ago, when war was declared, I urged that we Indians should be part of it. I believed then, as I still do now, that it was important, as part of the family of this empire, that her wars should be ours.' A hand rose from the audience.

'Gandhi sahib,' Kim said. 'You advised us to fight for the empire. Now that we have done this thing, what is our reward? I do not mean mine or his, but India's. What have we gained by our deaths for India?'

'The British have promised us greater freedom in ruling our own lives,' Gandhi said.

'And you believe their promises, Gandhi sahib?'

Gandhi chuckled. 'We must believe those who hold power, until the time comes to suspend this belief.'

'Why should they give us freedom when they have benefitted so much from us?' Kim said.

'We have died in France and Belgium and Mesopotamia for them. It will not be easy for them now just to turn around and say: "you are free".'

'You're not much older than I, but quite impatient. You obviously distrust the British.'

'I have learned well from them, Gandhi sahib,' Kim said. 'Their promises are meant only for convenience.'

*Praise for T. N. Murari*

THE IMPERIAL AGENT

'This novel conjures up a quietly vivid panorama of Indian life'

*The Guardian*

'A thoroughly meaty evocation of the sub-continent in all its pullulating diversity'

*The London Daily News*

'A bold novel of high adventure'

*Liverpool Echo*

'A fascinating read for lovers of the Raj'

*North-Western Evening Mail*

'A gigantic, colourful and wondrous backcloth . . . a first-class yarn'

*Sunderland Echo*

THE LAST VICTORY

'A fine book that looks without too much old-fashioned guilt, yet with a searching eye, at our long, vivid time in India'

*Manchester Evening News*

'A powerful, action-packed adventure . . . has all the compelling attraction of its predecessor, *The Imperial Agent*'

*Sunderland Echo*

'A novel of extraordinary sweep and power'

*Books*

'There is also an appropriate flirtation with demonology, adding to the mixture an exotic and intoxicating touch of the mystical'

*The Independent*

**Also by the same author,**
**and available from NEL:**

THE SHOOTER
TAJ
THE IMPERIAL AGENT

**About the Author**

T. N. Murari has written many acclaimed novels, plays, non-fiction works and screenplays as well as being a journalist. He is the author of the best selling novel, *Taj*, which has been translated into nine languages. *The Last Victory* continues the story he started in *The Imperial Agent*.

T. N. MURARI

# THE LAST VICTORY

NEW ENGLISH LIBRARY
Hodder and Stoughton

**For my Father, In Memory**



First published in Great Britain in 1988 by New English Library hardbacks

First New English Library paperback edition 1989

The author and publishers gratefully acknowledge permission to quote 'Fate the Magician' from *The Golden Pomegranate* by J. C. E. Bowen, published by John Baker Publishers Ltd.

**British Library C.I.P.**
Murari, T. N.
The last victory.
I. Title
823[F]

ISBN 0-450-50099-3



Printed and bound in Great Britain for Hodder and Stoughton paperbacks, a division of Hodder and Stoughton Ltd., Mill Road, Dunton Green, Sevenoaks, Kent TN13 2YA (Editorial Office: 47 Bedford Square, London, WC1B 3DP) by Richard Clay Ltd., Bungay, Suffolk.
Typeset by Hewer Text Composition Services, Edinburgh

*The Spring at its source may be turned with a twig;*
*When it is grown to a river it cannot be crossed by an elephant.*
*– Sa'di*

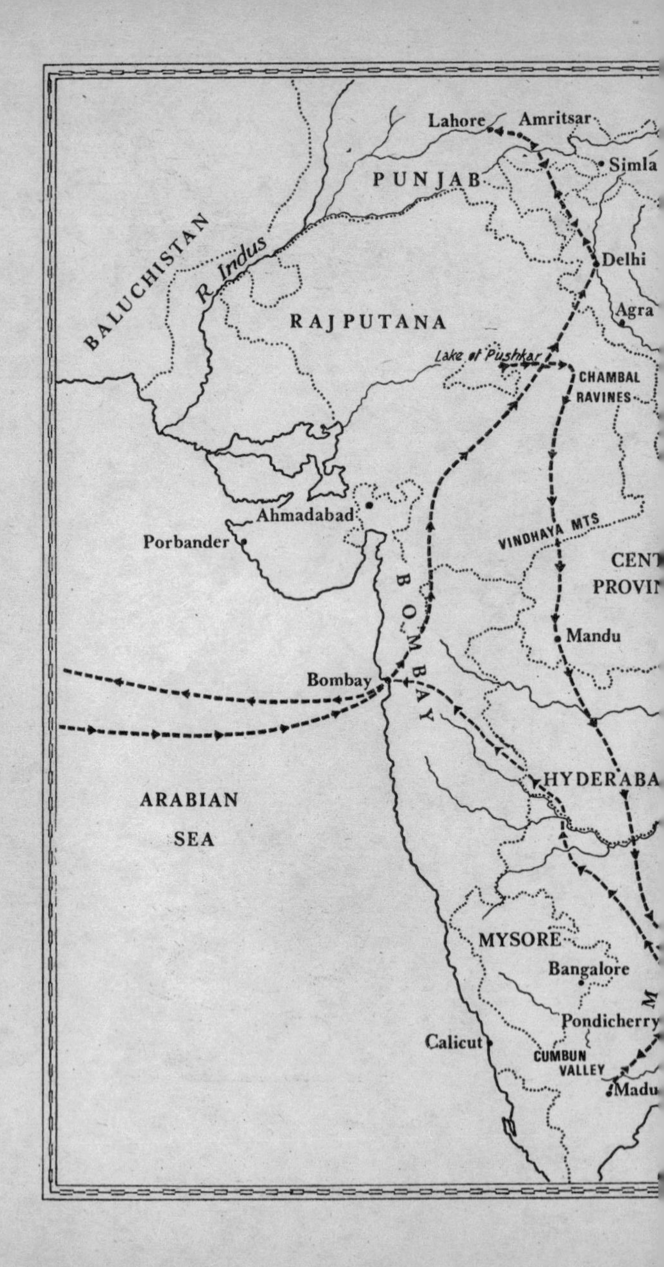
Lahore
Amritsar
Simla
PUNJAB
BALUCHISTAN
R. Indus
Delhi
Agra
RAJPUTANA
Lake of Pushkar
CHAMBAL RAVINES
Ahmadabad
Porbander
VINDHAYA MTS
BOMBAY
Mandu
Bombay
ARABIAN SEA
MYSORE
Bangalore
Pondicherry
Calicut
CUMBUN VALLEY

HIMALAYAS
NITED PROVINCES
cknow
Rae Bareli
Allahabad
R. Ganges
Benares
BIHAR &
ORISSA
Calcutta
BAY OF
BENGAL
0
300
Miles
Kim's route

# 1

# October 1910

The Colonel felt most lonely at breakfast. He now disliked a ritual which once had been pleasurable. Breakfast used to be the only meal he ate with his children.

"If I listen, I can hear them," he thought. "Their voices echo in this place, changing from shrill childhood to the deeper timbre of adults. Thank God it's only my imagination. Ghosts don't exist. If they did, and we could still hear, I'd be able to hear Richard's dying screams echoing down from the mountains . . ."

He suppressed these wounding memories and took his place at the table. There were only two chairs. The others had been taken away; he needed no painful reminders. His faced the verandah and garden, and from where he sat he could see a jacaranda tree, a bed of channas and a row of croton pots. He could watch the sparrows and seven-sisters hopping on the freshly watered lawn, listen to crows and squirrels scolding each other. He loved India most at this time, when it was full of promise and still innocent as a child. By midday it would be its true age, ancient and devious.

Abdul, his white uniform already showing stains from his morning's labour, placed the teapot on the table, bowed and returned to his position at the rear of the verandah. The *Englishman* and a buff-coloured telegram rested on the side plate. The Colonel was, even on Sunday, correctly dressed as always, in a freshly pressed linen suit, starched white shirt and regimental tie. He believed, as a European, that the native should never see him other than immaculate. Even his military moustache was trimmed daily.

The Colonel ignored the telegram as, unlike other men, he was used to telegrams. They were his daily means of communication and betokened no special urgency. He dropped it unopened into his pocket, half rose as his cousin Emma entered, and exchanged a courteous 'good morning'. Abdul brought in a tureen of porridge. Emma sat opposite, stiff and upright as a praying mantis. She was a distant and elderly widowed cousin who had managed the Colonel's household for many years. She lived a life quite separate from his, and was an almost invisible presence, hovering just within his range of vision, never intruding. She could barely be counted as company. To avoid the silence he had taken to skimming the newspaper at table.

The rambling bungalow was too large for him and Emma. When he had the time he'd look for something smaller.

He pushed away his half-empty plate, impatient to escape, excused himself, patted the dogs and strolled out onto the porch. His gharri was waiting and the syce held the door open. The gharri hadn't moved far up the road before it stopped and he heard his driver, Sen, ordering someone away. The Colonel stuck his head out of the window and saw a thickset man with an angry, sullen face holding the horse's head.

'Come here,' he ordered and opened the door. The man limped over, climbed in and squatted on the floor. Once the door was closed he couldn't be seen from the road.

'What happened?' the Colonel asked.

'Kim escaped us,' said Madan. He avoided the Colonel's eyes; they always unnerved him. Chilly, blue and circled by heavy eyebrows and pouches of skin, they reminded Madan of a predator. 'And my brother is dead.'

'I'm sorry. He was a good man.' The Colonel meant

merely that he was loyal; this surpassed other qualities. Madan's brother had been a cruel man, more dangerous than Madan.

'Who killed him?'

'Kim. I saw it with my own eyes. He would have killed me too, but I managed to escape.'

'It isn't within Kim to kill. I know him too well, like my own son. He killed only for a reason.'

'My brother killed his companion, the thin dark one.'

'Narain,' the Colonel spoke the name in a sigh. 'Narain was dear to Kim. Yes, he would kill for that. And the woman?'

'He rescued her from the island palace. There was a third man with them. I didn't see him at first but when I was running down the steps of the fortress, he came out of the shadows. He carried a sword. You didn't warn me about him.' Madan was aggrieved at this lack of intelligence. The swordsman had nearly run him through.

'I didn't know of him. Describe him.'

'He is thin and tall as a stork, with spectacles and . . .'

The Colonel silenced him. Isaac Newton. Newton was his intelligence chief in Bombay. How had he appeared in Ranthambor? He could not have followed Kim and Narain from Tihar Gaol. Or could Narain have telegraphed his uncle from Delhi to meet them there? Surely not. Which meant Newton had followed Madan and his brother from Bombay. His loyalty was now in question. Newton would have to be punished for this betrayal. Not immediately, but in time.

'Did he speak to Kim?' The Colonel asked, praying he hadn't.

'I don't know, Colonel sahib. There were two of them attacking me and I managed to escape only by the skin of my teeth.'

'They saw each other, then?'

'I think so.'

The Colonel felt helpless, not wanting to confront the inevitable. If Newton and Kim had met, then Kim knew Madan was his man. Madan had shot Kim years ago in

Bombay. It was an accident, admittedly, but Kim might have died.

'Did Kim recognise you? Was it dark?'

'It was very early morning, Colonel sahib. You could not see your hand in front of your face.'

'What difference does that make?' the Colonel said to himself aloud. He was convinced Newton had betrayed him, that Kim knew Madan was his man. 'It is a pity your brother was killed. He was a good man and not a fool like you. Can you take orders?'

'Order me, Colonel sahib. I will make no mistake again. Do you wish Kim killed? It will be done.'

'No, no, no, you fool. I never asked for Kim's death. I ordered your brother to watch and wait and follow Kim. Instead he gets himself killed and Kim now knows you work for me. Go back to where you lost sight of him. He travels with the woman and not swiftly alone. Find in which direction they are going, and report to me. Do not let him even suspect that you follow him. You understand?'

'Yes, sahib. But he will not be still in Ranthambor.'

'I know that,' the Colonel checked his exasperation. 'Ask and people will tell you. He has the woman with him. They will be noticed. This is a land that has no secrets that can't be discovered. He will probably go north. He knows the country there, and he has many friends. Many.'

'I need money,' Madan said.

The Colonel handed out a fistful of rupee coins. Madan counted them carefully before he slipped out and melted into the crowd. The Colonel hoped Madan wouldn't exceed his orders. He was headstrong and vengeful where his brother had been disciplined and dangerous, a useful tool but not perfect. Kim had killed him. He wondered how Kim, a spiritual man, would feel about this killing.

"What will Kim think now? He will know my plans and believe me to have turned against him. He won't understand that my loyalty is not to any man, even him, but to the Crown. I must use men to achieve our ends, even if it means their betrayal, their deaths. I must convince him of this loyalty, make him see that the India he loves can only be protected from chaos by England's continued rule. Once he understands this, I am sure I will win him back to serve me, serve the Crown."

The Colonel prayed he'd not lost Kim. Children one loves out of filial duty but what of the stranger? Kim was his third child, more special for being chosen than the other two. His affection for Kim was unfettered by duty; it was freely given. The pain he felt was worse than if Kim had died (for death grants forgiveness) because of Kim's disloyalty. The Colonel had chosen him, lavished attention on his upbringing; no prince could have been more fortunate. It was, admittedly, to the Colonel's advantage. The Colonel needed Kim, needed his ability to be an Indian and not an Englishman acting as one. And he believed Kim needed him to remind himself that he was British and to keep him from the squalor of an early death. The Colonel had trained him in loyalty to himself, to the Crown. They had played the great game on the North West Frontier well. But then the game had changed, and he had used Kim against India. The Colonel's mistake had been to believe that he had weaned Kim from his original mother, Mother India. The Colonel had asked him to choose and set him against his own people. But, the Colonel was certain, Kim still remained unsure of his identity. Indian? English? Kim teetered between them and was far too valuable to be discarded lightly. The Colonel had to find him, woo him again as he had done when he had first set eyes on that handsome, cheeky youth wandering in the company of an aged lama. He needed Kim even more now that India had begun to change.

The Colonel remembered the telegram and opened it, expecting a coded message. Instead it delighted him. He smiled broadly in the privacy of the gharri. 'CONGRATULATIONS ON THE ANNOUNCEMENT IN THE BIRTHDAY HONOURS LIST OF YOUR KNIGHTHOOD STOP

SUGGEST YOU IMMEDIATELY SAIL FOR ENGLAND TO RECEIVE HONOUR STOP ALSO REQUEST YOUR PRESENCE FOR IMPORTANT DISCUSSIONS STOP MORLEY.'

John Morley was the Secretary of State for India. He had visited India three years ago to work on legislative reforms with Lord Minto. Morley had wanted more Indians on the Governor's councils, until now the exclusive preserve of British advisers. The governors of the Indian provinces were almost viceroys themselves and ruled quite autocratically, having the power to veto their councils. The Indians, wealthy landlords and university graduates voted in by a limited franchise, would only have been figureheads. Lord Minto, his members in the Viceroy's Council and the Indian Civil Service, had managed to emasculate even this act of liberalism. Instead, Indians were elected only to the municipal councils. However, the Indian government had to concede to Mr Morley's appointment of an Indian to the Viceroy's Council. The Colonel, during Morley's stay in India, had been of great help to Lord Minto in successfully resisting the reforms, so the knighthood wasn't totally unexpected.

Even as he set foot in the sprawling maze of the Writers' Building, the administrative centre of the Indian government, the Colonel realised it had become common knowledge. Men shook his hand, clapped him on the back and suggested celebrations. The Indians bowed their homage. The Colonel accepted both with equal politeness and humility.

Once in his office, the elation vanished. No one really shared the joy of this honour with him. He felt empty. The feeling he had had at breakfast, that he lived among strangers, returned, together with one of regret that Richard was dead. He imagined the delight in his son's face. Richard would have whooped and danced and they would have sat up all night with champagne. The Colonel started to smile and stopped. Richard would never know.

The Colonel composed a telegram to Elizabeth on

board her ship: 'HAVE BEEN HONOURED WITH KNIGHT-HOOD STOP WILL BE SAILING FOR ENGLAND SOONEST POSSIBLE BERTH AVAILABLE STOP WILL TELEGRAPH ARRIVAL DATE AND STEAMER STOP LOVE FATHER.'

He wasn't sure what his daughter would think. They had parted with bitter words. She had been angry with him for his monstrous deceit.

The Colonel dismissed his daughter from mind. He had a mountain of work in front of him. If he had been summoned to London by the Secretary of State it was for a reason. They wanted a report, and on his advice as head of the Political and Secret Department, the Secretary and the British government would formulate a longterm policy on India. He summoned files and, though familiar with most of them, carefully re-read the intelligence reports from his agents, the police, political informants and from the secretaries of all the government departments. He worked all day, not even stopping for lunch. A peon brought him a sandwich and a pot of tea. By the end of the day, he had filled a notepad with jottings. He sat back, tired but satisfied. He believed he saw the pattern of future political movement in India, and had devised a formula which London could safely implement to contain it.

He rose and peered out of the window. The dark was velvety, with the flicker of thousands of lights. His clerks and peons waited in the outer office and he dismissed them as he passed through. He had forgotten they were waiting. The Writers' Building was deserted. His gharri awaited him under the porch and he climbed in.

'Home, sahib?' Sen called down.

'No. Dalhousie Lane.'

The gharri drew up in front of a darkened mansion. A light burned only at one window and the Colonel went over and tapped on the shutters. They opened, illuminating him in strips of light, and closed. He went to the back door and stepped inside.

'Colonel sahib, isn't it convenient I'm always at home to you?' Sushila laughed. He bent down to brush her cheek with his lips. Her skin was smooth and silken and he inhaled the subtle perfumes of sandalwood and jasmine. Her black hair was iridescent in the lamplight. She took his hand and led him to her room. He saw books scattered on her bed. 'I haven't seen you for weeks.'

'Busy, I'm afraid.' He took the whisky and water she held out for him. Her husband drank himself to death only on the best Scotch. They had lived separate lives from the day of their arranged marriage, she in Calcutta, he on his tea plantation 200 miles from the city. He was still a young man, but dying from overindulgence. The Colonel had had him investigated once, only as a precaution.

'Ah, the thankless task of running an empire. Do we natives ever appreciate your efforts, Colonel sahib?'

He frowned. Her oval face revealed only the innocent beauty which had first attracted him at the garden party in the Lieutenant Governor's residence. He still couldn't believe his good fortune. She had been in the company of other Indian ladies attending the farewell lunch party for Lord Curzon. She had smiled, so gently and softly, that at first he thought he had imagined it. 'Sometimes, Sushila, you can be too bold. I never know what mood you're in. At times you're soft and submissive; now you're trying to provoke me.'

'Colonel, no one could provoke you. I only commented on the efforts of the British to administer this country. We would make such a mess of it ourselves.'

'Of course you would,' he agreed, and saw her smile. Again beneath the sweetness he sensed the mockery. She had wanted him to agree. He laughed. 'You're in your political-freedom mood. It won't happen, my dear Sushila. You need us; we need you. We rule only because you allow us. If, as a people, you rose, there would be too few of us to control you. But I didn't come to talk politics.' He paused. 'I've been given a knighthood.'

She showed genuine delight, clapping her hands and swooping down to kiss his cheek and then linger on his mouth.

'Colonel Sir Creighton Sahib. Is that what you will be called?'

'Yes,' he assured her, not caring to correct her and spoil her pleasure. 'I've been waiting all day to come and tell you. I knew you'd be the only one to be really pleased for me. You are, aren't you?'

'Of course I am. And I have a special knighthood present for you.'

She brought out a thin packet bound in silk and handed it to him, suppressing her excitement like a child. He undid the knot. Inside was a sheaf of brittle papers. He carefully lifted one out. The writing was in Persian and on the second sheet was a beautiful water-colour, depicting a richly dressed man sitting beneath a golden canopy surrounded by courtiers. 'Those are the poems of the Emperor Jahangir. I found them through a friend. There are only a few of them that have survived the centuries, and they are very precious.'

'Jahangir,' the Colonel whispered the Great Mughal's name in awe and held the poems tenderly. He imagined the Emperor, seated on his silver throne penning them. He closed the package and thrust it back at her. 'Jahangir! No. You musn't give these to me. They're too valuable.'

'But I love you, and I want you to have them. They are my gift for all the times you have been my companion in loneliness. Please Jack, it's only a small present.'

He took the packet, reluctantly yet filled with pride. After their first meeting she had discovered his hobby was to translate Urdu and Persian poetry into English. The loving labour made him feel closer to India, made him a part of its endless history.

'I will treasure these with my life. Have you translated them?'

'I left that pleasure for you. Come, let's not waste time. It's been so long.'

Later the Colonel lay contentedly beside Sushila. With each breath, he took in the sandalwood perfume and luxuriated against the warmth of her body. He thought himself fortunate to have her; she made him feel he belonged to India and was part of it. All his life had been spent in India and at times he felt he was Indian, part of the weave of its history. And at other times, baffled, he found himself a total stranger. His thoughts drifted to Elizabeth. He had hoped her return from being educated in England would have rekindled her love for the country of her childhood. But Richard's death and that disastrous business with young Peter Bayley had forced her to flee back to England.

'I miss Elizabeth, you know' he said, and was surprised at his confession. 'You women know what is in each other's hearts. Do you think she'll forgive me?'

'She might, eventually. For a man of such wisdom, it was foolish of you to have concealed the fact that your wife was still alive. Did you really hate her so much?'

'Yes. She was an awful woman. She betrayed me and the children. A marriage should be sacred. Elizabeth just couldn't understand that her mother had broken this trust.'

'Yes, we women are always to blame, aren't we?'

'Are you taking . . . my wife's side?'

'No. I don't know her side, Jack, only yours. But men rule us with their rules, and when we break them we are punished. Yet men change those rules for their own convenience. What you are afraid of really is that Elizabeth could think her mother right and you wrong.'

'I hope not,' the Colonel said firmly. 'I'm sure Elizabeth will eventually understand. How long do you think it will take?'

'That I can't tell, Jack. She seemed a strongwilled girl. You must make the effort to persuade her.'

'I sent her a telegram to say that I would be in England soon for this knighthood.'

Sushila turned over and looked down at him.

'For how long? I'll miss you.'

'Not long. England always makes me uneasy. Will you really miss me?'

'Of course. Who else is there to make love to me?'

The Colonel would have stayed until dawn, but his

time was measured now. He had work to get done before he left for England. Sushila fell asleep at midnight, and he dressed by the flickering lamplight and let himself out. The gharri waited by the gate but the Colonel stepped past it, into the shadows where he saw a man rise at his approach.

'What do you see?' the Colonel asked the policeman.

'I myself have seen nothing, Colonel sahib.'

'Keep watching,' the Colonel climbed into the gharri, tightly gripping Jahangir's poems. He smiled to himself in the darkness, not at the pleasure of Sushila's beautiful gift, but that she was not visited by another man. He wasn't sure how he would feel if he discovered she had a lover other than himself. He had been betrayed once by a woman and he always feared it would happen again.

# 2

## October 1910

Kim's pain was emotional, not physical. He was barely aware of his surroundings, barely aware even of the woman he carried to safety. She lay still, hardly breathing, light as a child. He loved her and suspected she was dying from a spell cast on her, but even this couldn't lend urgency to his movements. He had loved one other in his life, a man whom he'd obeyed and respected as a father, a man who had guided his destiny as an Imperial agent since adolescence. He knew now that this man had deliberately manipulated and betrayed him. From the favoured position of a son he had been abruptly reduced to that of a pawn in the great game of ruling an empire. He was still shocked by this recent wound, not wanting to believe in this betrayal, yet knowing it to be the truth. The bleak landscape reflected his despair and he questioned his own worth, as would anyone who had suffered such a rejection.

"I was loyal to the Colonel sahib, I was loyal to the empire and served both faithfully. But the time came for me to choose between them and India, and I chose India. The fault lies neither entirely with the Colonel sahib nor with me. We serve the same country but to different ends. I changed. I no longer owe my blind obedience to the Colonel nor my belief to the empire. A part of my life has ended. I have lost a father, lost a calling."

High above, wheeling in great circles that encompassed half the earth, Jatayu watched over Kim. Brahma had granted Jatayu immortality for his fatal bravery against the demon Ravana and permitted him to change his form from a vulture to that of a more noble bird. The eagle watched Kim look up every now and then as he led him slowly eastwards.

An hour behind, two men, armed with rifles, jogged in pursuit. Kim looked back and, though he couldn't see them, knew they hunted him and the woman. Just rising above the horizon he saw the first wisp of smoke from the funeral pyre of his friend Narain. He hesitated, but knew he had to go on and leave the rites to Isaac Newton. Kim felt it was dishonourable to flee but the safety of the woman in his arms was more important. Silently he commended Narain's soul to God.

"What am I to believe as to this very fundamental riddle of our existence, Narain? As an Englishman I am taught to believe that your soul will rise to heaven like smoke, or descend to hell. Despite your sins in this life, I cannot believe that your soul will descend. But the Indian within me cannot accept such a simple solution to this riddle. I believe men are meant to be chained to the endless wheel of rebirth, until through their own efforts they escape and attain moksha. If such a thing as the soul exists, and men have spent centuries trying to prove this, then surely you will be permitted to evolve into a greater being. I pray that in your rebirth you will be born higher than the brahmin. I do not know who or what judges these matters so finely that he can direct a soul into the body of a cockroach or of a man, but I can only pray that you, Narain, will be reborn on a higher plane."

He looked down at Parvati, whispered her name and shook her. Her vacant amber eyes stared up at the sky. They were circled with exhaustion and the skin had turned black as though touched with kohl. Her delicate beauty was slowly setting into a death mask. Her body was fragile, brittle; he could almost crumple it to dust. There were moments when she woke from her trance and recognised him but the demons that possessed her reclaimed her immediately. His love was not enough to defeat them and set her free.

At midday he halted in the shade of a marble chaatri on the outskirts of a village. The chaatri was a small domed roof held up by six pillars and was the monument of some long forgotten prince or general; Rajputana was scattered with such memories. Parvati slept on peacefully. The heat shimmered, glazing the brown hills; the mustard fields were burning yellow and the air hummed with insects. Kim could have felt contentment if the woman who rested beside him were not in such danger. His heart ached as he looked down on her, and he felt helpless.

He waited for the heat to abate, and continued their journey. The land became harsh, brittle and dusty; goats and bony cattle scrounged coarse grass, so brown it seemed they were eating earth. Rajput villagers, the men wearing dazzling turbans of saffron and vermilion and the women in blood-red skirts, scraped and poked at the ground for sustenance.

At midnight, he halted. The land was empty; there was no village. He moved off the road to rest in a shallow ravine.

They were woken at daylight by a great clattering and banging, and a woman swearing obscenely yet poetically. Her command of language was profound and Kim lay for a moment, filled with admiration for such an imagination. Whom she swore at or what the clatter was about, barely interested him. The noise woke Parvati too. She smiled up at him and he saw her beauty in spite of the gauntness.

'Are you well?' he asked.

'Yes, for a while. God only knows for how long. I have two sorts of dreams. Those of peace and beauty, and then ugly ones that frighten me. I can't tell which are real, which not. Dreams can be our reality, and the waking our sleeping.' She caressed his face and twirled the ends of his moustache which drooped from neglect. '*You* feel real.' She sat up and peeped over the ridge.

On the road a gleaming yellow motor car stood with its bonnet open. Its headlamps were of silver, the seats of red leather. The two men standing nearby were reflected in the shining body. Sitting in the rear seat was a small woman, not much larger than a child, encrusted with jewellery and wearing a bright purple sari. Kim couldn't see her face but the voice was certainly a woman's, melodious and strong. She had still to take breath. The object of her scorn was the driver, who wore a white uniform, polished boots and a scarlet turban. He cringed and clenched his hands together, moaning for mercy. Beside him, less splendidly dressed, was the cleaner who could not hide his relief that he was not the target of the lady's anger.

'I will personally cut off your manhood and feed it to my peacocks,' she screamed. 'Your hands will be given to the monkeys and I will use your head to play polo, as my ancestors did with those who displeased them. Your mother will regret having lain with a langur and given birth to a creature as ugly and useless as you.'

Now Kim knew nothing about motor cars, but he was drawn from hiding to stare at it. He peered into a silver headlamp and saw his face twist and turn.

'And what does such a jungley want?' The woman turned on Kim. She was young but ugly, and Kim flinched at the cruelty of fate. Her nose was bent, her mouth twisted; she could have been reflected in the same headlamp that changed the shape of his face. Her eyes, however, were filled with great vitality. They dimmed the obscenity of her flesh. Also she was delicate as a bird.

'Have you never seen a motor car? Go away, go away.'

'Great queen,' Kim said. 'I came not to stare at the car but to be drowned in the beauty of your eyes.'

'You have a wise tongue. If you'd called me beautiful, I would have had you executed. But my eyes: yes, they're beautiful. Do you know anything about these machines?'

'I will look, great queen.'

He went to look at the engine. It was wondrous, but beyond all comprehension. The chauffeur stood sullenly beside him. Only Isaac Newton could have read these metallic entrails.

'Well, now that you've looked, what do you see? Or are you a badmash taking advantage of a helpless woman.'

'Maharani, no one would ever believe you to be helpless. Not with the power of such a voice and a wit to match.'

Kim saw a dangling wire and, knowing the British invented all things for a purpose, traced its path. Gingerly, he picked it up and fitted it round a copper button. It seemed the right distance for such a wire.

'What have you done?'

'If I told you, then you could do it yourself.'

'I'm not sure I like such boldness in a jungley. Who are you?'

'A man.'

'I like you less for such answers. Do you know who I am?'

'A great queen.'

'Yes. I am the Rani of Amar and you are in my state.'

'Then you should be grateful for men. All I have seen here is sand and rocks and thorns.' He ignored her snort, and told the driver, 'Start the engine.'

The chauffeur tried and immediately the car roared to life. He was a tubby man with a finely curled moustache. He gave Kim a venomous glance.

'Here,' the Rani said, removing a large ruby ring.

'I did not do it for riches. Give it to your driver who advised me so wisely.'

'You are no ordinary man. This ring would feed a village for a year.'

'And doubtless, a village starved a year to provide you with such a trinket.' The Rani slipped the ring angrily back on her finger. The driver stared ahead stonily. 'I wish one favour, Rani. I am in great haste. If you can take us but some distance, I would be grateful.'

'Why not? You will make pleasant company.'

'And the woman I travel with.'

Kim fetched Parvati from hiding.

'I will be honest with you, great queen. A spell has been cast on this woman, and her only chance to live is for her to reach the feet of the brothers Bala and Bala. They are east of here, but I do not know how far, and she is near death.'

He looked up; the Rani did too. He saw Jatayu circling, moving east. But the Rani saw only a speck in the sky circling ceaselessly, with the patience of all such predators.

Parvati namasted. She trembled from weakness but stood straight. Her spirit seemed to have returned. But if one looked closely into her eyes one saw the dread. She also looked away from the Rani's face, for it reminded her of the demons.

'I see nothing wrong with her, and I don't need a woman of her beauty to remind me of my ugliness. But she is very skinny.'

'She will veil herself from your eyes, but not from your generosity. Your eyes reflect your true beauty.'

'You have too silvery a tongue. Get in, get in. I have heard of Bala and Bala but have never heard them sing. I am told they are blind.'

'Yes. They have been blind since birth. I met them five years ago near Burhanpur and travelled with them some of the way. Their father was court musician to a rajah in southern India and was a bhakta of Lord Krishna. He prayed to Lord Krishna to give his son a wondrous voice and, when the twins were born, Lord Krishna granted the boon to them both. But, having given them such voices, he commanded that they should be heard by all of India, and since the time they could walk they have been travelling. Brahma, hearing of the boon bestowed on them by Lord Krishna, gave them sight but not sight such as you and I know, Rani. Their eyes remain shut and they see through their minds. If they both survive to their twenty-fifth year, they will lose their voices and regain their sight, and may return as ordinary mortals to their village. However, should one not survive the journey, then the other will die within a minute of his brother and their deaths will be followed by countless other deaths and great changes will happen that none can foresee. And whoever is responsible for their deaths will bring down the curse of Brahma upon their head, the heads of their family and upon the kingdom to which they belong. Though she does not remember, Parvati heard them sing in her husband's palace, and one of those songs was about us. I had told them of my search for Parvati. She gave them a message for me and with their voices they summoned Jatayu who found me and told me where to find her.'

'In the past there have been men with such voices,' the Rani said. 'There was Tansen, the Emperor Akbar's court singer, who could summon rain with his voice. And I am told that to the far south there is a temple in which the idol has turned completely around. An untouchable sang to the idol from behind the temple. The wall shattered and the idol turned so the singer could worship it.'

'I too have heard of such singers. If we are lucky, we will hear Bala and Bala sing and I pray to God their power will be great enough to drive out the demons in Parvati.'

The Rani promised to take them as far east as Pushkar, where she was to attend a marriage. She was a blunt-spoken woman and she told Kim that because of her ugliness no prince would marry her. Her mother, who had died at her birth, was a woman of great beauty and, because she had taken her mother's life, the prohit said God had cursed her with ugliness. Her father, the Rajah, was a more forgiving man than God. Her mother had been ugly within and he was relieved at her death. He was also a wise and just ruler. He had given his daughter the same education as her brother. They had had an English tutor, a Mr Weatherby, from whom she had learned not only to read and write, but also philosophy, French and geography. She played cricket, and polo too, and was a fine shot. One day her father died quite mysteriously and her brother was made Rajah by the British. Her father's death had deeply affected her, for she'd loved him and suspected that her brother had murdered him. In the same manner, a year ago, her brother had mysteriously died and the British had appointed her as ruler.

'Surely they suspected murder.'

'Surely. But the death of an Indian doesn't amount to much, unless it is to their inconvenience.' She chuckled at some secret which she didn't impart. 'Besides my brother was making such a mess. Do you know, the fool sent a letter to the Resident refusing to comply with his wishes? Naturally he denied this letter, but it sealed his fate. When he died, the government was only too happy to appoint me Rani of Amar.' She announced this title grandly, her voice rising above the roar of the machine. 'Now, who are you?'

'I am Kim, a friend of all the world. I was born in Lahore and my parents died when I was still a baby. I grew up in the bazaar. I have no family and no home.' He didn't tell her how he had met Colonel Creighton and been recruited as an Imperial agent, or that the police were hunting him.

At midday, to his surprise, he discovered that another motor car had driven ahead of them and set up a small camp, complete with a large tent for the Rani to bathe, eat and rest in comfort and privacy. This was a practice copied from the nomadic Mughal emperors. A meal had been prepared, and Kim and Parvati were invited to lunch. The tent was capacious and the Rani, bathed and changed, waved them to their places.

'She must not be given food,' Kim said. 'Give her rice water.'

'But I'm hungry,' Parvati said. 'I have a great pain in my belly.'

'Of course she must eat,' the Rani said.

'No,' Kim said. 'The food only feeds the demons. Rice water will sustain her.'

But faced with Parvati's pain and the Rani's insistence, Kim gave in. Food was piled on Parvati's silver plate and as they watched the first morsel pass her lips, she fell into her trance. The Rani cried out in fright. Kim ordered the food removed and fed her rice water. Parvati drank greedily but the demons spat it out; rice water was a thin and bitter gruel. If he had expected them to free her immediately, he was mistaken.

'I have never seen such a thing before,' the Rani said. 'Who cast this spell?'

'Her mother-in-law, Gitabhai.'

'Your mother?'

'We are not married.'

'Ahhh. She's another's wife. Whose?' The Rani loved gossip and suspected the husband would be of some importance.

'I prefer not to mention his name. He is too well known.'

The Rani graciously accepted his refusal but she carefully remembered the name of Gitabhai. The Rani rose, went to a corner of the tent in which stood an image of Durga and returned with a gold flask.

'This contains Ganges water. I will sprinkle some on her.'

The effect of the sacred water on Parvati was startling. The drops sizzled and burned the moment they fell on her skin. She screamed and writhed on the ground. Kim held her to prevent her hurting herself. Then, as suddenly, she fell silent and entered a deep, calm sleep.

'We must hurry to find these brothers,' the Rani said. 'I didn't believe you when you told me about this woman and her demons.' She clapped her hands and the car was immediately brought to the entrance of the tent.

They drove through the day and into the night, stopping only for fifteen minutes for the chauffeur to rest. Every hour, the Rani wet the end of her sari with the Ganges water and wiped Parvati's face. It acted as a balm, soothing the sleeping woman and protecting her.

They saw the lake of Pushkar gleaming in the dawn light. On the shore was a small cluster of temples. It is water that is granted sanctity by man, Kim thought, and they build temples on the shores and the water returns the sanctity to the land. The temple to Brahma was at the far end of the village and as the lane was too narrow, the motor car stopped outside the village. Already, the population of the village was seeping out to touch and stare.

'My car can travel no further,' the Rani said. 'Go with God. I pray to him that you will reach the brothers in time for them to save her.'

'Great queen, I thank you for your compassion. Surely God will bless you for this act of kindness.'

Parvati woke and stared dully. With each awakening she grew weaker. She had shrunk further; her face was all hollows. Kim picked her up and became the head of a procession. He passed many temples – to Siva, to Vishnu, to Durga, even one to Meenakshi. The narrow lane ended at the temple of Brahma. Above the entrance was a carved goose, his celestial vehicle. This, strangely, was the only temple to Brahma in all India.

'Dear Kim,' Parvati whispered. 'What suffering I have brought on you. If you did not love me, you would be free of this pain. We've spent so little time together and I know I am dying. I had lived, during our time apart, on the hope that one day my whole life would be spent by your side. My spirit will always be beside you.'

'You cannot die yet,' Kim said gently. 'We will find Bala and Bala very soon. I know they can save you.' He turned to the crowd. 'Has any among you heard of two brothers who sing so beautifully that they can turn stone to honey and still the fire and the wind?'

'Yes,' said a handsome man wearing a swollen red turban and a gold earring in each ear. Kim hadn't seen him before and he noted the wary distance between this man and the villagers. He carried a jezail and now pointed it towards the ravines. 'They are travelling east into the Chambal ravines. I have not heard them sing myself but I have heard of their miraculous voices. People travel many, many hours to hear them. I will accompany you. I am Kishore Singh.'

It was in the nature of Kim to attract strangers, men and women alike. He carried himself with jaunty dignity and in his face one readily saw the humour and piety of the man. There was no avarice written there, nor envy and, if he were willing to sacrifice himself for this woman possessed by demons, then Kishore Singh judged it worth his while to befriend Kim and help him find the brothers Bala and Bala.

The ravines were ridges of earth, like skin wrinkled in a deep frown, which stretched for nearly a hundred miles. An army could hide within their folds and for centuries dacoits had used them as a hideout.

'We can't waste time. She is nearing her end. How far are Bala and Bala?'

'A day, maybe longer. We'll find them. They travel very slowly.'

Kim followed him, carrying Parvati. It wasn't far to the edge of the ravines but the path was narrow and stony, with steep sandy walls on either side. They stopped often for Kim to rest. Kishore Singh didn't volunteer to carry Parvati. He considered it Kim's duty, his karma, to bear such a burden. Each man had his own and to share it unnecessarily was stupid.

'Dear, dear Kim,' Parvati whispered. 'You're a foolish man and I'm a foolish woman. I am always in trouble and if you did not always rescue me maybe all my troubles would cease. If you had not grabbed me on the platform at Delhi, I would have been captured by my husband's goondas. I would have ended my life then.'

'And I would have missed the delight of loving you. Don't talk. You must save your strength.'

'Oh, Kim,' she sighed. 'I feel so tired. I feel as if something inside is consuming me. I am going to die.'

By nightfall, when they halted, Kim thought they couldn't have travelled far. The landscape looked unchanged. They had followed a twisting, tortuous path and for all he knew they could well be back where they'd begun that morning. Yet he trusted Kishore Singh who moved so confidently through the maze of ridges.

'Wait here for me,' Kishore Singh said and strode into the darkness.

Kim lay back, weary. His arms ached from carrying Parvati and his throat was parched. He stared at the sky, clear and interminable, and couldn't keep his eyes open any longer. He slept, and dreamed of the mountains. He felt cold air on his face, saw the morning sun brush the snowy peaks. He heard the wind keen through the deodars and pine trees and tasted the cool waters of the mountain streams. When he drank, they numbed his lips and their icy touch tingled his cheeks.

He was woken by a sharp prod and saw the black barrel of a musket. He sat up. It was Kishore Singh. Behind him were three men, each carrying a musket. He did not introduce them.

'Bala and Bala are not far. If we leave now, we'll meet them at dawn.'

On the ground Kim saw a makeshift stretcher: two poles held together by a crude rope net. He carefully placed Parvati on it, and one of the men took one end and Kim the other. The silent procession wound through the ravines and Kim noted now an excess of caution in Kishore Singh. They stopped suddenly and Kishore Singh went gliding off into the darkness and minutes later returned to beckon them on.

'What is it?' Kim asked.

Kishore Singh didn't reply but moved even more cautiously. The ravines were black in shadow and each time they came to a rift of moonlight, they took turns to scurry across as though it were a stream of water. While the men who carried the other end of the stretcher took turns, Kim remained at Parvati's head. She was barely conscious and he worried that she might not last until dawn. She moaned once and Kishore Singh was quick to clamp a hand over her mouth. Kim wanted to tell them to hurry, hurry but he knew they were being careful for a reason. He was only certain they were moving west from the night sky. Dawn came gently, and as the stars began to fade Kishore Singh called a halt.

'Voices carry,' he whispered. 'I have an enemy in these ravines. We look for each other and pray the other will be unprepared when we meet. This man betrayed and murdered my father, Man Singh. My father was in Tihar Gaol and this man, who was his lieutenant, was meant to help him and his three companions, also one Anil Ray whom I don't know, to escape. Instead he set a trap and shot my father as he was escaping.'

'I too was in Tihar, but I never knew your father,' Kim said. 'Yet it is strange that in this cruel and desolate place, in this darkness, the name of a man I know and also helped to escape should be spoken. It's an omen. We will be bound together all our lives. It is another of my karmas. But I have no liking for Anil Ray. He is too embittered.'

It was an hour past dawn when they finally found the brothers Bala and Bala, walking east hand in hand, following the invisible line that had led them from their village in the distant south so many years earlier. The pattern of their journeying was to cross from east to west, walk north for a day, then move from west to east. In this way they traversed India and would eventually end their journey in the Himalayas. They had grown since Kim had last seen them near Burhanpur and down had sprung on their cheeks. Their faces, however, because of blindness, hadn't lost their unfinished look. The features were still soft, all but shapeless. Eyes, Kim had thought then, give the character to a face. With the blind it's impossible to see within. Bala on the right carried his ravanhatta; Bala on the left the cymbals. Their positions never changed for Bala on the right saw only the right half of the world and the other Bala saw only the left. If they should change, they would see nothing at all through their minds.

They recognised Kim and the smiles on their faces were identical.

'We thought we would meet you again,' they said in perfect unison. 'In the pattern we weave across the land, some men occur and recur in our lives. Our destiny is interwoven with the destinies of men such as you. You received the message we gave Jatayu to carry to you?'

'Yes. This is the woman who gave it to you. You must remember her. She is possessed and now near death. I know of no one who can drive these evil spirits out of her and you are my last hope. Jatayu led us to you. Look up and you will see the great bird.'

But when they all stared up at the sky, they saw nothing except the endless, cloudless blue.

'We remember her. She was in that island palace.'

They fell silent, looking neither at Parvati nor at Kim. Though their eyes were closed it was possible to feel their gaze. Kim sensed that they were conferring with each other silently. Kishore Singh and his men were too awed to notice such a subtle change in their appearance. Instead they squatted, mouths agape, staring at the boys who could see and talk in such harmony.

'We can try,' Bala and Bala announced. 'Bring her into the shade.'

Parvati was laid north-south in the shade of a tamarind tree. One brother sat at her feet, the other at her head. Her eyelids fluttered weakly, her breathing was shallow. In spite of the shade, the heat was suffocating. Kim and the men squatted to one side.

Parvati lay staring up at the sunlight winking down on her through the branches. She found it difficult to arrange her thoughts; she had never been in such danger.

"I am dying. My life wavers like those leaves. I pass from shadow to sunlight, fluttering and fragile as they. What did I do to deserve such an evil ending to my life? I am told this suffering was for my evil in a past life but I . . . the I who lies here now . . . was not responsible for that past person. Why do I bear his or her punishment? Should my wrongs be visited on a child in the next life? It is unjust. I escaped my evil husband and met Kim, who is more dear to me than this life, miserable and wretched as it is. Now I will be snatched from him. I had also re-made myself. From being a chattel I became a person. I worked, I earned a living, I thought great things and wrote of them. I had a cause. Now I have been reduced to shrivelling flesh. Are these demons real? Or have I invented them at Gitabhai's suggestion? I can't tell. I lose control over such thoughts. It's easier to believe in the evil cast by another person than the evil within oneself."

She felt Kim take her hand. His warmed hers; she wanted his strength. Her thoughts became distracted by the activity surrounding her. The air seemed sweet with incense and she sensed a ripple among the men watching and waiting for a miracle. She hoped to sense some movement within her, the drawing out of her spiritual poison, but felt nothing, except drowsier.

At the very first note of the slokas that sprang from the brothers' mouths, Parvati jerked rigid; her back arched, her eyes flew open and her mouth twisted into an ugly grimace. Kim looked away, not wanting to see such beauty defiled by the demons. Within an hour the air surrounding them had grown cold, for the mountains had sent the wind to listen and carry the songs back to them. In the second hour, the surrounding grass and bushes, which had been brittle and brown, turned green and lush; the fruit of the tamarind ripened and fell in abundance around them; the earth quivered in ecstasy as though Lord Nataraj danced. The tree filled with birds and scorpions sprang from the earth and ringed the small gathering, their tails flat and the deadly poison sheathed.

The brothers continued their singing and many hours passed. Parvati still lay contorted but Kim noticed that the air about her was changing colour. A brown mist rose from her mouth like a visible scream and slowly darkened. It rose higher, and swirled around as though the singing drove it upwards. Kim saw shapes in the dark mist, blood too and entrails, and deformed and demented creatures struggling to battle the forces summoned by the singing. Fierce fires darted like snakes' tongues and lightning danced in between. Even as the men watched in fright, they saw the creatures, who were so terrible to look on that they averted their eyes, vanquished one by one. As they fell, they evaporated and the mist grew smaller with each victory. And as it shrank, Parvati slowly relaxed. Her fists unclenched, her staring eyes grew drowsy, her legs no longer trembled but lay still. Her mouth remained open a little, as though to kiss. Evening came, but the boys did not stop their singing for a pocket of mist remained. It swung crazily back and forth like a pendulum, trying to escape the sacred power which had destroyed most of it. They heard the howls and dreadful curses directed at the brothers, but because of Brahma's shield the malignant creatures that had survived so long were powerless against Bala and Bala. When night fell, they caught glimpses of the evil power, lit by a pale violet light within the mist. It seemed as if it were too powerful even for Brahma to destroy but Bala and Bala continued their singing, summoning Lord Krishna and Siva and Vishnu to do battle.

When the sun rose, the air was clear, cleaned as if rain had fallen and washed it. Parvati slept peacefully and the brothers, slowly, softening their voices, stopped singing. For a long time nothing moved. The air sighed in regret and grew warm, the scorpions danced away with their tails raised and what had become green returned to being shrivelled and parched.

'How can I thank you?' Kim asked. He prostrated himself in front of Bala and Bala as they stood up, and touched their cracked and dusty feet. Kishore Singh and his companions too pressed their faces into the dust and touched those feet. They had witnessed miracles. The boys helped Kim and the men to stand up.

'Lord Krishna didn't give us these voices for us to be rewarded.' Each took hold of the other's hand. 'We must continue our travels now. But we know our paths will cross yours again, Kim.'

He watched until they dwindled and faded into the haze. Parvati slept calmly and they carried her as fast as they could to the nearest village. It was small and poor but when they asked for food it was given generously. Only one household had cooked meat that day and the local merchant gave a goat curry. When Kim had gathered enough food, he woke Parvati. She smiled at him with such delight that he couldn't suppress his happiness. Her face was at peace, all her fears had disappeared.

'Here, eat as much as you can. We'll stay here until you've regained your strength and then continue our own journey away from this part of the country.'

She took a nibble of meat and swallowed, waiting fearfully for the demon. Then she realised that the taste lingered in her mouth, and began to eat ravenously. With each mouthful, her strength returned, her colour heightened and once more she felt the pleasure of being alive.

# 3

## October–November 1910

It was not by chance that even as his name was spoken, Anil Ray should be moving slowly in the opposite direction through the ravines. Kim was right in his belief that they were bound by destiny to move within the circumferences of each other's lives. The ridges hid them from each other though they were no more than a hundred yards apart.

Kim would not immediately have recognised Ray. When they had parted, after their escape from Tihar Gaol, Ray had been bearded and long-haired, a frightening figure with angry eyes. Since then he had adopted the guise of a sunyassi, had shaved his head and face, wore the saffron robe of sanctity and carried a begging bowl made from a dried pumpkin, and a staff. In the bowl, beneath a rag and a banana, was a revolver.

Anil Ray was aware that rumour was transforming him into legend. He had yet to kill anyone, but stories about his spectacular revenge against the policeman who had killed his uncle were rippling across India. They exaggerated the deed, making him sound heroic and fearsome. As if to authenticate the stories, the government had placed a huge reward of 50,000 rupees on his head. Half the reward had been donated by Parvati's husband, Lal Bahadhur Ram Shanker, the first Indian to become a Member of the Viceroy's Council. The reward was large enough to make Anil suspect every man, woman and child he met. Yet he had no regret.

Anil watched the dawn. The shadows in the ravine were soft at this hour, the knife edges of the ridges blurred. It remained cool longer as the night air was trapped in these pockets. He was quite lost. Unlike Kim he found the sky strange to him, merely decorative. But he hoped he would soon be found by the man he'd come to kill. There was no escape from this duty; he had promised the dying Man Singh he would avenge him. If he had known that Man Singh's son also had sworn the same vengeance, he would have been relieved to have the duty taken from him.

He had asked at each village in the region for the whereabouts of the dacoit leader Ranjit Lal. 'We know nothing of this man,' the villagers would reply and then later, while he squatted patiently in the shade, they would ask: 'Why do you search for him?' Anil told them 'I am a sunyassi and have heard of his greatness. I come to give him dharshan.' Even villains wanted a god man to bless them. Word would eventually reach Ranjit Lal and he would find this sunyassi who wanted to bless him.

"Then what? Whom should I kill next? I wonder. I can't live a whole life of revenge. I feel it eating into me, as it has done all these years. How sweet my life would have been if my uncle had not been murdered in the foothills of Simla. Instead of these robes of humility I would be wearing a black silk gown, standing before judges to debate the finer points of law. I can't, I mustn't dream. Dreams are the luxuries of men who lead fortunate lives. I blame the British doubly. First for having forced me to ape them – for how else could I have fulfilled the ambitions of my father but to become a brown Englishman? Secondly, for turning me into this savage. They must be driven out of India, driven back to their tiny island. We cannot argue with them in courts of law or pick the legislative crumbs they throw us from their sumptuous feast. As long as they yoke us, we cannot stand. There are 300 million of us and we must arm ourselves and kill each and every one

– men, women, even children. From this moment, that is the direction of my life. I shall free India, free myself."

Such thoughts stirred him. He banged his staff on the earth as he walked, as though with every blow he killed an Englishman. But the banging softened as his thoughts turned to his cousin Sushila Basu. She had harboured him, comforted him, loved him when he needed it. Life could have been different once . . . quickly he suppressed the thoughts that tried to change the past, reshape a destiny already cast. He could never ever spend days and months and years with Sushila. At most he could only snatch an hour or two and preserve the memory of her voice and perfume and the touch of her hand on his face. There was no place for her by his side. She was lost to him, as was his country and all his inheritance. His would be a harsh life, a dangerous one and he could not subject her to such ugly discomforts. For him to remain long anywhere was to court arrest, eventually, inevitably, death.

He had been so absorbed in these thoughts that he failed to notice the shadow above him. A man with a musket squatted on top of the ridge and when Anil had passed he waved to someone ahead. Anil reached the end of one valley and hesitated. It branched left and right and he chose the right. From the shadows he could tell he moved west still. He had no idea how long it would take Ranjit Lal to find him but he had to remain in these ravines until then. He chose a shady spot to eat his banana. As he settled down, he saw five men waiting. They were unkempt, unsmiling, hard. One poked Anil with his musket.

'You're the sunyassi who seeks Ranjit Lal?'

'Yes. I wish only to give him dharshan. I've heard of his greatness and I'm told he is an Akbar among men for his wisdom and generosity.'

'Save your flattery for his ears. If you believe such things about Ranjit Lal, you deserve to meet him.'

The speaker was small and wiry, older than the others.

'How far is he?'

No one answered. Anil replaced the banana, which was spoiling in the heat, in his bowl and followed them. He no longer thought his life strange. Walking with bandits through a parched, dun-coloured land was only part of the same bad dream as his years in Tihar Gaol. He clutched the begging bowl tightly, surprised they had not peered in, but a holy man wouldn't be taken for an assassin. Finally, near midday, they stopped and Anil chose to sit beside the older man.

'How much further?'

'We wait here.' He leant back against the earth and closed his eyes.

'Doesn't he trust me?'

'He trusts no one. Since killing our leader, Man Singh, he moves only sideways like a spider. We have heard that Kishore Singh hunts him.' He sighed. 'It's best to let others deal with such a vile man. As long as I'm fed and have money, all leaders are the same.'

'Why don't you help this Kishore Singh?'

'What for?'

'Then you'd be free of Ranjit Lal.'

'You're a fool, sunyassi. Why should Kishore Singh be different? All leaders are the same. He may even be worse. Man Singh was the best and a son is never as good as his father.'

'What if Ranjit Lal is killed in action?'

'Then we'll see.' He studied Anil in silence. 'For a sunyassi you ask many questions.'

'The Gita advises not inaction but action. If there is injustice one must act. You could be leader if you acted.'

'That's true. But then I would have to sleep with my back to a wall. I prefer this position. Obey orders. Namaskaar the leader, whoever he is.'

Suddenly he snatched Anil's begging bowl. His eyes never left Anil's face as he held it and then gently removed the banana from the top. He hefted the bowl and without removing the cloth returned it to Anil.

'This is a heavy bowl for a sunyassi who should

possess nothing. Here, eat your banana. You're going to need strength to carry that bowl in front of Ranjit Lal.'

Anil Ray had to wait for Ranjit Lal until evening. The dacoit leader slid cautiously out of the shadows, followed by half a dozen men. They bristled with weapons and were as taciturn as Anil's companions. As they sat down, Anil noticed a seventh man, unarmed. He appeared to be a prisoner though his hands weren't tied. A gun was pointed continually at his back.

Anil had only glimpsed Ranjit Lal twice. Once he'd been a dour, cruel visage beneath a flash of red turban, recognised by Man Singh in the crowded Delhi streets. Ostensibly, Ranjit Lal had been reconnoitring their escape route. The second glimpse was more fearful, over the rifle sights as Ranjit Lal and his men shot down Man Singh and Charan as they ran from the prison work party. Anil had been fortunate that he hadn't died too in that betrayal. Now, he only hoped Ranjit Lal didn't recognise him from those encounters.

It was dark and he was safe a while longer. Ranjit Lal ignored him and instead sat in a huddle with his trusted men. Anil heard the whispers: 'kill him', 'no, listen to him', and believing they were discussing him slid his hand into his begging bowl and gripped his revolver. Then the man who was their prisoner was pushed forward, and Anil withdrew his hand from the bowl and edged nearer.

'Tell us why we shouldn't cut your throat,' Ranjit Lal was saying.

'Sahib, I have heard of you even as far to the north as Delhi, and your brave deeds have stirred my blood.'

'Am I feared?'

'Yes, sahib,' and the man took courage, seeing that his flattery worked. 'Very feared. And you are also brave and wise.'

Mahender, for it was Lal Bahadhur Ram Shanker's servant, thought Ranjit Lal a fool for believing such lies. It had been most unfortunate that in hunting Kim and

Mohini (the woman Kim called Parvati) he'd stumbled upon Ranjit Lal and his men. If his brother, Rajender, had been with him they could have opened fire and escaped. But he'd sent Rajender back to report to Gitabhai that they'd traced Kim and Mohini to Pushkar and there heard that the two were moving west with Kishore Singh.

'Good, very good,' Ranjit Lal's voice swelled with pride. 'I already knew all this before. You still haven't told me why I shouldn't cut your throat.'

'Sahib! Would money, a lot of money, maybe even a lakh, be a good enough reason to spare my worthless life?'

When necessary, Mahender could grovel. Inside, he raged at his ill luck in having been caught by this buffoon. Even as he cringed, Mohini could be moving out of reach. He had to catch her. She would be his reward, if Bahadhur sahib was angry with her for escaping again. A man can lose patience. Bahadhur sahib had promised, admittedly in anger, that if she didn't behave he would give her to his servants for their use. Mahender was driven by lust for her, intoxicated with anticipation of her beneath him. He could never forget seeing her bathe naked in the river after he and his brother had kidnapped her from the Congress Party meeting in Allahabad. Then she had arrogantly walked past him as if he were a rock with no passion, no physical yearnings. He prayed he would catch her again.

'You look too poor even to know of such a sum.'

'I didn't say I had it. But I know how you can get this lakh.'

'Tell.'

'In front of everyone?'

'Yes.'

The silence was expectant; men held their breaths. None of them had seen a lakh either and their minds were fired by this king's ransom. Anil heard the loud click of a hammer being drawn back.

'I am hunting a man,' Mahender said. 'He stole something of great value from my master. The man also is wanted by the police but if I find him before the police and recover what he stole, my master will pay a lakh as a reward.'

'What is the precious object this man stole? It could be worth more than a lakh.'

'It's only worth this lakh to one man. It's his wife.'

'She must be very beautiful.'

'Very. But if you should touch one hair, my master will kill you. He's a jealous man. He is very close to the British rulers and he will have them hunt you down and kill you and all your men.'

'The Angrezi don't frighten me,' Ranjit Lal boasted. 'He will pay a lakh for her safe return?'

'Yes. But I won't tell you his name. Otherwise you will cut my throat and go to him direct.'

'Then what is the name of the man you hunt?'

'Kim.'

"Why, if God exists, does he write my life in circles?" Anil thought. "Kim altered the course of my life like dynamite the direction of a river, and he atoned for that by helping me escape. Am I now expected to return this atonement by saving him from these men? I could warn him. But should I meddle with another man's destiny even though he meddled in mine? He is also an Englishman and I have resolved to drive them all, every one, from this land. Let him be the first to die in this resolve then, if not by my hand then by Ranjit Lal's. But I have come to kill Ranjit Lal. Fate thus sets me a subtle trap. If I kill Ranjit Lal, then Kim is saved. If I don't, I have betrayed the promise I made to Man Singh. Yet I can resolve that. I shall kill Ranjit Lal, but I shall let him kill Kim first."

'Where is this Kim then?' Ranjit Lal asked.

'Not far. He was half a day ahead of me. His companion is one Kishore Singh.'

'Kishore, Kishore,' Ranjit Lal called out. 'I will kill that devil too. Good, I like you. You have given me a reason not to cut your throat just yet. I will cut Man Singh's son's throat instead.'

"And now," Anil thought wryly, "if I delay in this killing, Man Singh's son will die. Can I live with such dishonour on my soul? Father and son? I can prevent the son's death if I act swiftly."

'Go and look for this Kim and Kishore Singh,' Ranjit Lal ordered, and two men rose and drifted into the night. 'Now where is this sunyassi who seeks me out?'

Anil rose and stepped forward. He tripped over a musket, trod on one man's leg, kicked another and groped to sit in front of Ranjit Lal. Ranjit Lal touched Anil's face and traced the bald head and shaven face.

'Well, sunyassi?'

'Sahib, unlike this man here I had not heard of you until one day when I was meditating by the Ganges, mother of all rivers, and a vision came to me of Durga riding the tiger. She called to me and said, "There is a man by the river west of here. He is a brave man and will one day be a great leader. Go to him and live in his shadow to give him the spiritual guidance he needs to fulfil his dharma. His name is Ranjit Lal." And when I woke from this vision, I immediately set out on this pilgrimage. I have walked many days and nights, and on the road I asked for Ranjit Lal and heard of your greatness.' Anil paused, pleased with his lie. A vision couldn't be denied; the promise of a great destiny would tempt even the most honest of men. The dishonest, because of their greed, would be more easily seduced.

'Durga herself!'

'Yes, sahib. She carried her weapons of war and the tiger she rode was large as an elephant. Her voice was sweet and melodious and I heard every word distinctly.'

'Stay by me then, and give me your dharshan, sunyassi.'

Anil raised a hand, palm outwards, mumbled a prayer and felt Ranjit Lal grope for his feet. His toe was clutched and released. Anil could have shot him then, as he bowed, but he hadn't expected the gesture and cursed the darkness.

# 4

## September–November 1910

Alice Soames was not one of those privileged to welcome the new Viceroy of India, Lord Hardinge of Penshurst. In fact, she was considered an undesirable. As a writer she constantly attacked rule in India and questioning this divine right made her an outcast. She wrote her heresy for an American newspaper, the *New York Herald Tribune* and, worse, for *Sher*, an English-language magazine published in Bombay. She was its founder and editor, and the publisher a native called Romesh Nairoji. Gossip, unsubstantiated, had it that they were lovers and this put her quite beyond the pale. Alice was amused by her reputation and certainly had no wish to be one of the stuffy, fawning party sweltering under the shamiyana. At its centre was the governor of Bombay Presidency, flanked by his council members and the Members of the Viceroy's Council, and all their memsahibs. Alice suspected her husband too was among the blur of faces. She knew of his knighthood and had composed the first draft of a blistering attack, not on him personally but, through him, on the government of India. He would not be pleased. And it could be dangerous.

She watched Lord and Lady Hardinge's arrival from behind the police cordon, pressed in by a large and curious crowd. The sea was a hard, flat blue, metallic in its stillness, and the glare of the ship's white sides glowed on the faces of the waiting dignitaries. As Lord Hardinge's foot touched Indian soil, trumpets heralded the momentous event and the cannons in Bombay fort, some distance away, began firing his fifty-one-gun salute.

The new king of India had arrived. No man, however rich and powerful he might be in England, could ever dream of the power and the glory of being Viceroy of India. The Viceroy led a life even more splendid and magnificent than that of his only superior, the King-Emperor himself, George V. On Indian soil even the Prince of Wales bowed in homage to the Viceroy. His retinue numbered hundreds and he would travel through his Indian domain with all the pomp and circumstance of a Mughal emperor.

Alice watched Lord Hardinge, a tall, spare, aristocratically handsome man with a high forehead, wearing breeches and a cut-away jacket under the Viceregal robe. It was sky-blue with an ermine collar and hem, and woven into it in gold thread was his decoration of Master of the Most Exalted Star of India. The plume in his cocked hat nodded with every movement, as he inspected the Rajput guard of honour. He looked hesitant and unsure, as if somewhat startled by his position. But that would pass once he grasped the extent of his power. As he moved along the red carpet towards the landau, shaded by a huge silk and gold umbrella carried by a bearer, Alice pushed her way out of the crowd. A squadron of Bengal Lancers on coal-black horses was lined up to escort the Viceroy on his drive to the governor's residence.

The ceremony stirred unhappy memories. Alice retreated to the shade of a hotel verandah, remembering the arrival of the previous Viceroy, Lord Minto. She had been accompanied by Mohini then. Her melancholy sigh attracted the attention of a bearer. Her handsome face was drawn and weary with worry, and she felt the seams of despair around her mouth. It had been her fault that Mohini had been abducted by her husband from the Allahabad Congress session. She should not have sent her to cover the story for *Sher*. Alice had reported Mohini's disappearance but the police, naturally, had done nothing. Mohini's husband, the first Indian Member of the Viceroy's Council, was too powerful.

She rose abruptly and strode towards a gharri as if to escape her morbid thoughts. She was a tall woman, and had been beautiful as a girl, but age and India had faded that beauty. Yet in the way she walked and held herself, she looked a strong and independent woman.

It was half an hour's drive to her small bungalow on Malabar Hill. She slipped into its peace and quiet, comfortable with the untidiness of a single woman's life. The bungalow reflected her pursuits. Books and magazines were piled on tables and chairs, and in her small study papers overflowed the rosewood roll-top desk.

To take her mind off Mohini, she sat down to work, and read the draft of her article for her editorial column in *Sher*.

> Loyalty, of course, must be rewarded. Without loyalty, the British Empire would collapse overnight. Loyal men have given their lives to perpetuate British rule over India, and those who do not lay down their lives but serve in safer occupations live to be amply rewarded for their faithful service to the Crown.
>
> No doubt such men as Colonel Creighton of the Political and Secret Department of the Indian government are worthy of their rewards. Colonel Creighton's name has appeared in the King-Emperor's Birthday Honours List. He is to receive a knighthood. Colonel Sir John Creighton has a nice ring to it. In the corridors of the Writers' Building and in the Viceroy's Council, Colonel Sir John will no doubt be even more respected than before. From the department's own title we understand the nature of its duties, though we see very little of its actual functioning.
>
> Political and Secret are dreadful words. They imply control, and worse, manipulation, hidden by a veil of

lies. The two words also imply suppression, suppression of ideas, suppression of hopes and dreams, suppression finally of the men who nurture such dreams. Doubtless the Colonel has done his job, whatever it is, well and deserves his knighthood for his continued service to the government of India. Though not the people of India.

Alice laid down the papers. She chuckled. How ironic! She could now call herself Lady Creighton. Looking out on the small garden she saw the mali empty a bucket of water over the bougainvillea and wanted to scream in irritation: I've told you a hundred times not to give it water! Resolutely, she turned away and dabbed at her face and hands with a small towel. The heat was moist and suffocating. It was only on days like this that she thought of summers in Oxford and afternoons spent on the cool river. Alice seldom thought of England, and never with any yearning or need to return. India was home.

Her daughter too occupied her thoughts. Elizabeth was now so far away. It was tragic that she should have waited so many years to meet her. Elizabeth blamed her mother for the estrangement, Alice the Colonel. He had 'killed' her in the eyes of her children. Her resurrection and sudden appearance in Calcutta had stunned Elizabeth. It was not an unexpected reaction but given time, Alice hoped, they would become friends. They could never be mother and daughter but she prayed for friendship at least. It wouldn't be the friendship of two women of a similar age but of an older woman, an aunt perhaps, with her niece. Alice was not a motherly woman. She was too bold, too restless for such a submissive role. Alice wished she had known Richard. There, in her son's tragic death for the empire, lay the seeds of lifelong regret.

She had promised to write to Elizabeth weekly, though not expecting any response. Even in that one brief meeting she had recognised her own stubbornness in her daughter. Picking up her pen, Alice hoped that these weekly reminders could soften her daughter's heart towards her, if not towards India. She knew Elizabeth would never return.

Alice sealed the letter and stamped it. She slipped her article into an envelope and addressed it. When Mohini had worked on the magazine, it would have been given to her. The mali was squatting by the gate, desultorily weeding, and she called him over and gave him precise instructions to post one and carry the other to the editorial office of *Sher*. There he was to hand it personally to Romesh Nairoji and bring back a signed receipt. She watched him stroll out of the gate, a tall, lazy man. He was useless in the garden but she hadn't the heart to sack him. She could have taken the article herself as she would be passing the office, but she didn't want to see Romesh. He would want to know where she was going, and if she told him he would do all in his power to dissuade her. Romesh was overly protective, an endearing quality in a lover but at times suffocating. He would have liked her to be as submissive as an Indian woman, not always but at those times when she did things contradictory to his wishes. This clandestine meeting would certainly not meet with his approval.

At the corner Alice hired a gharri for the evening. She was deliberately vague in instructing the driver and told him only to drive to the city. She would direct him from there. The ride into the city, along the beach road, was a pleasant one. The heat had abated and the evening breeze had sprung up. Had she looked back, she would have seen her mali patiently following the slow-moving gharri.

The gharri drove through the city and continued to the further outskirts. It was dark now and the driver lit his lamps. They came to a group of mud and thatch huts huddled tightly together. Oil lamps flickered here and there. The stench of open drains was suffocating, and Alice held a scented handkerchief to her nose. The driver grew nervous and argumentative. He was worried for memsahib. These people were poor, hungry and dangerous, and she shouldn't have come here. Alice ordered him to drive on and he reluctantly obeyed.

They passed the slum and then the mills, rising black and forbidding, no different from the 'dark satanic mills' of Birmingham or Manchester. The rutted track curved away to open ground and they travelled along it for another fifteen minutes before it dipped into a hollow. She sensed, rather than saw, the group of silent men. There wasn't even a candle between them. A man rose and approached the gharri cautiously.

'Miss Soames memsahib?'

'Yes.'

She got down and joined Arvind Joshi. He was a short thickset man who stood no higher than Alice's shoulder. Normally a jovial man, now he was grim and suspicious. He peered past her into the night.

'Did you tell anyone you were coming here, memsahib?'

'Of course not.'

'Don't be cross, memsahib,' Arvind Joshi said. 'You are British, we are Indians. None will harm you but we will be beaten and gaoled. Come.'

Alice sat down on the earth, cross-legged and looked out at the shadowy faces. More than a hundred men sat in silence. A beedi glowed, a man coughed. They waited patiently. Whites of eyes gleamed, she caught the flash of teeth, but none said a word as Arvind spoke. He told them about the need to create a union, a union such as men had in other countries. 'This memsahib is wanting to help us. It was she who made the suggestion that we should meet and discuss these matters before proceeding further. We all know that we are exploited by the mill owners. They pay us poorly and force us to work long hours. If we complain we are dismissed and cheated of what money we have earned. This memsahib works for a newspaper from across the kala pani, and she will write about our efforts to obtain justice.'

# 5

## November 1910–February 1911

'What then?'

'Soames memsahib told the men how they should form this thing called a union. She said it would be dangerous and that they would be beaten, even killed, by the mill owners. Whenever men band together for justice, they will be attacked violently. She said that in Am-er . . . Am-er . . .'

'Amer-ika,' Newton said.

'Yes, that is the word,' the mali said. He stood humbly just on the threshold of the room. 'In Amer-ika, when the coal miners formed this union and went on strike . . . what is strike?'

'A workers' bandh.'

'. . . strike, the owners had them beaten and killed. But the men should stand firm. Other men would be brought to work in the mills and they should dissuade them.'

'Ha! How, I ask you, can you dissuade hungry men from working? Do they care that they will be badly treated? Of course not. They want the wages. Go on. Then . . .?' Newton looked up from his note-taking. He sat cross-legged at a low desk with his back against a bolster.

'Soames memsahib spoke more about this union, about the rules, how they should elect a leader and a committee. They listened to her in silence. I saw no response, except from this Arvind Joshi. He is the trouble-maker.

When she finished, she got into the gharri and went home.'

'And Joshi?'

'I was instructed to follow memsahib. Not Joshi.'

Isaac Newton dismissed the mali. Stupid man. Stupid woman. What point, I ask you, in putting dangerous ideas in the heads of uneducated men? The ideas will run amuck. How will they form a committee when they don't know how to vote? The vote, the simplest of ideas, and we don't know how to use it. Stupid woman. I will have to write my report and the Colonel sahib will take action against his wife. He will have to. The article the mali showed me this afternoon about the Colonel sahib's knighthood is definitely seditious. No doubt about it. If an Indian wrote such blasphemy he would be quick-as-a-wink in prison, with a dose of flogging too. It will be interesting to see how the British will treat their own people.

Newton wrote his report in a precise hand. He took pride in his meticulous penmanship. An admirer of Walter Scott, he equalled him in the length of his sentences, one of which filled an entire page. When he finished his report on Alice Soames, he placed it carefully in her file. It fattened slowly. Scraps had grown to pages. He knew much about her, about her lover (and this shocked him, that the memsahib lay with a native) and her work habits and her thoughts. He locked the report in his safe.

He returned to his desk. A fortune in diamonds had lain under his file. He filled a palm. They were cold, and each one was worth more than the lives of all those mill workers. One especially, the size of a pigeon's egg, could have filled their bellies for a year. He studied it through his jeweller's glass. It was perfectly cut. He knew he was the best diamond-cutter in Bombay and he was modestly proud of his skill. Carefully he poured the diamonds into a cone of paper and tossed them aside.

His ancestral profession had long since palled. As a boy he had begun a passionate affair with machines;

they were almost magical for him. He wanted to invent wonders. He was so in love with western science that he had even changed his name from Gopal Krishnan to Isaac Newton. He had brooded long and hard over whether to add the 'Sir' but concluded it would be presumptuous. He would wait until he had one success. But this success still eluded him. The gap between imagination and execution remained yawning as ever. This room and the whole top floor of his house in Jewellers Lane was crammed with the evidence of his efforts. He glared angrily around at the bits and pieces cowering in the shadows.

Newton had also lost heart for his occupation as an intelligence agent for the Colonel sahib since the murder of his nephew Narain. Newton had cremated Narain in Ranthambor and immersed his ashes in the stream. How swiftly were men reduced to such small, fragile things. Ashes. Narain, a man once filled with blood and courage, had fitted into his cupped palms, fragmented and vanished into the water.

"And what, I wonder, has happened to my dear friend Kim? Did he elude his pursuers? Does he live? Does she – this woman for whom he has risked all? Every man's life is a story and we wonder what happens to them when we part. What is the next chapter? Will it be sad? Or happy? Is there continuity or, as with Narain, an abrupt 'the end'?"

Isaac Newton found himself thinking such dark thoughts because he was unhappy. He had served the Colonel sahib for thirty years. He had been a village youth when the young captain rode into his life like the hero of a mythical story. He looked like a god, resplendent in his uniform with shiny boots and belt, and the topi shielding his eyes from the sun. Gopal had never seen such a man before, one with skin so white and eyes the colour of the sky. He was inventing something then, neglecting his trade, and the sahib had watched with amusement. They talked about the invention, which had failed, and before leaving the sahib had suggested that Gopal listen.

To what? he asked. The sahib replied: The wind, voices, whispers, and if they should be interesting, come and tell me. He didn't know then what it meant but months later, attending at the command of a rajah who wished him to make a diamond necklace for his monkey – ugly brutes, both master and animal – Gopal heard him plot the murder of his uncle. He could have remained silent but he felt no loyalty to the rajah and suspected that if he were to mention this to the sahib, they would be rid of the rajah. In this assumption he was correct. The vile fellow vanished, and his uncle, a pleasant man with a religious mind, took his place. A year passed and Gopal was summoned by the young officer, who was no longer in uniform but seated at a desk. He thought Gopal's skills were wasted in a small village and moved him to Bombay and financed his business.

But now the Colonel sahib knew of Isaac Newton's part in Kim's escape. Putting two and two together, he would know that Isaac had followed his assassins.

In this business of deception, Isaac Newton thought, it is safest that only one person know all things and that there be only one spider to spin the web. Now my knowledge of the other parts of his web has placed me in jeopardy. God curse knowledge. If we remain ignorant, we are content. Instead, like the cat killed by curiosity, I followed the two men from Bombay, the one who limped and the dangerous one. The one who limped will have described me to the Colonel sahib and now he will know Isaac Newton disobeyed his orders and strayed from his speciality as agent in Bombay and poked his damned nose into business which was of no concern to him. Ahre bhai, what troubles will come on my head now! I am afraid for my life. And yet, this fear is overcome by outrage. Yes, outrage! Me, a man who has such scientific control over his thoughts and emotions! The Colonel plays his games with people, turning us on each other. So where does his loyalty lie, I ask myself. Is it to India? Or is it outside India to England? If it is outside, then how can I be expected to be loyal? He has always said he serves India, only India. But his masters are not Indians. We are his servants. His masters are those across the kala pani, men like himself.

Newton stopped. Such thoughts were treacherous and gave him sleepless nights. He would end up in prison if the Colonel could read his mind. Isaac Newton, a man who believed with utmost sincerity in British rule, now doubted it and that was what worried him most. If not them, whom? It was unanswerable. Though doubts harried him, he could not bring his mind to the possibility of Indians ruling their own country. His own inferiority had been so inculcated in him that the thought had never entered his head. Certainly he had heard Tilak's call for swaraj but it was a mantra only, not a plan or a blueprint for their own rule. He could only imagine a vacuum, an empty throne, and anarchy.

He needed diversion from such thoughts. Neither his diamonds nor his inventions held any appeal for him. Narain's last gifts to him stood wrapped in cloth. Stolen, doubtless. Newton unwrapped the first. It was a box-shaped machine with a cylinder and a lens, and within was a large bulb. He squatted and considered this for a while. It looked vaguely familiar; he had seen something very like it in a magazine and he went in search of it. In the next room, his books and magazines were stacked from floor to ceiling. They lay behind glass in rosewood cupboards, neatly catalogued. Newton, being of scientific mind, understood the need to have information at his finger-tips. He flicked through a leather-bound ledger and found his entry. Anything which interested him, and most things did, was entered here. He found the copy of the *Illustrated London News*, re-read the article and studied the drawings. Narain had given him a film projector. The other gift, which he unwrapped eagerly, was a moving camera. Newton had never seen moving pictures. He excitedly connected the projector to his generator, and watched a man walking, running and jumping. It was the most wondrous event of his life. He ran the film again and again. He had read that the bioscope could even tell stories. Narain had also scavenged a roll of film and Isaac Newton now carefully fitted it into the bulky wooden camera. It stood on a tripod and when he peeped through it he saw the room upside down. He resolved to take pictures of his street and would have gone down at once if a message hadn't come from the Colonel sahib summoning him to Government House. The summons was sudden and it worried him. He returned to his desk and carefully wrote a letter to his superior.

Newton changed into his only suit. It was ill fitting, one leg too long, a sleeve two inches short, and it didn't button in front. Newton's shape, thin and angular, stork-like, had defeated the skills of the local tailor. He slipped the MCC tie over his head and slid the knot to his throat. He carried his shoes and the report on Alice Soames in a cloth bag. At the gate to Government House, he put on his shoes and winced in. This could be a fateful meeting. The Colonel would dismiss him and, knowing the Colonel sahib's mind, Newton didn't want to think of his punishment. The Colonel hated disobedience. For him it only meant disloyalty. And disloyalty meant treachery.

The Colonel made him wait. Newton stood in the shade of a banyan tree, clutching his bag, until a peon rudely summoned him. He noted the peon's arrogance. By serving the sahibs, the low felt themselves elevated in front of their own people.

'Colonel sahib, my felicitations on your receiving such a great and wonderful honour from the King-Emperor. May you receive many more, including a lordship.'

'Thank you, Newton. Now what have you to report?'

The Colonel took the file. He sat back and read in silence. The punkah flapped fitfully, fluttering the papers on his desk. Newton perspired. The Colonel had made no mention of his disloyalty, yet Newton was sure he knew. If he is aware of it and yet not mentioning it, Newton reasoned, then he has plotted something against me. What, god knows. Who can read another's mind? It is a science greater than astrology, astronomy or biology. But as Newton thought this he saw a subtle change come over the Colonel's face. He recognised the tightening around the mouth and the lowering of the eyelids as anger. Alice Soames had angered him. Newton shuffled uneasily; he hated bearing news which made his superior angry. The Colonel snapped the file shut, rose and strode to the window. The sea's murmur soothed him. When he returned to his desk, he was calm.

'Good,' the Colonel said. 'Enough rope is what I've always believed in. Who is the printer of this magazine *Sher*?'

Newton consulted his notebook. 'Mohan Prasad of Lunar Presses.'

'I will have him arrested for sedition. That will stop all this damned nonsense. And what do you know of Arvind Joshi?'

'Nothing yet, Colonel sahib. It seemed harmless . . .'

'Nothing is harmless. Someone is putting him up to all this talk of a union. Find out who. I want a name. Quickly.'

'Yes, Colonel sahib. And Miss Soames? Should I continue the surveillance?'

'Yes,' was spoken with a hiss. 'Employ more men. I want to know everyone she meets. I suspect she could also be financing these things.'

'But she lives simply, Colonel sahib.'

'Women never live simply. I want the evidence against her.' He sat back and smiled. It was a warm, friendly smile. The anger had evaporated. 'And how are you, Newton?'

'Sad, Colonel sahib,' Newton said, prepared for the question. 'My nephew Narain was killed.'

'I'm sorry. I met him once. He was going to study law.'

'He was better at other things. He was a great help to me, Colonel sahib.' Newton took a deep breath. 'One of your men murdered him. I followed the two of them – the dangerous one and the one who limped – to where they waited for Kim. They attacked him and Narain. The one who killed Narain, Kim killed. Justice was meted out. I drove the other away.' He stopped. The Colonel stared at him, unwinking. They listened to the squirrels and crows, the swish of the punkah. 'But you already know of these things.'

'Yes. I am angry at your disobedience. Why did you follow my men?'

'Curiosity, Colonel sahib. It will kill the cat, but if I am to serve you well, I must know some things. From Kim's description, I knew the one who limped was the man who had shot him. I wasn't aware if you knew this, but at the time of the shooting I had searched for them. Now, having found them, I couldn't let them out of my sight.'

'You should have.'

'I will resign. I have my letter.' Newton placed it on the table. The Colonel glanced through it, crushed it and threw it in the waste-paper basket. It was meant to be a dramatic gesture. He couldn't allow Newton to resign. His head carried too many secrets. Only in the grave would they be safe.

'You're a valuable man and I need you.' He rang the bell twice. Instead of the peon a young British police officer entered and Newton knew this meeting was prearranged. 'This is Deputy Inspector Edlecliff-Johnstone, one of our new officers from the Indian Police Service. Christopher, this is the famous Isaac Newton.'

'The Colonel has spoken very highly of you, Mr Newton.'

Edlecliff-Johnstone crushed Newton's hand. Whereas Newton was thin and frail, the young man was stocky and muscular. He looked too young and innocent, his grey eyes brimming with life and his blond hair plastered down by the heat. He smiled at Newton as though they were old friends and Newton felt himself indulged, like an ageing parent.

'He's an Oxford man. Christ Church, was it?'

'Balliol, sir.'

'Ah yes. Balliol. And a first in your IPS exams?'

'Yes, sir. I joined the Criminal Investigation Bureau in

Bombay and then served in the Intelligence Department in Karachi where I was promoted to Deputy Inspector.'

'I'd like you to train the Deputy Inspector, Newton. Show him what you've been doing.'

'Everything, Colonel sahib?' Newton said and didn't look at Edlecliff-Johnstone. He noticed the man called the Colonel 'sir' and wondered whether he should too. But 'Colonel sahib' was a habit and showed greater respect than 'sir'. Maybe to ingratiate himself he should add the knighthood, 'Sir Colonel sahib', but it was a mouthful.

'Everything. I want him to run Bombay for me eventually. Thank you, Christopher.'

Edlecliff-Johnstone smiled pleasantly at Newton before leaving. Newton wished he could sink into a chair. But the Colonel hadn't invited him to sit so he remained standing, trying to grasp the implications of what he had just heard. If this pleasant young man took over Bombay, then Newton would be out of a job. But the Colonel had refused his resignation. It lay crumpled in the waste-paper basket. He admitted to himself now that when he'd seen Edlecliff-Johnstone he had thought he was to be arrested. Now what? What about his friends, his library, his precious inventions? He had been so excited about the moving camera. He had such plans to make moving films. Now what?

'Now what?' he spoke aloud.

'I'm transferring you to Amritsar.'

'Amritsar! What is there in Amritsar? It's a village.'

'You'll see why very soon. Once you've trained young Edlecliff-Johnstone, go to Amritsar and find a place to set up your shop. You must build up a network of informers.'

'But does this man have experience in such delicate matters?' Newton couldn't bring himself to mention the young man's name. He was a child and wouldn't be practised in deception.

'Just show him the ropes, Newton,' the Colonel said. 'He's quite brilliant, I'm told, and an excellent police officer. The Police Commissioner of Bombay recommended him.' The Colonel came around the desk and clapped Newton on the shoulder. 'Don't look so forlorn, old friend. This is a promotion. You'll see why in a few months' time. Meanwhile if anything vital comes up while I'm away, send me a telegram.' He personally opened the door and ushered Newton out, something the peon usually did.

The Colonel re-read Alice's article. He flushed, embarrassed that an Englishwoman – his wife! – should write such vitriol. It was her revenge on him. She was an embittered woman, nursing hatred, and now lashing out in a personal attack. He had not seen her since that fateful night so many years ago and imagined her soured, reduced from her proud beauty, something horrid and ugly.

Manipulation! Lies! She was demented too. Briefly, he thought of allowing the article to appear. It would certainly raise a chuckle among the Members and secretaries, who obeyed scrupulously the dictates of the India Office. Naturally, sometimes they knew better than London and would avoid acting on some of their more hare-brained suggestions. It was only for the good of the country. Suppression indeed! No, it would never see the light of day. An article of this nature would encourage the natives to write equally dangerous drivel. He decided not to arrest Alice for sedition, but only because she was a European. It would set a bad example and no doubt she would inform the magistrate that Colonel Creighton had once been her husband – that, indeed, he was still. It would be better to arrest the printer.

He watched the sea, green now but darkening as the light faded. He would sail at noon the next day. If it were not for the knighthood and the summons from the Secretary of State, nothing would induce him to make the journey. He had no fond memories of England, though his childhood and youth had been spent there. He had been sent as a child of six and left at twenty-one, relieved and happy to be returning to India. His father, a major in Skinner's Horse, had been killed in the Mutiny. His mother had died soon after, of a broken heart he still believed, but he was too young then to have known better. He'd been orphaned but not left destitute. Three generations of tea and coffee plantations had left him with enough money to live an independent life. During his minority, his wealth had been administered by trustees appointed by friends in his father's regiment. They had also sent him to his father's old school, Wellington. He'd never wanted to leave India but it was the custom to send one's children home to be educated. If he had been poor, he would have gone to St Lawrence in Sanawar or Bishop Cotton in Simla, and that would have satisfied him. He would have been among friends and the familiar. Instead he was condemned to cold exile.

The shock of loneliness had left its scars, a chill reserve that none could penetrate. The barrier had been raised on the very day of his arrival. The Evanses, an Anglo-Indian family, had advertised themselves in the Indian newspapers as a kindly couple with a rambling house in Brighton. They offered to look after Anglo-Indian children during the holidays. Captain Evans claimed to have been an officer in the Bengal Lancers, but he was profoundly ignorant of India, and a bully. His wife was no better. They had mocked his accent and the Evans children immediately stole his pocket money. When the little boy complained, Mr Evans boxed his ears. He wrote to his trustees begging them to find another family for him to stay with. They had interviewed the Evanses who feigned astonishment at his charges, and when he had to spend the summer with them after all they tormented him cruelly but subtly. They called it discipline; he knew it was torture. The child learned the craft of deception.

Prep school had been an escape from the wretched family. He could deal with boys his own age, though not with the masters. They encouraged the boys to consider Anglo-Indians inferior, as if they were Eurasian.

There were other Anglo-Indian boys at the school and he became their leader. He understood that leadership required aloofness. At Wellington, he had met boys whose fathers had achieved high rank in the army, many of whom were ignorant snobs. There developed several bitter animosities which lasted through the five years at Wellington and continued at Sandhurst.

He had never taken home leave in England, as others did every three years. He knew those memories would rise unbidden to torment him again. Now he went reluctantly, summoned by honour. And what should he report to the Secretary for India? The Colonel was not an imaginative man, he was too experienced in his work for that. But he was startled by his own realisation that he imagined a giant mind, something quite amorphous, awakening, a light here, a light there, spreading, like electricity illuminating distant parts. India was uniting slowly, not of her own accord, but at the direction of instigators. The people themselves, he believed, were content. Left alone, they were happy with British rule. Even the Congress Party didn't want swaraj; only a small share of power and they would be satisfied. It was another, malignant part of the mind that conspired against England, believed in rebellion. Rebellion. It made him uneasy. Fifty-three years ago a rebellion had occurred, and had been ruthlessly crushed. This time, they would be ready. They had learned enough of the events leading up to the Mutiny to prevent such a thing happening again.

The Colonel woke early, dressed warmly and went out on deck. If he'd expected to have it all to himself, he was mistaken. The decks were crowded with the passengers; on the upper European, below Indian. Their breath filled the air with mist but beyond the bow of the ship lay a thicker mist, denying their view.

"The sea changes us too," the Colonel thought. "But in different and opposite ways to the Indian who crosses these waters. They are coming outward to their rulers' land and with each passing day their past recedes. They must experience a freedom from the restrictions of family, caste, customs; chains fall away. But we lose something on this journey home. We grow quieter, less authoritative, less arrogant. We lower our voices as we leave Port Said and no longer bully the waiters and stewards and cleaners. The ocean levels us. From our great height as rulers we are reduced, mile by mile, to ordinary people. Yes, ordinary. We're no longer sahibs – those titles conferred on us one and all because we're English – but plain 'Mr', just like millions of others."

Suddenly he realised he was looking at England. A dark land loomed through the mist, lights sparkled, a murmur rippled through the decks. They had all seen the land. It wasn't dramatic or substantial. Like a promise yet to be fulfilled it faded. He heard tugs hooting and voices drifting across the water. They grew more distinct as the land slowly returned to view and remained. Wharves and docks drew nearer and pale faces stared up at the ship as it loomed against the quay. Ropes were thrown down and fastened and then a great silence settled on the ship. It was an eerie quiet. He had grown so used to the vibration of engines that it seemed the ship had died.

From Liverpool Street, the Colonel took a hansom cab to the Oriental Club. He preferred the Club to staying with friends. It gave him independence and he wasn't a man who could remain polite for long. He had retained his club membership all these years out of habit.

The Oriental club was off Oxford Street. It was an imposing granite building standing deep in a garden, the entrance flanked by Corinthian pillars. The drawing room hadn't changed, the same oil paintings of India and Hong Kong hung on the walls. Other India hands came regularly and the porters recognised them, but they'd not seen the Colonel before. He waited awkwardly while a porter went to check his membership and reservation. This surprised him. If he had visited

Simla or Rawalpindi, no porter would have barred his way into an English club. Of course, he realised, he was no different here from the man in the street. Here he wasn't a sahib and instantly recognisable. Momentarily he felt lost and diminished. London awed him. It had changed so much; there were new buildings everywhere and the bustle was intimidating for a man used to a slower pace.

The porter returned, apologised and took his cases. He followed the man through dimly lit rooms full of armchairs and dozing members. He wouldn't be surprised if he saw a familiar face among them when he sat down for dinner. He presumed members still dressed for dinner. Or had England changed beyond recognition?

While the Colonel was dressing for dinner, the porter brought up a note. It was from Elizabeth. 'Father, I'm sorry I cannot meet you. Rest assured I am well. Congratulations on your knighthood. Affectionately, Elizabeth.' The Colonel folded the note and tucked it carefully into his case. He felt guilty at his relief at not having to see his daughter. He had done his duty towards her as a father and she was now old enough to look after herself. She had an adequate income, transferred monthly from his account. There was nothing more he could do for her. He had no doubt she was still pursuing Peter Bayley, even as he did but for less romantic reasons.

He hailed a hansom cab outside the club. It was too dark to see anything but he noted how quiet London was. An Indian city would be full of bustle and noise at this hour and the air would be filled with exciting odours. The cab dropped him off in Trevor Square in front of a substantial family house. He rang and waited a while before the door was finally opened by an old Indian bearer. His beard was white and he peered out at the Colonel from beneath his turban.

'It's me, Dass. Colonel Creighton.'

'Yes, Colonel sahib; I recognised you at once.'

'How are you?'

'I am well, sahib, but I miss my country. It is already

a bad winter and I'm not used to such cold. Even when Murchison sahib went to Kashmir it was never this cold. I will tell sahib and memsahib you have come.'

India was vibrant and visible everywhere in this house. Silken kashmiri carpets covered the floors, Mughal emperors and their court hung on the walls, bronze Chola gods danced on tables, silver plates, inlaid with gold, glowed in cabinets, carved ivory chests which once held the saris of ranis were used as occasional tables, gold filigree swords, inlaid with precious stones, hung below shields of silver and bronze. A tiger snarled soundlessly from the floor in the hall and canes and umbrellas filled an elephant's foot. A silver temple door opened into the dining room. The Colonel touched the Emperor Shah Jahan's jade wine cup and the gold comb of the Maharajah of Mysore.

Beatrice Murchison rushed in one step ahead of her husband. She was a silvery haired, extremely pretty woman and the Colonel was flattered that she should greet him with a warm hug and a peck on the cheek. Stanley Murchison, a tall, cadaverous man, shook his hand firmly. The Colonel was pleased to see these familiar faces. The Murchisons, like the Creightons, had spent generations in India. Murchison would be able to advise him as to how he should approach the new Secretary of State for India, Lord Crewe.

The Colonel talked quietly and gave them news of mutual friends in India. He was vague as to births and deaths and marriages, which was what Beatrice wanted to hear. As to more irregular affairs, he remained discreet, though Beatrice was certain the Colonel knew who was carrying on with whom. His news was general and she knew he was waiting to be left alone with Stanley. Stanley was now a councillor on the Board of Control for India. The Board, composed of parliamentarians and men with great experience of India – they had to have lived there for more than five years – advised the Secretary of State on Indian affairs.

After dinner, Beatrice left them to brandy and cigars. They would discuss the India that didn't interest her.

'I shall need your support when I have my meeting with Lord Crewe,' the Colonel said. 'Hardinge's views I know, but Crewe's interest me more.'

'Naturally he's worried about the increasing unrest in India,' Murchison said. 'He's studied your suggestions for increasing the powers of arrest and stiffer sentences for conspirators, but he'd like to defer a decision for the moment.'

The Colonel took the rebuff calmly. He was used to the differences in London's thinking. Lord Crewe was a Tory and inclined to a more liberal attitude towards India.

'How would he deal with it then? Have us release Tilak and pat the terrorists on their heads?'

'Not quite. He feels we should find political solutions, not enact draconian regulations. Part of the unrest, especially in Bengal, rose out of Lord Curzon's partition of the province. He plans to re-unify east and west and place the province under a governor.'

'Re-unify! It's going to make it difficult to administer such a huge province. Also, the division of east and west was part of our continual policy of creating a check against the Hindu. Giving East Bengal to the Muslims did help to create the division we needed to control Bengal. Now the Muslims will feel they've been betrayed by us. Even if they don't, reuniting Bengal will make it a powerful single political force. The babus will believe they've won the day and that will encourage them to incite further violence because they'll think we've retreated.'

'It's possible,' Murchison said. 'When you meet Lord Crewe, I'd make those points if I were you. You might be able to change his mind.'

'But you doubt it.'

'His mind seems pretty well made up.'

The Colonel disliked retreat. He knew what the Bengali extremists would think: that the British had been persuaded by violence and that if it could be done once, then it could be done again to bring about swaraj. They already called for it and had been only diverted by the partition of Bengal. Now that they had achieved that, they'd return to swaraj.

It was drizzling the next morning, and the Colonel thought with satisfaction that some things never changed. He dressed warmly though he noticed at breakfast that nobody else seemed to mind the cold as much as he did. There wasn't even a fire.

It wasn't far to Whitehall from his club and he strode briskly in the increasingly heavy drizzle. It would pour down at any moment. He looked, in the London streets, a healthy man with a very military bearing and skin a shade darker than those he passed. Any observant eye would recognise a colonial on home leave.

The porter on duty directed the Colonel to Sir Gerald Bartholomew's office. It was on the second floor, overlooking the park. He didn't have long to wait before being shown in. Sir Gerald stood as straight as a Guards officer. His face was seamed and his thin lips lent him a cynical and somewhat sinister air. Like the Colonel, he had an unblinking and impassive stare. Though they had not met previously both men felt at ease with each other. They practised a similar profession and understood each other's minds.

'I'm sorry we lost your daughter, Colonel,' Sir Gerald said. Surprisingly, he was a soft-spoken man and the Colonel had to lean forward in his armchair to hear him distinctly. 'We did have your message to meet her boat. Our man followed her to the Murchisons and we kept a watch on her round the clock. She was very clever. My man followed her to Harrods where she went to the ladies' department. She chose three or four things to try on and went into the dressing room. Naturally my man waited in the main department. After half an hour . . . well, I must commend your daughter. If she'd taken one dress he would have been alerted in a few minutes but she took four so he thought it would take her a while longer. He asked an assistant to go into the dressing room, but she was gone. There was another way out which she'd obviously noticed, and she quite simply disappeared.'

'And did you manage to find anything on Peter Bayley?'

Sir Gerald picked up a thin file. He held it up and dropped it back eloquently.

'He's not what he claims to be, but he does know many influential people, both in the city and among the aristocracy. We questioned his acquaintances – he seems to have no friends – and they're all quite vague as to how they met him. Through introductions, that sort of thing. They all describe him as charming, and good company. He didn't go to Eton or any of the better public schools. We're checking on the others. He seems just to have appeared in London one day.'

'As he did in India.'

'You suspected him of being a Russian agent?'

'I'm not certain. Let's say I still have my suspicions.'

'I'm sorry to mention this, but it is important. You don't suspect him simply because you're concerned that he's . . . friendly . . . with your daughter?'

'Certainly not,' the Colonel said.

'Please don't take offence.'

'That makes me sound unprofessional. I am, of course, concerned as to her whereabouts, but also because she could lead us to him.'

'How long have you suspected him? He'd been in India for some time, hadn't he?'

'A couple of years, off and on,' the Colonel said and his face darkened fractionally. It was his only sign of embarrassment. 'He became friendly with my daughter, but he also knew many English families in Calcutta. He seemed to be a man of private means, and of course he came to India with impeccable introductions. Apart from that . . . well . . . he was so English.'

'And of course it's impossible to believe that an English gentlemen would be a Russian agent.'

'The ones we've caught before came down through the mountains. They would pose as hunters or botanists but they were easily spotted and apprehended.'

They fell silent. The sound of traffic along Parliament Street was muted. In this high-ceilinged, comfortable room, his explanations sounded threadbare. He was vague about Bayley, vague too as to how Bayley had insinuated himself within his own family. But in India, unless a European was an out-and-out scoundrel, eccentricities were tolerated. However, if a man let the side down he would be reprimanded and firmly advised he should leave the country. Bayley had behaved impeccably except in the matter of Elizabeth. That was far too close to home, and the Colonel felt his judgement clouded by his closeness to his daughter. Her lover could just as well have been another man. It was not having a mother that was to blame for Elizabeth's deplorable behaviour. He still wouldn't blame himself for driving Alice out of his home; her blatant indiscretion had nearly ruined his career when he had just been seconded into intelligence work. No, he blamed Alice.

'What next?'

'Elizabeth wrote a letter. It has a Trafalgar Square postmark, which means absolutely nothing. It could be worthwhile to watch the post office. The letter was also posted in the evening.' Sir Gerald jotted a note. 'As you may know, one of the reasons I'm in London is to be knighted.'

'I do and I am delighted.'

'Thank you. She won't be there, of course. But she is still my daughter and I'm sure she'll be curious. The day and the time of the ceremony will be announced in the court pages of *The Times* and she might try to catch a glimpse of me in front of the palace.'

'I'll have men posted in the crowd. They may spot her. Now, why don't we go and have some lunch?'

The Murchisons, as his only 'family' in London, accompanied him to the palace the following week. The Colonel wasn't a stranger to the King-Emperor,

George V. They had met in India six years earlier when the then Prince of Wales had visited India. The Colonel was flattered to be warmly remembered by His Majesty and after the ceremony he was invited to a private audience to discuss the situation in India. The King took a personal interest in his Indian domain and strongly disapproved of Lord Curzon's partition of Bengal. George V had enjoyed his visit but the attitudes of his English subjects resident there dismayed him. 'Evidently,' he wrote in his journal, 'we are too much inclined to look upon them (the natives) as a conquered and down-trodden race . . . the native, who is becoming more and more educated, realises this.'

The King was a short man and his skin looked pale and new compared to the Colonel's. He now confided to the Colonel that as King-Emperor he intended to make another visit to India in December that year. His coronation would take place in London in June and there would be another one in front of his Indian subjects. He had instructed Lord Hardinge to arrange a grand durbar in Delhi. The King-Emperor hoped he would have the pleasure of meeting the Colonel again in India.

Colonel Sir John Creighton and the Murchisons drove from Buckingham Palace to the Savoy, where they had reserved a table for lunch. The Colonel scanned the small crowd outside the palace. The faces were a blur and he couldn't see Elizabeth. He had been so certain, in Sir Gerald Bartholomew's office, that she would come, but now he wasn't. She had not written again. Do children ever forgive their parents, he wondered. He had not had his long enough to accumulate the pains and injustices, imagined or otherwise. Of course it was possible that Elizabeth couldn't care less about his knighthood.

He barely tasted the food, and for the first time in many years found himself slightly tipsy from too much champagne in the middle of the day. Later the porter at the club helped him up to his room and handed him the note that had been left for him. The Colonel stared at the scrawl, trying to focus. It was from Sir Gerald. 'My men saw your daughter outside the palace and followed her home. She has taken a room in Shepherd's Bush. We will keep watch for Bayley.'

The Colonel was delighted. Not because she had been found but because she had stood outside the palace on a freezing cold day to catch a glimpse of him. He felt forgiven.

The night before he sailed he had dinner with the Murchisons. The conversation was general until Beatrice withdrew and left the men to their brandy and cigars. The silence was long and companionable. Stanley Murchison finally broke it.

'Had a good visit?'

'No,' the Colonel said. 'Yes, in a way. It was an honour to be knighted, and of course, to spend a few minutes with the King. But what I find most disturbing is the total lack of interest in India. The man in the street is quite ignorant, but Members of Parliament are ten times worse. I had planned to discuss the Indian situation with some of them but they were irritatingly vague. Unless they understand how are we to enact the necessary legislation?'

'Creighton, a debate on India is the quickest way to empty the House of Commons. Only when something terrible happens in India will they pay any attention. As long as India doesn't cost the government money, no one will say a word.'

'But you're on the Board of Control for India. Can't you convince them how important India is to this country?'

'It's the diamond in our crown but we'll never realise that until it's too late. I'll support you in the Board as best I can but teaching an English MP about India is like trying to turn a jutka pony into a racehorse. They're ignorant about India, and they're proud of their ignorance. It's a distant and complex country and they feel the less they know the better. You people out there are really on your own . . . until a visiting MP gives you a lecture on how to run the country. It's really easier for one of the

Congress-wallahs to come here and meet them, than for someone like you.'

The conversation depressed the Colonel. It made him feel lonely and unappreciated. It summed up all his years, squandered in the heat of India. A knighthood was a crumb tossed out occasionally to placate all those who served the Crown there, to sustain their belief. But beyond that nothing else existed.

The Colonel walked slowly up the gang plank. He stood at the rail, looking over the roofs of the custom sheds, trying to fix in his memory this last view of England. He didn't see the grey, dark town but the green fields and rolling hills that were beyond his vision. He stood separate, ramrod straight, self-sufficient. There was a loneliness in his very erectness. It was a defiance of the pain he had created for himself. Others had companions, and they held each other. He gripped the rail. The siren echoed, a lonely keen; and its note reminded him of the Indian kite, a softer, shriller sound yet somehow similar.

There was no colour, only the noise of the band, the cries of goodbye. The sky and docks were grey, the air chilly. It began to drizzle, a last reminder for those leaving England. On the lower deck were a few girls, laughing and calling, throwing out streamers to the land. They were the fishing fleet; girls looking for husbands in India. They would arrive as they left here, ignorant of the life they would have to lead if they did catch a husband. A few would be left unwed, the 'returned empties'.

The Colonel left the deck and his space remained empty a moment, a poignant gap, until it filled with the shift of people. He should have remained watching but he wasn't a man to waste such emotion. He'd never liked England and was glad this departing day was cold and miserable. It would remain in his memory years from now. He knew without a doubt he would never return.

# 6

## February 1911

'I wish I could tell Alice I'm safe and well,' Parvati said. 'She must be so worried about me. I also want to tell her how Gitabhai cast a spell over me and how you rescued me again. I miss her friendship and my work at *Sher*.'

They sat in the spare shade of a hillock not far from the nameless village. Three months had passed since her exorcism and Parvati had gradually regained her strength. Kim knew her true story now and her true name, but couldn't bring himself to call her Mohini. She was happy to forget it too and thought of herself as Parvati, the daughter of the Himalayas.

For the first time in her life Parvati had come to understand the hardship and pain of her own people. The land here was cruel and it gave sustenance reluctantly. The villagers existed on a handful of millet, onions and hot spices which made such a meal palatable, though they burned her mouth. There was no water. The women walked over a mile to a dried well where water seeped reluctantly into their vessels. Yet the people were kind, and generous with the little they had. How could these people, so starved, so neglected, rise as one and throw out their oppressors? She felt guilt, humiliation and rage, all at once. In the city she had not thought of them once and now she would constantly.

And for the first time in his life, Kim had told another person his complete story. To others he had told only pieces so that his life remained a puzzle, for he never provided every piece to one person. Parvati's eyes grew large and round when he first began to talk of his childhood, and she scarcely breathed in case she interrupted the tale of adventure and intrigue. There were times when she wanted to interrupt with the questions that boiled in her but she remained patient. He had begun the telling one hot afternoon and went on as the shadows lengthened. When he finished, she could see every detail of his face silvered in the moonlight.

'I never thought you were an Angrezi. You behave so much like us,' was her first comment. It was difficult for her to digest this. She had written for *Sher* about the oppressors, and the man she loved was one of them. And yet, he never behaved as they did but as an Indian. She'd seen for herself his compassion and his singular lack of arrogance. 'You told me you were Pathan when we met.'

'And you claimed to be a boy,' Kim said. 'We all need our guises when we first meet. I cannot be held to blame for my parentage. I knew neither my father nor my mother and my childhood was spent in the bazaars of Lahore in the company of chokras who didn't care whether I was Angrezi or not. Even I didn't know what I was until the Colonel sahib solved the puzzle of my locket. Does it change your feeling towards me?'

'Dear Kim, if you were a creature from a distant star I wouldn't care.' She smoothed the creases on his forehead. 'In spite of what you know about me, you have never ceased to love me. And my sins are far greater than the accident of your birth.'

Because the village was too poor to offer the hospitality of a roof they slept some distance away in a shallow, sandy dip, which remained cool long after sunrise because it held a pocket of night air. The sand was their mattress and for covering they shared a torn blanket. Only a few stars were visible this night; the moon's glare hid the universe.

'Will you return to work for the Colonel?' Parvati whispered.

'I feel, and I mean this only in all humility, like Arjuna in the Gita. I have no charioteer to advise me but I have dismounted from the chariot now and stand on the earth between the gathering might of two armies. One is tightly disciplined and controlled, the other undisciplined and leaderless. Like Arjuna, I see my friends on both sides. I am part, by blood, of the disciplined force that rules this land. But by love and thought, I am Indian. Where does my duty lie in this coming fight? I cannot tell.'

'Our side,' Parvati said.

'For what?'

'For freedom, of course.'

'And what's this swaraj going to be? Who will rule this country? India will return to the chaos of her past; we will be ruled by despotic princes again.'

'No, we will learn from the British. Already a few have the vote and we'll elect our own leaders, as they do in England.'

'It's a dream that we can do such things. Until we know what we want, there can be no victory. The British rule has been just . . .'

'Unjust,' Parvati whispered fiercely. 'Now you talk like one of them.'

'It's possible,' Kim admitted softly, 'but so do Gokhale and our other politicians. They don't say: drive out the British. They only want to share the power. It's only men like Tilak who demand total rejection and he doesn't tell us what we shall put in place of the British.'

Parvati despaired. She could argue all night but only from blind emotion. She had no idea who would rule; she only knew she didn't want the British. In anger she'd accused Kim of thinking like an Englishman but so did many Indians. Even Mr Motilal Nehru scoffed at Tilak's call for swaraj. If an educated and rich man like him didn't believe in an India ruled by Indians, why should Kim be blamed for thinking similarly?

'Then don't you feel we should at least share their power instead of being treated like children? Things are done without our consent. We must have the right to consent to the laws imposed on us by the foreigners. Won't you at least fight for that?'

Kim stared at the sky and felt Parvati watching and waiting. 'I can, but one day there will come a point when, in the middle of the battle, a man will turn and question me: "Can we trust you? Blood is a stronger tie than love and one day you will betray us."'

'Never.'

'It will happen. You love me and are blind to doubt. Others will not love me and they will open a gulf of suspicion against me.'

'Then we won't be part of this battle.'

'You cannot remain indifferent, dear Parvati. Your passions are too transparent. If I suppressed this fight in you, it would one day turn on me.'

'I don't care, as long as I'm . . .'

Kim clapped his hand across her mouth. Cautiously, he raised his head above the ridge and stared out over the ghostly landscape. The light was deceptive, and it threw indistinct shadows. Nothing moved. Yet he had heard the familiar click of a hammer drawn back. Sounds carried in the eerie silence, sped across desert long before anything was seen.

'Men come. Stealthily. They're up to no good.'

'What for?' She peered over the edge and saw nothing. The earth appeared asleep and silent and she felt they were the only two alive. 'There's nothing in the village.'

'Nothing to you, but for them there is. I can't tell how many there are.'

'I see nothing.'

Kim saw a shadow move, swiftly scuttle closer to the village and then fall still. The men came west out of the ravines. His hollow was north of them and out of line of their vision. The village slept behind a thin defence of thorn bushes. The entrance was shut but the attackers would make light work of such a flimsy barricade.

'I must warn Kishore Singh,' Kim said. He scrambled up the slope and Parvati clung to his leg.

'You'll be killed.'

'I can't stand by and watch a friend die. He has been betrayed. Those are Ranjit Lal's men. Remain hidden until I return.'

Parvati would have cried out but Kim was gone, creeping along the thin shadow thrown by the rise in the land. He saw another shadow crawl forward and stop. It wasn't possible to tell the size of the attackers. His own movements, the crunch of sand underfoot, the roll of a pebble, all seemed unnaturally loud. Kim reached the thorn barricade. It was higher than a man and struck firmly into the hard ground. The thorn felt like a scorpion's sting and drew blood. Kim removed his shirt and bound it around his hand. He couldn't see the attackers but now heard them moving, muffled but distinct. Carefully he pushed the thorns aside, slowly enlarging an opening until there was just space for him to wriggle through. The thorns scratched his back and thighs, leaving thin bloody streaks. He crouched and scurried to Kishore Singh's hut. The man slept lightly. He came awake at Kim's whisper, and reached for his musket.

'It's Kim. Men come stealthily. I don't know how many. They could be Ranjit Lal's.'

'Which way?'

'West. Go north.'

The woman Kishore Singh dallied with woke and nearly cried out. He hushed her and moved out quickly. Two of his men shared a separate hut; he woke them and the four made their way to the opening. The land was still and silent but filled with shadows that took on the shapes of men. They imagined an army waiting beyond. Kim prayed Parvati had remained hidden and that she wouldn't come in search of him. They heard nothing, and one of the men wriggled through the opening and crouched on the other side, musket at the ready. As the second man was halfway through, Kim glimpsed the spark of a musket and the crouching man toppled over. A sharp crack followed his death.

Kim grabbed the ankles of the man trapped halfway through the barricade and pulled him back. Behind, the village stirred, a man called out a warning and shadows emerged cautiously out of doorways.

'We can't escape,' Kishore Singh said. He knelt and fired at the musket spark but it was a wild shot, an angry reply delayed too long. From east and south, the shot was returned by half a dozen muskets. No bullet found its mark. Kishore's man fired; muskets replied from the west now. The encirclement was complete and Kishore Singh cursed the trap. He would die because he'd remained too long in this nameless village with a woman. He had broken his habit of being constantly on the move to elude Ranjit Lal.

Parvati wisely lay still. Below the ridge was a thin, long shadow and she rolled into it and pressed herself into the sand. Her sari was dark and she wore no jewellery to sparkle in the moon's light. She felt like a frightened child, shutting her eyes tightly yet visible to all. She heard the shots and cries, and wanted to run to the village imagining Kim falling and dying and experiencing her own death in her imaginings. The pain in her heart was unbearable and she wanted to cry out but muffled her face in the sand. She didn't know what to do. Run to the village? Away from it? Stay? She stopped breathing at the sound of the scuff of a foot in the sand a few feet away and the heavy breathing of an excited man. Her face was turned away and she didn't dare turn back to peep but expected to be grabbed and her throat slit, or worse. If she had known that the man who crouched only an arm's length away was Mahender, she would have fainted in fright. If there was any man she hated more than her husband, it was Mahender. Only his master held his cruelty in check and she knew that if she fell into his hands again she would be abused and beaten. But she was fortunate. Mahender was intent on the village, intent on finding her again and relishing the long journey back when she would be entirely in his power. He already felt her flesh beneath him and the pleasure he'd take from her disgust at his touch. He would pinch and slap and bite until she pleaded and begged.

'If another shot is fired I will destroy the whole village,' Ranjit Lal's voice floated across to them. The village had assembled now, cowed and huddled in the centre. The seth, the only one to value his property more than life, called to Kishore Singh.

'Do what he says or we'll all die.'

'None will mourn your death, money lender.' Kishore turned to Kim and whispered. 'What shall I do?'

'I see no escape. It's open ground and we'll be shot down.'

'Throw your guns over the barricade,' Ranjit Lal called out. There was no mistaking the satisfaction in his voice. 'All of them. Now. Otherwise we'll fire and God mustn't blame me.'

'Will you be responsible for the deaths of the women and children?' the seth whispered fiercely from the very middle of the huddle. He was young, bald and plump.

'I would happily be responsible for ending your life,' Kishore Singh said, planning to hide one musket. He would kill Ranjit Lal even as he died.

'Seth sahib,' Ranjit Lal called out. 'I know you value your life and wish to have nothing to do with our quarrel. And being wise too, you will ensure that all the guns are thrown out. If even one should remain, I will kill you.'

'See,' the seth spoke in a voice wrung with panic. 'He also wants to kill me. Doesn't he know my brother is the thanedar sahib in Jaipur?'

'He's only a constable,' a voice replied from among the villagers and the seth tried to identify the speaker, marking him for another two per cent interest should he come for a loan.

'Throw out your guns,' the seth commanded.

Kishore Singh threw his over the barricade in disgust. He wasn't concerned for the seth's life but for those of the innocent villagers. His companions did the same. A few villagers had country jezails and those followed.

'Are those all, seth sahib?'

'Yes.'

'We come then, and if a shot is fired we'll kill you all, and cut your hands off so you won't be able to count your money.'

Men rose from the earth and approached cautiously. Kishore Singh counted nineteen and stepped back into shadows and drew out his knife; Kim picked up a goat herder's cane and tested it. Many years ago in Lucknow he had learnt the martial art of kalari-payyatu from a great teacher called Kutty. It was an acrobatic form of combat and Kim knew all the vulnerable points, the kulumarmams, of a body. He could kill or maim with a lightning touch and rain blows on an opponent at the rate of three a second. He planned to get close enough to the dacoits to disarm and maim three or four and cause them to panic.

The seth ordered a villager to throw open the gate. He was bold now and hurried forward to welcome Ranjit Lal. The men had gathered, impatient now, and prodded their muskets through the thorns.

'Hurry, hurry. We must be gone before dawn,' Ranjit Lal said and when the barrier opened, pushed two of his men ahead to test the seth's veracity. 'Where is Kishore Singh and where is the man called Kim?'

'I know of no Kim but Kishore stands there in the shadow,' the seth spoke quickly. 'There is a man with him who might be this Kim.'

'How does he know of you?' Kishore Singh whispered.

'I don't know. We have both been betrayed.'

Anxiously, Kim searched for a man with a limp among the group of dacoits filing through the opening. In this light they all appeared to walk normally, in spite of their collective swagger. He noticed one man with a cane and a begging bowl and the shaven head of a sunyassi and was surprised to see a holy one among such evil men. Another man carried no gun, while a third carried two. Kim had never seen Mahender before and paid him no further attention. He looked in Parvati's direction and was thankful to see no movement. No doubt she had heard every word and knew Ranjit Lal wanted him too.

'They are both there,' the seth pointed eagerly and the men ringed them, muskets pointed, from a safe distance.

'Let me see Man Singh's cub's face before I butcher him. Or is he afraid of me too?'

Kishore Singh stepped out of the shadow, holding the knife behind his back. Kim joined Kishore in the open, placidly leaning on the harmless cane. He noticed in the shuffle of men stepping back at their approach that the holy man had moved closer to Ranjit Lal, as if for protection.

'You are Kim?'

'Yes.'

'Where is the woman then?'

'If you believe this staff is a woman, then it is a woman,' Kim said and knew now his hunter wasn't the Colonel's men but Mohini's husband's.

'He's lying,' the unarmed man said.

'She's dead,' Kim said dismissively. 'A spell had been cast on her which was too strong for any person to drive out and she died. She is now ashes.'

'Seth sahib,' Ranjit Lal called without turning. 'Does this man speak the truth. Is there a woman?'

The seth, despite cowardice, knew it would be unwise to betray a woman. He calculated his chances. The villagers wouldn't betray her, and if he should deny she was alive, he would climb in their esteem. He made this calculation rapidly.

'Lal sahib, I saw only Kishore Singh, this man Kim and two of Kishore's men.'

'You swear it?'

'I swear.'

'It's a pity then, because we could have shared a lakh between us, you and I. That is the reward offered for the finding of this woman.'

Greed had its own sound: a falter in breath followed by a moment's silence, almost spiritual in its intensity, and then the hiss of this breath released. This night it was a collective sound followed by Ranjit Lal's chuckle. Kim knew what the villagers thought. A lakh was unimaginable. It was an ocean of milk in which they could cleanse themselves of all hunger and longing. They could rejoice in good land and buffaloes and goats, extravagant marriage ceremonies for their children and a lazy and secure old age. It was what they dreamt of all their mean lives. Talk of this lakh nourished these withered dreams and Kim awaited betrayal. Which man would speak first?

The seth spoke first and swiftly. He recognised the sound of greed and hurried to claim his share of the money before the others spoke. The thought of a villager richer than him made him feel quite ill. He would lose all respect. Besides, what did they know of money? They spent their meagre earnings foolishly. Money was a seed to be planted and nurtured. The poor had a fixed destiny in life, to remain poor. Without the poor how could men grow rich?

'Lal sahib, how do I know this money exists? Will you be paying it?'

'I'm not as rich as you, seth sahib. Where will I find a lakh? No, this man here promises that his master will pay the lakh.'

For the first time, everyone's attention turned to Mahender. He stepped forward and they felt him staring at them, willing them to speak. The seth couldn't see him clearly and shuffled forward. Mahender looked most unprepossessing and the seth thought he would feel safer with Ranjit Lal than with this man with the fierce, brutish face.

'And who is his master?'

'I asked but he refused to tell,' Ranjit Lal said. 'I even threatened to kill him. I believe he tells the truth, otherwise he would have babbled any name.'

'He looks a liar."

'And you look a fool,' Mahender shouted. 'A lakh is what my master promised. What can you people lose by telling me where she is? Only point and I will remember who pointed.' He waited, no one stirred. Instead they looked to the seth as though this were a play. 'If there is no lakh, Ranjit Lal will kill me if I'm lying. If there is, you gain.'

Kim heard him in despair. When a man's greed was aroused, only gold could dampen his lust. He had no gold to offer. Mahender swung towards him, peering through the gloomy light. Kim heard him rumble as though he meant to speak but only a growl carried across to him. Even if Parvati heard every word, where could she hide? These men knew the ravines. Two men had followed them from the island palace. Where was the other? Out there, waiting? Kim remained staring at Mahender although he wanted to see if Parvati was still safe. Mahender would follow the direction of his glance and know in which direction Parvati was hidden.

'Instead of talking to these fools, let's search,' Mahender said.

'She won't be far from this man. Her lover.' He spat in Kim's direction.

Kim expected the seth to speak, to claim his blood money before he was cheated by a search. Instead, he stepped back and lowered himself to the ground. He had weighed the matter and now doubted the money existed. Pragmatism overcame greed. How would he collect his half of this reward from Ranjit Lal? The man was a dacoit and would sooner cut this throat. Besides, he reasoned, who would squander a lakh on a woman? If one died, there were always others; always younger, always prettier. 'It's a pity I know of no such woman,' the seth said from the midst of the villagers. 'Kim came alone.'

The village sighed in disappointment. Whatever else they thought of the seth, they knew he was cleverer and greedier than they. If he could turn away from a lakh, the money was an illusion.

Mahender knew he'd lost. He knew stupid villagers, only because he had been one once. 'You are fools,' he shouted. 'One lakh to any of you if you tell me where this woman is.'

'And one lakh too for Ranjit Lal,' a villager mocked. 'Ahre, you're generous with your master's money.' The laughter banished the greed.

'At least she is saved,' Kishore Singh whispered.

Kim had been studying Mahender and saw a sullen and stubborn persistence in this man. He would remain at their heels as long as breath remained in him. He was obsessed, possibly by loyalty to his master. Kim didn't know Mahender's obsession was with Parvati.

'Enough of this,' Ranjit Lal said. It was growing light now and their faces emerged out of the shadows. 'Kishore Singh, come here.'

Kishore touched Kim's arm in farewell. One hand still gripped the dagger and Kim tightened his own grip on the cane. The moment Kishore lunged, he would hurl the staff into the bunched men, driving them back.

'It's best you die, Kishore. This isn't of my making, but because I killed your father this vendetta will continue. With your death, the line ends. I can sleep in peace and not be haunted and hunted by your sons.' He jerked the rifle up as Kishore kept coming. 'Stop there.'

Ranjit Lal's attention was diverted by Kim twirling the cane. It became a blur and hummed. As Kishore lunged forward, Kim released the whirling cane. It cut a swathe through the men even as a shot was fired. The cane struck Mahender across his face, cutting his forehead, then hit a dacoit across the nose. The two men stumbled back, throwing the others off balance even as Kishore reached Ranjit Lal and pushed the dagger into his belly. For a moment, they stood as if embracing, then Kishore Singh, in some surprise, stepped back and Ranjit Lal slowly crumpled to the ground.

'He was already dead,' the sunyassi said. He turned his revolver on the other men, who were too surprised to retaliate. Mahender moaned, clutching his forehead. The other man gurgled through blood. 'Drop your weapons or I'll kill.'

Anil was still numb from killing Ranjit Lal. It was the first time he had killed and the act, a shot into Ranjit

Lal's left side, had been mean and cowardly. He would have preferred Ranjit Lal to have seen him and to have understood. There hadn't been time. He'd planned to jam the barrel into Ranjit Lal's side and force him to drop his rifle. He had actually done it but in the confusion Ranjit Lal, too intent on killing Kishore Singh, hadn't noticed.

'Who are you?' asked Kişhore Singh.

'I was with your father in prison and he died in my arms. He made me promise to take revenge. I have fulfilled that promise.'

'It was a timely fulfilment.'

'We are bound together by our acts,' Kim said.

'I won't lie to you, Kim,' Anil said. 'If Ranjit Lal had wanted to kill you, I wouldn't have fired. We are even. You freed me from prison, now I will let you escape from here.'

'There is no such thing as "even". Life isn't arithmetic though we wish it were. A good act doesn't protect us from the evil acts of others. Our lives will touch again. It is karma.'

'You, an Angrezi, are more superstitious than I.'

'Because you, an Indian, are more of the Angrezi than I. This killing,' he glanced down at Ranjit Lal, his face still frozen in surprise, 'began years ago when you made your vow. You will continue to kill.'

'Not Indians ever again. Only you British.' And then in an impeccable Etonian accent, strange even to his ears for it belonged to another person, he added, 'Go on, Kim. Get out of here. Go back to your own people.'

'These are my own people, more than they're yours.' He turned to Kishore Singh. 'I'd like one favour.'

'Name it.'

'Hold this man for a week,' he pointed to Mahender. 'Then free him.'

'It would be safer for you, Kim, if I cut his throat now. He is a dangerous man and will continue his search for you and Parvati.'

'No. I won't buy our safety with his death.'

Kim found Parvati crouched in her shallow hiding place, fearfully peering over the edge. At first she didn't move and then, when she recognised Kim, she jumped up and threw her arms around him. Her face was damp with tears.

'I was weeping because I thought you were dead. When they cremated you, I was going to throw myself on your pyre.'

Kim laughed. 'Suttee is forbidden.' He kissed her. 'We must hurry. I asked Kishore to hold your husband's man for a week but I suspect he is too wily and bold, and will escape.'

'Which one?'

When Kim described Mahender, Parvati shivered with fright.

'You should have killed him. He wants me, Kim. He won't ever give up.'

'You too are bloodthirsty. He won't know where we go. Come.'

# 7

# May 1911

Kim, who understood the nature of evil only too well, was right twice over.

On the fifth night of his captivity, when the moon was but a thin crescent and a man could barely see his hand in front of his face, Mahender rose from the ground. He remained crouched and wary, feeling the rope that bound his leg to a dacoit. He inched forward and held his breath as he stealthily drew the dagger from the guard's belt. A man tossed and turned and returned to sleep. Mahender suddenly clamped his hand over his guard's face and drew the blade swiftly across his throat. The soft gurgle went unheard. He cut his rope and took the man's jezail. For a moment, he considered killing Kishore Singh but that would be risking too much. He was already five days behind Kim and Mohini and had to hurry.

At daybreak Kishore Singh's men hunted for him, but he had vanished into the ravines.

Kim was right too about Anil Ray.

Once the shock had worn off, Anil exulted in the act of killing. It took him some weeks to grasp the horrifying truth. He spent his days wanting to prove Kim wrong and wrestled to suffocate his true feeling. The scarred desolate landscape matched his bleak mood. He ate and drank little and the austerity of his life awed his companions. They believed him a true sunyassi in his self-denial. But killing a man had changed him. It had been too easy. It was seductive, it freed his rage at the world. The exploding bullet spent him as though he had been massively drained sexually. He had thought that once he'd fulfilled his vow, he would escape further violence, escape his cursed past. His father had wanted him to escape to America, to fashion a new life and never look back on India. But his mother and father were dead, both from broken hearts, and Anil couldn't escape. He had taken a new vow, to kill the British. It seemed futile, one man against many, but the revolver made all men equal.

He needed to carry out a spectacular killing, one which would shake an empire. He could walk into the bungalow of a collector on any night while the man lay drunk on his cot, and shoot him. Others did, not often but frequently enough to alarm the British. The newspapers and the government spoke of cabals, conspiracies and secret societies. There were none. Only lone men like him, passionately hating. But still the British read meaning into each death as though they were looking for a single, simple answer to these murders. They peered suspiciously through the veil of memories of '57. That mutiny too had begun with single killings and then exploded into bloody massacres. It would happen again; they knew it, they waited for it, prepared this time.

Despite his resolve and the clear expression of his future intent, Anil didn't leave the ravines or his new companions. Kishore Singh, now the leader of the dacoits who were only too pleased to switch allegiance and not be executed, owed Anil his life and wished to serve Anil's every whim. But Anil wanted nothing except the rough comfort of these men. They didn't look beyond the ravines and cared little who ruled India. He took no part in their robberies of trains and caravans, and wanted no share of their meagre loot. Though he would have denied it, Anil was waiting for a sign, a signal, like the starter's gun on Sports Day at school, to guide him.

Men often misjudge the impact of their own acts. Anil Ray was notorious. He had been woven into myth by beating Inspector Goode in Lucknow. His name had travelled swiftly, the deed exaggerated, other deeds laid at his door. Stories accumulated while he sat quietly and was ignorant of such things, until two men found him in the ravines.

They were in search of a hero, a leader, and they believed in Anil Ray. One was Satish Mukherjee, a quiet, spectacled Bengali youth who would have passed unnoticed in an empty room. He was stooped like a cobra's hood, undernourished and aged beyond his years. His companion was a queer one. He was simply called Bhai, brother, and Anil couldn't discover anything further. He was dumb and only Satish could communicate with him. He was a lout, a man of simple strength with a child's face which had yet to take on the lines and character of intelligence and in this simplicity Anil thought he detected duplicity. He also thought they wore each other's faces.

Satish and Bhai had spent months searching for Anil Ray. It hadn't been easy for there was no trail except the rumours, like a deep undercurrent, that flowed through India. They had swum in these currents, this way first, then that, and slowly floated west to the ravines where they heard the stronger whispers of Ranjit Lal's death. One of the dacoits, hearing them make enquiries in a village by the Chambal river, brought them to Anil at gunpoint. If he had not, they would never have found him but instead floated past, dragged by another rumour in another direction.

'What do you want with me?'

'To guide us,' and they prostrated themselves and touched his feet. Anil jumped back. He hated worship, this Indian habit of elevating ordinary men to the extraordinary.

'Since I have no plans, where should I guide you?'

'Wherever you choose,' Satish said and blinked. He seemed vacant-minded as well but between those blinks,

Anil caught a glimpse of a bright mind. He waited. 'I have a plan. I'm not capable of carrying it out. We chose you out of all the others.'

'What others?'

'Men like you. But they didn't fill my needs. You do. We know your background; we know your deeds.'

'What do you want me to do?'

'Kill someone,' Satish blinked, his voice and face innocent of such murderous intent. He added, 'An Englishman. I have made a plan.'

Anil laughed. 'If you have made the plan, you kill him. And what have they done to you that you want to kill them?'

'They are here. Isn't that enough? Nothing has happened to me or my family as has happened to you and yours. I know your father and mother died of broken hearts. I've thought deeply on this matter. I'm not brave. I'm not strong. Bhai protects me as he has done ever since my schooldays. We must drive out the British as Tilak and Bannerjea have said. We must strike such a blow that they will be afraid.' He spoke with the intensity and passion of a man with an empty life searching for something to fill it. This had meaning, this was a cause.

'And whom do you wish me to kill?' Anil humoured him.

'This man.'

Satish reverently drew out half a sheet of newspaper from a deep pocket. He unfolded it carefully and passed it to Anil. On one side were advertisements for labrador puppies, a report on a test match in Birmingham and the racing results of the Royal Bengal Race Club. Anil turned it over. On the other was a detailed article about the forthcoming coronation of George V. Many Indian princes had been invited to the event.

'So?'

'The last line.'

The last line announced the King-Emperor's decision to hold a durbar in Delhi in December. Anil re-read it and was excited. Yes, the King-Emperor would be the man to kill. His assassination would bring chaos to the empire. But first they would have to plot and plan, and he would need to learn how to shoot with a rifle.

# 8

## June 1911–December 1911

Once again Parvati vanished. It happened the very day she left the nameless village. Kim bought her baggy pi-jamas, a long loose kurta and a black waistcoat embroidered in faded gold thread, from a travelling merchant who spread open his bundle of clothes, old and new, in the shade of a ruined temple. The waistcoat had a suspicious black stain on the back and the thin tear had been expertly mended. Kim suspected it had been removed from a corpse but the merchant disclaimed all knowledge of murder. He sold them a blue turban too and Kim tied it expertly in the Gujerati style, a tail of cloth snaking down to the waist, on Parvati's head. In this disguise she passed for an adolescent youth.

'We women can never ever be ourselves,' Parvati said. 'We play parts to please our men, fathers, husbands, even brothers, never to please ourselves. I have been a boy, a Muslim woman, a wife and now this Gujerati.'

'It's for your own safety,' Kim said. 'People will only see two men travelling south. If you remain a woman, we will be easily discovered.'

'But you will be recognised as the fair, handsome man who walks boldly as though he owns the world. Mahender will ask "have you seen Kim?" and the fingers will point to us.'

'What would you wish me to do to myself? Turn ugly and creep through the world as though I were afraid of it?'

'Walk with humility. Not like a prince.'

'I can't change my walk. Nor can you yours. I notice the sway of your hips although you are meant to stride boldly.'

They travelled slowly on foot and by bullock cart, once at heady speed in a tonga. They could have raced south by train but they would have been trapped in narrow corridors of timetables and ticket inspectors and railway police. Kim wanted to cross the Narbada river before the monsoon broke. The sky was still clear and sunny but the time of the year was approaching and when he lifted his head he smelt rain in the far distance. But Parvati delayed them. She could see Mandu dimly in the distance. Like every fortress in ancient India it hovered above the earth like a levitating sadhu. They were a few miles from the ruined city and she insisted on visiting it.

'How can I pass by the place where Rupmati died?'

'We can come back,' Kim said.

'No. Only a few days will be lost. We'll hurry.'

The road up was steep, almost perpendicular and wound through passes. The city had been built on a plateau high in the Vindhaya mountains, part of a rocky barrier separating north from south. They weren't snow-peaked and blue but stubby and yellow, like bad teeth. Kim and Parvati crossed the savage gorge that formed a moat around the plateau by a narrow bridge. When they looked down they saw the Narbada in the distance, a thin twisting line, and the mountains fading into a shaded sky.

The walls of the City of Joy petered tiredly away around the rim of the gorge and only the Dehli darwaza and the turret remained intact. They passed under a pink sandstone archway decorated with deep-blue enamelled mosaic, the ancient wooden gate rotting on rusty hinges, and down a narrow dusty road. The ruins were silent, pink and white and open to the sky. The palace lake was a green fever of lotuses and on the north side the ruins rose in tiers of balconies. Thick dust had settled on the floors of the halls and choked the ancient baths. The sky was dun coloured and a faint drizzle coated their faces. The Jahaz Mahal, its walls curved to resemble an ancient sea vessel, sailed in the ripples of the water. Opposite, the Hindola Mahal, built like a palanquin, seemed to swing and sway. The wind picked up strength, ruffled the water, and sighed through the skeletons. The sigh sounded like a song, still lingering in the ruins, haunting them with the memory of a beautiful woman. Parvati too sighed, her breath in tune with the wind.

They spoke in whispers, for both knew the story of Rupmati, a beautiful Hindu singer at the court of the Muslim sultan Baz Bhadur, and how they had fallen in love. He built her a palace, some distance from the city itself. Kim and Parvati slept the night in the tiny village bordering the ruins. The villagers only vaguely knew the history or the legend. For them the high plateau was no more than a place to survive.

At dawn Kim and Parvati explored the Jami Masjid. The mosque had long been abandoned and bats clung to the walls like damp leaves. Beside it was the exquisite marble tomb of its builder, Alif Khan Hoshang Shah Gori. Monkeys and bats now inhabited the frozen splendour but its dome had been copied by Shah Jahan and placed on the Taj Mahal. It took them half the day to reach Rupmati's palace, only to discover that it was now a low stone mound, overgrown with weeds. But the sandstone pavilion was still intact and standing under it they felt they could look across the whole of India.

Rupmati's beauty had been her downfall. The Mughal Akbar had sent his general, Adham Khan, to conquer Mandu in 1562, and Baz Bhadur had been killed in the battle. Adham Khan had then marched into the haram and demanded Rupmati. Legend had it she sent him wine and sweetmeats and sang for him from behind the jali. Then she appeared in all her silks and jewellery and fell dead at his feet. Adham Khan discovered she had hidden poison in her hathphool, the elaborate hand ornament, and in rage at this denial, he had thrown the other women to his soldiers and razed Mandu. For this destruction, Akbar in turn had had Adham Khan hurled from the walls of the Lal Quila. And when he didn't die immediately, he was dragged up and hurled down again. Death had soaked into the very earth and the broken walls of Mandu, and when Kim and Parvati left, they felt the relief of leaving a graveyard.

It took them another week to reach the banks of the Narbada river. The dark sky pressed down on the land, a roiling belly of clouds with creases and fat folds of rain waiting to split and drown them. In places a silvery light filtered through. The air rumbled and lightning flickered in the distance. They sat on the bank, waiting for the boatman to take them over. He was drinking tea on the far side and waiting for passengers. They didn't wait alone; villagers gathered in small groups, carrying sacks and leading goats. They all feared the rains and Kim wished the boatman would hurry. He called out twice but the man didn't stir. The Narbada was still gentle, a silvery murmur, cooling, rolling through its banks. Once the rains fell it would swell monstrously and suddenly, and swallow men and beasts and land. The silver would turn to a blood colour. Then they would have to wait weeks for it to shrink and become tame again.

The boatman finally came, thin as the pole he used. The boat was frail, planks bound together with frayed rope, and water lapped in the bottom. The others now hurried down the banks to make the crossing, looking up and praying for safety. It was the very stillness they feared. At any moment, mid-stream, the stillness could break, the wind would be swift and violent, the placid waters would rise and snap at the boat.

'Hurry,' they all said. 'Hurry.'

One was a small peacock of a man in a pure white turban; he had an inquisitive face, sharp and ferreting, and Kim knew he would ask questions. He announced, to none in particular but intending his words for Kim's ears, that he was a pundit, a sanskrit teacher who was held in high esteem.

'And you are travelling far?'

'Not far, pundit-ji,' Kim said. 'We are on a pilgrimage. My brother was struck dumb by a vision, and God ordained that for his cure he must visit every temple in the land. And so we spend our lives endlessly toiling for his salvation. Maybe our journey will end tomorrow at the next temple which God has chosen for his tongue to be loosened. Or else we will grow old and never complete our journey. Truly we are on the wheel of life, for only one of these temples holds the cure.'

The story pleased his listeners; it promised salvation for those who persisted, and confirmed their belief that God set out puzzles for men to decipher. The story took their minds off the rain. They suggested this temple, then that, old ones, new ones, ruins too. But which? India had a million temples, as life itself had a million meanings. It kept them occupied until they crossed the river and parted on the opposite bank. Kim and Parvati received their good wishes and two of the women asked the youth for dharshan because he had seen a vision. It was shyly given. The pundit and the villagers hurried away, pleased with the tale they could carry; the tale would spread and change and be known by every village in the district before the next night fell.

Stories remain long after the teller has vanished into the endless labyrinth of India. This one hung in the air and fell now on Madan's ears. He was sheltering from the storm in the hut of a village head man and resting his swollen ankle. The pain was a constant reminder of Kim and with each limp, he vowed to find him. The rains made it ache more, as the damp seeped into the splintered bones. The Colonel's instructions were explicit: find Kim. He intended to disobey. He would find and kill. Kim had killed his brother and this was a vendetta. But he'd lost all trace of Kim. He had followed Kim and the woman into the ravines and lost them there. It was by chance, a month later, that he heard of Ranjit Lal's death and of a man and woman leaving a nameless village.

When he heard of the two travellers on their endless pilgrimage, he paid little attention at first. The air was full of such stories; miracles and curses and cures abounded. Visions were seen constantly, gods descended disguised as men or beasts to ravish women or grant boons. Out of politeness he listened to the story and by now in its telling, Kim's description was exaggerated. He'd grown fairer and taller, while Parvati was smaller and thinner and darker. The youth had even fallen into a trance, the sar panch said, and predicted that the pundit's wife would give birth to a girl child on the next full moon, which she did. This was a part of the exaggeration but it came near the truth. Madan had heard in Pushkar that the woman remained in her strange trance and couldn't be cured.

'The man you say was very fair. How fair?'

'Fair as a woman should be,' the sar panch said, 'fairer even than wheat.'

'Well built, supple, with a luxuriant moustache and eyes the colour of evening smoke rising against a clear sky?'

'Yes, yes,' the sar panch said.

'Was this boy who fell into a trance pretty?' Madan asked. 'Did he have delicate features?'

The sar panch, who had not seen either of these strangers, nodded eagerly. 'Yes, his face was delicate with his vision.'

'In which direction were they travelling?'

The sar panch waved southwards and Madan gambled and planned to cross the Narbada, once it stopped its thunderous roaring.

Though Madan couldn't see Kim and Parvati sheltering in the village some fifty miles away, where they had stayed for the last two months, other eyes did. High above, the giant eagle Jatayu watched Kim and Parvati. The eagle, once mortally wounded by the demon Ravana, Sita's abductor, had impressed Brahma by his bravery and been granted the boon of immortality. It was a twofold immortality, for his deeds had been woven into the imaginations and dreams of all who lived below the span of his great wings. He was carved, painted and worshipped. Jatayu was now the eye of the dwarf Vamana, the avatar of Vishnu, who had summoned Kim and given him the stone that he wore around his neck in a leather pouch. It was an ordinary looking pebble but it gave Kim the power to summon Vamana when he was in desperate need. The dwarf had already saved his life once, drawing out the bullet that Madan had fired into Kim's heart.

What Kim and all men and women did, Vamana knew through Jatayu's eyes. He saw all things, from horizon to horizon: Madan waiting for the rains to stop, Mahender sheltering in a village, Anil Ray preparing to kill a king. The rains had trapped them all in place, turning the earth to mud and the mud into lakes and roaring rivers. Roads, bridges, pathways, vanished. No one dared move until the monsoons ended.

The rains began to falter. The land was lush and fresh, like the body of a young woman. They continued on their journey. The sky was their roof and that night they watched the slow movement of the stars. The country they were in was strange and new. They no longer understood the language and had to communicate with signs and gestures.

Jatayu circled patiently and noted how Kim often looked back north. He was leaving his past. All his life had been spent there, criss-crossing the land; like a spider's web his path wove together mountains and valleys and plains and roads and bazaars and cities. Friends and enemies too were entangled in that web, remembering him even now as he thought about them.

'I don't wish to take you away from what you know,' Parvati said. 'Each night and dawn you look north. I am to blame for this break in your life.'

'No. You have escaped your husband, I my past.'

'You miss your old life then?'

'Yes. I will miss it,' he said eventually. 'I will miss my friends especially but also the familiarity of the country I passed through so often.'

'Then we'll go back,' Parvati said and immediately

rose. They carried only a blanket each and a change of clothes. 'I cannot bear to see you unhappy.'

'No. You don't understand that if I didn't miss the past that would make it worthless. Come. Sit. I want you to understand my own nature which made me behave as I once did.'

'You are a good man,' Parvati said. 'Surely you can't regret that part of your life.'

'It's the use one man makes of another that I think about,' Kim said. 'I was a child when I began my work for the Colonel. He told me that what I was to do was honourable, and that it was honest in its intent. I loved him as I would have my father, and needed to believe in him and believe in the profession he allotted to me. He spoke of kings and empires and great games. An agent must be given beliefs. Without beliefs his life is empty. Money alone cannot fill it or make it worthwhile. The Colonel gave me these beliefs. He spent days telling me the history of my people, of which I knew nothing. Until then I was an Indian, one of a conquered race. My heroes were an Indian child's heroes, mythical men and events so distantly past that I could scarcely imagine them. I knew the story of Rama and Sita; I knew of Bhima's great strength and bravery; as a child I re-fought the battles of Udai Singh against the Mughals. But then, all our past ceased, and we whispered only of our defeats. We were proud of the Rani of Jhansi who led her soldiers into battle against the British and died fighting, proud of the rebellious sepoys, but we were defeated. You must understand, I was not ashamed of these defeats. We died bravely, recklessly. I thought this was my only past. Then suddenly I was given another. The Colonel filled me with the glory of Clive and Hastings, the triumph of the Mutiny, the bravery of Nicholson, the boldness of vision that conquered this land, and an empire stretching from one sunrise to another. I was a child, and children only wish to belong to the winning side. Victory in itself is a belief. It's stronger than God even. The belief he gave me was that I was part of this history; he wove me into the fabric of this newer heroism and glory. It was natural that as a boy I should thrill to such tales, more natural still that I should wish to belong, not to the ruled but to the rulers. I wanted to be an Englishman. The Colonel divided men into Englishmen and those who were not. One day I was a "not"; the next I was an Englishman. It was like a reincarnation. As he believed, so I believed. And once he saw my belief in these things, he gave me a purpose. But as an Imperial agent I betrayed men, I led them to believe I was one kind of man, a friend, but I was truly another, the enemy. Some deserved it, others not. Those who did not deserve betrayal now lie uneasily on my conscience. They were as honourable in their cause as I in mine, except that their interests lay against the interests of the empire. I was taught that it was honourable and just to lie and to cheat, because in these lies were greater causes served. They had a meaning and pattern which I was too small, not only in age but in position, to understand. You must understand that for years I served the Colonel blindly. I did his bidding, without questioning why he bade me do this and that. I knew of course that he had more trust in me than in any other. I was of his blood but could pass through the bazaars and travel the roads without being known for an Englishman. But with each betrayal I grew less. I dwindled in my soul. I felt it shrinking within my body and I knew it was time to escape if I was to live with myself.'

'What would you have done otherwise?'

'Nothing. I had no direction until he found me. I moved at whim, ignorant of all purpose in life. The Colonel gave me one; the lama another. I tried to fulfil both but there was constant conflict in me. One asked me to serve the empire, the other God. The war within never ceased.'

'And now? Are you calm and at peace?'

'Peace comes with forgiveness,' Kim said harshly. 'Who is there to forgive me? Men lie in prisons and graves because of me. Anil Ray will never forgive me.'

'He is not important. Will the Colonel?'

'Yes. I will write him a letter of resignation. He will understand.'

'He won't accept your resignation. He has put too much of himself in you. You are what he wishes he could be. He needs you and will use you again, dear Kim. He took a boy and corrupted him for his own purpose. He saw in you the way into India. We are strangers to them. They live in their cantonments, too remote to understand us. And no king can hold a kingdom like that. You are the Colonel's ears and eyes, the only ones he has ever trusted. There will be no forgiveness.'

'I know him well. A father will always forgive.'

'Only if he isn't forced to choose between a son and his duty,' Parvati said. 'And what will you do now with me? You're not a man who will sit quietly. You will look north always; you will yearn for the excitement of your past.'

'I yearn for innocence once more, not excitement.'

Kim longed suddenly for the days he had spent on the Grand Trunk Road with the lama. The lama was innocence. He had led a full life and still looked at the world through a child's eye. That was Kim's goal but he knew his child's eye had darkened.

In December Kim and Parvati reached Madras. Though it was a relief to be nearing the end of their journey, Kim yearned even more for the north. This yearning was physical now. He'd never experienced such heat. The air was moist and seemed too heavy to breathe. They moved in the damp heat of a hammam.

'It will be worse in Narain's village,' Parvati said. 'There'll be no sea breeze.'

'He said it was cool.'

'For a south Indian cool only means standing in the shade.'

As Parvati had been drawn to Mandu, Kim was tugged to the squat, granite fort facing the white-hot sands and a sea as blue and hard as the sky. Fort St George was a drab grey shrine, crab-like, in a dry moat with small cannons pointing out to sea. In his mind he had pictured it as awesome and magnificent as the Lal Quila in Delhi or Agra. This fort had been built in 1644, the first English foothold in India, on land given by the Rajah of Chandragiri. The grant was inscribed on a plate of gold.

The fort was no ghostly ruin but bustled with life. The stately white mansions inside housed the secretariat of the Madras Presidency. Carriages and the occasional motor car crowded the narrow lanes, officials strolled down long verandahs and peons in white with red cummerbunds and turbans jumped to attention at their passing. Kim reverently entered the small white chapel, shaded by a huge banyan tree, beside the parade ground. It was cool and quiet inside and the walls were covered with marble and brass plaques.

One of the plaques commemorated the marriage of the English hero, Robert Clive, and Parvati watched Kim carefully reading the faded old English script. Nearly every square inch of space commemorated a captain or a major, a wife or a child, who had died in India. She felt the calm and quiet of the chapel. Here, amidst this past, she became truly aware of Kim's English identity. It was all his history, not hers. There was nothing familiar for her and she was confused by this shrine, resenting its existence and its hold on the man she loved. In her arms, his difference was unimportant. Now he had stepped away, too far for her to reach. He belonged to the race of the conquerors and she felt a sense of her own betrayal in loving him. If she'd had the courage of Rupmati, she would have swallowed poison. But she had been taken by love and not force.

Kim noticed her confusion.

'This too is part of India.'

'No. There's nothing I recognise.'

'Why is it different? If you can stand in the ruins of an Afghan fort and feel it Indian, why not this place? The marble and brass are Indian, the stone underfoot and the trees above, all Indian. These people served India too. Look, so many died here.'

'But they're English.'

'And they belong here. You can't unravel one thread and pull it out of the weave. You'd destroy the fabric, destroy India. This is part of India, as much as the Mughal past, the Afghan, the Turkish. You may resent their rule but you cannot deny their place in Indian history. To do so is to be false, to be blinded by resentment. They've shaped our minds and changed our future by their presence. There will come a day when history will be rewritten to deny their existence, but that history will be written in their language.'

'You speak of "them", but you are one of them.'

'I'm not ashamed. I can't be blamed for an accident of birth, as others can't be blamed that they are born untouchable or Christian or Muslim. And like them I consider myself an Indian but of a separate caste, another community.'

'But I was watching you, and I saw pride light your face. I could never feel that. I feel diminished here. I feel suffocated between these walls.'

They stepped out into the sunlight and walked along the beach road towards the towering minarets and domes of the Madras High Court. A carriage passed them at a smart pace and they caught a glimpse of two Englishmen in the dim shadows.

'Am I one of those?'

'No,' Parvati said.

He had become Indian for her again, blending back into the land and the people. This didn't lessen her confusion. It only left her with a sense of unease, doubting what she had seen in the chapel but knowing that he'd moved away from her.

Madras, a sea of green shady trees stretching out like a canopy over the white bungalows, lay on the very edge of the sea. It was a city only recently established, and the roots here were more English than Indian. The fort was the dropped pebble, and the streets and buildings rippled out from it. There were no ancient forts or chowks; the bazaars were called Flower Bazaar or Rattan Bazaar, and the town centre was George Town. Mount Road stretched straight as an arrow from the rear of the fort as far as the eye could squint into the terrible glare. These were the real names of these places, not anglicised, for there had not been an India here before.

It was in the shade of a rain tree in the compound of the High Court, which had once been a nawab's palace, that they heard of the King-Emperor's durbar. It was to be in Delhi, in a week's time. A writer told them that the King-Emperor intended to move the capital from Calcutta to Delhi. He repeated the ancient curse of Delhi: when a dynasty built a new capital in Delhi, that dynasty would fall. He also told them the estimated cost of the spectacle and whispered 'six hundred thousand pounds' in awe. A special crown had been made for the King-Emperor, the Imperial Crown of India, and he would be crowned Emperor of India at this durbar.

'We are a poor people. Why should we have to pay for such things? The Emperor also intends to re-unify Bengal once more but it's not enough,' he confided, as though he were a Bengali and not a small, dark Madrassi with a snow white moustache and a gaunt face. 'We must have swaraj.'

'And what will you do with this freedom?' Kim asked. He was surprised that in this place, so distant from the turbulence in Bengal, a man should voice such thoughts. 'Some maharajah will rule you again and impose a heavy burden on you, and there will be chaos and darkness.'

'Then it is of our own making,' the writer said. 'Times are changing, my friend.'

He studied Kim curiously and from his bearing and the difficulty of language knew him to be from the north. He also admired the lightness of Kim's skin and that of his young companion who said not one word.

Before him was a low desk and the instruments of his trade: ink, a steel pen, a collection of nibs, a blotter, paper and postage stamps. He wrote letters and petitions for those who could not, and though neither

Kim nor Parvati was illiterate Kim felt this man had the necessary equipment for the writing of this important letter of resignation.

'Do you write English with a fine hand?'

'I am a most beautiful writer of that fine language. Even the Chief Justice has admired my hand. My writing alone has swayed his judgement in very important cases. The letters I write earn the men who send them great jobs in the government service. Tell me what you wish to say and I will couch it in such a flattering manner that you will be granted your every wish.'

'I'm not a man given to flattery. Only write what I tell you. I can read and write but your hand will be better.' He waited for the writer self-importantly to organise his materials, choose a fine nib with great care and fix it to his pen. When he was ready, Kim began: 'Colonel sahib . . .'

'No, no. You must address it. Who does it go to and where? I know the form. Otherwise this good gentleman will not read your letter.'

'Write as I tell you. "Colonel sahib . . ."'

'You should be more respectful to this sahib,' the writer said. 'I will write Dear Most Reverent and Wise Colonel sahib.'

'Write what I tell you,' Kim repeated. '"Colonel sahib. I have thought deeply on this matter and have not taken this decision lightly. The death" no, say "the murder – of Narain by one of your men affected me greatly. Until then, I was unaware of the deception involved in this matter. I served you loyally and did not expect your betrayal. I will not discuss this any further. You and I know what I mean. I do not deny the worth of this empire and the great measure of order it has brought to India. Nor do I deny the blood that flows in my veins. Yet the very heart which pumps this blood through my body is tugged in a different direction. I was, as you know, a child of India and would even now possibly be dead, a victim of disease or, worse, starvation if you had not found me and discovered my true identity. When I first served you in the beginning, we played the great game against another empire – the Russians, for whom I had no love. Like you I feared their intentions towards India. But once that game ceased and you turned your attention within the country, and moved me like a pawn in the new game against the Indian people, I lost heart for the game. I cannot betray my own people. Nor can I betray you. I wish only to remain without commitment to either cause. I hereby tender my resignation. What I have done in the past and all the things I have known will remain as silent as the deepest and darkest night. I remain your most humble servant . . ."'

The writer paused, waiting, and finally looked up. His eyes were veiled, giving no indication whether the words he wrote had lodged in his mind.

'And your good name, please?'

'I will write it myself. Give it to me.'

Kim took the letter. The man wrote with a fine, flowing hand. It looked impressive and he was quite pleased. Parvati read it over his shoulder.

'It's a foolish thing to resign a good government job,' the writer said. 'And more foolish to do it in such a disrespectful manner. This sahib will never forgive you. Let me write it again and couch it in language of humility.'

'Writer sahib, I attend to my work, you attend to yours. Here is another letter for you to write. "My old and dear friend, how are you? I don't know whether you are still alive. I left you mourning Narain's death and gathering wood for his pyre. I saw the smoke from a distance, and prayed to God to accept his soul and allow him to be re-born on a higher plane. I am writing to tell you that I have resigned from the service of the Colonel sahib. I find I cannot lift my hand against India, and what is to happen will happen whether I am part of this new game or not. It was Narain's death, more than the manner of his dying and the betrayals that led to his death, that brought me to this decision. I do not wish the Colonel to know where I am. He will not harm me nor try to dissuade me, but Parvati's husband may come to hear of our whereabouts and send his men once more in pursuit. I beg you, and know you will, keep the postmark of this letter a secret. I will not remain here long either. Please re-direct the enclosed letter to the Colonel sahib. I will always remain your affectionate friend."'

Parvati leaned over and whispered into Kim's ear. He turned to the writer and dictated one more letter. This one was brief. 'Dear Alice. I only write to tell you I am alive and well. I was rescued from certain death by the same man who saved my life before. I cannot tell you where I am for I still fear my husband. I only hope this finds you well too. I will write at great length at a later date telling you of all my adventures.'

Kim paid for the writer's service and they strolled down the beach road to the main post office, a dark red Victorian building with white arches and pillars. The streets leading off were small and narrow and crowded with commercial establishments of every description. Eager young Englishmen, commercial types, box-wallahs employed by the British companies, mingled with natives on the streets. The Englishmen wore topis and some wore spine pads, an invention meant to protect the wearer from sun stroke. It marked them as newly arrived.

The writer followed Kim and his young companion. He loitered fifty yards behind, having left his desk and implements in the safe custody of a tea-kadai. He mumbled continually to himself and if one had listened, one would have heard Kim's letters word for word. He was committing them to memory. As a writer he was privy to many small secrets, most of little use: coolies writing to their villages, young men applying for jobs, others petitioning the courts, a few telling of twisted deeds in the commercial establishments and reporting them to distant people who could profit. He made use of this knowledge in his own small way; it was his dastur for having the skill to be a writer. He sensed the importance of these letters and the greater importance of the man he followed.

The writer saw Kim enter the post office and take up a pen tied by a string, and sign the letters. He saw him blow the ink dry and not use the blotter provided, and this frustrated his attempt to discover his name. Parvati did the same with her letter to Alice.

Kim bought three stamped envelopes. He carefully wrote 'To Colonel Creighton', placed the Colonel's letter in this first envelope and sealed it. He slipped it in with the second letter and addressed that to Isaac Newton. Parvati understood the need for a writer as she carefully addressed her own envelope. Kim's handwriting was atrocious.

'Didn't they teach you to write properly in school?'

'I didn't stay there long enough,' Kim said. 'Though I was young, within I was already a man and couldn't spare time for such niceties.'

He would have sent his letter then but, turning suddenly, he caught sight of the writer standing at the telegram desk. His back was to Kim but Kim never forgot the stance or build of a man. He made no mention of this to Parvati and when they left the post office, they rested in the shade, cooled by the sea breeze. The writer came out a moment later and Kim watched him search the road. If he did finally notice Kim, he made no sign but walked slowly back to the High Court. However, once he turned the corner, he summoned two chokras who ran errands for anyone who paid them. He gave them two annas, described Kim and his companion, and told them to follow him.

'But be careful,' he told them. They were small and dark and wore only ragged shorts. 'He is a man who notices all things and if he should see you he will remember your faces. Remain separate from each other and, if one is noticed, send another to follow.'

When Kim passed the High Court, he saw the writer absorbed in his profession. The railway station wasn't far and when they walked there in the cool of the evening, he kept frequent watch to see if they were followed. Chokras abounded like flies, and even his practised eye couldn't tell if any followed them. Like all railway stations and all government buildings, this one was painted red. This uniformity of colouring was meant as an official badge, for police stations too were red.

'I wonder why red?' Parvati asked when they were inside the cavernous hall, 'And not blue, to match our sky. I suppose red is an Imperial colour.'

'Purple,' Kim said. 'But it would be expensive to use so much indigo for the paint.' He posted the letters and bought two tickets for Madurai.

The writer later heard nearly every word and knew the time the train had departed and in which carriage they sat. Though it was late and the darkness intimidated him, he set out along Poonamalli Road. He was a thrifty man, and walked rather than hire a tonga. The road was straight, with barely a curve, and led all the way west to Bangalore. Madras soon petered out and it grew darker still for the road passed through a tunnel of trees. During the day, he would have welcomed their shade but now their shadows made him jumpy and fearful. He hurried, peering around nervously. He was in the country, and the road was flanked by rice fields. He only slackened his pace when he saw the entrance gates. A chowkidar stood on guard and inspected the writer carefully by the light of his lantern. The light fell on the name carved on the plaque on the gate: T.V. Naidu. The chowkidar unlocked the iron gates and permitted the writer to enter. From the road, he couldn't even catch a glimpse of the house. The drive curved gently between trees and set further back were immaculate lawns and flowerbeds. He heard water flowing and it soothed his nerves. He caught glimpses of fountains and small canals, the water blacker than the earth in the moonless night.

He rounded the final curve. The mansion loomed suddenly, a white cliff glowing with lights. A hundred yards further along was a low bungalow, connected to the main house by a passage. Dogs barked and rushed and he stood stock still, terrified, but they only sniffed his heels and servants came to pull them away. He was permitted to wait on the large verandah that surrounded the house like a moat and a servant brought him tea and biscuits.

The writer rose and namasted when T.V. Naidu finally came out of the house. He was a slim, athletic-looking man, clean-shaven, with gold-rimmed spectacles. He was young, in his mid-thirties, and his calm face always impressed the writer with its intelligence. He wore a crisply ironed white dhoti and a long silk shirt, and smelt of soap. The writer felt unclean beside him. A servant walked behind T.V. Naidu, holding a silver tray on which were a tin of Gold Flake cigarettes and matches. T.V. Naidu himself carried only a new cricket ball, which he spun constantly as though it were a coin. He listened carefully to the writer's report.

'The only names in these letters are Narain and Parvati and the Englishwoman Alice. Yet there was no woman present, only the silent boy. Could he have been this woman?'

'He was delicate.' The writer squeezed his face into thought. T.V. Naidu waited, spinning the ball. It shone in the lamplight, red like all the buildings but polished as an apple. The suggestion took shape in the writer's mind; the youth changed into a woman. 'Yes, yes. It was a woman.'

'Colonel sahib. Which Colonel? He is no longer in the military and plays great games. Those were the words, great games?'

'Great game, sir.'

'Against the Russian empire. This Colonel then is a political man, one of importance. Some months ago, a Colonel Creighton was knighted. The newspaper failed to specify what he did.' The writer watched the fall and rise of the ball; it was hypnotic and he kept nodding in time. 'They don't knight military men until they become generals. Creighton possibly, then. I'll make enquiries about him. You couldn't find out the name of the letter writer?'

'No, sir. My boys never heard it spoken.'

'But he's an Englishman?' Naidu said.

'Sir, he did not look like one or behave like one. I thought he was from the north, but never an Angrezi.'

'Which would make him ideal for the Colonel. But he's unhappy with his Colonel sahib. He could be of use to us. He has secrets . . .'

'He intimated as much in this letter. "Silent as the deepest and darkest night" he will keep them.'

'Secrets are a government's heart and soul. Send a telegram to Srinivasan in Madurai. Tell him to wait for the train and follow this man and the youth.' He gestured and the bearer stepped forward with the tray. He took a cigarette and the bearer lit it. 'Alice! It's a familiar name. I know it from somewhere.'

'Only the main post office is open now,' the writer said, worrying about how he was to get there at this hour. He'd hoped to spend the night here and return to the city in the morning. His heart sank at the thought of the long walk.

'The motor car will take you,' T.V. Naidu said and ordered a servant to fetch the car.

The writer wasn't surprised by this gesture. T.V. Naidu was known to be quite eccentric. The poorest villager, even an untouchable, could, in an emergency, commandeer one of Mr Naidu's motor cars. He had also built the local school and made education compulsory for every child, male and female, and his kitchens supplied them with lunch daily. And any bright but poor young man, as long as he understood even the rudiments of cricket, could win one of Mr Naidu's scholarships to study in England.

They sat in silence, listening to the hum of insects in the garden. The ball spun continually. The writer noted his fingers: they were long and delicate and supple. He caught a glimpse of headlights through the trees long before he heard the engine.

He rose when the car stopped beneath the porch. It was a great gleaming machine, and he'd never ridden in one. T.V. Naidu rose too but made no move to accompany him. Instead he pulled out a fistful of coins from his pocket and without counting let them fall into the writer's cupped palms.

# 9

## December 1911

From the steps of the Jama Masjid, the huge mosque built by the Mughal emperor Shah Jahan, they watched the preparations for the great durbar. On all sides the past lay in ruins; here the fortress wall of a Lodhi king tumbled down like a child's bricks, there crumbled the tomb of a Persian soldier. The legacy of conquest peeped out of the faces of the men and women around them. Like the fragments of a broken mirror they reflected a Greek profile, a Turk's eyes, a Persian's nose, a Mongol's cheek bones, a European's skin. The city, like an old woman forgotten and hidden away in a neglected palace room, stirred to life. It was being adorned and painted and jewelled. Yet there was a sense too that nothing had changed. Other citizens, over the centuries, had watched such preparations for other monarchs.

It was a cold day, with thin, fine sunlight which barely warmed them. Around Anil and Satish milled devout Muslims, some intent on prayer, others, like them, drawn to the activity.

Across the vast maidan, half hidden by the dust raised by the movement of men and bullock carts and elephants, rose the massive walls of the Red Fort. It too had been built by Shah Jahan and completed by his son Aurangzeb. Though it was truly of another age, it had never lost its purpose. The fort still housed an army and the British flag flew above the Amar Singh gate. The interior had been partially razed during the Mutiny but the British had checked their vengeance short of the marble palace overlooking the Jumna river.

Anil Ray had never witnessed such frenetic activity. A town of stone and tents was rising on the brown plain, not an ordinary one but elaborate and magical. It stretched as far as the eye could see and then further, a township of lanes and avenues, bungalows and mansions, servants' quarters and stables, all made of cloth to house the guests. It was so extensive that a special track was laid for a train, to pick up the guests and carry them to the fort. The town was also to have its own special monuments which were rising swiftly beside the walls of the Red Fort.

'Those are two concentric amphitheatres,' Satish explained from his notes. 'There will be many activities – parades, polo games, singers and dancers – to entertain Their Imperial Majesties and their guests.'

He had planned carefully. His notes had been copied from his father's files every evening while his father slept. Anil had been attracted to this plan by Satish's meticulous attention to such detail. Satish's father was a clerk to the army engineer in charge of constructing this magical city. His files contained not only the plans of the city but also the seating arrangements and the order of the processions. Men and animals alike were placed in precise positions. Here would be the governors, there the lieutenant governors. The Indian princes would start on the procession at specified times, their places determined by the gun salutes accorded them by the British, from twenty-one for Baroda down to none for the minute principalities. The King-Emperor and Her Majesty, enthroned on an elephant, would make their entry into Delhi. They would proceed into the Red Fort and mount the steps to the battlements above the Amar Singh gate. There, on a marble platform, beneath a gold canopy, they would sit on their thrones and view the march past of their subject people. The King-Emperor would wear a special crown made for this occasion, the Imperial Crown of India. Once His Majesty was crowned and the durbar over, the Imperial Crown of India would be removed to London. This was to prevent any usurper stealing the crown and proclaiming himself Emperor of India.

The police, of course, would guard every foot of the route and surround the durbar ground. None would be admitted without special passes and these would be issued only the day before. The killing couldn't take place within the durbar arena; only outside.

They scouted the route and finally found a tiny storeroom above a silk merchant's shop that looked out on the road. The merchant was glad to rent it to Satish for twice its value. Satish told him it was to store spices sent from Calcutta. His roof was joined to countless others. The old city flowed and spread like a great river and it was easy to move from one building to another, and jump the narrow lanes and gulleys. Escape would be swift.

Anil paced the distance from the building to the road where the King-Emperor would pass. A hundred and ten yards. Too great for a revolver with any accuracy. Anil returned to the dealer who had sold him the revolver and haggled over a brand new .303 Enfield rifle. He bought it for three hundred and fifty rupees, provided by Satish, and hid it, wrapped in sacking, in the storeroom.

They were careful. They spent only an hour each day studying the preparations. Otherwise, their idleness in the bustle would attract attention. Anil had a room in a serai and was grateful not to have to spend all day with these new companions. He found them unsettling. Satish said little, except occasionally to discuss a detail of the assassination of His Majesty. His past was blank and he had no other interest. This intensity depressed Anil. Satish was also humourless and quite bloodthirsty. He wanted Anil to shoot off the King's head but Anil intended to aim for the body. On top of an elephant the King would be an easy target.

Satish's father, Mr Mukherjee, a spindly man with an unnaturally large stomach that resembled a clay pot, was immensely satisfied with his position as a clerk. A government job was coveted by all. It was well paid, secure and carried a pension. It also gave one status and a certain, if limited, amount of power. Friends and relatives envied him. During office hours, perched at his desk, he was obsequious and humble. Outside, he walked with a swagger and bullied his wife, his nine children and everyone else within range of his authority.

So he almost succumbed to sheer fright when he found Satish's copies of all his files hidden in a corner of the small tent that had been put up for government servants. He didn't understand the reason for their existence and couldn't believe his son capable of any mischief. Satish was his eldest boy and he expected him also to become a clerk.

'Why are you copying my files?' he demanded.

Satish had anticipated the discovery. The tent was too small for any privacy. 'I'm only practising my English so that when I apply for a job, I won't fail.'

The answer should have satisfied his father, but only the day before an Inspector of Police, named Goode, had lectured them on the importance of protecting the life of their King-Emperor. Satish's father was proud to be working for the King-Emperor and each morning at work bowed in homage to his portrait. Inspector Goode was a thin man with a bristly red moustache. He wore a permanent smirk but it was the setting of his broken jaw that distorted his face and leaked a thin dribble of saliva from the corner of his mouth. He constantly dabbed at it with his handkerchief. Mr Mukherjee knew who had broken his jaw and hated men such as Anil Ray who gave them all a bad name. Of course he didn't suspect Satish but the boy was impressionable and could have shown the chart with the seating arrangements and the exact timings of the King-Emperor's entry into Delhi and his route to the durbar.

He didn't want to get Satish into trouble and spent the whole night agonising over the problem. When Satish and Bhai went out in the morning, the file went with them. His father followed them and when he saw them meet Anil Ray on the steps of the Jama Masjid he knew immediately that Satish had been coerced into this treasonable behaviour.

'Who is that man you met this morning?' Satish's father asked the moment he returned.

'A sunyassi. He is my guru.'

'Then why is he interested in the arrangements for the durbar?' his father demanded. When Satish didn't reply, he slapped him. The blow wasn't hard, as he wasn't a strong man but it shocked him. It was panic and worry that made him strike out. 'He's forcing you to bring him these papers. I know that.'

'He isn't forcing me. He's just a sunyassi.' And Satish sullenly refused to discuss it any further. He knew his father's pride was this job, working for the English, and held him in contempt, even though the job gave Satish a comfortable life.

Mr Mukherjee made up a story before he approached Inspector Goode. He went humbly, hands clasped in supplication, dressed in his best suit. He had rehearsed his story and knew he had to be believed. Selfishly, he thought it was to save Satish but it was to save himself from future repercussions. He waited in the shade of Goode's tent for the interview, perspiring profusely.

Inspector Goode was a different man. His views had been changed by the beating. He no longer loved India, but hated it. He hated the people even more and viewed Satish's father with distaste and cruel dislike. Before the event that had not only distorted his face but twisted his heart and soul out of shape, he would have been patient, as a parent would with a child. Now he lived with his humiliation, but barely, because he knew it had become public knowledge. He knew that Europeans pitied him and wished he had died instead of embarrassing them all with his continued presence, while Indians smiled behind their sly faces. The sole reason he hadn't resigned and left the country was Anil Ray. He dreamt of killing Ray, gloating over the terrible agony he would inflict. Ray's death wouldn't cleanse him; it wouldn't straighten his face nor iron out the twists in his soul. But it would finally free him from India.

'What the hell do you want?' Inspector Goode said. 'You could have spoken to my deputy but I gather it's very important. Be quick, and get your dirty hide out of here.'

'Inspector General sahib. . . .'

'And stop your bloody flattery. I'm an Inspector, you stupid little nigger. Come on, out with it. You're stinking up the tent.'

'Inspector sahib, I only come to report something that might be of some importance to you.' Mr Mukherjee was flustered by such rudeness. His own superior, Colonel Nichols, was a polite and considerate man. 'There is a sunyassi, but he only pretends to be one, and he is very interested in this durbar.' He waited for some comment, shying away from those unblinking blue eyes. They kept staring. 'My son has nothing to do with this. He was forced to show him the map of the route and the timings. This sunyassi has a hold over him. He has hypnotised my son who is a very good boy.'

'You're lying about your son. You're all bloody liars, the lot of you. What's this sunyassi's name?'

'I do not know, Inspector sahib.'

'Fetch your son. Quick. Now. Get out.'

Satish wasn't afraid of Goode, though he didn't reveal this feeling. He kept his head bowed, furious with his father for this betrayal.

'Who is this man?'

'Inspector Sahib, he is only a holy man. He is a great admirer of the King-Emperor and wished to know where to stand in order to get the best, clearest view of His good Majesty. I helped him with my advice.'

'What's his name?'

'Swami Anand.'

'Bring him here. Immediately.'

Anil Ray learned of Inspector Goode's presence with satisfaction. The beating had achieved what he had intended, stripping Goode of the outer layer of hypocrisy and revealing the true inner man, the hater.

'What should I do?' Satish asked.

'Tell him Swami Anand has gone away and you can't find him,' Anil said. 'And we mustn't meet again until after the assassination.'

'Where will we meet then?'

'Delhi railway station,' Anil lied. He meant to disappear completely and reappear as another man, still intent on killing.

Satish reported Swami Anand's disappearance and blinked rapidly in the icy glare of Goode's eyes. They hurt, like sunlight. Goode dismissed him; he already knew Swami Anand had remained in Delhi, and was living in a small room in a serai behind the grain merchant Lal Chand in the Chandni Chowk Bazaar. He had sent an assistant superintendent to follow Satish, expecting him to lie. He would arrest Satish later.

The assistant superintendent in question, Neil Dumaine, was an ambitious young man. He was aware that there were only a couple of rungs more for him to climb before his career stopped. He would never rise any further. Only Europeans held higher posts. Four generations of Dumaines had served in the Indian Police. His great-grandfather had been Inspector General of the United Provinces, but times had changed. Dumaine had a thin stream of Indian blood in him and this faint colouring prevented him rising to such heights. He was bitter about this taint and dreamed often of how different his life would have been if his great-grandfather had not married an Indian woman. She had been a Jat princess, fair and lovely, but in the eyes of his superiors his great-grandmother was reduced to a 'native', and he to a 'chi-chi'. It took a special eye to note his colouring; his skin took to the sun easily, never turning to the raw and angry red that marked a true European. He had blond hair and grey eyes and stood head and shoulders above the Indians. Like an Englishman.

He was meticulous in his duty and felt that responsibility for the King-Emperor's safety rested entirely on his shoulders. He day-dreamed of dramatically saving the life of His Majesty and receiving the KCMG.

He made his report to Inspector Goode on Satish's meeting with a sadhu. They had spoken at some length and then the sadhu had wandered over to the steps of the Jama Masjid. He had sat there for an hour, watching the final preparations for the durbar.

'What does this man look like?'

To Dumaine, Goode was barely polite. Goode always noted the mute pity in his men's eyes. They followed him everywhere and even if he were posted to Cape Comorin some policeman would have that look. He hated it.

'He's bald and clean-shaven. About five feet six. Quite muscular. He's quite indifferent to the people who ask him for dharshan.' He'd noted Anil's reluctance to bless the people who asked for it. He'd wave his hand vaguely and dismiss them.

'Keep a close eye on him and report back.'

Goode was frantic with last-minute preparations. Guests had already begun to arrive and take up residence in their tents. There were already complaints of petty theft and he had increased police patrols. On the twelfth, in two days, the King-Emperor would make his entry into Delhi and police were already posted along the route.

Neil Dumaine decided a disguise would be best, otherwise he would be noticed. He chose to be a Kashmiri; his fair hair and grey eyes suited this role. The city was filling with people, many of whom had been sent in large parties by the district collectors to show their allegiance to Their Majesties.

Anil spent the final day in solitude. It was almost a religious feeling, an ecstatic experience. He made no move to go to the rooftop and instead sat contemplative and serene by the Jumna river, feeling the calm of the water. He wasn't yet practised enough to notice Dumaine following and watching him. Anil took a final stroll around the durbar site, wanting to catch a glimpse of Inspector Goode. He was drawn to this man now, trapped by their intertwining destinies. As with Kim, life drew him within this man's circles, playing with him as though he were a puppet. To his frustration, he couldn't see Goode.

He woke early on the twelfth while it was still dark and cold. The city too was already awake and tingling with anticipation. Officials, who normally moved at a sedate pace, were hurrying, shouting instructions, conferring. The Imperial train had arrived in Delhi Station, and on the outskirts of the city a vast array of princes and their entourages was gathering. When their turn came they would bow in homage and obedience to this foreign king who sat on the throne of India. Almost every regiment had sent a contingent to appear in the durbar procession too. Policemen and soldiers in full uniform, mostly drawn from the Sikh and Jat regiments, lined the route colourful as paintings on biscuit tins. The crowds had begun to knot and swirl, but were kept at a distance from the Red Fort.

Anil ate a light breakfast and noticed the Kashmiri who gawked around like some jungley fellow who had never seen anything larger than his own village. Anil paid him no further attention, distracted by the cold. He wore a shawl but no coat. It would spoil his disguise and he wished he'd chosen something more practical. The revolver lay in his begging bowl.

The crowd was festive and good-natured. He drifted through it, moving slowly towards the cloth merchant's shop. 'The King-Emperor comes,' the whisper ran through the crowds, a wind rippling and pushing them forward. The police beat them back with lathis; mounted English officers patrolled the narrow passage, ordering and pointing.

Anil slipped swiftly into a gulley some distance away from the cloth merchant's and climbed the narrow stairs past a tailor's shop which, like everything else on this day, was shut. He waited a whole minute crouched in the shadows to see if he had been followed. The stairs remained empty and he vaulted over a parapet and jumped onto the adjoining rooftop.

Dumaine was excited. This was the sadhu's first suspicious move. Until now, he had behaved in an orderly and open manner. His swift movements spoke loudly of mischief. Neil thought of summoning a constable or at least sending the man to make a report to Inspector Goode. But he had no definite proof. So he waited, letting the crowd push and pull him, as he stared at the empty stairs. He felt the revolver under his loose shirt and country jacket, and cautiously followed Anil.

Anil only glanced at the glittering plain spreading out from the Red Fort, bright with gold and silver, with flags and pennants and shamiyanas of countless colours. He smelt the dust and the odour of horses and elephants and people. Such a squandering of money was criminal but it had brought the King-Emperor within the sights of his rifle.

He unlocked the tiny room and closed the door, not locking it. He opened the window, which was small and set quite high in the wall. It narrowed the world to a rectangle, slightly above the King-Emperor's head when he passed in his howdah on top of the elephant. It was a perfect angle. If the Emperor was on horseback, Anil would need a greater elevation to shoot down. He unwrapped the sacking from the rifle. It felt good in his hands, strong and powerful. There were five rounds in the magazine and the sight had been set for 100 yards. He levered a round into the chamber then squatted patiently, the rifle against the wall, the begging bowl at his feet. He was waiting for the great roar of the crowd to signal His Majesty's approach.

The murmur below remained muted, peaceful as a drowsing beast. It changed a note or two, buzzed louder, and Anil stood up and peered through the window. He saw a shifting of heads in the distance and a waving of flags, but there was no sign of the King-Emperor's elephant. He would instantly recognise the gold and jewelled howdah and the Imperial flag. It was by sheer chance that he caught a glimpse of the Imperial ensign borne aloft by a lancer riding ahead of the Emperor.

Anil cursed. Why was the King-Emperor riding on horseback? In the orders of the day, His Majesty was meant to be on an elephant. Anil wasn't to know that the Emperor had decided at the last moment that it would be more symbolic to enter Delhi on horseback, as he would have in London, than on an elephant. This had caused consternation among his advisers and the reason why the crowd remained muted was that only those in front could see the King ride by. Anil grabbed the rifle and, standing on tiptoe, tried to aim downwards. The angle was too steep. He needed a chair, a stool, anything. Too late. The King-Emperor and his escort had pranced out of view.

Anil slumped down, bitterly angry at this twist of fate. He dropped the rifle and, head bowed, didn't notice the door slowly opening. Light spilling into the room jerked his head up.

'Don't move,' Neil Dumaine ordered. He pointed his revolver and while Anil watched, slowly bent and pulled the rifle towards him.

'Who are you?'

'Anil Ray,' Anil said deliberately.

'Ray!'

Dumaine couldn't hide his amazement. He had won himself a promotion and the reward money, as well as the gratitude of Inspector Goode.

Anil saw the man's attention slip. He couldn't contain his excitement at this capture and already he foresaw fame and reward and promotion. Anil squatted still and calm, watching the policeman tug the rifle out of reach. His own hand rested lightly on his begging bowl. The policeman gripped the rifle and turned slightly to step back out of the tiny room. Anil's hand slipped into the bowl and before Dumaine realised what had lain hidden under the saffron rag, he glimpsed the flash of the revolver and felt a tremendous blow hurl him out of the room.

# 10

## April 1911–February 1912

Alice laid down her pen, and slumped back. Every muscle ached. She was so tired, even sleep brought no relief. She and Romesh had been working round-the-clock to bring out the new issue of *Sher*. The government had arrested their printer and gaoled him for six months on a charge of sedition. *Sher* had been closed under the Indian Press Bill passed by Lord Minto. More than forty Indian-language newspapers and magazines had been closed, but not one English-owned paper. Her article on her husband's knighthood had caused the poor printer to lose his livelihood. Someone had informed on him. The printer had been arrested even as he was typesetting her article. What angered her most was that the printer himself was not to blame. The government should have arrested her but, because she was English, the printer's arrest had been a warning.

Neither she nor Romesh was intimidated. They had searched Bombay for another printer but none wanted the work. They then decided to buy the press from the imprisoned printer who was glad to be rid of such a dangerous liability. Alice had never felt so close to Romesh as when they worked hard to bring out the issues. They had shared the burden of writing and production, and Alice felt a deep sense of satisfaction. It was good to work hard for a cause, good to see the results. But the pressure aged her more than it did him. Only his eyes darkened in exhaustion while she felt her whole body sagging and fissures cracking across her face. She hadn't dared look at a mirror recently.

They'd had no time for intimacy and neither thought about it. But now the February issue had been put to bed, their thoughts turned to each other. As a celebration and reward, they were going to have champagne with dinner. Alice lazed in the tin tub of warm water, knowing that once they had made love, she would sleep all night and all day and finally wake replenished.

Dressed and powdered and perfumed, Alice sat on the verandah with a glass of wine to await Romesh. She smelt the dust mingled with jasmine and the odours of her dinner from the kitchen. The garden was noisy with cicadas and bats swooped out of the shadows. She felt at peace, at home. India breathed its humid warmth into her, and already she felt renewed.

But she didn't want to brood tonight and poured herself another drink. Romesh was more than an hour late. It was unusual for him, as he prided himself on his western sense of punctuality. As a Parsi he was more westernised than other Indians. The Parsis had escaped Muslim persecution in Persia eleven centuries ago and made their home in Bombay. They were known as astute businessmen, scholars, intellectuals and sportsmen, who assiduously retained their identity and traditions in the land of Hindus. Romesh's uncle, Daddhabhai Nairoji, partly to prove an Indian's ability to transcend being a subject race, had represented the London constituency of Bethnal Green in the House of Commons. Alice had met Romesh eight years earlier while interviewing Daddhabhai Nairoji for the *Manchester Guardian*. Their attraction had been instant, though she did know that he was married to a Parsi girl. Romesh had provided the bungalow on Malabar Hill for Alice.

When another half-hour had passed and she thought the stars were blurring from the effects of the wine, she began to worry. Only once before had he been late, when his wife had fallen ill. He had sent his peon with a message and Alice had accepted the role of waiting mistress. By ten thirty, when there hadn't even been a message, she thought of sending the cook to fetch a gharri. But what could she do? Turn up on his doorstep? She felt helpless and angry. Bloody man, she thought, and sat down angrily to a solitary dinner. The bottle of champagne drowned in a bucket of melted ice and she picked at her food. Before locking up, she took one last look down the road. It was full of shadow and moonlight, but deserted.

The insistent rapping on the shutters frightened her. She came awake in pitch blackness and the noise was foreboding.

'Who is it?'

'Nairoji sahib's peon, memsahib.'

Alice sighed in relief. A message at least. There was nothing so terrible to a woman as neglect. Her head was aching from the wine and her weariness felt like lead. She opened the front door, her lamp held high, and recognised the old man. His mouth was tight and grim. He carried no note.

'What's happened?'

'Nairoji sahib has been arrested by the police. They take him to central prison. He tells me to tell you.'

'When did this happen?'

'Evening. I can't come earlier because of problems.'

'But why have they taken him?'

But he couldn't tell her. The poor man had walked miles and was already setting off to make the return journey. Alice told him to sleep on the verandah and in her panic hurriedly threw on some clothes and ran out of the house. She stopped at the gate. It was still night; the sky hadn't even lightened. She went back indoors and looked at the clock. It was three thirty in the morning. There was nothing she could do. She slumped back onto the bed fully dressed. Romesh's arrest felt like a physical blow, close to her heart. The government was carefully cutting away the ground around her, toying with her, gobbling up the people close to her, leaving her isolated.

She dozed and had nightmares of Romesh being beaten in prison.

It took Alice two days to get permission to visit Romesh. The prison was the same granite, gloomy building outside which Elizabeth had waited while her father went to interrogate Peter Bayley's bearer Rao. It was the same visiting room too, sparsely furnished with two chairs and a table.

Alice expected to find Romesh handcuffed, instead he entered alone. He also looked recently groomed. He wore a clean shirt and trousers and his black hair gleamed with oil. He remained a handsome man in spite of his ordeal, whereas she was sure the last two days had changed her; she felt shrivelled and tired.

He didn't seem pleased to see her. There was a familiar sullen line around his mouth which reminded her of a spoilt little boy. He nodded curtly and she was hurt.

It was when she touched his hand that she knew he'd changed towards her. His hand had cringed and though he didn't move it out of reach, she felt the muscles tighten, the quiver of control.

'What has happened?'

'I'm in prison . . . that's what's happened.'

'You know what I mean. I can feel it in your hand.' They looked down at those connected hands as if they belonged to other people. 'You want to draw it away.'

'No,' Romesh said and she felt him make an effort to relax. He avoided her eyes; his own, pale brown, liquid and expressive, couldn't hide his emotions. She saw a wound bleeding there, and didn't know how she had caused it. 'Don't you understand why you remain free? I do, I do. And that is the problem. Because you're an Englishwoman and I'm a native. You're the ruler, I am the oppressed. Alice, the time is coming for us to separate. I can't be seen with you, talking to you, loving you.'

'Stop babbling, Romesh. I'm your lover, I'm your friend. We've fought hard to bring out *Sher*. I believe in everything you believe in – even the freedom of this country.'

'For you, India's freedom is an intellectual exercise. For me, it means this prison, these four stone walls and the degradation of being ordered around like a slave. How can you understand what I feel? Even when I'm released, I'll always know that here in my own country you will always be treated differently from me. I will be the native, you the ruler.'

'I'm not one of them,' Alice said desperately. 'I live my life absolutely apart from them. You know that. I have very few English friends. I'm a pariah. If you turn against me, who will I have as a friend? You must trust me.'

'Must I? One of the policemen told me it was you who told them where to find the printer.'

'And you believed him?' She was furious with him now.

'No, I didn't. I knew you'd never do something like that. But there might come a time when I'd be forced to believe such things of you. When I look at you, I see an Englishwoman. We're nearing a time of extremes, Alice. It will be dangerous for us both. For us to be seen together, as friends, would make us both suspect. I need my purity, Alice; I have to prove myself to my own people.'

Alice felt the tears, the ache in her eyes, and dabbed them with her handkerchief. She was determined not to cry here in prison. Romesh's eyes glistened too and when she passed him the handkerchief, he dabbed at them. Indians were a sentimental people, laughing or crying easily like children. She suppressed the thought, not wanting to be so English in this parental attitude.

'Can't we at least still work together?'

'It's possible,' he said. 'We must give it time. When I'm beside you I'll want you, and I can't afford to. I must learn to forget.'

She wouldn't beg or plead; she was too old for that, and too wise to deny him his martyrdom. She should have expected this, his reach for an identity that had to exclude her. From love they would descend to uneasy friendship, then cool aquaintance, finally, if the bitterness increased, enmity. She prayed it would not happen. She didn't ever want to be excluded from India. What home would she have if she couldn't have India?

'I'll weep later,' she said and leaned over and pecked his cheek. 'I'd better leave the bungalow.'

'Please keep it. A gift.'

'Romesh, Romesh. You can't give me a bungalow and not be accused of corrupting yourself. Your purity will finally depend on how much you hate us all.'

Once in her bungalow, she shut the windows and doors and screamed out the suffocating pain. She wept like a small child, nearly making herself ill, and took to her bed for two days. On the third day, like a resurrection, she rose briskly from bed, determined to get on with her life. She penned a brief note to Romesh in prison, informing him that she would be leaving the bungalow and hoped he would retain the morality he had discovered in prison.

"But it's so easy to corrupt the Indian leadership," she thought. "Tilak is a rare man, unafraid of the British, and he's paying the price of his defiance in prison. The others only want power and are quick to compromise. The Morley-Minto reforms dangled the carrot of pretended participation in government and they grabbed it. Look at Lal Bahadhur Ram Shanker, Mohini's husband, a Member of the Viceroy's Council, the first Indian in such an august body; yet it means nothing. He will nod his head when required and one day be knighted. He isn't a patriot but a man pursuing his own venal ambitions."

She had heard of Mohandas K. Gandhi's campaign in South Africa. She felt Indian in her pride in him. There, she thought, was a moral man. He had stood up to the violence of the South African government without betraying his principles. Could he do it in India? It would only be a moral man who could win India her freedom. His morality would have to be like steel and not bend to the enticements of the government or fear of the government when enticements failed. He would need this morality in order to be trusted by men of every community, caste and religion in the country. She wanted to meet Gandhi, to hear him and judge for herself whether he was such a man. It would have been so simple to get on a steamer and visit him. She'd heard he welcomed strangers to the ashram he had built outside Durban. But once she had left India, would she be allowed to return?

She stood at her window watching the gardener watering the flower pots; his expertise was limited to carrying water back and forth. Her study was in chaos. Trunks and suitcases lay open, books and papers were scattered all over the floor. The furniture had been hired from Lawrence & Co. It was starkly functional; chipped and scarred with use. Mr Lawrence promised to move most of it to the flat and she was expecting the bullock cart that day. Though Romesh had yet to ask her to leave, she was too proud to remain living off his charity. She had found a flat on Church Gate, small but adequate. She would miss the garden and the view of the sea.

A motor car stopped at the gate, trailing a heavy cloud of dust. India, she thought, wasn't meant for such vehicles. A carriage would have passed silently without the furore of dirt and dust. An English chauffeur in a white uniform and gleaming black boots opened the rear door and a slim, elegant Indian stepped out. Fastidiously he waved away the dust with a silk handkerchief, stared at her bungalow, then strolled up the path. Alice waited for Lal Bahadhur Ram Shanker to knock twice, before she went to open the door. Mohini's husband looked old. His skin, stretched over the bones, had the texture of parchment. No wrinkles showed and those stone black eyes were unwinking.

'Come in, Mr Shanker. I'm quite honoured to have a Member of the Viceroy's Council call on me. In fact, I was just thinking of you.'

'Favourably, I hope.'

'Of course not.'

Alice smiled as she said it and he giggled, unsure whether this was the English sense of humour or an insult. He was never certain if he was being made fun of. He had tried to develop this sense of English humour, as he had the mannerisms, but it eluded him. Alice saw his hesitation.

'You take yourself too seriously, Mr Shanker. Come in.'

He refused her offer of tea and perched on the edge of a rattan chair like a bird of prey. Delicate thin hands rested on the knob of his silver walking stick. His nails were manicured yet she imagined his touch would be scaly and she cringed at the thought. Poor Mohini had been married off to this creature as a child. He looked around, and she noticed his sneer. Lal Bahadhur was constantly surprised that his rulers lived in such spare and humble surroundings. Even the Colonel sahib lived as simply, though in a bigger bungalow. The English never understood the advantages of power; at least some didn't.

His attention finally turned to her. He saw a pale perspiring woman with blonde hair streaked faintly grey. She had steady eyes, of an attractive blue, which met his stare without sliding away. She wasn't a beauty, unlike her daughter, but there was passion in the shape of her mouth. He thought she had a strong face and strong hands; he was sure the mons of her palm would be firm and swollen.

So this was the Colonel sahib's wife, the secret that had been revealed to the daughter when the son died. Lal Bahadhur also knew of her lover, Romesh, in spite of their secrecy. He supposed the Colonel did too and felt a twinge of compassion for the proud man. His wife with a native! Lal Bahadhur had brooded long how to use this information to his advantage. It gave him power over the Colonel. If he revealed it the repercussions would be harsh. The British stayed in their enclaves to protect their women from sexual contact with the natives. A glance, a touch would be looked upon with horror and rage, to violate would bring down murder.

Their women are the symbols of their superiority, he thought. They bring them out at great expense, like their dinner services made in Sheffield or their guns, and to be without one is a terrible disgrace. The Englishman would prefer to wither and die than marry an Indian woman, beautiful and loving as she can be. It's this act of self-denial that sets them above us. In protecting their women against our sexual promise, the men prove themselves as men. And if the woman should go voluntarily with a native, it's a deep and grievous wound to the pride of the Englishman. Even one such choice is proof to us that they are ugly, ugly and inferior. A sexual distance between their women and the native must exist to prove, and to protect, their superiority. If the woman sleeps with the native, it destroys the sanctity of that superiority.

He didn't know the affair was over, and that in the next room lay the wreckage of a life ending.

'Do I meet with your approval, Mr Shanker?' Alice asked, and saw him tighten his grip on the cane.

'I didn't mean to stare, Miss Soames.' He didn't like women of such boldness. Mohini had grown bold, and he had taught her a lesson. She would have grown meek if he had had her within his clutches longer.

'I'm busy, Mr Shanker. Obviously you've come for a purpose.'

'Obviously you also know the reason, Miss Soames. I'm looking for my wife, Mohini. I know you harboured her when she ran away from my home.'

'Of course I harboured her.' Alice couldn't admit she had received a brief note from Mohini. It would only make him more persistent.

'I'd do that for anyone connected with you. The last I saw of the poor girl was when she left for the Allahabad Congress meeting. I gather you attended that and I'm surprised you didn't see her there. In fact, I thought you had abducted her.'

'I did,' he said abruptly. 'But someone stole her away. My love for her is not a prison, Miss Soames. I'm her husband by law and she is my wife. If you do know of her whereabouts, you must tell me. Otherwise . . .' He allowed the silken threat to hang between them. Alice stared at him lazily, knowing he would grow uncomfortable. Despite his high position, the English still made him uneasy.

'What?'

'I could take legal action against you for interfering between a lawful husband and wife.'

'Is there a Hindu law for that? I'm surprised. I'm sure you could do worse than that, Mr Shanker. You're the sort of man who'd prefer violence, committed by another, naturally. I'm afraid I can't help you. I haven't seen hide nor hair of your wife.'

'Have you heard from her?' In the plea she heard the heart of this cold man. He did love Mohini, for all his monstrous faults. 'Miss Soames, you know what it feels like to love someone. I love my wife and my heart aches for her. She may have told you bad things about me. I must accept the blame only because I loved her too much. Is that wrong, I ask. It was love at first sight. Her beauty robbed me of all my senses and when she's near me, the air is clear and cool and fresh as if I were in the mountains. Then I thought only of my own good fortune. Now I can think only of her. I wish only to make her happy. As a woman you'll understand a man's passion. Explain to her that I beg for her forgiveness. I will place my head on her feet should she see her way to returning to my side. I . . .'

Alice held up her hand. 'Mr Shanker, if you were any other man I might have believed you. Your tongue is as silvery as the cane you grip so tightly. I've no doubt that should Mohini fall within your grasp, you would punish her cruelly.'

She didn't flinch at the sudden surge of malignancy in his eyes. They were fixed on her, beating her down with his hatred. She had made a terrible enemy in him and felt a little afraid. She held his stare, praying he'd never find Mohini and Kim.

He rose abruptly, swiftly. 'I shan't keep you any longer, Miss Soames.' He opened the door and stopped. 'I've forgotten the name of her friend. It's . . .'

Kim, she could have told him, but kept silent. Like his question he hung on the threshold, balanced between the glare outside and the cool gloom of the room. He slipped out then without a goodbye and she watched from her window as he climbed back into the gleaming machine and trailed his dust like a regal train.

On the day she moved into her flat on Church Gate, she received a drab, khaki-coloured envelope with 'On Indian Government Service' printed along the top. Inside was a curt note requesting her to call on Mr C. J. Edlecliff-Johnstone at the Secretariat. He had no title or department.

She dressed carefully and formally, and wore no jewellery. She wasn't kept waiting in the corridor. A peon immediately ushered her into the cool, high-ceilinged room. The door, unlike others in the corridor, bore no name or title. The office was sparsely furnished as though the occupant had only recently moved in. There was a file on the desk; hers, she suspected. Mr C. J. Edlecliff-Johnstone sat with his back to the window, overlooking the distant sea, reading *The Times*. He rose, a thickset man, tanned and fit, handsome in a schoolboyish way. He was in his early thirties and she felt slightly resentful that India hadn't soiled him as rapidly as it did European women.

'Miss Soames, it was very kind of you to come.' He had a grin, not a smile, which emphasised his schoolboyishness, yet she sensed a sterner person behind the façade, someone watching her as if through a keyhole.

'It was a summons, Mr Edlecliff-Johnstone.' Alice felt the dreary formality of officialdom. Once she'd sat in one of the row of chairs facing him he retreated behind his desk. She waited patiently for him to arrange the things in front of him and noticed a spinsterish preciseness. 'By the way, who are you?'

'I beg your pardon?'

'Mr Edlecliff-Johnstone, I am very familiar with the workings of this government. Everyone is proud of their titles. And their departments. Your note and your door bear neither.'

'Ah.' He grinned ruefully. 'I've just taken over this job and haven't got round to the calling cards and my own stationery. I'm a government servant with the Home Office.' He sat forward to take away her initiative. 'Now . . .'

'And how did you discover I had moved? Your letter coincided with my arrival.'

This time, he made no effort to grin. Instead, he had the grace to blush. The pink innocence failed to have any effect on Alice. Like the grin, she felt it was the man's façade, quite controlled. It seemed menacing and Alice knew he was watching her. She was uneasy now at her own hostility. Maybe she should have adopted the manner of a supplicant.

'As we're both busy people, I'll come to the point,' Edlecliff-Johnstone said. 'I've been asked to convey the government's displeasure at your reporting, Miss Soames, especially for the newspaper you write for abroad. The Americans are an ignorant people and your colourful accounts will influence them the wrong way. Your comments in this little Indian magazine, *Sher*, too will influence people the wrong way.'

'Are you censoring me?'

'Not yet. We just feel you should be more objective. We're not all villains, Miss Soames. We have the enormous burden of ruling India and your constant criticism doesn't make our task any easier.'

'I try to write as honestly as I can about India's aspirations.'

'They haven't the faintest idea what they want,' he said. 'Tilak called for violence and look what it led to. The murder of a policeman at His Majesty's durbar and then the brutal murder of Mr Noel Jackson, the collector for Nasik. I knew him. You couldn't have met a man who loved and cared for India more than he did. But Tilak's writing inflamed the mind of young Kanhere, and he shot Jackson down in cold blood. Is that what they want? Murders? Is that swaraj?'

'There are going to be any number of victims in the coming years, Mr Edlecliff-Johnstone,' Alice said. She wanted to tell him he was looking at one. Another kind of casualty, not from a bullet but the looming rejection. 'Some will be as innocent as your Mr Jackson. Others may not. My writing isn't going to change the future of India. All I can do is try to explain their cause.'

The peon interrupted with tea and the interruption seemed to allow Edlecliff-Johnstone to regain his composure. He fussed with the pot and biscuits and sat back with a contented sigh, nursing his cup.

'I've done what I was ordered to do,' he said. 'In many ways, I do sympathise with the Indian cause. You look surprised. Why not? Indians will one day govern themselves with our guidance. And I do look forward to that day, Miss Soames.'

'We seem to have only subtle differences in our views on India's future.'

'Which can be worked out. Have you been reading these articles by Valentine Chirol, Miss Soames?' He tapped the folded paper and offered no further opinion, watching her through those candid grey eyes. She knew he was testing her.

'Poppycock. I met him while he was here,' Alice said. 'A whirlwind tour, meeting the sahibs and garnering their learned opinions of the natives. You like his articles because they represent the government's line of thinking.'

'I didn't say I liked them. I only asked your opinion. Between you and me, I also think they're poppycock. He's written from the opposite extreme to yours. People rushing in to make snap judgements on India don't please us either. There is a middle road. This swaraj nonsense, your extreme, is only perpetuated by a tiny handful of politicians . . .'

'One of whom you've imprisoned.'

'And rightly so. We are the legitimate government of this country. And when a man calls for violence, any government, whether here or in Britain, will have him imprisoned. How many Tilaks are there? A dozen? Let's be generous, a hundred? The population of this country is 300 million. They're not calling for swaraj. They're grateful for our presence. India was in bloody chaos when we came. And it will return to chaos should we ever leave. Admittedly, it was our mistake to bring in western-style education to this country but it was our duty to educate the Indians. A few of them now have high-flown ideas that because they speak our language, they should rule in our stead.'

'It is their country, Mr Edlecliff-Johnstone,' Alice said, adopting his sudden formality. He had regained the chill manner of an official again, and was confusing her with his agreements and disagreements. He was clever. 'We are an Imperial power and don't belong here. We could if we wanted, but the decision not to become Indian was made a long time ago. Swaraj will grow. It is the irony of learning that men aspire to greater things only once they discover they exist. And no doubt this government's repressive measures will grow to keep pace with these aspirations.'

'How on earth could we become Indian, Miss Soames? We're of a different race, and superior at that.'

'We didn't think so when we first came to India. We've changed since then.'

'That wasn't our doing. The Mutiny changed everything. We won't leave the people to the Indian politician. Don't forget this country is ninety per cent villages. We won't betray them.'

'That is most patronising. Have you asked them?'

'Of course we have. They are content with us, trust us more than they would a Hindu. Swaraj is all a Hindu movement. There's not a single Muslim involved. The Muslim will never allow the Hindu to rule him.'

'And I'm sure the government will sow that seed in the Muslim's mind. It's already done so through Lord Minto's encouragement of the formation of the Muslim League to divide Congress.'

'It wasn't intended to divide, Miss Soames; it was to protect the minority interest,' he spoke with increasing impatience. Her persistence was irritating him. The Colonel's wife was certainly a nuisance.

'Then why not a Christian League and a Buddhist League? Because they're not powerful enough to be the wedge the government requires. Only the Muslim League is.'

'Miss Soames, I have read your reports and have never agreed with your assessments of this country,' he said brusquely and tidied his papers, the interview coming to an end. 'You intellectuals have never understood India or its problems. Thank you for coming to see me.' He rose and came round to escort her to the door.

'I want to travel to South Africa.'

'We're not Russia, Miss Soames. You have the freedom to go. I don't understand why you should have to ask my permission.'

'I'm not asking your permission to go, Mr Edlecliff-Johnstone,' Alice said. 'I only want to know whether the government would allow me to come back.'

She waited. His face had hardened imperceptibly.

'You won't, will you? Be honest.'

'Miss Soames, to be frank, we'd be delighted to see you leave India. And I doubt this government will be foolish enough to permit your return.'

'Thank you. You could have allowed me to leave and refused me entry later.'

'It's not in the nature of this government to behave dishonestly,' Edlecliff-Johnstone said primly, as though accused of some perversion. She rose and at the door, which he barely held open, he added: 'The government also feels you should only report events and not get involved in affairs which are no concern of yours. It could become uncomfortable.'

'I'm used to discomfort, Mr Edlecliff-Johnstone.' Before he shut the door she said: 'You must send me your card when your position becomes official. I would like to know what you are in the government.'

He closed the door firmly. At least she had succeeded in rattling him. Then disappointment and depression set in. A trip to see Mr Gandhi would have been a welcome relief from her personal life. He could have given her a little hope, though, looking at Mr Edlecliff-Johnstone, she wondered whether anyone would have the strength to shift men like that out of their chairs and offices.

On the street, she squinted through the glare. Now who had he had watching her? She wasn't practised in this profession of spying but knew she was being followed. Brown faces and white flowed around her, all apparently indifferent to her. It wasn't a long walk back to Church Gate and in spite of the heat and glare, she enjoyed the feeling of being part of India. In Edlecliff-Johnstone's office, she'd felt herself detached and disconnected.

She climbed the flight of stairs to her flat and stopped. The door was slightly ajar, the padlock broken. She pushed the door gently. Her sitting-room, which had been in chaos anyway after the move, looked as though a cyclone had swept through it. Her trunks and suitcases were open and her papers were scattered all over the place. The motive wasn't robbery. She possessed only these papers and a few hundred rupees in her bank account.

'Dorairaj,' she called out for her cook and held her breath, praying for a response. She heard him reply from the rear balcony, where he slept. At least he was all right.

She knew who had searched her flat. Mr Edlecliff-Johnstone's men, she thought, looking for more incriminating and inflammatory articles. At first nothing seemed to be missing and it took her a week of sorting and filing away her papers to discover that she had lost Mohini's letter. She felt quite afraid. Mr Edlecliff-Johnstone wouldn't have stolen it. Lal Bahadhur Ram Shanker had sent his men to find something written by Mohini. There was no address and nothing to indicate in which direction she and Kim were travelling, yet the unease persisted. Lal Bahadhur would find his wife eventually, and Alice wished she could send Mohini a warning.

# 11

# July–October 1912

Lord Hardinge of Penshurst, Viceroy of India, was too much of a gentleman to reveal irritation in front of the bearers. He neatly folded the *Englishman* and dropped it to the floor. It was quickly retrieved and gently replaced by his plate. His twelve-year-old daughter Diamond giggled and Lady Hardinge smiled sweetly from across the table. They were long used to servants but not as many as were provided for the Viceroy. One bearer stood behind her chair, another behind her daughter's, two behind her husband and three at the door. She was a pretty woman, as tall as her husband, and with the same aristocratic bearing. It seemed perfectly natural to her that her husband should be Viceroy. His grandfather had been Governor General in 1844, when India was ruled by John Company, while her own uncle Lord Northbrooke had been Viceroy in 1872. India gave both their families a sense of continuity. They were meant to rule.

The breakfast room, looking out on the verandah and the cluttered garden, seemed overcrowded on this hot summer day. The air was difficult to breathe, hot, still and dry. They would have retreated to Simla as was the summer custom, but her husband was too busy in Delhi. Other wives had long fled the plains for the hill stations. Winifred Hardinge, however, was an exceptional woman. She was considered more intelligent than her husband and she was often consulted on administrative matters. Without his wife beside him, Lord Hardinge would have found his job intolerable.

'They'll never stop whining, my dear,' Lady Hardinge said. 'The sooner you ignore them, the better. It's such a relief to get away from them!'

Lady Hardinge had little patience with the Calcutta European community. She thought most of them a selfish, self-centred lot. However, as Vicereine she had to get on with them and managed to do so with effortless courtesy and charm.

'Reading this drivel, anyone would think I was to blame.'

King George V's proclamation that the capital of India was to be moved from Calcutta to Delhi had caused an uproar in Calcutta. What had begun as rumour had become an Imperial edict and Calcutta was outraged at the insult. For over three centuries it had been the capital and swaggered with the arrogance of a young, lusty city founded by Europeans for their own needs.

Lord Hardinge had been booed out of Calcutta and though six months had elapsed the fury still beat about his head. He was relieved to be temporarily beyond the reach of the Calcutta business community. They were the ones making the most noise as their own interests were hurt. At this distance they wouldn't be able to influence or badger the government to make decisions favourable to them. Naturally, even the Calcutta Indians objected but the reunification of Bengal muted their protests.

The Viceroy now lived in cramped humility in the Circuit House in Delhi. It was a large rambling bungalow, intended for important visiting government officials and not as a permanent residence for the Viceroy and his staff. The garden was crammed with tents housing his personal administrative staff, and their proximity heightened Lady Hardinge's feeling of claustrophobia. Whichever way she turned she was tripping over someone or other. Beyond the high compound walls rose a makeshift town. The dust of activity hung in the air and even the slightest breeze would waft this yellow vapour into the Viceregal residence to settle on everything, furniture, clothes, hair. Somewhere in the haze, the government of India functioned as best it could. Secretaries of departments shuffled their dusty files while masons and carpenters moved among them, hurrying to put up one kutcha room after another. From living in spacious bungalows in Calcutta, the government officials' living space was reduced to a room or two, with a dining-room shared with others. Imperial edicts, they muttered among themselves, were all very well but did anyone stop to think of the consequences? Unlike the Viceroy's, their families had escaped to the hills, which was fortunate for they would have been driven mad by the chaos. It was fine now during the summer, but once the monsoons set in the garden would turn to mud and half the tents and houses would collapse. They all wished the Viceroy would stick to tradition and govern from Simla.

Lord Hardinge would have preferred nothing better, but King George V was taking a personal interest in the plans for his Imperial city. New Delhi was to be grander and greater than anything conceived and built by previous emperors, Mughal or Lodi. The Viceroy's palace was to be more magnificent than the Mughal's in the Red Fort. It would dominate the skyline of this new Delhi and would radiate the power of his office. The commission appointed to find an architect for this city had chosen two men. Sir Herbert Baker was to design the Secretariat, the Council Building and the residential quarters while the layout of New Delhi, the Viceregal Lodge and the Great Place were the concern of Sir Edwin Lutyens, a forty-three-year-old self-proclaimed genius.

Each time Lord Hardinge thought of the arrogant man, he felt a deep well of self-pity. He had not only to rule India but to oversee the building of this new city and do battle with Lutyens. Lutyens's conception was already racing beyond the budget and efforts to reduce his expenditure were fruitless. The damned man already knew how to manipulate Lady Hardinge and would appeal to her if Lord Hardinge protested about his designs. It was intolerable. Hardinge couldn't stand Lutyens's bluster. He was an extremely shy man who hid his shyness behind a cold reserve which made him appear unfeeling, but his family knew him to be warm and loving.

The Viceroy's Council still met weekly. Instead of the sombre conference room in Calcutta, with its large oil painting of Lord Hastings hanging behind his chair, Lord Hardinge took his place at a long scarred, chipped table in a sunny sitting-room. His back was to the French windows. The sitting-room had been the guest suite.

Despite the heat and inconvenience, the Council Members were in a jovial mood. They reminded Lord Hardinge of schoolboys on an outing; they swapped tales of hardship and misadventure, all trying to outdo each other. As young men they would have been used to such discomforts when they made their winter tours of the country. This huge makeshift camp evoked their youth and zeal as young district collectors or deputy magistrates.

The sole Indian member, Lal Bahadhur Ram Shanker, was also trying to join in the gay mood. He wasn't as inconvenienced as they, for he had a house, one of several scattered about the country, in Delhi. The Viceroy liked Lal Bahadhur. The man was an obvious gentleman, always immaculately attired and courteous. He had a sharp mind and promulgated a moderate political view in reforms. Though he had no power in the Council, however, his views were barely tolerated by the others simply because he had been foisted on them by the Minto-Morley reforms. Hardinge disapproved of the Members' coolness and did everything possible to encourage Lal Bahadhur. He was the forerunner of the other Indians who would one day also sit in the Council.

Further down the table, staring absent-mindedly across the lawn, sat Colonel Sir John Creighton. Hardinge had learned early on that his domain was private and jealously guarded. Because of the nature of his business Creighton was a secretive man and Hardinge distrusted him. It was impossible to control him and he was the only one at the table who made the Viceroy feel uneasy. Those deep hooded eyes revealed nothing and promised even less.

The Council was discussing the Annual Finance Bill when Lal Bahadhur caught Lord Hardinge's eye. The Viceroy waited for a suitable moment and signalled his permission for Lal Bahadhur to speak.

'Your Excellency, may I add a note of objection to the discussions?' Lal Bahadhur lounged in his chair, as did all the others when they spoke. The Council was more of an exclusive club and informality was encouraged by Lord Hardinge. Under Lord Curzon's steely gaze Members had risen to their feet and stuttered. 'The cost of building this new monument for the King-Emperor is bound to be more than my poor country can afford. I have yet to see the budget for this new Delhi but I've heard the rumour of many crores. Over a million pounds. I approve of the move from Calcutta. Delhi is the natural capital of India, as it has been for many centuries and for . . .' he smiled '. . . many empires. But I cannot see why the Delhi that now stands not too distant from us cannot be modified to suit the needs of the government. This vast expenditure is certainly wasteful. And this burden on my people follows the one hundred and eighty thousand pounds spent on His Majesty's durbar. Can India afford such extravagances, Your Excellency?'

'Mr Shanker, His Majesty thought that India, moving swiftly into the new century, should have a capital befitting this new age. We did consider Delhi as it stands now, but it's not adequate for the seat of government. It's too old and holds too many memories. We would still have to erect new administrative buildings, new homes for the officials, a new Viceregal Lodge. I feel we should start anew, break new ground.' The Viceroy paused a moment, to hold Lal Bahadur's attention. 'New Delhi will also benefit India in countless ways. Though the architects are British, all the building work will be done by Indians. The money isn't being squandered in a foreign country but spent in India on Indians. I am sure you will see the benefit to your people.'

Lal Bahadhur did. He had merely spoken for the record. A minor objection made him feel less of a puppet, satisfied his pride. He distinctly saw the advantages of this new Delhi. Quite a few of the acres on which it would be built were owned by him. He had heard the rumour of the King's decision to move the capital and had secretly bought plots widely scattered around old Delhi, but never so many as to arouse suspicion. The land was either owned by ignorant villagers or consisted of jagirs granted by a Mughal, which had long since lapsed. He couldn't even begin to think how many lakhs he would make on the investment. Contractors, builders, raw materials – his mind spun hazy dreams of accumulating a vast fortune from this folly of the British. He did consider it folly, like castles built on sand or on remote hill tops. He considered it a vanity too, a vast mausoleum to their rule.

He brooded on the legend of Delhi and the ending of dynasties. If this dynasty ended the next would be Indian. The thought of dynasties turned his mind to Mohini. She should have borne him a child, a son to continue the line, to rule this country. He needed a son, many if possible. He was getting older and his obsession with his wife had blinded him to the need to ensure the future of his family. He would never give up his search nor his revenge for his humiliation. But he would divert his sexual energies into another woman, one who would bear him children.

When the meeting adjourned Lal Bahadhur looked for the Colonel and saw him hurry out. He dawdled a while longer, arranging his papers, savouring his own importance. Even this simple drawing-room, with its flowered curtains, empty vases and framed paintings, was transformed; it appeared larger, more sombre, now that it had heard their debate. His own voice lingered on, resonated within these walls. He would have liked to stroll out in the company of the others; such familiarity would have gratified him. But he walked out alone. The others had gathered in groups on the verandah, gossiping and joking. Lal Bahadhur knew they would fall politely silent if he joined them. He remained indecisive, wondering whether he should hurry away as if on important business.

Some distance away, between two tents, Lal Bahadhur glimpsed the Colonel deep in conversation with a police officer. They looked up once, to scan the perimeter of the Circuit House. He followed their gaze and noticed several police constables posted at regular intervals. He had heard a soft whisper, a mere ripple in the hot breeze, that an attempt had been made on His Imperial Majesty's life at the durbar. It wasn't an official whisper, only bazaar talk. But a policeman had been killed. If the rumour were true, Lal Bahadhur wished these stupid attempts by his countrymen would cease. Each violent act only made his own position most uncomfortable, and Lal Bahadhur didn't like that.

'Mr Shanker, I'd like a private word with you, if I may.'

Lal Bahadhur found himself addressed by Lord Hardinge and immediately straightened his shoulders. He always felt reduced to a child in the presence of the Viceroy, as though he were about to be admonished.

'Certainly, Your Excellency.'

Lord Hardinge held Lal Bahadhur familiarly by the elbow. Lal Bahadhur wanted the others to notice but they were too absorbed in their conversations. The only people he could have impressed were his fellow Congress politicians but they were excluded from such august company. He and the Viceroy strolled to the end of the verandah, and Lal Bahadhur waited in respectful silence while the Viceroy watched the activity in the garden. The Viceroy stood a whole head taller than he.

'It's certainly not the way to run a country,' Lord Hardinge said, 'from tents. But I suppose it used to be once, when the Mughals were on their interminable travels.' He sighed. 'And this makeshift HQ certainly won't change during my time in office. Building this city is going to take years and years. I'd love, one day, to stand in the centre of this new Delhi but I probably won't be alive to see it finished. Men begin great tasks and leave them for others to complete. And God alone knows how this one will turn out. Lutyens, I fear, is going to make a thorough mess of it. It'll be beyond everything if he has his way, a gigantic Brighton Pavilion. Did you ever see it?'

'No, Your Excellency.'

Lal Bahadhur was enjoying this tête-à-tête but wondered where it would lead. He perspired at the sudden thought that the Viceroy might know of his land speculation. Nearly half the city would be built on his land.

'Ghastly. A princely folly set on a cold English beach. India influences us in such strange ways at times. Do you believe in that legend, Mr Shanker? That when a dynasty builds a new Delhi it will fall?'

'Of course not, Your Excellency.'

'Pity. I do.'

Lal Bahadhur was surprised. He had never expected the Viceroy to admit that this empire would come to an end. It was a confession and only he was there to hear it. He waited for the Viceroy to continue, but Lord Hardinge remained silent, his face drawn, dreamy. He was imagining this new Delhi; it already stood around him, shimmering like a mirage on the plain.

He imagined standing on Raisina Hill and looking east to the great mosque, the Jama Masjid, opposite the Red Fort. Immediately on either side of him were the towering new Secretariat Buildings. Behind was the Viceregal Lodge with its huge copper dome and four residential wings. Beneath the dome would be the marble Durbar Hall, while slightly to the north would be the circular Legislative Council Building. And there to the south were the bungalows of the Members and secretaries of departments. New Delhi would breathe; it would be imperially spacious, not cramped and crowded like the old one. There would be broad avenues radiating out from a concorde, and great parks and fountains, and every building would be a perfect blend of past and present, old India and new. The materials would be the traditional marble and red sandstone, the same as the Mughals used in their buildings. But they had only imagined their Delhi on a small scale. This Delhi would be massive, covering many square miles.

Lal Bahadhur squinted into the sun and saw only dust and the stubby horizon of trees. He had little imagination and had no idea what this new Delhi would look like. He thought only of the past, his immediate and familiar reference. Another Calcutta, another Agra. It could even be another Bombay, with a huddle of new buildings, winding narrow lanes and the occasional maidan to relieve the clutter. Whatever it was, it would, ultimately, only be another cantonment, a grand enclave for the European to shut himself up in.

He cleared his throat. 'Surely the British throne is safe?' He hadn't thought that the throne could fall, but what else could the Viceroy have meant by his remark? But the Imperial Crown of India worn by George V at the durbar had been removed to England in case a usurper crowned himself king of India.

'What? Of course it is. Ah, I see what you're getting at, the end of a dynasty. Not in our lifetime, Mr Shanker. Not in the next either. But there comes a time when every empire must bring down the curtain. Roman, Greek, Mughal, to name but three. It could take centuries and I hope certainly this one's end will be in the very distant future. But I've been prattling on, and you must be wondering what I wanted to discuss with you.'

Instinctively Lal Bahadhur sensed that the Viceroy wasn't telling him his true feelings, his true prescience that had let slip the remark. Lal Bahadhur believed some men sensed the future. Lord Hardinge had the delicate features of a seer. He saw an end.

'It has already been a privilege, Your Excellency, to spend even a few minutes in your company.'

'I've suggested you for a knighthood. I'm hoping the acceptance will be a mere formality, but you can never take these things for granted. I feel a man of your political persuasion should be given every encouragement and honour in the eyes of his countrymen.'

'Th-thank you, Your . . . Your Excellency,' Lal Bahadhur couldn't believe his ears. He could scarcely even breathe. 'I had no expectation of such an honour. I am only serving my people and the government to the best of my ability.'

'I'm sure you are.' Out of the corner of his eye, Lord Hardinge noticed Colonel Creighton and a policeman hovering for attention. 'I wouldn't say anything until it's confirmed by the palace, you understand.' Abruptly he shook hands and left a stunned Lal Bahadhur speechless.

Inspector Goode snapped to attention and saluted the Viceroy. Though staring past the Viceroy's shoulder, he felt the man's careful examination and wished he were not so disfigured. He knew people winced within when they saw him. He held himself rigid and humiliatingly felt the spit dribble from the corner of his mouth. It burnt a path down his chin and he clenched his jaw tighter, to no avail, and believed the Viceroy cringed from this repulsive deformity.

'Your Excellency, this is Inspector Goode,' Colonel Creighton said, and Goode found himself shaking hands with the Viceroy. The kindly, humane gesture made him feel slightly more at ease. 'He is the officer in charge of security arrangements, and I gather he thinks there is a conspiracy afoot to endanger your life.'

'I'd have thought the Bengalis would calm down after reunification.' Hardinge scanned the walls and noticed the extra men. 'It's so tedious to be watched over like a small child.'

'The Bengalis have calmed down, Your Excellency,' Goode said. 'But there is one man I think will make an attempt. He's a revolutionary, dedicated to throwing us out. I have an informer who tells me this man, one Anil Ray, will try. It was he who killed Sergeant Dumaine at His Majesty's durbar.'

'Are you sure?'

'We're positive. He was identified by Dumaine, who gave us a description just before he died and I recognised the man as Anil Ray. He was in the guise of a sadhu, a holy man.' Goode could scarcely contain his rage and frustration. He could have caught Ray; he had had him in the palm of his hand. Instead he had sent an inexperienced officer. He felt no remorse for Dumaine, only regret that he had not confronted Anil Ray himself. He would have shot him point-blank.

'I suppose I'll have to put up with you people looking over my shoulder.'

'I think it's best,' the Colonel said. 'With the building going on, and all these peons coming in and out, it makes our job even harder.'

Dismissed by the Viceroy, Goode saluted, spun on his heel and went on a tour of inspection, then returned to his tent. He hurled his soiled handkerchief on the ground and took out a clean one. His bearer kept the tent as tidy and clean as possible but the grimly silent Goode ignored his efforts. They hardly communicated and the bearer felt he was serving a dangerous man. Once Goode sahib had been a kind and considerate employer but Anil Ray had changed him, twisted his heart like his face.

Goode lay on his camp bed, indifferent to the heat. He breathed through his mouth, sucked at the air as though it were a teat. On a low stool stood a small photograph of Rebecca. She looked solemn and serious, but that didn't disguise her prettiness. He had proposed to her only hours before Anil Ray had so viciously attacked him. It had been his stupid romantic preoccupation that had prevented him from reacting in time. Rebecca and he had planned to marry in the winter and take their honeymoon on his home leave. He couldn't bear the thought of her now. How could any woman want to marry a man with a warped face, a warped heart? He touched his nose, tracing the break. He no longer looked in a mirror; he didn't want to see the ugliness. Rebecca had wept and sworn she still loved him, but he knew she cringed at the sight of him and felt herself only bound by obligation. At the first chance she would have broken off their engagement to marry a handsome man, an unbroken one. Goode only kept her photograph to remind him of his hatred of Anil Ray. Ray had denied him his happiness. It was impossible to be at peace while he still lived. Goode knew he was in Delhi; he sensed his presence in the very air. He rose abruptly, and left the tent.

At night Delhi flickered in lamplight. Goode watched from deep within the shadows. He stood in a doorway, studying the jostling throng. In each he saw some familiarity – the colouring, the nose, the mouth, the stance. He followed men at random on the off-chance that he might stumble across Anil Ray. And when he tired of this pastime, he visited Tihar Gaol. He kept Satish Mukherjee and Bhai in separate cells. They had been held on charges of conspiracy since the previous December. Goode always conducted his interrogations after midnight.

He woke Satish abruptly, slapping the thin youth and shaking him as a terrier would a rat.

'Where did you meet Anil Ray?'

'In the Chambal ravines.'

'How many are there in his gang?'

'He works alone. Always alone.'

'Did he tell you where he would go after he killed the King?'

'He said the railway station, but he never came. We waited and waited for him.'

'He abandoned you, didn't he?'

'Yes.'

'Now, think carefully. Did he mention where he would hide?'

'No.'

'The ravines?'
'Yes, yes. The ravines. The dacoits shelter him.'
'And then what was he going to do?'
'Kill every Englishman.'
'Did he mention the Viceroy.'
'Yes. The Viceroy.'
'Did he ever talk about me? Did he tell stories about me?'
'No, sahib. He never mentioned your name.'
'You're lying. He must have laughed, cracked jokes about what he did to Inspector Goode.'
'No. He was always silent as to that.'
'Did he talk about anyone? A man? A woman?'
'Once I heard him mention the name Kim. Anil Ray hates this Kim.'
'That's a European name. Who is this Kim?'
'I don't know. It is his karma to be tied to Kim.'
'Does Anil Ray have a woman? Here? In a village?'
'He never spoke a woman's name to me.'
Though the answer seldom varied, Goode persisted. Somewhere in Satish's memory was the key to Anil Ray. He knew where Ray hid, who his friends were. One night, Goode was sure, Satish would let the answers slip.

# 12

# December 1912

In the moonlight filtering through the carriage window, Anil Ray thought he recognised the young man who slept opposite him. The light played on his face, shading it darker then lighter, tantalising Anil. He was a face from the past, but couldn't be placed. He was a few years younger than Anil, quite handsome in repose, with fine cheekbones set in a narrow, sensitive face. He locked as if he had never wanted in his life; fine, delicate hands, carefully manicured, rested on his lap. Like Anil, he was dressed in a three-piece linen suit. His was the latest fashion and well cut, while Anil's was secondhand, bought in the bazaar and a size too large. The suit was an effective disguise: in it, Anil was a hardworking, ambitious babu, travelling on business. He wished he could remember exactly where he'd met this young man. In Calcutta? In the hill stations? England, possibly? Memory was vital to a wanted man. He could betray himself so easily if he forgot a face, a gesture, a place. The man distracted his mind from brooding on his next assassination.

He dozed, lulled by the monotonous rhythm of the train.

Anil was returning to Delhi. He had escaped from the city an hour after shooting the policeman, and made his way on foot to the sanctuary of the Chambal ravines. He knew the railway station and the trains would be searched and watched. Kishore Singh had welcomed him back and given him shelter. Anil had spent a few quiet and contemplative months in that harsh stretch of land. But inactivity irked him, and he felt adrift in this remote fastness. He wanted to discover what was happening, read, talk to people whose horizons encompassed politics, philosophy, history, revolution. His dacoit friends still lived on the narrow trail of robberies and murders, pointless murders, not revolutionary ones which would drive the British from India.

To distract himself, he bought a cheap notebook from a travelling salesman and began to write. 'Each man is force . . .' were his first words and he stared down at them in surprise. He couldn't remember the last time he had written anything and the pencil stub felt strange in his hand. His childhood returned; images of a small boy shaping alphabets and words in a strange language. "a,b,c, . . . dog, England . . . amo, amas, amat . . ." Chalk-dust and perspiration filled his nostrils. He suppressed memories of those days of innocence, and bent his head to the task of transferring his thoughts to the child's lined notebook.

In four months he had filled it, then another; then he drifted south to Bombay and took a room in a cheap boarding house. Most of the lodgers were students from the newly created Bombay University. They were intense and intent young men. Their horizons were also narrowed by their greed for the mastery of knowledge and the English language. He saw them only as peons for their British masters. He wanted to sneer at them but remembered his own past, his own eagerness to succeed.

But not all the students were from the same mould. A small group were followers of Tilak. Tilak was still in Mandalay Gaol and a weak flame flickered in his memory. These students were a lost little band, and Anil spent the evenings talking with them. He gave his name as Chandra and was accepted into their company. Their discussions were endless and, eventually, boring but they were better company than the dacoits. They showed him respect, not only because he was older but because they suspected he had killed. It showed in his manner, in the tension and the angry hardness.

Their revolutionary zeal was confined to publishing pamphlets which they handed out surreptitiously, and one day Anil shyly showed them one of his own essays. They were delighted with his contribution, and he found himself in print on cheap paper signed with his pen-name, 'Chandra'. Their childish conspiracies amused him.

One evening, they invited him to accompany them to a secret meeting. They spent more time in these clandestine meetings and drinking endless cups of coffee than taking action. The meeting wasn't to be in some dark and depressing room tucked away in a warren, but instead on the outskirts of the city. Four of them, including Anil, were to take part and they carefully arranged to arrive at the rendezvous at different times and from different directions. Anil accompanied one of the students and the circuitous journey took most of the evening. At dusk, they cautiously approached an isolated bungalow on Juhu beach. It was some distance from the road, and the ground between was sandy and bare. No one could approach without being noticed. Behind it lay the flat, limitless sea.

Anil froze on the top step when the door opened. The man silhouetted in the doorway was distinctly European. Anil smelled a trap and stepped back. His hand instinctively reached under his shirt and gripped the revolver.

'Do come in,' the European said, and stepped aside.

He sounded very English and reminded Anil too much of a prefect he had fagged for at Eton and heartily disliked. This man had the same brazen confidence and was at ease with these motley students, as he would have been in any elegant drawing-room. He was taller than any of them, thickset, and with tightly curled brown hair. Anil suspected he would be successful with women. He had the looks that they would think handsome. Anil thought them merely pretty.

'I'll wait out here,' Anil said.

Peter Bayley, whom the students knew as Andrew, was also acutely suspicious of Anil Ray. He was too old to be a student, and there was an animal danger in the way he carried himself. Bayley marked this stranger as ominous, not easy to manipulate. For a fleeting second, Bayley thought he could be a police informer, but that would be too obvious. He had noticed Anil's eyes swiftly searching the shadows with the instinctive caution of a hunted man.

'Suit yourself,' Bayley said. He left the door open and went in. He beckoned to a student. 'Who is he?'

'His name is Chandra.'

'I didn't ask his bloody name. Who is he?'

'A revolutionary. He hates the British. That's why I didn't tell him what you are. He wouldn't have come. But he's a very strong man. He's done things but he never speaks of them, and his body is scarred from beatings. I think he's been in gaol too. I judged it worth your while to meet him.'

'We'll see. Next time ask me first.' Bayley hid his anger behind a kindly smile, but the pat on the student's back was more a hard slap. It stung.

In deference to 'Chandra', the meeting was held on the verandah. Anil merely listened. 'Andrew' did most of the talking, guiding the woolly thinking of the students. He was articulate and reeled off the facts and figures of British exploitation and how India was being bled dry. He encouraged seditious pamphlets and small and petty acts of sabotage. Minor irritations, nothing major. He also exhorted them to recruit more students to the cause of overthrowing the British. At the end of the meeting, he doled out money for their expenses in printing pamphlets and buying materials.

Anil would have left with them, but Andrew said: 'Why don't you stay a while, Mr Chandra? We could talk.'

'About what?'

'Oh shoes and ships and sealing wax. I have some

excellent Glenfiddich. I'll see the rest of you later,' he dismissed the students who trooped out. Bayley went in and returned with a bottle and two glasses. 'Neat or pani?'

'Neat.'

He poured, and they stood warily studying each other. Anil sipped. The last time he had drunk this Scotch had been in Sushila Basu's bedroom. For some reason the taste then had been different. It had had a special flavour. Sushila's sweetness had permeated the whisky and softened his palate. Now it tasted harsh, bitter.

'Who are you, Mr Chandra?'

'No one. And you, Mr Andrew? An agent provocateur?'

'Not for the Indian government. Let's say, for another one which would like to see certain changes here. That government believes in India's freedom.'

'For its own advantage. You don't sound Russian.'

'Why should I? I went to a decent public school. And I suspect you went to an even better one, though you're making a great effort to disguise your accent. Eton, I'd say.'

'Yes.'

'It will take time, but there couldn't have been that many Indians at Eton. I'd say you're in your late twenties. All I would need to do is look up the records to find out who you are.'

'Take the time then.'

'You're extremely cautious. Maybe you're the agent provocateur.'

'No. Just a patriotic Indian.'

'I've told you who I am, and placed my life in your hands. You could easily betray me to the authorities. I'm wanted by them, you know.'

'Meaning I am, too?'

'Your animal instincts are obvious. Well, why don't we put our cards on the table? We can both escape this deserted beach. I won't be here at dawn; nor will you. But if we do have mutual interests, we could arrange a meeting tomorrow and discuss what we should do.'

'I'm listening but tomorrow's too soon for me. Let's say, in a week's time.'

'I can't wait that long. I'm leaving the country in a couple of days. I feel we can be of some use to each other. You need a friend in this world, Mr Chandra. I know what it feels like to be very alone in one's work.'

Anil drew out the revolver. The butt was slippery with sweat. He'd been gripping it tightly all evening.

'I thought you were carrying a gun.' Bayley drew up his shirt. In the pale light, his belly was unnaturally white and soft. 'You see I'm unarmed.'

'Good. Now step back five paces to that chair and sit down facing me.' Bayley sat, quite at ease, whisky in hand, legs outstretched. 'I'm Anil Ray.'

'Ah!'

Anil felt a small triumph. So his name meant something to this man. Once he'd dreamed of it having another meaning; that of a successful, wealthy lawyer, famed for his eloquence and his belief in the rule of law.

'Now I understand your caution, Mr Ray. I believe we could work together.'

'Printing pamphlets?'

'Those are for children. We are of another world, Mr Ray. I only give those students toys to play with. To you, I'll give the real thing.'

'And who are you?'

'Let's say my name is Peter Bayley. It's the name I've lived with the longest. My true name . . .' he fell silent, brooding and melancholy as if the words had conjured up the vastness of his homeland '. . . I will reclaim when I return to my country. Many years ago my British father was a professor in Moscow University. My mother was a Russian countess. I was born in Moscow but educated in England. I spent a few summers on our family estate near St Petersburg. I was truly happy there, Mr Ray, but fate decreed another life for me. Through my father's connections I was recruited as an agent. I was ideal material, with a Russian heart and soul and the external surface of an Englishman. At school and university I made many friends, and they all believed me to be one of them, an English gentleman. There was always enough money at my disposal to cultivate and entertain and, of course, to recruit. Naturally, India is of great importance to us. We are only interested in helping Indians win their struggle for liberation from British rule.'

'I doubt that,' Anil said. 'Empires, of whatever hue or whatever period, are entirely single-minded in their suppression of people's freedom. Any agreement to work together will be only for my convenience. I have no love for Russia, and have no intention of seeing a king-emperor replaced by a tsar. Both titles are an abomination to my ears.'

'At least you're frank.'

'You deserve that, Mr Bayley . . .'

'Peter.'

'. . . as you have placed your life in my hands with your revelations. It's obvious that this isn't your first visit to India.'

'I have been here before.'

Often, he could have added, and each return grew more dangerous. He had been foolish and reckless on his first visit seven years ago. He had seduced Elizabeth Creighton, the Colonel's daughter, and placed his life in jeopardy. He had been attracted to Elizabeth at a dinner party in Bombay. Her cool, almost austere, presence had been a challenge. He remembered brushing her thigh with the back of his hand under the dinner table and feeling the searing heat of her skin through the silk. With that touch, he knew he had to seduce her. But the seduction could only take place on a second trip and the affair in Calcutta, conducted discreetly, had been as sexually exciting as he could have hoped. In bed and in the Indian heat, her icy superiority had turned to greedy passion. An added pleasure of the affair was knowing how he skirted danger. Colonel Creighton was the head of the Political and Secret Department, the very man who had played the great game against his countrymen on the North West Frontier. He knew she was in London and haunted Half Moon Street in search of him. But he'd also spotted the detectives, using her as the bait to draw him out and he'd avoided her. Maybe when they finally tired, he'd renew that delicious acquaintance. Since the affair he travelled around India, a perfect English gentleman, but at each place he visited he sought out revolutionaries and financed them handsomely to buy guns and bombs and print seditious pamphlets against the British.

'If you should be going to Delhi soon,' Peter broke his silence, 'I'd like you to meet a friend of mine. A Marwari businessman who will supply whatever you need.'

Anil woke with a start, the sun scorching his face. It felt like live coals and he lifted his hand to shield his eyes. The young man opposite him frowned, and Anil realised he'd been studied too. Suddenly, the man clicked his fingers and smiled in pleasure. 'Anil Ray. Eton. You scored a century against us at Lord's in the Eton and Harrow match.'

'Were you playing for Harrow?'

'No,' the young man smiled ruefully. 'I went to Harrow but was only in the audience and very proud that an Indian should thrash the bowling as soundly as you did. I remember you hitting a glorious six into the pavilion – a straight drive that bounced into the second row.'

'I remember.'

It had been a murky day with a fine intermittent drizzle which left a sheen, like perspiration, on everyone's faces. The ball was swinging wildly and Eton had lost their first two wickets cheaply when Anil went in to bat. As he strode out of the pavilion, he knew this was his stage, this his moment. He was absolutely confident. He picked the first ball off a length and drove it for four. Runs then flowed from his bat. He still remembered every stroke. The sweetest sound was the clapping of the boys and their parents, rising to their feet, as he carried his bat back to the pavilion having won the match. He too had been proud that they cheered an Indian. After the game, he'd been mobbed by admirers and he now recalled a young Harrovian shyly pushing through to congratulate him on his innings. They had spoken but that conversation had been forgotten.

'Nehru,' Anil said out aloud. 'Jawarhalal. I thought your face was familiar.'

'You remember!' Nehru seemed inordinately pleased. 'Are you still playing?'

'I'm afraid not. No time.' This polite conversation, two Indian gentlemen recalling their English schooldays, amused him. 'How long have you been back?'

'Not long. I went up to Cambridge after Harrow.'

'Oxford.'

'Then I studied for the bar. I intended to stay on a bit longer but my father wanted me to return and practise law here. I'm afraid I'm not going to make a terribly good lawyer.'

'I read for the bar as well.'

Jawaharlal Nehru noticed Anil's suit. In the cruel sunlight, it was shiny at the elbows and revealed crude darning. He was disappointed that his schoolboy hero looked so unsuccessful. He wondered for a moment whether he should give him some money but one glance at Anil's face told him the gesture wouldn't be taken kindly. Anil's eyes made him uneasy. They stared unblinkingly at him with ironic amusement.

'Are you practising?'

'No. I'm not a great believer in English law. But I'm sure you'll be a great success.'

'I don't have your confidence. But I feel I can't just spend the rest of my life practising law and becoming selfishly rich while India continues to be ruled by Englishmen. They have an iron grip, not only on our bodies, but on our minds and souls. We must free ourselves.'

'That sounds seditious.'

'Are you going to report it?' They passed the Mughal emperor Humayun's tomb, the train was nearing Delhi.

The tomb was huge and sadly forlorn. Monkeys scampered in the overgrown garden and stalked the parapets.

Anil laughed out loud, much to Nehru's puzzlement. 'No. I won't report this conversation to the next policeman. Will you use violence to achieve this great objective?'

'If necessary. But I'm not a violent man. My father's contented with their rule. He thinks it's brought us peace and prosperity because he's grown rich and successful. But the price has been high.'

'What are your own plans?'

'I'm joining the Congress Party. Even they are puppets, but at least they're our voice in this wilderness. To be honest, I really have no idea. I can't see which direction I should take. Will my becoming a Congress member free India? I don't think so, but I don't know what else to do. The power to grant us freedom lies with the British.'

'You're wrong,' Anil waved to the land beyond the window. 'It's out there. Rouse them, Nehru, if that is to be your way. There are 300 million of us, ignorant and crushed. Awaken us. We are the army who will drive out the British.'

'But how?' Nehru looked out doubtfully. 'It's an enormous task.'

'Go and live among the people, not in the cities where you are the European. I was like you when I first returned, a stranger.'

'But you still wear a . . . suit.'

'Oh, this is my fancy dress,' said Anil and laughed again.

Standing on the platform of Delhi Station, immersed in the people and the noise, Nehru noticed Ray put on a soiled solar topi and hold a crumpled handkerchief to his face. Nehru didn't think the air that dirty. It smelt like any railway station: of food and steam and disinfectant. Ray carried a cheap tin case, and when a coolie tried to take it from him he pulled it back violently. Nehru permitted the coolie to carry his two monogrammed leather suitcases and the two men threaded their way to the exit. Ray handed Nehru his ticket, muttering that he didn't feel very well. When they passed the ticket barrier, Nehru handed in their tickets and Ray slipped by with the handkerchief still pressed to his mouth.

'You're looking pale.'

'I'm all right,' Ray said, already moving away as though carried by an invisible current. He was fading from sight, quite mysteriously.

'Here's my card,' Nehru shouted and hurriedly thrust it into Ray's hand. Ray waved and vanished into the flowing mob of people and Nehru lost all sight of him. 'Peculiar chap,' he said aloud to himself, and followed the coolie to a tonga.

It took half an hour for Nehru to reach his destination through the narrow, winding streets of Delhi. From the outside, the house had a high drab, yellow wall, streaked black by the rains. It didn't look promising and even less so when the chowkidar, a sullen Sikh carrying a lathi, refused to let him enter until a message had been carried inside announcing the arrival of Jawaharlal Nehru. While he waited, Nehru found himself watched suspiciously by the Sikh. Finally a small door set into the large wooden gate opened, and a bearer, dressed in white with a blue cummerbund, emerged. He was deferential and took Nehru's cases without saying a word.

Nehru stepped out of Delhi into an enchanting garden. He clapped his hands in pleasure. Stretching away from him was a large immaculate lawn with a marble fountain in the centre. The lawn was surrounded by great shady trees and flowering plants. On one side was a huge banyan, stretching out its limbs like a lazy giant. Nehru calculated that it must cover half an acre. He strolled behind the bearer, admiring his surroundings. All the city harshness faded and he heard the birds and squirrels clearly. The house itself was magnificent. He stepped up onto a marble verandah and passed through high-ceilinged rooms, some wood-panelled, others decorated with shards of mirrors that reflected broken images of him. He considered this slightly excessive. Within the house was yet another, smaller garden and a smaller marble fountain. He was led up stairs, along verandahs and finally shown into a vast bedroom. The bed had a headboard elaborately carved with demons and serpents intertwined and Nehru shuddered, hoping he would not have nightmares. Comfortable easy chairs faced the large French windows which looked out onto the exterior garden and a large ornamental lake. Swans floated serenely under his window. On the far side was a strange building. It was quite high and built entirely of granite. At first he couldn't put his finger on why he found it strange. Then he realised it had no windows.

Before bowing himself out, the bearer handed Nehru a folded note.

"Please forgive me for not welcoming you. Make yourself at home. I'll be back for dinner. Drinks in the library at seven. Lal Bahadhur.'

Nehru's rest revived him but as time passed, he grew uneasy at the silence. He had welcomed it at first, but now it felt oppressive. He heard no sounds and, staring out of the window, he saw very little sign of human existence. In the far distance he thought he saw a mali at work but could have been mistaken. He gazed at the swans as they moved regally from one end of the pond to the other, leaving scarcely a ripple in the water.

He was relieved to hear the bearer knock on his door at ten to seven. Once more he trailed the man mutely through a length of corridors, his own footsteps echoing. They passed through many rooms and in the glimmer of lamplight he saw priceless paintings, Mughal and European. He paused to admire a Rembrandt sketch and the bearer waited patiently. The floors were covered with silk Persian and Kashmiri carpets; light glowed on silver and ivory, shone on polished rosewood and teak. He had hoped to hear sounds of other guests, even the host's family, but he met no one on this long voyage through the labyrinth of uninhabited rooms.

The bearer finally opened a door and permitted Nehru to slip in before shutting it. The room was lined from floor to ceiling with leatherbound books. Their polished brown spines and gold lettering shone in the light. Nehru was drawn to them, and walked around pulling them out and wishing he could spend the rest of his days locked in this room, reading. None, he found, had been read. The pages were still uncut.

'I thought you would like this room,' Lal Bahadhur said. He had entered so quietly that Nehru hadn't heard him. He stood in the very centre of the room beneath the ornate chandelier, possessively surveying his books.

'It's an impressive library, sir,' Nehru crossed quickly and shook Lal Bahadhur's cool hand. 'Even my father doesn't have such a collection.'

'I'm delighted that at least I can boast of a better library than Motilal's. Come.' Nehru was guided to a deep leather armchair. A tray of crystal decanters stood on a table. 'Whisky?'

'A claret, if you have one.'

'I remember your father's preference.' Lal Bahadhur poured the claret and Nehru sipped an exceptional vintage. 'How is your good father?'

'Very well. Naturally he sent you his best wishes.'

'Thank you. I received his note. I gather you plan to join the Congress Party. He wanted me to guide you with whatever advice I could offer.'

'Yes. As a Member of the Viceroy's Council, Father thought you'd be the best man. Of course he'd like me to follow in his footsteps in law, but I don't see myself practising it very well. I'm more interested in politics, and as the only opposition to British rule here is the Congress Party I wanted to become an active member.'

'Well, as a Congress man I certainly welcome young blood. We old ones will one day have to bow off the stage. But I certainly hope you're not going to be one of these revolutionary young men.' When Nehru remained silent, he continued, 'I feel that if we continue along this path of legislative reform we will eventually win our goal. The British want us to mature slowly so that we can understand the democratic process which they have perfected through centuries of effort. Eventually we'll rule, with their guidance and advice.'

'And they will still remain our masters.'

'I see. Jawaharlal, I know you're young and impetuous.' In fact Lal Bahadhur thought the opposite. He saw a dreamy young man, a dilettante like his father. Jawaharlal would be more suited to the gentle pursuit of composing poems than the corrupt world of constant betrayal that was Indian politics. 'British rule is a fact. Violence will only be met by greater violence from their side. But if we move judiciously along the path of reform, India will gain the freedom to rule herself. Overall policies will naturally be formulated by Westminster, but we will run our own day-to-day affairs.'

Word for word, Jawaharlal thought it was the same advice given him by his father. These were men set in their ways, satisfied with the pathetic progress of this 'self-government' under Westminster's paternal eye, old men who couldn't imagine a free India. Nehru felt he belonged to a new generation, the new blood Congress needed to set it alight. He only half listened, not wanting to enter into a debate with this slim, powerful man. He knew that Lal Bahadhur could politically help or hinder his own rise in the Congress Party. Gradually he managed to steer the conversation away from Lal Bahadhur and his political views.

'This is a beautiful house. Do you live here alone?'

'My mother lives with me. I was married . . .' he hesitated, wincing inwardly at the thought of Mohini, '. . . but my wife couldn't bear children. I remarried last month.'

'Again!' Nehru couldn't hide his surprise. Lal Bahadhur was as old as his father, though drawn and steely. He wondered where she was. 'I congratulate you.'

'Thank you. I enjoy the company of a wife. I'm sure you will soon, too. My mother, of course, arranged this second marriage – a young girl from a good family, an orphan. She isn't as beautiful as my first wife, though. Has your mother arranged a girl for you yet? You mustn't wait too long.'

'Yes,' Nehru said glumly. 'But I can't agree with these old customs. How shall we enter the twentieth century if we continue these traditions?'

'Why should we change? Come, let's eat. I prefer an early night.'

They dined in a banqueting hall, with tapestries and shields on the walls, which reminded Nehru of a mediaeval castle. The rosewood table ran the full length of the room and could seat forty. Lal Bahadhur and Nehru perched at one end, served on silver plates by a lone bearer. If there was an army of staff, Nehru saw none of them. His own home in Allahabad was noisy and chaotic with family, friends and an enormous retinue of servants. But the food was delicious and came out of mysterious kitchens in a steady flow. Lal Bahadhur ate sparingly and swiftly.

'You had a good journey?'

'It was comfortable. But we don't have even the privilege of travelling first class. It's injust that in our own country we should be second-class citizens. But there was a very pleasant coincidence. I met, not a friend, but a boy I'd admired tremendously during my schooldays. He was an excellent cricketer and played for Eton against Harrow. Unfortunately, he looked as if he'd fallen on hard times.'

'With an English public school education? He must be pretty incompetent. Who was he?'

'Anil Ray. We had a chat about . . .'

'Anil Ray! My dear fellow, why didn't you mention it earlier?'

'Why? Do you know him?'

'Anil Ray is being hunted by half the police in this country! I have personally placed a reward on his head. Dead or alive. And you travelled with him! Did he say where he'd be staying?'

'Ray! A terrorist?' Nehru blushed, remembering his

remark about sedition, and understood why Ray had laughed. 'I never knew that.'

He suppressed his excitement and felt the resurgence of hero-worship. His boyhood hero hadn't failed him after all, though his heroics were now dangerous. Then he felt sad too, thinking of that swashbuckling cricketer being hunted by the police. It had to be a damned lonely existence, Nehru thought. My God, he used me cleverly to get past the ticket barrier. If he had been spotted, bullets could have been flying around my head. I suppose he must have had his gun in that cheap tin case.

'Well, for God's sake don't even mention the fact that you know him or met him. You'll be down in their books as a fellow conspirator and end up in prison.' Lal Bahadhur pushed his plate away. 'It's too late to inform the authorities now. I'll do it early in the morning. Inspector Goode is in charge of His Excellency's security. I won't tell him how I know Ray's in Delhi. I'll make up some story to protect you. But Ray's a very dangerous man.'

'What has he done?'

'He attempted to assassinate Lord Curzon. Then he escaped from Tihar and badly beat up an English police officer, this same Inspector Goode. I've heard that he also killed a policeman when he was attempting to assassinate His Imperial Majesty at the durbar. He's extremely dangerous.' He rose and Nehru, who hadn't finished, hastily pushed away his plate and followed Lal Bahadhur out of the dining-room. 'By the way, I managed to get a special seat for you at the welcoming ceremony for the Viceroy. It's his official entry into the new capital of India. A total waste of money, this new Delhi. He's been on tour and it's going to be a big tamasha, with the Viceroy entering on an elephant. The seat was very difficult to get and I had to use a tremendous amount of personal influence.'

'I do appreciate it. I'll be up early.'

'Not a word now about meeting Anil Ray.'

The bearer waited to lead him back and Nehru felt somewhat like a prisoner.

While Nehru slept, curled as far from the headboard as possible, Gitabhai, Lal Bahadhur's mother, was wide awake and standing below his window. She had no fear that Nehru would wake and see her. He would sleep like a child until dawn.

She moved quietly around the pond to the granite building. The door on the far side was made of iron with a heavy padlock. The key hung at her waist. She opened it and slowly pushed the door open. Though it had no windows or lamps, the room glowed with a yellowish light. A great gust of terrible noise burst into the night, setting all the pi-dogs within hearing distance howling in fright. She closed the door quickly and slid the bolt into place. Streams of shadow swirled around, flickering with sparks and smoke. Demons and serpents danced and writhed, changing shape and form even as they moved in the stream. Gitabhai ignored the dreadful shrieks and screams and sat down cross-legged beside a damp sheet which covered a shapeless mass.

'Hurry, hurry, hurry, hurry,' the demons chanted.

'Be patient, my friends. It won't be long.'

She spoke politely, disguising her relief at soon being able to rid herself of the malignant host. She had to succeed, for her own life was in danger from them and they had long outstayed their welcome. She'd summoned them to visit a terrible and frightening death on Mohini but instead, like cowards, they had flown out of her body, exorcised and defeated by the sound of two boys singing. They hadn't returned to the netherworld but instead had descended on her head, whining and complaining that they had fought the divine voices of Bala and Bala but that the boon given them by the Lord Krishna with the protection of Brahma was beyond their powers. 'Why then did you in the first place permit that man to steal her from my power?' she enquired as politely as she could. 'Because,' they screamed in unison, 'he wasn't afraid of us, and was also protected by a divine power. We were helpless to stop him.' Gitabhai believed she had summoned incompetents to do her bidding and that the gods conspired to defeat her.

She had not slept since the night Kim had stolen Mohini from her. On the surface she remained serene and youthful and lovely. The only outward sign of the ferment was the darkening circles around her eyes but even those, cleverly dusted with powder, made her appear unchanged. The demons had re-entered her after their defeat by Bala and Bala and in order to escape their whining din she had built this granite chamber and disgorged them. She had thought that in time they would tire and return to their own black world and then discovered, to her horror, that they were trapped on earth. Their only routes of escape were either her – and they would take her down with them in revenge – or else through Mohini's death. Gitabhai far preferred the latter. She had offered them other women, young, lovely village girls who had fainted immediately at the sight of them. But they had been summoned by her to destroy only Mohini and they couldn't accept a substitute. Gitabhai thought their bureaucracy as inflexible and stupid as the one that ran the country.

'Why don't you find Mohini then? You have the power to fly around the world. Surely, she can't be far.'

"Because, you ignorant fool, we will be seen. There are 330 million avatars of God in this land. One god and one-third for every soul in this country. And if we are seen by any one of these avatars we will be destroyed. There are sunyassis too who can reduce us to dust by a mere glance. Either find Mohini for us and take us to her. Or else . . .'

Gitabhai tried to summon Mohini to her and failed. She tried to find her whereabouts through magic and failed. Gitabhai had to search for another way.

She spent her days and nights immersed in the study of black magic. She consulted evil men from far and near, and begged their guidance and advice. They taught her new spells and unearthed ancient mantras, for a price, but none worked. Gradually it dawned on her that the power protecting Mohini and the man was greater than she had ever imagined. No lesser deity could have frustrated her spells or curses. It had to be Siva or Vishnu who protected them, and Gitabhai went into such a screaming tantrum at this discovery, that she almost frightened the demons back to their own black world. She wouldn't tell them the cause of her ill temper, for if they knew who stood against them, they would have accepted defeat and killed her.

Having reached this conclusion, Gitabhai realised that the only way to defeat this protective power was to appeal to the very god who had bestowed it. Since Brahma had created as equal both good and evil in the universe, he would grant both good and evil boons to the true believer. There were many instances in which evil men had attained as great a power as the holiest from one and the same god. But it would not be an easy path. Gitabhai knew that only through intense devotion would the god answer her appeal and reveal the way in which she could find Mohini, transport the demons to her and destroy her and her lover. She spent months in prayer, fasting herself to skin and bone and leading a life of deprivation and severe austerity. She knew that eventually Brahma would hear her and send a messenger with his boon.

One day a leprous woman came to the gate asking for her. The woman carried a filthy bundle and only parted with her precious gift in exchange for Gitabhai's eight gold bangles, her emerald nose studs and emerald earrings. Gitabhai opened the bundle in her granite sanctuary and found an ancient, rotting document written on papyrus. It almost turned to dust at her touch and she was all but overwhelmed by the vibrations of its malevolent power. It was written by a sage whom Siva had turned into a squid for his evil deeds. She studied the writings carefully and learned Brahma's greatest secret, the creation of a living human.

So Gitabhai summoned the demons and revealed her plan, not telling them that it was Brahma who'd come to her aid. It was best that they believe she herself had this power. They cackled in sheer delight and promised to install her as their deity once they escaped the earth.

On this very auspicious night, Gitabhai removed the sheet and stared at the mound of damp clay. It had been brought from the banks of the holiest river, the Ganges, and on each grain she had blown and whispered the special mantra. She took a handful and began to knead it.

Lord Hardinge woke with a sense of unease. He lifted the curtain, it was still dark though the first faint streaks of light were visible on the horizon. His ceremonial entry was due to begin in three hours and he hoped the feeling would disappear after a bath and breakfast. He rose carefully so as not to waken Winifred and put on his dressing-gown. He moved through the ornate sitting-room of the railway carriage, opened the door and stepped out. It was decidedly chilly and he shivered. His Imperial bodyguard and the two police constables standing on the platform on either side of the door snapped to attention. Beyond them stood a further ring of policemen and bodyguards. He hoped the unease was no more than indigestion and stood awhile watching the night sky slowly lightening. He enjoyed the clear clean smell of an Indian dawn. The silence was soothing and all around him, slowly, India began to come awake. He stood awhile, and returned to the bedroom.

Winifred sat up.

'What's wrong?'

'A touch of indigestion. It'll soon go away.'

In the dressing-room his valet had laid out his ceremonial uniform, a blue cutaway coat complete with decorations and the Garter ribbon. His cocked hat with its plume was still in its box and the cloak of his office was draped over a tailor's dummy. Wearing that would be suffocating in the heat. Though not as elaborately jewelled as a Mughal emperor's sarapa, it was meant to remind Indians of a similar Imperial power.

At precisely eight thirty Lord Hardinge, followed by Lady Hardinge and Diamond, stepped out of the Viceregal railway carriage onto the red carpet laid out on the Number One platform of Delhi Station. There was a splendid turn-out of dignitaries waiting to welcome him, and he passed through their ranks chatting and laughing, though he had never felt less like it.

'Oh dear, I feel that something absolutely dreadful is going to happen,' Lord Hardinge whispered to his wife.

'Nonsense, dear,' Winifred said. 'It's only your indigestion.' She tried to reassure him, though she too felt her husband's unease.

His ADC led the way out to the kneeling elephant. On its back was a gold and jewelled howdah. Behind it knelt another, far less opulent. Collins helped the Vicereine and Diamond onto the second elephant.

Anil Ray waited in the crowd. He clasped a Trichnopoly cigar box very carefully against his side. He had chosen to stand by a pillar which gave him protection from being jostled by the crowd. The cigar box contained a small vial of nitroglycerine packed in cotton wool. Surrounding the packing were countless small nails.

The nitroglycerine had been supplied by Peter Bayley. He had given Anil the name and address of the Marwari businessman in Delhi. This was a test of faith for both men. If Anil picked up the nitroglycerine and carried out his assassination, Bayley would know he had found a perfect weapon in him. If Anil was arrested by the police, he would know Bayley had betrayed him.

Anil had approached the address cautiously. The house was at the end of a small, narrow lane. There weren't many people about but Anil watched for an hour. When would the trap be set? After the collection, or before? He circled the house – the other rooftops were an easy jump apart – before knocking on the door. He felt himself being studied through a grille and finally the door opened enough to allow him to slip in. His eyes took a moment to adjust to the cool gloom. A fat, perspiring man led him down a corridor and into a sparsely furnished back room. He locked the door and dabbed at his face. Anil guessed the man was also quite prosperous.

'You are Anil Ray?'

'Yes, Mr Bayley sent me.'

'I am most delighted to meet you, Mr Ray,' the Marwari shook his hand. 'I have followed your career since the tragic murder of your uncle by the police. I wish I were as brave as you but, being an outright coward, I do what little I can to help our freedom movement.' He fell uneasily silent when Anil made no effort to reply. 'Here is what I have for you.'

He went to an earthenware pot in the corner, plunged his hand into the water and carefully drew out a small bottle, its top sealed with wax.

'For God's sake and my life, don't drop this. It will blow us all and this house, my ancestral home, to smithereens.'

Anil held the bottle carefully. Despite the water it felt warm and alive. The Marwari's eyes were fixed intently on the bottle and sweat trickled down his face. The house was silent and Anil strained to listen for an alien sound.

'Do I just throw this?'

'No, no. In the open it will only go bang and do superficial damage. It must be made more lethal.' He picked up a cigar box from the table and opened it. In the middle was a wad of cotton surrounded by rusty nails. 'We place it here. Now when it explodes, the nails will fly in all directions. Just imagine them tearing into flesh and bones.'

'You are a bloodthirsty man,' Anil said. He hefted the box. 'It's awkward to throw.'

'But you were a great cricketer.'

'This isn't a cricket ball. Carry it for me to the end of the lane.'

'Me? Mr Ray, I am a coward. I could drop it.'

'In which case you would have served a good cause,' Anil said. He drew out the revolver. With a sigh, the Marwari carefully picked up the cigar box and carried it in front of him, like an offering. Anil followed half a dozen steps behind. It was a clear, chilly night. Shadows flickered in the lamplight and Anil imagined them holding men waiting for him, and tensed for the eruption of gun fire. The Marwari reached the end of the lane, saw that he was alone and nearly dropped the box. Anil kept his gun ready and moved carefully into the lane. He reached the Marwari who thrust the box into his hand and bravely stood his ground to prove there was no trap.

Inspector Goode crouched in the minaret of the Jama Masjid, scanning the crowd below him with binoculars. He'd placed a dozen officers with rifles on rooftops all along the route. Extra police had been drafted in and he watched them slowly beating the crowd back, moving it as far from the Viceroy's path as possible.

He had to find Ray, had to. He was within reach, a dark and evil face in that crowd. Goode covered the crowd, face by face. He had given the other men the best description possible but only he would instinctively know Anil Ray. He doubted whether Ray would still be a sadhu; it was too conspicuous and he was too intelligent. Even so, Goode didn't dismiss a single flash of saffron. What would he be? A Punjabi, a Sikh, a Muslim, a Kashmiri? India had so many disguises for her people. Goode squinted and again swore at Lal Bahadhur Ram Shanker. He was sure the bastard was protecting someone. How did he know Ray was in Delhi? Which train had he travelled on? Who had been his travelling companions? But Lal Bahadhur had been bland, merely repeating that he had heard from a reliable source that Ray was in Delhi. If Lal Bahadhur hadn't been a Member of the Viceroy's Council, Goode would have taken the bastard to the lock-up and beaten the truth out of him.

Goode swung to watch the Viceroy's stately progress. The Chief Commissioner of Delhi and the Royal Horse Artillery led the procession. Behind them rode the Inniskilling Dragoons. Next came the Bodyguard wearing scarlet and gold, followed by the Imperial Cadet Corps, twenty-five strong, escorting the Viceroy. On either side of his elephant were bearers carrying great silken umbrellas to shade the Viceroy from the morning sun. A thin line of police constables pushed back the crowds. Goode focused on the people nearest the Viceroy. He went over the scene inch by inch, looking for a suspicious movement, a hand waving a gun, a rifle poking out from a window. Suddenly it came. Something sailed through the air.

The bearer carrying the umbrella nearest him vanished from sight. It took Goode a moment to understand what had happened. He heard the 'tumpf' of an explosion seconds later and the bloodied headless body fell back to earth like a rag doll. He shifted quickly to the Viceroy, who remained upright. His elephant had stopped. Slowly, even as Goode watched, Lord Hardinge fell over to one side.

'Cordon the crowd, cordon the crowd,' Goode screamed down to his subordinates. 'Don't let the bastard Anil Ray escape.'

# 13

# July 1912

It was a black night with no moon and faint stars. Kim and Parvati could see the beckoning glow of a distant village. Even as they watched, the lights were extinguished one by one leaving them alone in the immense darkness.

Kim crouched beside a boulder. Parvati knelt behind him, her face pressed wearily against the warm stone. She could barely see Kim a foot away. He gripped a cane tightly with both hands, leaving enough of a gap between to slip it over the man's head, jerk back and snap his neck. Kim had seen the young man scanning the crowd in Madurai Station and when he'd spotted Kim and Parvati he'd immediately looked away. It marked him as inexperienced.

They both had reason to fear this stranger. Parvati had at once taken fright, believing him to be one of her husband's goondas. But the man merely followed them out of the station, and when they left the town on foot he remained alone and made no attempt to attack.

'He's the Colonel sahib's man then,' Kim said. 'Though I've no idea how the Colonel could have traced me here so swiftly.'

Kim, having worked all his life for the Colonel, had an almost superstitious belief in his powers. That belief had been instilled and sustained by the Colonel who knew the Indian half of Kim's mind was easily awed by mystery. It needed the supernatural, an authority greater than man, to control it.

One spring, when Kim was still at school, he'd slipped out of the dormitory, climbed over the wall and escaped into the Indian night. On such excursions he seldom wandered far. He needed to be immersed in the people he knew best and to escape the stuffy company of English schoolboys. This time he'd met a group of pilgrims outside Lucknow railway station. They were setting out on a pilgrimage to Badrinath, one of the holiest shrines, high in the Himalayas. Badrinath stood at the source of the Ganges. The temple closed when the snows set in and re-opened when they melted. The first thaw was an auspicious time for a pilgrimage. An old woman, being cheated by a fruit seller, drew his attention. He bargained on her behalf and, when he helped her onto the train for Delhi, he couldn't resist the impulse to accompany her some of the way. She offered to pay for his ticket but Kim preferred to escape onto the roof, in the company of other poor travellers, each time the ticket collector came. On reaching Delhi, the point at which he planned to return to school, his heart was moved by the old woman's plight. He knew she would never survive the arduous journey alone.

Nirmala had bright brown eyes and still moved with grace though age had stiffened her limbs. She had been a devadasi, a temple dancer, in Hyderabad and had no family to care for her in old age. Kim knew she was dying. He saw death dimming the brightness of her eyes even as the days passed. She entertained him with wicked stories about priests and princes, the wealth she'd made and squandered, the men who'd grovelled for her favours and showered her with gold.

From Hardwar, the last railway station, the journey became more hazardous. Kim bought a scrawny pony for Nirmala to ride and led it along the narrow and tortuous path which wound and rose through gorges and mountains. There was a cold and eternal beauty all around. He cooked what little food he could scrounge or buy from the poor villagers along the route and worried that Nirmala would never complete the pilgrimage. She dwindled visibly daily. He encouraged and cajoled her, pointing up to the jagged horizon, and the salvation she had come in search of. Finally, they reached the great temple and Kim carried the feather-light woman up the steps and helped her perform her pujas. Nirmala died that night, smiling beatifically, and Kim pawned her gold bangles and diamond nose-stud to pay for her funeral. What remained of her money he donated to the temple. He grieved all the way back to Hardwar. In his boy's mind Nirmala had become the mother he'd never known.

The Colonel had awaited him at Hardwar and Kim was awed by his detailed knowledge of his journey. Kim broke down and wept in his comforting arms. The kind and fatherly Colonel had accompanied Kim back to school. Years later, as Kim understood the nature of his own profession, he realised he'd been watched by the Colonel's network of spies all along the way. But that initial impression of the Colonel sahib's almost mystical knowledge couldn't be erased, even now.

Kim distinctly heard the panting breath of the hurrying man. He was also muttering to himself, and Kim knew he was afraid of this immense blackness and that his gaze would be intent on the distant village and safety. As he passed the boulder, Kim rose and softly stepped up behind him and slipped the cane over his head and pulled back.

The man leapt and would have screamed in terror if he hadn't been choking. His hands involuntarily clutched at the cane and Kim jerked him back a step. He was light and thin.

'Lower your hands or I'll kill you,' Kim said. The hands half dropped and fluttered at waist height. 'Who are you?' The man gargled and Kim slowly released the pressure. 'Stand still. If you make one move I'll break your neck. Now answer.'

'I'm . . . I'm Ravi Srinivasan, iyer.'

'Should I know you, fool?'

'I have been following you,' Ravi said, as if this were

all that was required to prove his good intent. Kim sighed and removed the cane. Ravi fell to one knee coughing and massaging his throat. He was young, not more than twenty, and very inexperienced.

'Who sent you?'

'I was given instructions by Mr T.V. Naidu of Madras, iyer.'

'Who is he?'

'A very learned and rich man, iyer. He owns much land and speaks eight languages, including French and German. He is also a cricket . . .'

'Are you such a fool?'

'Yes, iyer.'

'Who does he work for? The Colonel sahib?'

'He has no need to work for anyone. And I know of no Colonel sahib. And if this Colonel sahib is a Britisher then certainly never would Mr T.V. Naidu be in his employ.'

'Why is Mr Naidu interested in me?'

'I do not exactly know. But I have instructions to follow you and to give you a message. The message from Mr T.V. Naidu is that I must offer, on his behalf, all and any assistance and help you may need. This includes financial help as well. See.' Ravi drew out a bag of silver coins.

Kim made no attempt to take them. 'Why?'

'Iyer, you may ask whys until the cows go home but I do not possess the answer. You must be an important man and that is all I know. It is possible he wants your help.' He turned to stare up at Kim, still brandishing the cane. 'And I pray you won't thrash me, as I abhor pain.'

'Get up, you fool. But remain exactly where you are.'

Kim returned to Parvati's side, 'You heard?'

'Yes. Who is this Naidu?'

'I don't know, but I do know how he found us. The letter writer informed him. Like a fool, I hinted at my profession: "deep and dark secrets".' He called out to Ravi. 'Ahre, are you a nationalist?'

'Yes, iyer,' Ravi said with pride and repeated the slogan. 'Bande matram, Free Mother India.'

'Mr Naidu wants my secrets; he wants the names I carry in my head.'

Parvati, deeply relieved that this man wasn't one of her husband's nor the Colonel's, now felt akin to Ravi and felt her blood stir at his call to free Mother India.

'Give them to him, then.'

'Don't ask me to betray my past. I have eaten the Colonel sahib's salt and I cannot now turn traitor. I will always remain silent – and that is the guarantee for my safety. But once I open my mouth the Colonel will spare no effort to have me killed. I would be an example to others who might think of betrayal.'

For Parvati, nothing was worth Kim's death, not even a free India in which she would be alone and grieving for the rest of her days.

'Then be silent, my Kim. Neither I nor the child I carry could bear to live without you.' She wished she could see his face but, caressing it, felt the hesitation and then the wide grin.

'How long have you known?' He kissed her.

'A few days now. I had no wish to burden you with yet another worry. Once we were safe I was going to tell you, but now I wonder when we will ever be safe.'

'Soon. I don't think Mr Naidu will betray us. He will wait patiently, hoping I'll help him. I now have his name and I can equally betray him to the Colonel sahib.'

'What is happening?' Ravi suddenly asked and they found him peering at them from not a foot away.

'I told you to stand where you were.'

'I heard whispering and believed you might be planning to cut my throat. So I had to find out.' He peered at Parvati and then at Kim. 'I saw you kissing this boy. Are you that kind of man?'

'She's my wife,' Kim said. 'We must help her. She's with child.'

'Ah. I thought the boy walked in a strange manner.'

'There's lots of time,' Parvati said but both men tenderly helped her to her feet and she leant against Kim, with Ravi hovering uncertainly on the other side, as they made their way to the village.

It took them a further three days' walking and riding in bullock carts to reach Narain's village. Kim was still surprised by the south. During their travels the land had been lush and emerald with rice and coconut groves; water sparkled in canals and boys swam in tanks. The Cumbun valley was ringed by cool and misty hills. From a lifetime spent in the north near the mountains, he had imagined the south to be a barren, blistering furnace.

Ravi was as solicitous of Parvati as Kim, and insisted that neither lift a finger. He had received instructions to help them and it was his duty now to buy and cook their food. They learned that he was a student who, through no fault of his own, had failed his examination but was determined to try again once his small college in Madurai opened.

Narain's village was securely remote and a pleasure to their eyes. It was small, and all the houses were of mud with thatched roofs. They formed a brown island in an endless sea of green. The village stood on the banks of a man-made lake, surrounded by a shady coconut grove, and the only sound apart from the sigh of the breeze was the water tumbling from a canal down into the lake.

Kim asked a naked small boy for Narain's brother and was led along the bank of the canal to a man directing a group of labourers digging a channel.

'Narain! Narain! Why should I welcome a friend of my brother's? That no-good, good-for-nothing loafer left a big mess for me. A big one, I tell you! I have to manage our land; I have to feed his wife who never ceases to complain about him to me. As if I had anything to do with the shaping of that loafer's character! Instead of staying here, all peaceful and quiet and raising children and coconuts like a good man, he runs off to Bombay.'

In Kumar, Kim saw the ghostly semblance of his dead friend, even though he was a year or two older than Narain and plump whereas Narain had been bony and angular. He wore only a dhoti and his breasts quivered in righteous anger. The labourers had paused to watch the drama, wondering too who the three men, dusty and weary and very obviously from a distant part of India, were.

'He's dead,' said Kim.

'Ahhh . . .' Kumar expelled a gust of sadness instead of a further tirade. Surprisingly, tears immediately coursed down his cheeks and into his carefully oiled moustache, the only splendour left for the man. He sat heavily and lifted his glistening face to the sky.

'Ram, Ram, if you are still listening, please understand I didn't mean one word against my brother. I am, as you well know, a liar and I was very fond of him. Except, he did make my life a burden by his disappearance.' He paused for breath. 'Ram, Ram, naturally you understand our properties are all mine as he left no issue. At least not in this village. What he left in Bombay only you know, but they can have no rights here.'

Kim sat with his back to a coconut palm while Parvati dangled her feet in a small channel of water, surrounded by curious village women bearing brass pots on their heads. They were both the focus of this small, remote village's attention. Even from far afield, he saw men and women hurrying to stare at them.

'How did he die?'

'He was stabbed.'

Kumar sighed again. 'He found life here dull but he wouldn't have died so young here. What misadventure brought down this terrible death?'

'It's a very long story,' was all Kim said.

Kumar blinked at him, mouth screwed in calculation. He turned to the workers. 'What's this? A tamasha? The company isn't paying you to stare at these men. Work, get to work.' Reluctantly the men returned to their labours. 'And who's that man?'

'My wife.'

Kumar stared at Kim and then suspiciously at Parvati. It took him a long time to decide finally that Kim spoke the truth. The man did indeed have very delicate features and was facially hairless.

'Then why is she dressed like that?'

'For her own safety. You know how dangerous the roads are.'

'Full of thieves and molesters of women and stealers of children. Where is your village?'

'Near Bangalore,' Kim fibbed.

Kumar translated to the crowd. 'He comes from north of those hills.' That was as far as any of them had ever travelled. Their lives were circumscribed by this valley and beyond the rim of hills, India was vague and insubstantial. The Himalayas, which none had seen or could imagine, existed only in mythology.

'Does the collector visit frequently?' Kim asked.

'Who knows? I've not seen him for four years. Only another Britisher named Farson sahib.'

'What Englishman do you speak of?'

'He works for the company that owns all that you see from here to the hills and beyond too, I'm told. He is very important. Even the collector is careful of this Farson sahib. And if we do anything wrong, we can be put in the lock-up.'

Kumar led the way to his home trailed by Kim, Parvati, Ravi and most of the village which had no intention of missing this opportunity to break the monotony of their lives. All the homes were of the same size; Kim counted about two dozen and noted a few standing in a separate huddle. Kumar's mud walls were painted white but the thatch roof rose higher than any other. Beside the entrance was a low mud platform and Kumar, after shouting inside to his wife, settled cross-legged on it. Kim and Parvati joined him.

'And what are your good names?' Kumar asked.

'Kimathchand and Parvati,' said Kim.

'And who's that?' His stubby finger pointed to Ravi. 'He looks like a man from around these parts.'

'He's a nationalist.'

'This is the second time in my life I have heard this

strange word. The first time I couldn't show my ignorance but now I can. Is it a new caste? Another religion?'

'He can speak of this better than I.'

Ravi stepped forward eagerly and squatted in front of Kumar so that he also faced the encircling villagers. His face took on the intensity of a preacher called to spread the message of salvation. Kim glanced at Parvati. She leaned forward eagerly, silently encouraging Ravi.

'India is crushed by British rule,' Ravi began. 'We are enslaved by foreigners. All the money we earn is sent away from the country and this is one of the reasons why we are poor and oppressed. I heard you talk of this Britisher who owns all this land. The money you make for him doesn't stay here to benefit you but goes to fill the pockets of strangers. It is men like him who must be cast out from this land.'

'That's all very fine talk. But we're poor and ignorant people. We don't have the power. He does. He brings the constables with him.'

'That is what we must change. The money you pay in taxes doesn't come back to you here. It doesn't come to build you schools, roads, give you medicine; it all goes away to this distant land called Ing-land. We have no rights as to what they do with our lives, our money.'

'Who does?' an old villager asked. 'Only God has the right and he can be a most difficult person.'

'Why don't you all listen to him?' Parvati said angrily. 'The lives of your children and their children depend on us winning our freedom from British rule.'

The villagers fell into an embarrassed silence, not because she scolded them but because no woman had ever spoken in the company of men before. The men looked at Kim to see whether he would admonish his wife but instead he smiled at her in encouragement.

Kim understood Parvati's and Ravi's frustration. This village was too remote, 200 miles from Madurai, and living in a previous century. One ruler to them was as bad as another, though his skin might vary in its colour. All exploited them. They saw little of their rulers. Since only 30,000 Englishmen ruled the whole vast country, this village seldom set eyes on one except for this company man who passed through infrequently. Kim remembered that even Bala and Bala, because they only travelled the countryside and not the towns, had never seen an Englishman. Those directly responsible for these people's ills would be the local tashildar or the constable, both Indian. With little or no communication with the outside world, they would be entirely ignorant of the rise and fall of empires. Empires never touched their small lives.

Ravi had fallen silent, plucking at his lip as though it were a stringed instrument. He couldn't summon up the patience to explain, to teach. He was angry at their ignorance and stupidity. They deserved to be left to their miserable fate. In the city, it was much easier to talk to people about Indian nationalism.

'So who is this other nationalist you know of? Surely he must have told you a great many things about the evils of British rule.'

'Iyer, we are only ignorant villagers and he doesn't talk to us of such things,' Kumar said. 'The Zamindar only stops here on his way to and from Madurai and expects us to feed him and his whole party for no payment. He is also a friend of this Britisher. But he did mention once, when talking to a companion in front of me, that he was a nationalist. I saw him give a bundle of papers to this companion, secretively. He talked of "freeing India" to this man but I didn't dare ask from whom or why.'

'This zamindar's name is . . .' Ravi asked, heartened now that a man of such importance was a member of his enlightened group.

'He is the Zamindar of Puducheri. He is a chettiar.'

Kim recognised the name. His trained memory saw it clearly written in the Colonel sahib's files. He was one of the Colonel's agents who regularly sent in reports on the meetings of nationalists or visits by Congressmen. He also wrote about the workings of villages in his area, who the village headman was, whether he was loyal to the British, whether this or that man was contaminated by a Congressman's visit. Kim flicked through his memory as easily as the file he'd once held in his hand. Constable Doraiswami's petty corrupt practices had been reported with the suggestion that they should continue as he was loyal to the Zamindar and would obey orders. Kim recalled another line: 'Please note I am following your instructions to disburse, without reading, the seditious literature you sent me to carefully chosen influential people in order to note their reaction. Most show total disinterest. I have also advertised myself as a nationalist in front of people whom I consider to be influential in their own small villages but they've revealed total ignorance and never approached me. I will continue to follow your instructions until ordered otherwise.'

'I must meet him while I'm here,' Ravi said eagerly. 'There are so few of us in this ignorant part of the country. How far away does he live?'

Kumar pointed up into the misty hills. 'Four or five days' walk in that direction. Sometimes he spends many months in Madurai. He is a trustee of the Meenakshi temple and a very religious man.'

Ravi looked at the hills. The distance was daunting. Four or five days there, four or five days back. He decided that meeting the Zamindar would have to be postponed. T.V. Naidu had not instructed him to go off on little jaunts.

'I will leave it for another time,' he said.

Kim exhaled slowly. The postponement was a reprieve. He knew that Ravi, in his eagerness to impress the Zamindar, would have mentioned his assignment. He would also have betrayed the mysterious T.V. Naidu. Kim was certain that eventually the Zamindar would descend from his lofty palace to examine this stranger and describe him in the next report to the Colonel. Kim considered moving on, out of the Zamindar's range. There were other places nearby he could move to. Periyar or Tinuveli or . . . elsewhere. Then he considered it had been some years since he'd read those files and new names would have been added. He'd stay. At least here he knew the Colonel's man.

Kumar's wife emerged from the hut bearing tea. She was as round as Kumar and a few inches smaller. She had a kind, motherly face and a diamond stud glittered in her nose. Hidden behind her, shyly peeping out, were two small girls.

'I have five boys too. They're visiting their aunt in the next village.'

Kumar handed the clay cups to Kim and Parvati, ignoring his wife who remained as mute as the onlookers. He hoped Kim would follow his example and control his own wife's tongue. Kumar was enjoying his role as the centre of attention. Entertaining these strangers increased his importance in the village.

'How long do you wish to remain here?'

'We would like to live here,' Kim said. 'We will cause no problem. I will work in the fields like the other men.'

'You don't look as if you've done such work,' Kumar said shrewdly, glancing down at Kim's hands; they were slim and strong but without the scars and callouses of labour. 'But if that is what you want to do, it's possible you'll find work. We will have a meeting and decide whether you can be permitted to remain.' He winked. 'But I don't think there will be any objection.'

His conspiratorial grin faded and soured when a young woman pushed her way through the crowd. She was lithe and quite pretty except for sulky eyes. She was panting and perspiring from having run some distance and stood, arms akimbo, in front of Kumar and Kim. She stared first at Kim and then at Kumar. Visibly, Kumar shrank back, and Kim guessed that this was Narain's wife. He had known Narain for many years and had learned only on the day of his death that he had a wife in this village and had run away from her. This one would make any man abscond.

'I'm told this man knows that useless husband of mine.'

'He did,' Kumar said. 'He tells me the sad news that my brother, your husband, Narain, is dead.'

'Ha! He couldn't have done a better act in his life. Now I'm a widow and his mark has been left on me. Who'll want me now? Who'll look after me? Of course, as his widow I'm entitled to all his properties.'

'How can that be?' Kumar said. 'As a widow you have no rights at all. What we own is a joint property and it cannot be divided. I have worked his fields while you've eaten our food like a maharani.'

'I want to remarry, and I need a dowry. His properties will fetch me a good husband. It's the least the useless man can do for me. If his body lay at my feet I would spit on it.'

'The property can't be divided,' Kumar said stubbornly.

'We'll see. Let Shesha decide for us.'

Kumar's eyes widened in fright. His already dark skin turned muddy and broke into sweat.

'No, no. The panchayat can decide.'

'I want Shesha to decide,' and there was venom in her insistence.

'The magistrate then.'

'Shesha.'

Kumar appealed to Kim though Kim had no wish to be drawn into this family squabble. 'See what I have to deal with. Instead of discussing it with the family she immediately wants to go to Shesha. What chance do I have? That crooked priest who feeds Shesha will decide in her favour only because she'll lift her sari and show the old priest that thing between her legs. And any man who places his thing there knows it will wither and die.'

'You only say that because you've tried.'

The crowd drew in its collective breath and Kumar darkened. He stood and drew himself up to his full height, still a good head shorter than Kim.

Kim spoke quickly. 'Kumar must be a wondrous man if he can father seven children and still have the strength to force himself between your legs.'

The crowd chuckled and Narain's wife glared at Kim, turned and pushed her way back through the crowd. It closed ranks and Kim saw her furious head gradually receding.

'Thank you,' Kumar whispered as he resumed his seat.

'Shesha? Vishnu's serpent?'

'Yes.'

'But he exists only in stone.'

'So does God, as we see him, and isn't he all around us? Shesha too is alive.' Kumar whispered and lowered his voice still further. He licked his dried lips. 'One of us will take in our offerings to him and one of us will die. That is the way Shesha chooses. I know I am ignorant, but how can a serpent carved from stone make such decisions? It's that priest who cheats us, because he knows we're afraid of such things.'

That very afternoon the village men gathered to decide what to do about Kim and Parvati. They liked Kim. His quick wit had prevented an unsavoury quarrel, and they fervently hoped Narain's widow would meet a man from some other village and leave them all in peace. Because of this, and also because Kim was not of any caste they knew of and no one could therefore object to his presence, they voted to allow him to live in the village, as long as he didn't become a burden.

Kim spent the afternoon wandering around the small village, trailed by innumerable little naked boys and girls. They should have been plump and playful but instead he saw their ribs, and their silence oppressed him. He knelt to speak to them but they fled in shyness. Gradually, he knew, he would win them over. The small crooked lane on which Kumar lived was the high caste area. On the outskirts, with their own well and crushed in a misery of castelessness, the untouchables lived. They had no part in any decision-making. They were even barred from the temple that stood, mute and white, on the crown of a hill some distance from the village. Kim accepted such a division, though he knew it to be unjust. Caste and castelessness – his own condition since he hadn't been born Hindu – were preordained and none could escape the judgement made on men and women born into the world already marked. If they were most fortunate, they wore the sacred thread which assured them of comfort and security and respect.

But he also noted that whatever the caste, the village was poor. There was little food stored in the big clay jars for the times when the monsoon failed; their clothes were torn and faded by constant washing; the men and women were as thin as the children. Apart from working the fields there was no other activity to occupy them, which surprised Kim.

Ravi Srinivasan had anxiously been awaiting the village's decision. Now that he knew Kim would remain in one place for a while, he could safely return to the civilisation of Madurai and send in his report to T.V. Naidu.

When he came to say his farewell, he begged Kim: 'I will leave tomorrow at dawn. Please let me know immediately if you move. It will save me time and trouble not to come and search for you. And keep in mind, Mr Naidu will be most grateful for any help you can give him. I was instructed to give you his address once I believed you to be a trustworthy person.' And he slipped Kim an embossed visiting card.

'How can you be sure I am that?'

'I have seen your fair behaviour in all matters and know I am not wrong in this judgement.' He also wanted to leave the bag of silver coins, lighter now, but Kim refused such a gift. It would make him beholden to Mr Naidu.

After the simple evening meal eaten in Kumar's house, they sat out in the cool darkness. Parvati remained with Kumar's wife, helping her with the cleaning. She was grateful to have been allowed to escape her male clothing. Kumar's wife had given her a cotton sari and the act of bathing and swathing herself in a sari made her feel she was truly a woman once more.

'I've noticed that despite the richness of the land you

are all poor,' said Kim. 'You have no grain stored for the drought, and the children are weak.'

'Have you ever seen a rich village?'

'No,' said Kim. 'Only rich landlords. But surely this company gives you enough for your labours.'

'Not a pice more nor a pice less than other landowners in this area. But those other villages at least can make a number of things they require. We are not permitted. This village was once famous for the cloth it made. Fine cotton saris with wondrous designs which we sold in Madurai to pay for our needs. We no longer make them. It's been many years.'

'Why?'

'We must buy the cloth brought to us by the company man. He comes with his chaprassis who sell us cloth and other things we need. They forced us to stop making these saris as they said it was against the law. When we continued, they sent the police who broke our looms and burned them and beat some of us. We are frightened people, and cannot fight the police.'

'Then you must start again.'

'You don't know what you're talking about,' Kumar peered at him through the weak lantern light. He sucked on a beedi and mulled over Kim's words. 'The police will only be sent again.'

'Secretly then. Some distance from here we can set up a small place for the village to weave once more and make those fine saris.'

'With what money? We have none now to buy the raw cotton. It's a dream we all dream, but how can we save enough?'

'I can get some money. But we must tell no one until it is all ready,' Kim said.

He woke Ravi. 'You have Mr Naidu's money and you believe in the freedom of Mother India. You cannot free India until you free her people from poverty. I want that money, not for myself, but for this village. Will you give it?'

'Gladly,' Ravi said and handed over the bag of coins.

Kim didn't mention this plan to Parvati yet. He had acted on impulse and had yet to puzzle out why. This village wasn't just another shelter on his endless journeys along the roads of India; he had committed himself to it. He saw the people now as his own, his neighbours, his eventual friends, who would labour beside him in their fields. The decision wasn't a conscious one taken against the British. He thought that even if an Indian prince had forced them to do the same thing, he would have moved against him. But that it happened to be the British disturbed him again, as it had done in that village in the north when he'd been arrested and beaten.

'It can happen again,' he thought. 'And I expect it will if I persist in my actions. Like the wheel of life itself the past recurs, cycles described within cycles. This village, so like Rae Bareli where I defied the authorities, is but one example of such a cycle. There will be many others.'

Despite himself, he felt as if his faith and belief were being slowly eroded and he wanted somehow to hold on to the tattered remnants. He wanted purity in the people of his blood, not the greed of the Indian. He kept this struggle, these doubts that shook him, hidden, not wanting to confide in Parvati until he was prepared.

Kim chose to have their hut built at the far end of the village, off the road and somewhat hidden by the undergrowth and shaded by a tamarind tree. He wanted it large enough for the men and women to be able to occupy it for a few hours every day to make the saris. Parvati thought such space was extravagant and pulled his leg that like a Britisher he imagined this would be a bungalow.

The builder was an ancient, half-bent old man. Kim helped him to carry the river mud and slowly pack it tightly to form a large rectangle. When the walls had reached a height of four feet, and this the old man decreed to be the tradition, he and Kim cut bamboo poles and built the skeleton of a high sloping roof. There would be more than enough space to stand and within this height the warm air would rise and escape through the roof. They carefully selected palm fronds from those scattered around the village and placed them, layer upon layer, on the poles.

Within the day, Kim and Parvati had a clean and simple home. They surveyed the bare interior. In one corner Kim had built a raised clay oven, and by the entrance Parvati had placed a clay statue of Lord Genesh, the god of good fortune and learning. Kim felt satisfied with what he had made.

'This is the first time in my life I have ever had a home,' said Kim, and Parvati noted the faint surprise in his voice. 'In Calcutta, where I remained for some time, I stayed with the Colonel's friends, but it was their place, and heavy with furnishings. Otherwise, leading the life of an Imperial agent, I've never remained long under any one roof. And they've always belonged to others.'

'With the first rains, it will collapse,' Parvati said. 'But while it stands we will be happy here. I need nothing except some pots to cook for you and a mat to sleep on.'

'You women always want,' Kim said affectionately.

Kim and Kumar kept their secret as long as possible, but it emerged when the carpenter finally delivered the spinning wheel and the loom he had made and kept hidden a mile from the village. He brought them surreptitiously in the dusk and laid them out on the floor of Kim's hut while Parvati was cooking. Her eyes widened in curiosity.

'Do you think I cannot keep a secret?' she asked indignantly when they told her what they planned.

'It was my own doubts,' Kim said, 'which made me remain quiet. Even now, I wonder if this is wise.'

'It will be a test then, won't it?' Parvati said. 'We will see if the British will prevent them from earning their livelihood.'

'It isn't the government . . .' Kim began.

'The company and the government are one and the same,' Parvati said and softened her tone. 'I only hope they will not hurt this poor village and punish them.'

'Us,' Kim reminded her.

# 14

## October 1912–March 1913

The Colonel disliked enforced intimacy. That the other two men who shared the Rani of Amar's Delhi guest house were men whom he'd known professionally, and as acquaintances, for years, failed to lessen his displeasure.

Each man lived in a distant part of this ornate and rambling building. Its pretence to humility was immediately apparent. The guest house bore a vague resemblance to the Palace of Versailles. It was smaller of course, but here and there the detail was exact. The Rani's father had no doubt envied and imitated its opulence. The floors were of white Italian marble, the rooms large and magnificently decorated and the Colonel thought it all too rich for his blood. His bedroom had huge French windows looking out over a manicured lawn neatly divided by paths into precise squares. The bathroom was of yellow marble, complete with a marble bath and wash basin. The taps were of gold and such extravagance and waste appalled him. The cupboards were all of rosewood and his small wardrobe was lost in the cavernous interior that stretched from one end of the room to the other and smelt of mothballs.

The guest house had been lent by the Rani to the Indian government as a residence for the Members. There were other 'guest houses' scattered around Delhi, lent too by various princes who felt that such a gesture would keep them in favour with the men who slept under their roofs. The Colonel was separated from Sir Oscar Haggard, the Member for Opium and Salt, by at least fifty yards of verandah and rooms, and from Sir Arthur Stoneham, the Member for Home Affairs, by an equal distance, living also a floor below. It wasn't that they were cheek by jowl but that they took their meals, breakfast and dinner, together in the mirrored dining-room. They could gaze at their reflections or each other. The Colonel chose silence but the other two were gregarious men and chattered throughout the morning meal. The three had reached an unspoken arrangement. The Colonel sat at one end of the long dining table, Sir Arthur and Sir Oscar at the other. Different bearers served them. The Colonel had considered taking his breakfast out on the verandah but thought that such behaviour would be considered too rude. So he silently tolerated the murmurings drifting down the table, past his raised newspaper.

'The Viceroy really is going a bit far . . .' Sir Arthur was talking. '. . . I know he considers himself an expert on India and always gives the impression of loving the native more than the European, but I gather now he's sending Gokhale to South Africa to talk to this Gandhi chap.'

'I don't trust *him*!' Sir Oscar said. 'He'd no right to start that agitation in Durban. After all, it's their country, not his, and he shouldn't be interfering with their policies. Hardinge shouldn't have said all that about the sympathy of India going out to South African Indians and "Gandhi's resistance to invidious and unjust laws". It'll only encourage Gandhi and with Gokhale now going to give him a hand, you know what'll happen next, don't you? This Gandhi's going to end up on our doorstep doing the same thing.'

'We're not South Africa,' Sir Arthur said. 'We'll know how to deal with him. Won't we, Colonel?'

The Colonel lowered his paper reluctantly. 'We'll keep a close eye on him should he return. Seems a stubborn chap though. But so was Tilak.'

'And he's still in Mandalay. A good stiff prison term should keep this Gandhi in check.'

The Colonel raised his newspaper, confident that Gandhi would cause little trouble. Sending Gokhale to meet Gandhi in South Africa was a clever gesture on Hardinge's part. Gokhale wasn't a firebrand but a man of compromise and considerable stature in India and sending him would appease Indian sentiment. It meant the Indian government was unofficially sympathising with Gandhi. Still, he felt uneasy. Gandhi shouldn't be over-encouraged; he could bring his campaign of non-violent resistance to India. The Colonel considered it a double-edged, subtle weapon and he saw a deeper echo in its simplicity. It depended on the word 'violence'. He doubted something so idealistic and moral would work in India, where there was no morality and every movement exploded into bloody rioting, mayhem and slaughter. In South Africa, Gandhi led a handful of people; the Indians there were cohesive. In India, where there was no cohesion and people so easily divisible, this non-violent resistance would fall apart. No, the Colonel decided, Gandhi would be just another passing politician. And once he was offered a little power, his greed would overcome his scruples and he'd stretch out both hands to grab it, just like Lal Bahadhur and the other politicians now sitting on the provincial councils. Tilak was the only one to keep an eye on when he was freed from prison.

'I say, Colonel, you must know something about this Gandhi wallah,' Sir Oscar's voice interrupted the Colonel's thoughts.

'If he doesn't,' said Sir Arthur, 'no one will. You have your finger on every pulse, don't you, Colonel?'

'Not all, by any means,' said the Colonel brusquely. He folded his newspaper regretfully. 'His full name is Mohandas Karamchand Gandhi. He was born in 1869 in Porbander, a small state in Kathiawar. His father was the diwan of the local ruler and the Gandhis are vasih, a merchant caste. They are, strangely, closely associated with the Jain sect who practise ahimsa, non-violence. Gandhi doubtless is adapting that to his own non-violent movement. He was married as a boy to a child-wife and sent off as a young man to study law in London. I gather this caused quite a stir in his community. As you know, by crossing the kala pani, a Hindu loses caste. Gandhi was quite a dandy in London, dressed in top hat and tail coat and was a bit of a peacock. He left London the day after he was admitted to the bar and came back here. He wasn't a great success in practising law and I gather a leader of the South African Indian community hired him to represent them in a case. He's been there ever since, apart from a couple of brief visits to India. His wife and two sons have since joined him out there.'

The Colonel rose, nodded to the two men and strolled out to his gharri. The heat and glare felt as though he'd walked into a wall. The impact drove his breath away. He shaded his eyes. The blue was sullen and the whiteness of this sunlight made it unbearable. His linen suit felt tight and uncomfortable and he wished they could wear casual clothes for these summers, but he knew this would set a bad example to the Indian.

'Colonel sahib,' a woman called, and he looked round. At the far end of the verandah he saw a flutter of green silk through the marble jali. He approached slowly, deferentially, and bowed to the unseen woman.

'Your Highness. I didn't realise you were in residence. I must thank you for permitting us to stay. I hope we aren't an inconvenience.'

'Of course you're not. Are you in a hurry to go to your office?'

'Only files await me, Your Highness. They are quite patient things.'

He moved around the jali and entered the cool, gloomy room. The Rani of Amar rose, reaching only to his elbow. He bowed again and waited until she'd perched on the chair before he sat carefully. She was decidedly the most ugly woman he'd ever seen but he liked her lively eyes and quick wit. She was also extremely loyal to the

Crown and a straightforward woman. He'd known her father well, had been his guest on shikar a few times. When the moment had come to choose between her and her brother the Colonel had advised the government to appoint her ruler. She was aware of this and had always shown her gratitude whenever she could. She ruled well, kindly and firmly. Each morning she held a durbar in the palace which all her subjects could attend. She would listen carefully and give judgement, or pass the problem on to one of her ministers to deal with.

'You are comfortable?'

'Very. Government servants are not used to living in such splendour, Your Highness. It might spoil us and it would be impossible to return to our bungalows.'

'A taste of riches always helps men to understand what can be achieved. Our existence is a service to the poor.' The Colonel caught the quick gleam of laughter in her otherwise solemn eyes. 'We give them something to aspire to or else to destroy. Wealth is a focus for one or the other. Naturally I hope I only inspire to aspire. I note that a man called Lenin advocates the overthrow of the Russian Imperial family. If he should succeed what will happen to us lesser kings and queens?'

'The Tsar is too strong to be overthrown by mere words, Your Highness. Is it that which worries you?'

'No. I'm sure the British Lion will protect his humble subjects from men such as Lenin and Trotsky. I am, at the moment, struggling to read an economic work called *Das Kapital*. It is exhausting but I see the glimmer of what Mr Marx means. The distribution of wealth from each according to his ability, to each according to his need, would attract those men who have no ability but insatiable needs. I have such a man in my cousin. He's my father's brother's elder son and he married into a very minor Maharati princely family. He's been seen in Amar, speaking to some close friends of my late lamented brother. I've no wish to suspect him of any designs nor do I want an accident to befall him in my state.'

In the silence, she blinked sweetly up at him. A bearer brought a tray of coffee and the Colonel reluctantly took a cup and sipped. He wished the Indian mind were not so elliptical in its thinking. She'd set a puzzle and he tried to decipher it. Was she warning him that a follower of this Lenin was operating in Amar? Was her cousin this man? And if not, what did she want the government to do about the cousin? Or the follower of Lenin? Was she planning murder and also forewarning him?

'I will pass on this information,' he finally said neutrally, hoping to keep the matter pending until something definite occurred. 'I'm sure the Indian government doesn't want to lose a loyal subject.'

She stood, ending this brief audience, allowing the Colonel to work out the conundrum, smiling all the time which made her face even more lopsided. The Colonel bowed and allowed her to pass, waiting until she'd left the room. She stopped at the door. 'What happened to that extremely attractive young man to whom I gave a lift to Pushkar? His wife was very ill.'

'I gather she's recovered. Thank you for so promptly informing us as to his whereabouts.'

'I found him quite enchanting. Bold too. A very silvery tongue.'

'Yes, he does have that.'

He wished she'd not reminded him of Kim. Kim hovered continually in the back of his mind, the ghostly errant son, lost in this huge land. How was he? Would he remain silent with all his secrets or would he, without the Colonel's influence and guidance, succumb to the seduction of India?

The Colonel's mind wandered as the gharri moved slowly along the narrow streets to his office in the Viceroy's grounds. He felt his age, felt his exhaustion. He'd served all his life, and the tiredness was at times almost overwhelming. Sometimes he wished to sleep and never waken to the daily intrigues of his office. He had a year and a half to go until his retirement. Doubtless, it could be extended for a year, a special concession in his case.

He would not take that extension. He'd always known where he would spend the remaining days of his life. Far to the north, nestled in the foothills of the mountains, was Kulu, the valley of flowers. He imagined a small bungalow, which would be cheap, and a simple life of riding and reading and writing. He would translate the countless Urdu poems piled up in his trunk. Let other men carry the burden, deal with the Gandhis and Lenins of this world.

Such a man waited for the Colonel in his makeshift office, a large two-roomed tent. The clerks were crowded on top of one another in the main one and rose in unison when the Colonel ducked into the hot, dusty gloom. Inspector Edlecliff-Johnstone stood too and the Colonel noticed about him a heaviness, not of weight but of authority. The young IPS man was no longer the eager policeman. A secretive air clung to him. They shook hands and the clerks only resumed their seats when the Colonel and Inspector Edlecliff-Johnstone entered the small office at the rear. It had a little window which threw a patch of sunlight onto the Colonel's desk.

'Do sit,' said the Colonel and took his place behind the desk.

'Thank you, sir.'

'How are things in Bombay?'

'Running quite smoothly, sir,' said Edlecliff-Johnstone. He carried files and began to untie the red tape holding the papers to the stiff cardboard. 'Alice Soames is still a nuisance. She continues to write her articles despite the government's warnings. And we have noted she continues also to keep in touch with the union leaders. They've met twice recently and she has encouraged them to strike for higher wages. She's doing most of the organising – strike fund, constitution etcetera. I have copies of all her correspondence here.'

'I'll look at it later,' said the Colonel brusquely and took the file.

It was thick and heavy. Alice was definitely a nuisance. He had hoped the official warning and the arrests of

Nairoji and the printer would have tempered her missionary zeal. She was the same stubborn wilful woman he'd married so many years ago. She won't change, he thought bleakly, and I can foresee her destruction. We just can't tolerate such behaviour. I wish she had taken that trip to South Africa to meet Gandhi, then we could have prevented her coming back. Unfortunately, there's no provision for expelling her from India as she isn't a foreigner. Even if we could, it would cause an unholy row, especially from her American newspaper. When she wrote for the *Manchester Guardian*, I could have controlled their opinion through Gerald Bartholomew. But the Americans, naïve, fervent, still championing every cause, are beyond my power. The alternative is to arrest her on a charge of sedition, the first European ever.

'The file is incomplete, sir,' said Edlecliff-Johnstone. 'I'm not sure of the background of this woman Soames. Newton was extremely lax in not keeping his early reports.'

'That was on my orders,' said the Colonel. He tossed the file onto a table.

Edlecliff-Johnstone straightened and met the Colonel's stare. 'Sir, if I'm to control Bombay, I do need to know the background of the subject under my surveillance. Who she is, how she came to be in India. And,' he paused delicately, 'she is also in correspondence with an Elizabeth Creighton. I gather . . .'

'Yes, she's my daughter.' The Colonel took a deep breath. 'I used to be married to Alice Soames. She reverted to her maiden name when we separated. I don't think you need to know any more than that at the moment.'

'Of course, sir,' and Edlecliff-Johnstone thought he'd won a round by getting the wily old man to make such a personal and secret admission. He'd known it all along but needed the Colonel to confirm the relationship verbally. He looks weary, Edlecliff-Johnstone thought; he knows it's time to step down. A few years ago I would have been broken and posted to Nicobar for being so impertinent. Poor beggar, having a wife who causes such a bother.

The Colonel startled him by saying, 'I'm not that much of a poor beggar. I hope you understand that.' Those cold eyes fixed on him and Edlecliff-Johnstone squirmed, shaken by the Colonel's ability to read his mind so easily.

'Yes, sir.'

The Colonel's 'Good' was a whisper, filled with menace. He couldn't abide pity. It demeaned him in the eyes of the giver of such a cheap sentiment. He thought Edlecliff-Johnstone bold to have challenged him so openly about Alice. That was a brave act, he thought, but he must understand that a man must wait until he's in a position of power before becoming too reckless. It was a black mark against him.

Unlike the Colonel, Edlecliff-Johnstone had no Indian background. He was the first member of his family to serve in India. He's one of the new breed, I suppose, the Colonel thought; a bright, ambitious young man who sees India as a career, not a calling. It will take years for India to soak into him, for him to understand Indians and how to deal with them. Still I'm confident he'll eventually make a good head for the Political and Secret Department.

'As you know from my reports, I've been cultivating some contacts among the students in Bombay. Most are decent chaps but there are a handful who are followers of Tilak. I couldn't quite get a hand on something as my man was excluded from a meeting. It wasn't held in the usual place, one of the student's rooms, but on the outskirts of town. From what my man could gather, only after the meeting, the students met a European. I couldn't get a description of him. But one of the men also at the meeting was called Chandra.'

'Was he with the European?'

'No. He went with the students. Youngish man but older than the students. I tried to get a meeting arranged with this Chandra but he vanished and my man couldn't find him again.'

'Chandra vanished after meeting the European?'

'Yes. My man was pretty certain he was an Englishman.'

'I wouldn't count on that. Every European in India is considered an Englishman. I'm interested in this man.'

'So am I. He gave the students some money, not terribly much, to finance the printing of pamphlets.'

'He sounds less and less of an Englishman. And what did he give this Chandra then, I wonder?'

They fell silent. The Colonel dismissed 'Chandra' temporarily from mind. It was such a common name, it would be like hunting for a needle in a haystack. But the 'Englishman'? He narrowed his focus, imagining the meeting between him and Chandra. More than money would have changed hands. Weapons, possibly? But why would the 'Englishman' act against the British? To overthrow them? To agitate, to unsettle? And where was he now? The Colonel lifted his eyes to the map of India hanging on the canvas wall. It was multi-coloured, dividing the land into provinces, and so huge, an empire in itself.

'No name?'

'Only "Andrew".'

'You've studied the passenger lists?'

'Oh yes. Inward and outwardbound. But whom do we pick up? There were quite a few single men going on home leave, a few who'd been touring and visiting friends or relatives. Quite a few on business, too.'

'Well, just keep an eye peeled. I don't like the sound of him.' The Colonel reached for a file dismissively. He had considered inviting Edlecliff-Johnstone to dinner but it would be awkward. The man was too young for the company of Sir Oscar and Sir Arthur. Besides, with the Rani in residence, he preferred discretion. She had sharp ears and a sharper mind. 'You comfortable here?'

'Yes, I'm staying with an old friend from Cambridge.

I'm taking a few days' leave to go on shikar in the Kumaun.'

The Colonel sighed inwardly, sad. Richard had shot his first panther in the Kumaun and the Colonel tried to suppress the memory. His son's excitement, however, reached across the years and touched his heart, causing unbearable pain.

'I'm hoping to bag a tiger,' Edlecliff-Johnstone said but noticed the Colonel wasn't listening. His eyes were distant, filled with deep melancholy. Edlecliff-Johnstone waited patiently, allowing the seconds to pass until the Colonel noticed him again with a flick of displeasure.

'Who is Kim, sir?'

'Why do you ask?'

'Some time ago a letter came for Isaac Newton. Thinking it was official business, I opened it. There was also a letter addressed to you which I didn't open.'

'Where is it now?'

'I re-sealed the letter, with the envelope, and posted it to Newton.'

'It'll reach me eventually. And what did the letter to Newton say?'

Edlecliff-Johnstone carefully extracted a sheet of paper from his file and placed it on the desk. The Colonel glanced through it.

'This isn't the original?'

'No, I copied this . . . personally.' He waited but the Colonel remained silent. 'Should I know anything more about this Kim?'

'No.' He saw Edlecliff-Johnstone stiffen and deep red spots appear on his cheeks. 'When you get to my age and are running this department, you too will keep your secrets to yourself. I, and only I, run Kim.'

'Ran,' Edlecliff-Johnstone corrected coldly. 'He says he's resigned.'

'Temporarily.'

'He must be very special.'

'Very. I hope you have a good shikar.' He waited

until Edlecliff-Johnstone had reached the outer office and called out. 'Where was the letter posted from?'

'Madras . . . sir.'

The Colonel watched the stiff, damp back recede until it stepped out into the glare. A peon deferentially lowered the flap but the Colonel still stared at the last spot he'd seen Edlecliff-Johnstone. Now what would I have done with a sealed envelope accompanying such an intriguing letter? I would have weighed it up, re-read Kim's letter and then steamed the sealed letter open. Intrigue bred departmental intrigue too. Edlecliff-Johnstone knew the contents of that sealed letter, all right, had probably copied it too. And this infuriated the Colonel. He banged his bell once and a clerk materialised, notebook in hand. The Colonel dictated a telegram to Isaac Newton, summoning him to Delhi with the letter, and dismissed the clerk.

His eye travelled over India, caressing her contours lovingly, and alighted on Madras far down on the south-eastern coast. What was Kim doing there, so far from his familiar haunts? The Colonel had expected Kim to go into the mountains, snuggle into a cool valley. Or else Lahore, where friends would shelter him. South, he knew no one. Or did he? It was a long way from Delhi. Madras! He searched the coloured landscape. Kim would have moved on. In which direction? Further south? Into the interior? He must know someone there. Kim always moved with a purpose, drawn by something or someone. The woman Mohini? No. She was from Delhi. The Colonel began re-reading Kim's letter to Newton and stopped at the name 'Narain'. It was a south Indian name. Newton would know the location of Narain's village and if it were anywhere near Madras, the Colonel was sure he'd find Kim. He winced. Who else had read this? And what had Kim written to him? Newton he trusted, but this had already been read by one other man – Edlecliff-Johnstone. Now he knew Kim was very special too, apart from having secrets. Edlecliff-Johnstone would try to find Kim, to discover the secrets – the names of every agent – and to run Kim himself.

Isaac Newton disliked Amritsar, for the same reason he disliked Benares or Hardwar. The concentration of religion unsettled him. As he told himself, even the daily sight of a temple gopuram made him nauseous and each day he had to stare out of his window at the huge complex of the Golden Temple. As a scientific man, Newton distrusted the intensity of religion. It bamboozles people, he muttered to himself daily, watching Sikhs file through the great doors. It robs one of will, and also of one's earnings. If God is so omnipotent, I ask myself, why can't he support himself or else like the government print his own money instead of begging us poor humans to feed him, clothe him and build a golden roof over his head? How I yearn for Bombay. There none care for God unless they're very rich and frightened they will lose all, or too poor and coveting riches. Otherwise, Bombay is a greedy city, naturally human in such attributes. Dog eat dog. For the pious like those flowing around me piety is only a cloak for their inhumanity.

His shop, Karam Singh Jewellers, was in the narrow gulli adjoining the west wall of the Golden Temple. He didn't care whether he did business or not though occasionally a client would find his way up the steep narrow stairs, across a pile of bricks and bring him a trinket to pawn, a small gold bangle, a nose-stud. Newton would engage the seller in conversation and if the man should be of some use – the cousin of a police constable, the father of a jawan, the village headman's brother, the nephew of a priest – Newton would pay a reasonable sum for the trinket and recruit the man as his agent. Others, the poor without even such small influences, he regretfully turned away. Newton wasn't hard-hearted. He would have liked to give the money to such poor villagers but once word got out that Karam Singh was a fool, he would be buried in trinkets. No, he always mentioned such a low price that they cursed him and left.

Newton carefully sifted through the nuggets of information he heard and compiled a report to the Colonel sahib in his neat, spidery writing.

From : Karam Singh, Jeweller, Amritsar.
To : The Colonel sahib.

As you well know, Colonel sahib, the Sikhs are most hard-working and industrious people. They have served well in the Indian Army and the government has rewarded them most generously for their loyalty. In other words, there has been always a trust between the British people and the Sikhs. However, from the information I am receiving, I believe this trust must not be taken for granted much longer. The Punjab suffered greatly from the continued failure of the monsoons from 1905 to 1910. This drought caused great hardship to the poor farmers who to survive fell into the greedy clutches of money lenders. The government, unfortunately, didn't respond to their pleas. Due to this intense hardship, many Sikhs have left the Punjab to seek employment in the far flung corners of the globe – Singapore, Hong Kong, Canada, America. Why Canada? Because a Sikh regiment returning from the Jubilee celebration of Her Most Imperial and Gracious Majesty, the Kaiser-i-Hind, Queen Victoria in 1887, saw it was a good country. Now they are remitting their earnings from those lucrative corners to the people at home and also titbits of information. Because they have succeeded so well in Canada, they are now facing the jealousy of the native people there. The Canadian government has passed legislation dispossessing the Sikh from voting and also introduced further legislation barring all people of Asia from entry. All this I learned from the cousin of a Sikh farmer, now a well-to-do merchant in Vancouver. His information has been confirmed by many, many others. He also told me that he has a cousin in California and that the American workers are attacking and killing them because they work harder than the Americans. Now these Sikhs living in this other part of the empire are reasoning that if they cannot be treated equally outside India, the reason lies in their unequal treatment within India. What is happening in Canada and America is rippling back into the Punjabi villages like the flip of a stone thrown into a deceptively calm lake. Cousins are telling strangers, strangers other strangers. I have heard too that the Sikhs abroad are forming a political party, Ghadar, to redress their grievances. What makes this party dangerous is, I have heard, that they intend to liberate India from British rule by force of arms. This I believe to be rumour and cannot yet confirm. Sikhs, as you know, cannot combine for two minutes without falling upon each other. I do not believe there is cause for alarm. But measures should be taken to rectify these grievances and win back their loyalty to the Crown.

On the day Newton received the Colonel's telegram summoning him to Delhi, he was in a high state of excitement. That morning, he had received back from the developers in Bombay the print of his first moving film. He considered film-making itself quite frivolous. It was a waste of his intellect and energy. However while watching the film he noted the jerky movement. The hand couldn't crank the handle at a constant speed. He would invent a small motor to fit in the camera and turn the film at a regulated speed.

He was working on this invention on the Frontier Mail to Delhi. It was only when he was within sight of the Viceroy's residence and the crush of tents that he carefully pulled his tie over his neck and slid the knot tight. His Adam's apple bobbed in protest. He sat on a stone and squeezed his feet into his shoes, shook out his jacket and slipped it on.

The Colonel made Newton wait for an hour, and Newton knew he was in the Colonel's disfavour because of the withheld letter. Not withheld, delayed. He carried it in his small cloth bag, alongside his report.

'Colonel sahib, you must forgive an old and faithful servant for his worry over this matter,' Newton said the moment he appeared in front of the Colonel. 'I did receive the letter from Kim and the enclosed envelope for you. When I read Kim's letter to me I worried deeply for him as only a father can for his son. I did not want him to be in disfavour in your eyes. I remained silent, hoping and praying I would hear from him to cancel this letter to you.'

'Very eloquent, Newton,' said the Colonel, and merely held out his hand. He read Kim's letter and glanced up at Newton. The thin, dark face was creased with genuine concern for Kim. 'You should know me better by now. I'll take this letter with a large pinch of salt. But you failed to do your duty in not forwarding this to me immediately.'

'Colonel sahib, it took a long time in coming. It came via Bombay and I suspect it was opened and read.'

'Both?'

'Yes, Colonel sahib. I carried out scientific tests and discovered that the glue had been unstuck and re-stuck with new glue. It could have been accidentally opened by Mr Edlecliff-Johnstone.'

'It's possible,' said the Colonel. 'Have you tried to find Kim?'

Newton felt the tie tighten of its own volition under the Colonel's stare. The eyes were baleful, simmering with anger. He knew he was on the brink of a tongue lashing, or possibly worse, sacking, arrest. But he'd promised Kim to keep his destination a secret.

'No, Colonel sahib.'

'Do you know where he is, then?'

Newton now felt those eyes ferreting in his mind, peering into the dark corners, looking for the answer. He actually thought he felt them physically in his head and tried to squeeze his mind shut.

'No, Colonel sahib,' said Newton.

'Well, then, you must know where Narain came from? He was in your employ.'

'Yes, Colonel sahib,' said Newton, fitfully breathing in

relief. 'But he was a casual employee. You may remember I requested him to be made permanant but I received no reply. Being casual, I didn't ask him to fill in requisite forms. Son of, village, etcetera, etcetera. He told me he came from south India, near Madras. Beyond that I knew little of him.'

'I'm not sure I believe you, Newton,' the Colonel sat back. 'What was the name of his village?'

'Colonel sahib, what village has a name? It is near a lake, he told me, and within a valley. Beyond that he didn't confide. He was ashamed of his village. He wished to belong to Bombay only.'

'Has Mr Edlecliff-Johnstone questioned you?'

'No, Colonel sahib.'

'Good,' the Colonel smiled but Newton felt neither comfort nor warmth from it. The eyes remained cold. 'I'll give you until nightfall to remember the specific location of Narain's village. My old friend, I will not tolerate betrayal. Your loyalty is to me, not to Kim. If you don't remember, I'll dismiss you from my service and place you under arrest on charges of treason to the Crown. Do you understand?'

'Yes, Colonel sahib,' Newton's whisper was soft and sad. He knew it wasn't necessary to wait until nightfall. All his life he'd served the Colonel sahib and now couldn't bring himself to defend Kim any longer. Despite his agnosticism, he murmured a brief prayer begging forgiveness. 'He will be in a village in the Cumbun valley, Colonel sahib. It is by a lake. Beyond that I cannot be more specific.'

'Thank you, Newton. Now what do you have to report?'

The Colonel took the file on the Sikhs and read it carefully.

'I don't like the sound of this one bit. Armed invasion? Are you sure?'

'It is rumour, as I pointed out, Colonel sahib. Only rumour.'

'But it is a method which would appeal to the Sikhs.

They're martial people and love theatrics. I'll send a cable to London to keep a close watch on the Gadhar party and report back to me. Meanwhile, you keep a constant record of all you hear.'

He studied the map. The Punjab sprawled virtually all the way from Delhi to the North West Frontier. There had been two brief but bloody wars with the Sikhs in the late 1840s before the British annexed the Punjab. Lord Dalhousie, then Governor General of India, felt that the Punjab's proximity to the frontier made it too vital to allow any further risks, and annexed it for the East India Company. It still remained a sensitive area. But the Sikhs were a minority in the province. The majority were Hindus and this Sikh mutiny could be the fuse that would send the whole area up in flames. Then, like dry tinder, the Colonel continued his reasoning, the flames would fan out through India. He already saw the spectre of 1857 repeating itself. He immediately planned to plant more agents in the Punjab, but he wouldn't make any mention of this to Newton. The less Newton knew, the safer.

'Old friend, don't look so sad,' the Colonel rose and put his arm around Newton's bony shoulders. 'We've been together many years. I understand your deep affection for Kim. I too feel it. But Kim, like you and me, is frail and human. We all serve the empire, which must command our loyalties over and above those to any individual. Our passing will not affect its existence. You chose right in telling me where Kim is. I mean him no harm. I only wish to protect him from the possible harm others may cause him because of who he is. You do understand?'

'Yes, Colonel sahib. I also wish to tender my resignation from your service.'

'Nonsense. This is the second time, and each time it's because of your division of loyalty between Kim and the Crown. You serve the Crown, and you're too valuable for me to let go. This is a very important report you've brought me. I intend to mention it to the Viceroy and send a copy to the Lieutenant Governor of the Punjab. Obviously Amritsar will be the centre of their activities. You must keep a close and careful watch on everything that happens there. If necessary we will make a lesson of the Sikhs if only to teach the rest of India how foolish it would be to rebel against the Crown.'

'A lesson?' Newton felt uneasy. The Colonel sahib made the people sound like children. They were grown people, aspiring people. It was the wrong time for lessons.

'Yes, a lesson,' and the Colonel savoured the fervour of his own loyalty.

But Newton gave no further thought to these lessons as he trudged along the road back to Delhi Station. All thought too of his new invention had escaped his mind. He could barely carry the weight of his thin body. He sat on a stone, removing his tie and shoes and carefully folding his jacket. Tears began coursing down his cheeks as he thought how, like Judas, he had so easily betrayed Kim to the Colonel. It hadn't been for thirty pieces of silver but because of his duty to the Colonel, and he was confused as to which was the dearer.

Sushila Basu patiently awaited the Colonel. She'd written to him regularly since he'd moved to Delhi. For every three she wrote, she received one in reply. Her letters had been filled with love and the pain of missing him. His were cautious, skirting such romantic emotions. He dealt with the practical world and his daily life. His last note had been a brief scribble, announcing his impending visit to Calcutta. Since he had gone to Delhi, Sushila seldom saw the Colonel except when he swooped down to Calcutta on a brief visit.

The house felt emptier, like her no longer tense with the expectancy of his nocturnal visits. The silence enclosed her, as though encasing her like a curio in a glass cabinet. Her life too had taken on another urgent expectancy, the waiting for death. Her sister-in-law had informed her that her husband was certainly dying.

Sushila had paid him a brief visit and had been sickened. Her husband no longer recognised her. He was thin and drawn; death was twisting him into a fibre of flesh and bone, draining him of blood. He ate sparely, if at all, and his speech was slurred so she understood only a word or two. He suckled now only on the expensive Scotch whisky which had drained the family fortunes. Seeing this reality had frightened her. Her ghostly widowhood drew nearer, breathed his dying into her vibrant body.

She felt she didn't have the energy to battle this impending doom without the help of her lover. The Colonel could give her the strength to resist the evil Hindu customs of widowhood, the donning of white, the shaving of her head and her slavery to her husband's family. No, she'd retreat to her own family. Her father would give her sanctuary, leave her in peace to live out her days as a woman and not as an abused chattel. These were the plans which her fevered and frantic mind had spun on her journey back to Calcutta. They had sounded simple and easy; the ease of the escape had at first astounded her.

Now another complication had arisen and only the Colonel could resolve it. He could lead her out of her loneliness, out of this life and into a new one. Despite her doubts, she dreamed of a life with him, being near him, nurturing him as he would her. She didn't think beyond this salvation, uncaring of what her own family would say. She felt reckless and brave, but only when she thought of the Colonel. He instilled her with this courage, by his attention to her, by his love.

"Does he love me?" Sushila thought. "I'm never certain. We are intimate; I know his heart, but I'm not sure. I have spoken of love and his caress and his longing have been the reflection of his own unspoken love. But he's held back by what he is. A Britisher. He cannot escape that mould, cannot free himself from that stiff and formal conventionality. I know he loves me though. He must. A man and a woman cannot be lovers all these years only to find that there is no love, just convenience, just lust.

I know I couldn't, but that is because I am a woman. I'm not experienced enough with men to know their secret thoughts and motives."

But the Colonel never came. Instead Sushila heard the faint and distant explosion of the bomb thrown at the Viceroy of India, Lord Hardinge. Calcutta tensed, the Europeans snarled at the native, suspicious of all now. The police clamped down a curfew and the city waited for the distant repercussion of his death. Slowly the news reached them that the Viceroy hadn't died. He'd received superficial injuries to his back. The only death was that of the umbrella carrier. The newspapers praised the bravery of the Vicereine. She had dismounted from her elephant and in the ensuing panic directed the operation to rescue her husband. Because of the fearful bang, the Viceroy's elephant had frozen with fright and refused to kneel. The Vicereine sent men rushing to the nearby shops to bring crates. These were piled up against the elephant's side and a policeman had climbed this shaky ladder and carried the Viceroy down. He'd been taken to the Residence but because the staff were out awaiting his entry into Delhi, and unaware of the outrage, the Vicereine and her daughter had attended to the Viceroy's wounds themselves. He was, the paper reported, resting comfortably. So far, the police had yet to apprehend the dastardly miscreant who had hurled the bomb but expected to announce an arrest very soon.

The Colonel only arrived a month later. He came at night, at his usual time, and knocked on her window. Sushila threw herself into his arms the moment he stepped over the threshold.

'I have missed you, Jack. How I've missed you. I've never known such pain. The thought of you alone gives me such pleasure.' She kissed him on the mouth. 'You have missed me too, haven't you?'

'Of course I have, my dear Sushila. Delhi is dull without you to relieve the monotony of my evenings sitting and listening to Sir Arthur and Sir Oscar.'

'I could come to Delhi,' she whispered. 'You could

hide me away in a house in the walled city and visit me every evening.'

'What a delightful idea. But I'm not sure it's a very good one.'

'Why not?'

He looked around her bedroom. 'What about all this? What on earth will your family say if you suddenly run away to Delhi?'

'I don't care what they say,' Sushila tossed her head.

At times, the Colonel thought, she could behave like a precocious child, reckless and impetuous. He felt a surge of paternal affection for her and permitted her to cling to him. Her body was so malleable, it moulded itself against him. The very act of stroking her hair and her skin never ceased to give him pleasure. He drew strength from her. Alice had never been this pliable. And he still remembered, though exaggerated with his emotions, the rough hew of her body. He had walked in wearily, burdened by the worry of the attempt on Lord Hardinge's life, but here in the cool, shadowy room, he felt his pulse quicken. Sushila always renewed his vigour, made him feel physically virile.

'Why this sudden urge?'

He settled in a cane armchair and accepted a glass of whisky and water, sipping it appreciatively. Even a drink from her hand tasted different from his daily peg. She rescued him from the dry, draining existence he led. He had missed her and this surprised him. In Delhi when his mind had strayed to her, he had swiftly suppressed the longing that arose in him. It was the damned weakness of the flesh and he was not going to allow such flaws to weaken his concentration.

'My husband is going to die soon and I will be trapped. I will become a widow and it will be too late then.'

In their long familiarity, he had half forgotten her husband. As long as he lived he remained the reason for them to live apart. Now he was dying. Neither felt any pity. Her tears glistened in the lamplight and he felt an urge to protect her from this dreaded future. But how? He couldn't set her up in Delhi. The secret would be discovered. It might be forgiven in a younger man with less responsibility. But European society would spurn him, force him to give up the liaison. It was absolutely forbidden to keep an Indian mistress. He yearned suddenly for the past when such behaviour was accepted, when Englishmen married Indian women and were proud of their half-caste children and raised them to run their empires. It had all changed.

'I'm sorry to hear that.'

'Is that all?'

Sushila's heart fell. His face was half-shadowed and she saw him flinch at her harshness.

'What do you want, dear Sushila?' He reached for her hand. It remained inert in his, and he felt helpless.

'I don't want to marry you. I know that's impossible. It would destroy you and I wouldn't be able to live with that. I want sanctuary – I'm like Esmeralda in *Notre Dame de Paris* – sanctuary from the custom of my people. I want just to be with you.'

'We will be together, even if you live here. We'll find another house for you and . . .'

Sushila looked down at their hands, his strong and thick, hers brown and frail.

'I'm going to have your child.'

'Oh, Lord!'

He felt the breath driven out of him by the revelation. Her eyes were on him, huge beams of light, watching closely. He felt even more helpless suddenly, caught up in an event already out of control. He should have foreseen such a consequence, and cursed himself now. The outside world, the one he played with in his great games, was tightly controlled by his dictates. Men acted and reacted according to his commands, his manipulations. Now he'd lost control. He checked his anger. She shouldn't have become pregnant. Women could control such things. He had heard of medicines, of methods. He went over her exact words. 'I'm going to have *your* child.' How certain could he be that it was his and not that dying husband's? Not another man's? She was alone here in this huge mansion, and only one man at a time kept watch on her. In the same way, he'd had Alice watched in Arcot.

But at the same time, he felt proud that life could still spring from his loins. He knew for a certainty that the child she carried would be a boy. Of course, he would never be another Richard. He would be dark, bruised with her colouring. He couldn't send this child to an English public school or to Sandhurst. He'd never be able to join a decent regiment. What could the boy do, but go to waste in the no-man's land between the two races which the Eurasian inhabited? Already he felt sorry for his unborn child – if it was truly his. This doubt hardened him. The child frightens him, Sushila thought. His skin has become taut and I can feel the chill in his hands. His heart beats here, I can feel it, but it's twisting for escape and the steel in this man will never bend or break for love.

'How long?'

'Four months. That's how long it's been since your last visit,' said Sushila, not allowing him that escape. She felt detached, watching herself, watching him. She couldn't help it. The flow of love was drying like a trickle of water in a river bed, shrinking in the glare of his refusal to accept their child.

'Can't you . . . do something? You know.'

'No. I want this child. Don't you?' she added cruelly, and saw his mouth tighten. She wanted to cry out: 'Say "yes"! Give me hope!'

'I will support the child financially, naturally,' said the Colonel. He could do it through a standing order at his bank.

'Naturally,' Sushila said dully.

She had not thought of financial practicalities. Her mind was clouded with questions of death and birth. For another woman it would have been a natural thing, for her it was a stigma, a curse. But she wouldn't curse the child. It had been conceived in love and if she should now start to hate the Colonel it wasn't going to affect the child's life. She would keep her love and her hate apart from each other.

The silence was tense. Vaguely he heard the distant ticking of a clock, the breeze sighing in the trees. He wondered what Elizabeth would think of this little half-brother, not a fair English baby, but one subtly stained by his mother's blood. The Colonel was ashamed of these thoughts but couldn't check them. They'd been inculcated into him from childhood and, faced with this fear of racial contamination, they rose unbidden.

'I think you should go,' Sushila broke the silence.

If the Colonel had insisted on staying, there would have been a glimmer of hope that he might change his mind. Instead he rose, not swiftly but heavily, and carefully placed his glass on the sideboard. He looked around him with regret. This had been a secret sanctuary, and he knew he was now expelled from it for ever. He wondered whether he would see Sushila again, wondered too whether he would ever see his child. He would certainly always be in a position to know of its progress through his informers. Naturally, he would use his influence to ensure that, within India at least, it was given every advantage. He wanted to touch Sushila a last time but couldn't force even this gesture out of himself.

Even as he slipped out of the room, despair rushed, but Sushila began her weeping only when she heard the door close. She wanted to cry out and scream but instead only shook silently, the agony of her pain twisting her into a small bundle on the floor. She wept with her mouth open, her eyes clamped tight shut, but the tears gushed down and she moaned and cradled herself. She prayed the pain would kill her, the bitterness take her life, her tears turn to acid and scar her face for ever. Gradually, as she grew weakened and exhausted, her moans subsided to a melancholy croon.

She heard the outside door open and footsteps approach. She lay still; then the gush of hope pushed her to a sitting position. A man stepped into the room.

'Jack . . .?'

He didn't move. In the low circle of light, she saw his shoes and trousers and her hope flickered and died. The shoes were cracked and muddy, the trousers wrinkled and grubby with dried glass clinging to the cloth. This man was a stranger. He came forward slowly into the light.

'Anil!'

She saw in his face not pity but compassion. He knelt, and lifted her to the arm chair. Silently, he poured a glass of whisky and made her drink it. She gulped and coughed. Anil looked tired. There were lines now around his mouth, and his eyes, bloodshot and weary, belonged to a far older man. They looked wiser than she had remembered.

'I saw him leave,' said Anil. 'He walked quickly and didn't look back. There's been a man watching this house for the last two days. Sometimes he sits across the street; at other times he enters the garden and prowls around. The man who left here, spoke to him. And when the European left, the watcher did too. I wasn't sure whether there were other watchers and had to be careful.'

He poured himself a drink and pulled up a chair. He carefully wiped away Sushila's tears, smearing them across her cheek. She tried to smile but couldn't. Her face hurt.

'I want to hide here for a couple of days. Then I'll be gone. I've never forgotten you. Wherever I've wandered you've always been my last thought before I fell asleep.'

'Oh Anil, Anil,' Sushila leaned her head tiredly against him. 'I am the wrong person to think of, to dream about. My life is in ruins.'

'Tell me about such ruins. "Let us sit upon the ground and tell sad stories of the death of kings . . .".'

'I shall be a widow soon, and you know what that means.'

'Yes.' He took her limp hand, held it and kissed it. 'But it only releases you from that drunkard husband for me now. I'll marry you.'

'No, Anil.'

'Because I'm a wanted man and hunted? I understand.'

'No. Because I'm going to have the child of that man you saw leave here. The European.'

'So, another outcast. That'll make three of us. Three only, among so many outcasts in this land.'

He removed his jacket and dropped it on the floor. Sushila saw the revolver tucked into the waistband of his trousers. He pulled it out. It looked black and evil in the lamplight. Anil spun the chambers, carefully dropped the hammer on an empty one and placed the gun on the table within reach. She knew it to be a habitual gesture, the last act at night before he shut his eyes. 'What is the name of this European?' he asked.

Sushila shook her head. 'I can't tell you. Please never ask me again. I will pray daily for God to avenge me.'

# 15

## January–March 1913

The saris were magical in their colours. They were woven with the sky and the sun, the earth and the flower, the water and the field. The patterns flowing through the cloth were intricate and mysterious; the men who wove them invested them with their dreams and visions. The old weaver Gopalan was inordinately proud that his stiffened fingers had not forgotten the magic and skill they had had once. He now taught his three sons his craft, as he had learned from his father, and knew that on his death the tradition would continue on as it was meant to. The saris filled not only the hut with their vibrancy but the whole village. The very sight of them seemed to nourish the villagers who came daily to watch them grow on the looms.

Every action a man performs is political, Kim thought. His action doesn't need to be seen by thousands of people, like a political orator who can sway multitudes. It can be small and private and its result will be small and private. What I do now is political. This small act of spinning thread from cotton to help this village earn a living is political. It can be interpreted as a gesture of defiance though my action is intended only to fill children's mouths with food.

Kim was content even though such thoughts flowed through his mind. By the very action of spinning thread, he was weaving himself into the life of this village. He was a part of its daily existence, and that in its turn gave him an identity that had been denied him all his life by his wanderings. To belong to one particular place was the birthright of every man. He no longer needed to invent a place to belong to should he be asked: 'Which village do you come from?' At last he could truthfully answer: 'This one.' And his child would be able to say this with even greater certainty: 'This one.'

Parvati sat awkwardly beside him, also spinning thread. Her belly was huge, her face aglow with joy. Her terrors had been stifled, her past deliberately forgotten. The child was due very soon; in another ten days, the village women calculated, possibly earlier. Like every woman she prayed only that this child be a son, another Kim.

Once a month Kim, Kumar and one or two other men would travel by foot to a market in a large village at the entrance to the valley to sell the saris. Men and women from as much as two days away came to the market. They bartered and bargained rice, goats, calves and cows in exchange for their own needs. The saris were sold for cash to a merchant from Madras who was delighted that the village was once again making the saris, which had been extremely popular among the city women. With the money, the men would carefully purchase the village's needs – seed, salt, sugar, raw cotton.

Kim would have been completely content if it had not been for Kumar. With the passing of each month he grew bleaker and was dwindling in front of their eyes. Narain's wife had fulfilled her threat. She had made a pilgrimage to the distant temple and requested that Shesha arbitrate in the matter of their property. The priest, who spoke for Shesha, said he would consider her request and inform her whether Shesha would sit in judgement. Kumar had virtually ceased to breathe with the suspense of the wait. He prayed daily that Shesha would ignore so petty a squabble and decline to give judgement. Surely he would be occupied with weightier matters.

'Why are you so afraid?' Kim asked.

'You are a stranger and know nothing of Shesha's powers. The priest will choose me to enter the temple with the offerings, and lock me in for the night. She, as the accuser, will wait outside. And during the night Shesha will make his choice – her offerings or mine.'

'So?'

'Kimathchand, my new-found friend, the person who spends the night within never leaves alive,' Kumar was near to tears. 'Never have we heard of anyone coming out alive. I know I will die.'

'The priest might choose her for the ordeal.'

'Apart from being the accuser, I know she's already spoken to him and bribed him with her favours and the promise of money when she inherits the property. I will offer a bribe too, but it will be of no avail.'

'Why don't you speak to her, then?'

'She refuses to see me. I am willing even for the magistrate to judge this matter, but it's too late. Even if he should decide, we will have to present ourselves to Shesha. That is, if he summons us. I am praying he will not.'

'Give her half the land then.'

Kumar snapped out of his despair for a moment to announce haughtily, 'This land belonged to my great-great-grandfather and my great-grandfather and my father. One day it will pass to my sons.'

'It is better to possess your life than to possess land.'

'But without this land, I am nothing.'

'You will be nothing dead.'

Kumar considered this wisdom. He was a shadow even of the man Kim had first met. In his thinness now, he reminded Kim of Narain. Narain was emerging from his brother as he shrank each day. If Kumar continued to dwindle, on his death Kim would be looking down on his old friend Narain.

'You speak to her,' said Kumar. 'Offer her half; no, a quarter.'

Lalitha had returned to live with her father. Their village was half an hour's walk away and Kim made the journey on Kumar's behalf. When he approached her home, she immediately retreated inside and ordered Kim away.

He sat down calmly at the entrance. 'I will wait all day and night, and the next day if necessary. You will have to come out at some time.'

Her father, a tenant farmer who eked out a living working the company's land, came hurriedly, having received word of this stranger sitting stubbornly outside his home. He was a thin, tired-looking man and Kim could count his ribs as he sat down in front of him. It was hard to believe that this pretty but hard woman had sprung from such skin and bone.

'I know why you have come,' he said. 'I too am unhappy that my daughter has appealed to Shesha. It only causes bad blood between our families, between our villages. I begged her to withdraw but she is a stubborn girl. She feels she was wronged by Narain and insists on compensation.'

'How old was she when she married?'

'It was in her tenth year.' He called into the hut. 'Lalitha, come out.'

'No.'

They both waited patiently, the father grateful for the brief respite from labouring in the fields. Kim gave him a beedi and they smoked and talked about the daily routine of village life, the price of rice, the cost of this and that. His wife had died in childbirth some years ago and Lalitha looked after him and the younger children.

'You are Kimathchand?'

'Yes.'

'We have heard of you. You have started the weaving again. It could be dangerous if the company sahib discovers what is happening.'

'He will only hear from one of us,' Kim said. Nothing, in these villages, could remain secret for long. Gossip and news travelled swiftly as men passed each other in the fields.

Eventually, as they both knew she would, Lalitha

emerged sullenly. She stood with her arms folded, gripping her body tightly and stared down at Kim. He had planned to flatter and cajole her, praise her beauty and use his wiles as a seducer. But when he looked into her eyes, he saw her hatred. He was Narain's friend and there was no forgiveness. He couldn't help thinking how a man's actions reverberated long after his own death, twisting the lives of those who still lived.

'Kumar has sent me to ask you to withdraw your appeal to Shesha.'

'It's too late. I am waiting to hear from the priest.'

'He's also willing to share his property with you. A quarter of all he owns. Remember that if Shesha doesn't want to judge this matter, then you will get nothing.'

'He will,' and she said it with such certitude that Kim knew she had bribed the priest with her body or with the promise of future money. She continued bitterly, 'It's all Narain's fault. I went to his home as a bride and have lived my whole life in the disgrace of a woman without her husband. How do you think I have felt? I was pitied and scorned. I am already getting too old to bear children and who will support me in old age? Tell Kumar I will await only Shesha.' She smiled sweetly. 'He too could win the judgement if he is still alive the next morning.'

'Take the quarter,' her father urged. 'Let us have peace.'

'No.'

'Half then,' Kim said.

'No. All.'

'Take the half,' her father said once more.

'All.'

When Kumar heard her demands, he first buried his face in his hands and then screamed a torrent of curses on her head. He would prefer to die, he said, for at least then half the property would be inherited by his sons.

And it was on that same day that the village heard from the priest that Shesha would sit in judgement on this division of the property. Kumar and Narain's widow were to bring with them a pitcher of milk, a pot of ghee and a bag of sugar as offerings to the five-headed cobra that supported the Vishnu on his coils in the cosmic ocean. It was an expense none could bear, but they managed to collect the offerings from every house in the village in small amounts. The whole village wanted to accompany Kumar and, they knew, to return with his ashes. Parvati wanted to come too but Kim forbade her to make the journey. Her time was too near, and the other women agreed.

On the evening before their departure for the temple, Kumar was visibly a shade paler and perspiring. His wife and children huddled around him and he could scarcely speak. He looked around him, at his small quiet village, with longing. He'd known no other existence and wondered why, having had a life of such simplicity, he should now be faced with certain death.

'Will Shesha take another?' Kim asked.

'Yes. But only a fool would stand in my place.'

'I am that fool then,' Kim said. 'I wish to know what goes on in there, and why men should die. Are their throats cut?'

'There's not one mark on them, not even Shesha's bite.' He added hurriedly. 'Are you sure?'

'Yes.'

Kumar's face lit up with joy and then turned melancholy. He finally shook his head. 'I'm frightened, but I cannot permit you to take my place.'

'I insist,' Kim said. 'And do not say anything of this to Parvati.'

The temple was a day and half away and most of the village accompanied Kumar and Lalitha. She too had her supporters now, among them a few young men who eyed the small piece of land she could inherit. The women rode in the bullock cart with the children.

They reached the temple the following noon. It stood atop a low hill and they had to climb three hundred and fifty granite steps to reach it. Breathless from exertion, they stood at its imposing doors, looking back along the way they'd travelled. They searched for their own village in the blur of green that lay at their feet but it was lost to view. But they caught the glitter of the lake and imagined they could see their village after all.

The Brahmin was smooth and round, glistening with health. His face was fleshy and strong, and a tuft of grey hair sprang from the top of his shaven head like a question-mark. He sat cross-legged in the shade, a princely figure in his pure cotton dhoti with the sacred thread diagonally crossing his chest. The villagers prostrated themselves before the priest, all except Kim, who met the Brahmin's baleful glare calmly.

'Who are those who ask Shesha to decide?'

'I didn't wish to trouble the Shesha,' Kumar mumbled hurriedly. 'But my widowed sister-in-law insisted. If it's too much to ask . . .'

'If one party has made the request, the other party must accept. Where is your sister-in-law?'

Coyly, Narain's widow stepped forward and touched the priest's feet. Kim saw his eyes light appreciatively on her and knew the priest was familiar with those hidden curves and sweet vales. He caught Kumar's despairing look. It couldn't disguise his hope and fear, the hope that Kim would keep his word, the fear that he had changed his mind.

'You must take the offerings to Shesha,' the Brahmin said to Kumar. 'He will make a decision in this matter, and you will see for yourself how his great wisdom works.'

'But . . . but . . . no one ever emerges alive to tell of his decision.'

'That is only because Shesha has punished them. I assure you, if your case is just Shesha too will be just. If you do not step out alive when we open the doors, then half your properties will belong to your sister-in-law.'

'But what if he does remain alive?' Kim asked.

The Brahmin's hard squint settled on Kim. 'Then the matter is settled in his favour.'

'Can another represent his case?'

'Whoever wishes may plead to Shesha,' the eyes had

turned malignant at Kim's boldness. 'Do you wish to stand instead of him?'

'Yes.'

'Then you are a fool.'

'I have Vamana's protection around my neck,' Kim said and held the pebble, now pierced with a small hole and threaded with cord. 'And my cane. One will protect me from evil spirits, the other from evil men. What else is there to fear?'

He knew there was a long and dark list of dead men who'd preceded him. The villagers clustered around him tightly, praying for his protection, and when he went down to the temple tank to bathe, they followed and watched sadly as he dipped himself three times in the water. Kumar came and embraced him and, though still afraid, once more, in front of the villagers and the Brahmin, offered to enter himself. It was his property, after all.

'I'm curious to know what happens in there,' Kim said and turned to the Brahmin. 'Pundit-ji, have you ever spent the night within?'

'No. I don't know what will happen or what you will see.' Brusquely he pressed sacred ash on Kim's temple and offered arthi. When he was closer, he whispered. 'But I know you will die. You look like a man who deserves that.'

'I will see you at dawn, pundit-ji.'

The Brahmin rang the bell hanging above the temple door thrice and Kim, carrying the two trays of offerings, entered the inner temple. The Brahmin alone accompanied him and instructed him to place one tray to the left and the other to the right of the stone idol. Shesha was carved out of black granite. Even in the gloom, Kim could see the delicately etched scales. The cobra's long body lay neatly in coils but instead of Vishnu lying on them there were only garlands of flowers. Above the coils, to a height of three feet, rose the massive spread hood and five heads, splayed and curved like the fingers of a giant hand. The eyes were set with rubies and in the flickering lamplight they seemed to follow the movements of the two men.

'Other men I bless and comfort,' the Brahmin whispered. 'You I leave alone to your coming death.'

He stepped quickly across the high stone threshold and pulled the heavy doors shut behind him. Kim heard the key turn in the lock and the fading scrape of his bare feet. A weak light glowed in front of the idol, the flame still and straight. The shadow of the five hoods on the wall behind loomed larger and blacker. The silence was oppressive. He could hear nothing, within or without. It was suffocatingly hot and when Kim leant against the granite wall, the stones themselves sweated. The air was also heavy with the lingering odours of jasmine and camphor and joss. Kim slid down to wait, holding his cane out in front of him. The hour passed slowly and his mind focused on the stone idol. It shone with oils and was yellowish with light. When he closed his eyes, Kim still saw it in the centre of his mind.

Kim suddenly came awake, eyes wide open. He had heard a sound, deep in his sleep. He looked at the idol and saw it was gone. He squinted, thinking it a trick, and shut and opened his eyes, but the idol no longer stood at the end of the room. Cautiously, Kim rose to his feet. He heard the whisper of movement again; something slithered along the floor towards him and his every hair stood on end. He shielded his eyes from the lamplight and glimpsed movement on the floor halfway between him and the flame. Something dark rolled and flowed towards him and Kim felt the sweat break out all over his body and turn chill. He couldn't control the beating of his heart and the pain in his chest was almost unbearable.

Ten glittering rubies, a few inches from the floor, flowed towards him. Five pale tongues flickered out, tasting the air, sensing him pressed against the wall. Behind those eyes and heads, the body coiled and uncoiled, propelling Shesha closer and closer. That body seemed endless, for it trailed right back to the sanctum and even in that moment, when his mind had virtually ceased to function, Kim judged Shesha to be twenty feet long.

The five-headed serpent stopped, but the body continued to gather itself, catching up with the heads. Slowly, the body coiled and the heads rose slowly, hypnotically, the ten eyes never leaving Kim's. They seemed to encircle him for his own tried to escape the gaze but whichever way his eyes flickered Shesha's were there. The heads reached waist height, swaying from side to side and backwards and forwards in the familiar dance of the cobra. The hood now spread out to ten times its original size and Shesha looked gigantic. The heads didn't stop rising and reached shoulder height and Kim found himself staring straight into the eyes and into the five open mouths with their flickering tongues.

With a great effort of will, Kim shut his eyes and called aloud to Vamana, the dwarf who'd given him the stone which protected him. He expected to die at any moment but instead, out of the silence, a voice entered his mind.

'I know you've been granted Vamana's protection,' the voice in his mind was dry and quite musical. It took him almost a moment to realise it was Shesha's voice. 'Why do you pray to him so fervently?'

'To protect me, of course.'

'From me? I am Shesha. I won't harm you.'

'But so many have died.'

'Some died from fear,' Shesha complained. 'They didn't have your power. I approached them only to give them my dharshan. It isn't my fault that I was given this fearsome body by Brahma.'

Kim slowly opened his eyes. Shesha swayed now at eye-level. He smelt the serpent; it gave off a sweetish odour. The hood remained spread and swaying and Kim opened both eyes wider. He felt the hairs settle back against his skin and the sweat turn warm. His heart no longer beat so painfully. 'I will accept your dharshan, Lord Shesha,' said Kim.

The serpent swayed towards Kim and for a moment he was in the shadow of the hood. He could have touched the pale underbelly of the snake. When it swayed back, he felt a huge sense of peace and confidence, as though afloat in light.

'You said "some", Lord Shesha. What happened to the others?'

'They fainted, and that fat Brahmin who tends to my worship poisoned them before they recovered.'

'And you have permitted him to soil your name all these years without punishing him?' Kim was shocked.

Shesha seemed amused. 'You expect too much from god, Kim. If we struck dead everyone who uses us for his own avarice there would be no one left alive to worship us.' Kim felt a chuckle vibrate through the serpent. 'Maybe one or two. But no more.'

'But is murder no worse than avarice? I believe it is worse. Let him get fat in tending to your worship, but what right does he have to take men's lives?'

'Life is mere illusion, as is death. People cling to these gossamer things. Brahma is real.'

'It's all very well for you to say life is illusion. You float in the cosmic ocean, wherever that is,' Kim said. 'We are shackled to earth and for us this body, this existence, is real. We dearly value our time on earth, despite the pain and sorrow, and we are aware that we must strive to attain release from the eternal cycle of existence. I have performed tapas in the temple at Benares and have seen visions which have guided me. But I cannot dismiss life so easily as illusion. I have a woman whom I hold dear and who will soon give me a child. Should I abandon them in pursuit of becoming one with Brahma?'

'Each man must define his duty for himself. I cannot advise you to abandon or remain. You have free will; you must exercise your choice from deep within you.'

'But what is my karma?'

'Karma is only man's word for an event which has already occurred. Karma merely justifies tragedy or joy, and throws the blame or praise on god. You have choice.'

'And what choice does the untouchable have?'

'Brahma did not create the caste system. Men did.

And for the untouchable to escape he should convert to another religion. In Brahma's eyes all religions are one and the same.'

'But it's unjust that men should be untouchable. It's unjust that a priest should do murder in your name so that people walk in dread of you.'

'Just, unjust. Why do men blame god for their own misdeeds and then mention the words just and unjust as an accusation against god for not intervening? Brahma is. That is all. There is no good and evil, only the positive and the negative. One force cannot exist without its opposite. And both exist in Brahma.'

'So if I punish this priest by killing him for what he has done, it will be justifiable?'

Shesha sighed and rose slowly. 'Men can justify every action they do. If you see it as your inner duty to kill this man, then the act is justifiable in your own eyes. Far worse has been committed by men in god's name.'

'God is evasive,' Kim said in exasperation.

'We only reflect men's evasiveness. He is all around. You yourself tell me of your visions; you yourself have travelled with the lama, you yourself have communicated with Vamana, you yourself now speak to me. Yet you yourself cling to the woman and child and doubt every action. Why then accuse Brahma of being evasive? You see your duty to the people around you as stronger than that of devotion.'

Kim sensed a vibration, at first elusive and faint, then gradually becoming louder. Shesha was humming. The air danced, the stones shivered. Kim found himself physically held as though bound. He couldn't move hand or foot, yet there was no force holding him. The room's blackness faded and it grew so light he could see the grains in the granite, the ripple of the pulse in Shesha's throat. And as the humming faded, Kim felt as if he'd been cleansed within. Then the darkness returned and he could see Shesha no more.

'My time is over. I must return to stone.'

'What about your drinking and eating from those offerings?'

'Why do I need sustenance? The priest eats and drinks.'

Kim caught the glow of the markings on the back of the cobra's heads. Gradually, they grew brighter. They swayed mesmerically and his eyes followed the five markings, unable to resist the hypnotic swaying.

The voice in his head was receding: 'Make a small statue of me and hide me under the floor of your home.'

'I am already protected by Vamana,' said Kim sleepily.

'You are, but no one else. And soon, my friend, you will need the protection of Vamana because you will be entering a hell that no god created. Only men can create such terrible things . . .'

When Kim woke, Shesha was back on the pedestal, and the dying flame threw the serpent's grey shadows on the wall behind. Kim remembered a dream and went up and examined the idol. There were tiny grains of sand on the belly. The ruby eyes stared down at him, unwinking.

He heard the faint scrape of stone against stone and felt the cool touch of fresh night air from behind the idol. He stepped away swiftly and pressed himself against the wall. Part of the apparently solid granite wall slowly swung open. A light was thrust into the sanctum and a moment later the Brahmin stepped in. He ignored the idol and lifted the light high to look for Kim and when he couldn't see him lying in a heap he moved further into the room, perplexed. When he'd taken three steps into the room, Kim quickly slid past the open door. The priest whirled at the sound of movement.

'You're a . . . alive . . .'

'Pundit-ji, Lord Shesha gave me his dharshan. You may now wait and receive it.'

'No . . . no. I will give you anything . . .'

Kim grabbed the iron ring and heaved on the stone door. The Brahmin darted past the idol, hurling the light away in order to hold the door open. But the stone was smooth and his fingers had no purchase. As the door closed, Kim heard his screaming and weeping. Once it was shut, showing no trace of its existence, he heard nothing at all.

It was considered a miracle by everyone that at dawn Kim should be sitting calmly outside, warming himself in the morning sun. He wouldn't explain to Kumar or the others how this had come about. Kumar wept in relief and embraced Kim. His eyes were sunken and dark with sleeplessness.

'I prayed mightily that no harm should befall you for my sake, and god heard me.'

'We will see how else he has intervened,' Kim said.

Lalitha was dismayed to see Kim alive and her glance darted anxiously around the temple in search of the Brahmin. She knew now that she had lost all claim to the property and cursed the priest for his betrayal. Her hatred of Narain now settled on Kim and her stare was poisonous.

Kim, with the other worshippers who had arrived to perform their morning prayers, waited patiently for the priest to open the temple. But when he didn't appear, they sent for the trustees, who came in their full authority to investigate his inexplicable behaviour. All watched them open the lock and slowly push open the doors. The sun poured in, rippling over the priest lying with his arms outstretched in worship of Shesha. There was no mark on him and he was dead.

An occurrence such as this lifted Kim's veil of anonymity.

Parvati heard all that had happened, even as she entered the last hours of her labour.

The whispers, like swift streams, swept past the village to the edge of the valley and flowed up the hills and entered the palace of the Zamindar of Puducheri, who sat on a throne of ivory the colour of fading sunlight. The whisper entered the Zamindar's left ear, interrupting his conversation with Richard Farson.

Farson saw the flicker of concern in the Zamindar's

face. It was full-moon shaped with equally round, though slightly crossed, eyes. The head rested on a large shapeless body draped in a voluminous saffron-coloured silk robe. He also wore a silk saffron turban a foot high, with a tail that fell down to his waist, like a woman's tresses. The Zamindar never wore any other costume as he believed himself divine. Farson was forced to tolerate this delusion as he had no alternative. The Zamindar was the company's dubash. And he drew his salary not from heaven but the company's coffers.

Every British company had a dubash. The title was hereditary. Like his forefathers the Zamindar was employed to act as translator in all the company's dealings with the natives. He also received a share in the company's profits. Thomas, Wilson, Whitehead & Company, though vague and anonymous to the ear, was extremely rich and powerful. It had been established in Madras in 1726 to export pepper and cotton back to England. Thomas, Wilson and Whitehead had died enormously rich men. The company now dealt in virtually any and everything, owning vast tracts of rice fields, sugar-cane, coconut plantations, cotton mills, cotton fields, tobacco fields, as well as importing machinery, and buying and selling agencies. It also owned its own fleet of cargo ships. Richard Farson was the company's area manager.

Farson, a man only in his mid-twenties, sprawled arrogantly in a leather armchair. It was less elaborate than the ivory throne but was raised to exactly the same level. Suddenly, he slapped his riding crop against his boot and both the Zamindar and the whisperer, who delicately held the Zamindar's bejewelled ear, started.

'I presume this is important?'

The servant faded from view, bent from the waist, softly floating away out of the corner of Farson's vision. The Zamindar turned his attention back to Farson.

'I've just learned of a most disturbing happening. You might know of the temple built to Shesha, the five-headed cobra on which the Lord Vishnu rests. It seems that a man who spent the night there appeared alive at dawn but . . .' His eyes seemed to become even more crossed. 'The priest was found dead inside.'

'Fascinating,' Farson murmured; his blue eyes were half closed, shaded by pale, almost white, lashes.

He signalled to his servant who undid a bundle, unfolded three saris and threw them like fishing nets onto the marble floor. They stained the floor and filled the room with their vibrant colours. The Zamindar looked down on them, a ripple of perplexity spreading over his calm forehead. The saris were indeed beautiful.

'So?'

'So, my friend,' Farson said, flicking at the saris with his riding crop. 'These have found their way back into the shops. An associate of mine bought them in Madras. They are made right here, he learned, so I've been told to take action. You do recognise them, don't you? Somewhere in that god-like memory, you do remember?'

'Yes, yes; they're from the village by the tank. I had the police destroy their looms.'

'Thank you,' but Farson's sarcasm was lost on the Zamindar who was only grateful for being appreciated.

'But there are only three saris, Mr Farson.'

'I can count,' Farson said. 'Obviously there are more being made even now. Other villages, who are watching what is happening, will soon start making their own – if we do nothing. And then other villages. Three will become three thousand, then three lakhs. Our own cloth won't be necessary, either to the villagers or to the townspeople. And if we don't sell our cloth, we will be losing money. And if we lose money I will get a very stiff reprimand from Head Office. So we must make an example of this village and its people to discourage others from following in their footsteps.'

'Yes, yes, yes, I understand,' the Zamindar said, and his frown was meant to be fierce but instead he looked wounded as though the saris were insulting him. 'I will send the constable with men to investigate the matter.'

'I think we should go ourselves,' Farson said and rose immediately.

The Zamindar sat a moment longer, then realising he was meant to accompany Farson, reluctantly stood up. He wanted to postpone the matter until he'd investigated the temple story. Who was this man who had spent the night in the sanctum with the dread form of Shesha and lived? The Zamindar, despite his belief in his own divinity, had no such courage. Now he saw himself undermined and his god-like stature threatened. And how did the priest die? The priest was his personal friend and he was deeply distressed. He had appointed the priest to that temple and received one tenth of the donations in return, which amounted to half a lakh annually. Unless he could appoint another man loyal to him, he would sorely miss this revenue.

However, the company and Mr Farson awaited. He smiled obsequiously, cursing British impetuosity. But they considered this little matter important and he would prove his loyalty not only to the company but also to the Colonel sahib. Sir Colonel sahib, he corrected.

Farson well knew it wasn't a matter of simply striding out of the palace, mounting his horse, and riding down into the valley. The Zamindar demanded all the pomp and ceremony of a deity when he moved. Farson doubted whether they'd get started before dawn.

The Zamindar rang a silver bell and immediately his servant re-entered. He approached as he'd left, half bent in deference. He had a thin, narrow face, and a bony chest. His skin, from the waist up, was smooth and supple as a woman's and his eyes feminine in their swift appraisal of Farson. The Zamindar leant on him and, wafting a trail of rose perfume, majestically negotiated the expanse of the reception room.

'Immediately,' Farson called out and the Zamindar waved a handkerchief in acknowledgement.

Richard Farson's guest room was in a separate building, smaller than the palace but equally ornate, with domes and cupolas and pillars. He was the only guest.

He stripped, donned shorts and listlessly turned the pages of a Sherlock Holmes story, 'The Speckled Band'. He wished he were back in Madurai. At least he could spend the afternoon at the club and at five play a couple of chukkas of polo. But he had to spend ten days of the month, except in the rainy season, touring up-country – like any government official, except that his interest was not administrative but commercial – to inspect various estates, check that the natives were not cheating the company, attend to harvests and plantings, weighings and shippings, buying and selling. Higher up in the hills, there were European managers on the tea estates and he'd spend pleasant evenings with them, drinking whisky and water and talking of Blighty.

This was a life quite different from the one he was born to. He had been born in Chelmsford, and on leaving school had joined the company as a clerk in its London office, a cramped, stuffy building in Leadenhall Street, crammed with files. His uncle was the chief shipping clerk and had helped Richard get the job. It had been a dull but secure life. He was, in England, of the lower middle class, and he had made friends only with the other young clerks in the office. When a vacancy had occurred in the Madras office he had applied and had landed the job. The day he sailed from England was the most exciting of his life. He had read up the history of the company. The privately printed book written by the original Thomas's grandson, though dry and pedantic, filled his head with dreams of the fabulous fortunes to be made out in India. He knew, deep down, that the days of the old nabobs had passed. India was ruled by the Crown and companies like his could no longer free-boot their way to great fortunes. They couldn't make or break princes, start wars or sign peace treaties. It would be tame but at least different from the dreariness of London. He arrived in winter and dreaded the thought of summer. As a bachelor, he shared a bungalow in Egmore with three other junior company officers, and according to European social custom presented his card to the managing director's wife who was the most senior lady among the box-wallahs, in Madras. He was duly invited to tea, with other new commercial arrivals, examined and dismissed. As a box-wallah he joined the Gymkhana Club, the only one permitted to him by European society. He couldn't even set foot in the Madras Club on Mount Road. That was reserved for army officers only. Even so, Farson led a princely life and forgot his humble past. He wasn't paid a princely salary but it was enough for a polo pony; he'd never even seen the game before in his life.

Solitude and silence made him uneasy. He rose and examined himself in the blurred mirror. His tan ended at his neck and forearms. His body looked strange. He curled his moustache, grooming it carefully. He thought himself handsome, with his squarish, open face and a dimple in his chin. Some of the young ladies in the club enjoyed flirting with him. He couldn't afford marriage until his next promotion and hoped Miss Cynthia Alton, the deputy managing director's daughter, would accept his proposal then. They would marry before his next home leave in eighteen months' time. He couldn't wait to spend the autumn of 1914 in England.

The Zamindar was ready at dawn. Farson mounted up, accompanied by his bearer, syce and cook. The company paid for them and for the hire of a bullock cart to carry his gear. The Zamindar travelled far more elaborately and Richard Farson understood the importance of ceremony. It was meant to fill the viewer with awe and through awe gain his obedience. However, he thought the Zamindar's conveyance, a chariot drawn by a white horse, quite extreme. He thought it must be vaguely Roman but the Zamindar assured him that the Lord Krishna had driven such a vehicle for some prince whose name Farson had deliberately forgotten as the managing director's wife had advised him never to get involved with native nonsense. The chariot was painted gold and decorated with fresh flowers; the charioteer was a pretty youth, against whom the Zamindar leaned lovingly. Apart from the chariot there were elephants and bullock carts and more than a hundred worshippers dressed in pure white. The Zamindar rode the chariot only when he expected a sizeable audience. On this occasion his whole household, including his wife and other womenfolk, gathered to bid him farewell. Once out of sight, the Zamindar would mount his elephant and recline in the shaded comfort of the howdah. Richard Farson rode ahead of this embarrassing cavalcade with his rifle, hoping to bag a bird or two for the pot.

If the whispers of Kim's deed had flowed up the hill into the palace, now the whisper of the Zamindar and Richard Farson's journey flowed down and out into the valley. Everyone knew their intention. The Zamindar had mentioned it to his adviser, the adviser to his servant, the servant to others.

Kim heard at midday, even as he watched his daughter asleep in his arms, when Kumar, shivering with this new threat, whispered it into his ear. The baby lay asleep and naked and the whole village admired her not for her beauty, which she undoubtedly had, but for her fairness. Kim cared little for such things. This was his child; his blood now flowed in her veins. Kim had never seen or held something so delicate and beautiful ever in his life. He crooned and hummed to the baby and when she opened and closed her tiny fist, she took a tighter hold on his heart.

Parvati, however, was bitterly disappointed at not having borne a boy. This need for a son was too deeply ingrained in her, despite her professed belief in the freedom of women from male authority, despite her own strength of character and her ability to earn her living in Bombay as a woman without degradation.

'You must treat our baby as equal to a son,' Kim said.

'But a boy would have grown into a man such as you. He would have brought us a good dowry.'

'Ah, that's it,' Kim mocked. 'How can you women be considered equal when you yearn so longingly for sons and look on a female child as a burden? This child will grow up as beautiful and intelligent and bold as you. What more can we wish for?'

'A son,' Parvati said, and was determined the next time to bear a son.

Kumar couldn't bear Kim's calm acceptance of the news that the Zamindar and the company sahib were riding down on them from the great height of the palace – with a platoon of police, according to rumour. Such a combination of power and punishment frightened the whole village. They followed Kumar into the hut, crowding out the light, stopping the air. Their faces mirrored Kumar's anxiety. They weren't brave, only humble people who were frightened of the whispers.

'What shall we do?' Kumar wailed.

'Hide everything,' said Kim. 'We must dismantle everything immediately, so there is no sign of saris being made here. There is a place I have discovered by the hill, a small cave hidden by bushes.' Kumar smiled in delight and a collective breath of relief swept through the hut. 'But no one must tell the Zamindar or the company sahib anything. If they should ask about the saris, say "What saris? We are not making saris." And once they are gone, we must find a place further from this village, and go on making them.'

'But how did they discover we were making them?'

'The saris are distinctive.' Everyone stared accusingly at old Gopalan whose skill was now held to blame for their predicament. Kim had no words of blame for the old man. 'I think it would be wise, Gopalan, if you too were to hide for two or three days. Go on a pilgrimage, so that we may truthfully answer the Zamindar that Gopalan, the maker of saris, is no longer in the village.'

His good advice was eagerly accepted. It was an easy task to dismantle and hide everything, for the equipment was simple. The loom was a clumsy wooden structure with ropes and pulleys, spindles and a presser. The cotton was spun on small wooden wheels and the thread dyed in clay pots. They all worked quickly, though they knew the Zamindar and the company sahib were still two days away from the village. The floor was swept clean and where dye had stained the mud, the women quickly covered it with a layer of cow dung and water.

By the next day, nothing remained of their sari-making, and the whole village took a vow of secrecy. Children were threatened with demons and kidnappers should they open their mouths. If there was an exaggerated silence in the village, Kim was sure it wouldn't be noticed by their expected visitors. They were used to the awe their presence struck in villagers. Kumar was chosen as spokesman to answer questions though he would have preferred Kim, whose nerves were far stronger than his, to do it. But, as Kim pointed out, he was a stranger and would immediately arouse suspicion. If Kumar trembled and sweated in their august presence, it was only to be expected.

While awaiting their arrival, Kim occupied himself making a small clay statue of Shesha. He had little artistic talent and what he fashioned was a crude imitation of the serpent. The heads were thin, the body fat and lumpy. When he took it to the potter for firing in his kiln, the man chuckled at the sight. Hardened in the kiln, it took on a dark and fierce colouring. Kim painted the cobra markings on the back of the heads and while Parvati and the baby were out of the hut, he dug a hole in the corner and buried the idol.

In deference to the Zamindar's delusion, and also because he was the dubash and supposed to translate between the company and the natives, Richard Farson permitted the Zamindar to ride before him. The chariot swayed and creaked into the village and the Zamindar accepted the prostrated homage of all the villagers. They'd heard of this vehicle but never before seen it. The Zamindar was gracious and aloof, as a god should be. Kumar and two other men approached and garlanded him, and gave him their offerings of coconut. Kim sat on the ground behind Kumar and watched the European ride up and stop beside the chariot. Behind them both were three police constables.

'Show them the saris first,' Farson ordered.

'The sahib has told the Zamindar to show us the saris,' Kim translated in a whisper.

The saris were brought and the bearer threw them down in the dust and spread them out. Here they looked like the skins of exotic beasts, captured and destroyed.

'Do they recognise them?' Farson asked.

Kim whispered that Kumar should first examine them and only then admit recognition. Kumar and two others rose and approached the saris. They circled them, picked them up and studied them, and Kim thought they acted well. He watched Farson; the open face looked stubbornly patient.

'Yes,' Kumar said. 'Long ago we made saris like this, but it's been many years since we've seen such fine material.'

They returned to their places, while the Zamindar translated back to Farson.

'Search the village.'

The villagers remained in their places, turning to watch the police constable moving from hut to hut. They only looked in quickly for the women were inside. It didn't take them long and they returned to the Zamindar emptyhanded. Farson's eyes were narrow and angry, and for a second he seemed to be staring straight at Kim. But Farson saw only a blur of indistinguishable dark faces.

'Ask them where their weaver is.'

'He went away,' Kumar said and was grateful for Kim's foresight because Constable Doraiswami would have recognised Gopalan. 'There was no reason for him to live here, and he took his skills elsewhere.'

The Zamindar was happy to accept the explanation but Farson demanded a search. This time Doraiswami examined their faces. He saw Kim, frowned, continued. He reported that there was no Gopalan. The villagers were cross-examined for half an hour, but they stuck to their story. Farson thought it was indeed possible that Gopalan had taken his skills to another village, and cursed. It would take time to track him down. He would question the merchant in Madras when he returned.

Quite deliberately he nudged his horse forward. It stepped on the saris as he rode around the huddled villagers, and he saw that they were cowed, all except for one man who met his stare without flinching. But he immediately then lowered his eyes in deference. Deliberately, Farson rode back over the saris.

Kim had lowered his eyes to hide his rage. Farson's act of desecration made him ashamed of his race. He saw what was meant by it – power and contempt. Farson knew he could destroy this village and the lives it contained. The company no longer had the guns and the soldiers, but it had the money to buy retribution. It could change the laws, could circumvent them, and since it paid the men who made the laws, the Indian had no control over his own destiny. Nor did Farson care that his horse trampled on something of beauty, that ancient skills handed down from generation to generation had been woven into it. But, Kim admitted, it was an inert beauty, an ancient one, that couldn't rise of its own accord to strike back.

'I don't think we're going to get anywhere with these niggers,' Farson said and spurred his horse past the Zamindar.

Kim didn't translate, though Kumar asked him to. The chariot turned too, running over the saris. The villagers collectively flinched at this added cruelty and Kim knew the Zamindar had done it to prove his loyalty to the ruler. The bearer scooped them up in a bundle and ran after the chariot. No one moved. They watched the little party slowly moving down the dirt road, trailing dust that remained hanging long after they were lost to sight.

The Zamindar and Richard Farson dined together on this last evening before they parted company, the Zamindar to go to the temple, Farson to Madurai. The tent in which they reclined was richly elaborate. Persian carpets covered the earth, gold lamps hung from poles, and the interior walls were lined with silk. In a corner the Zamindar had installed an idol of himself, wreathed in garlands. Small, pretty boys served dinner on silver plates.

They spoke little. Farson had nothing to say to his dubash and made no effort. He read while he ate. The Zamindar, used to Farson, spoke in whispers to his adviser who had been sent to the temple to discover the identity of the man who had survived the night with Shesha.

Outside, a murmur gradually rose into an argument. One voice was a man's, the other a woman's. The Zamindar's face flickered with displeasure and a boy was sent to quell the disturbance. He returned to whisper to the adviser, who whispered to the Zamindar. 'Bring her to me, then,' the Zamindar said. 'Mr Farson, I apologise for disturbing your reading, but there's a young woman who wants to talk to us privately.'

'About what?'

'Saris, Mr Farson. Saris.'

Lalitha entered apprehensively and stared around her in awe. She'd never imagined such riches and was bitter that some should be so fortunate. She was intimidated, too, by the two men who stared at her coldly. The European held an open book which he carefully placed aside. The Zamindar fondled a boy who fanned him with peacock feathers.

'Well, what of the saris?' the European asked.

'I know where they're hidden,' Lalitha told the Zamindar.

'So the village is making saris?'

'Yes. They've hidden the looms and dyes.'

'Where?'

'I'm a poor woman,' Lalitha said. 'And a widow. The saris are so well hidden that the police will never find them without my guidance.'

'Ten rupees,' the Zamindar said.

'Two hundred,' Lalitha demanded, having calculated the riches here. The Zamindar would have ordered her stripped and thrashed by the police but Mr Farson wouldn't have approved.

'The man who leads the village is also the one who spent the night with Shesha. Two hundred rupees isn't much for two such important pieces of information.'

Kim was woken in the grey dawn by the cruel prod of a rifle, and dragged out of the hut by Constable Doraiswami and his two men. Parvati clung to Kim's legs and the baby, frightened, screamed and cried. The whole village gathered silently, clinging to each other in fright. In the centre stood the dismantled loom, pots, saris, spinning wheels. Farson held his horse beside the heap while a servant poured oil over it. The Zamindar stared down from the lofty height of his elephant. He wasn't used to being up at such an early hour but this Kimathchand drew him. The man made no attempt to struggle and passively joined the villagers, wife and crying child huddled beside him. He wanted to question him but that would have to wait until Mr Farson completed his tamasha.

When the saris and the wood were well soaked with oil, Farson took the blazing torch and dropped it on the heap. The flames began slowly, then found the cloth and burst into fire. The light blazed on the villagers and their shadows leapt and danced on the houses. Their faces were impassive.

Kim felt the heat and smelt the wood and cloth. The fire ran through his veins too. He watched the small and insignificant heart of this village in flames and realised that even something so small could threaten an empire. Force, as it had been in Rae Bareli, was the empire's only response. What had the Colonel sahib spoken to him passionately many years ago? 'They aren't going to nibble at the edges. I won't let them.' And Kim saw, too, the Colonel sahib as a force more subtle than arms and flames, and even more powerful as he corrupted the men who served him.

The sun rose and the pall of smoke drifted lazily across

the green rice fields, fell and faded. The flames turned white and ashes rose and covered Farson, the Zamindar and the villagers, darkening them too. The loom wasn't totally destroyed. Parts remained untouched, looking like wounds in the black ashes. Passing travellers stood on the outskirts staring mutely, as Farson had expected. They would carry the message across the valley and beyond.

Farson nudged his horse and stared down at Kim, still gripped by constables. He now distinguished Kim from the others and wondered why he hadn't noticed the differences before, his height and fairness, his bold stare. Farson didn't like this Kimathchand. He made him uneasy. His power depended on his own superiority of race, but staring down he felt himself studied not even as an equal but as something inferior, with the same contempt he used when looking at a native. This made him squirm. Only another Englishman, one superior in rank or breeding, could make Farson squirm.

'Take him to Madurai,' he ordered Constable Doraiswami. 'And if he escapes I'll have you hanged.'

'On what charge?' Kim asked Doraiswami.

Doraiswami was a portly man with a moustache that spread like a creeper from beneath his nose to disappear into his turban. Below, his mouth and neck were cleanly shaven.

'On what charge, sahib?'

'That of illegal manufacture of contraband items. Also sedition, making utterances against the ruling authority. Others will be framed by the company's legal department in Madurai.'

'May I speak to him?' the Zamindar called down. Farson waved a generous hand, spurred his horse and moved at a trot down the road towards Madurai.

Doraiswami pushed Kim forward until he was within reach of the elephant's trunk. Doraiswami didn't trust the beast. It had been known to strike a man in rage.

Kim and the Zamindar stared at each other, each memorising the other's face. The Zamindar needed to be accurate in his report to the Sir Colonel sahib. Naturally, he would take all the credit for unearthing a seditionist. But he also stared out of fear. Kim stripped him of his self-proclaimed divinity. The chariot, the saffron robes, the golden howdah, all were hollow and he saw his own empty posturings. And if he did, others would too. Kim had to be destroyed to preserve his power. He beckoned Kim closer until he touched the elephant's flank.

'Why didn't you die?' he whispered.

'Only to prove you false, Zamindari,' Kim instinctively knew his fear, and goaded him. 'Will you report this to the Sir Colonel sahib?'

The Zamindar opened and shut his mouth. His eyes became more crossed as he tried to read Kim's mind.

'How do you know I report to him?'

'I know these things, Zamindari. Tell the Sir Colonel sahib too that the priest was murdering those who spent the night in Shesha's sanctum, only to magnify their fear of god.'

'I've heard that Shesha comes alive. Does he?'

'Why should you believe me?'

'Because you live and the Brahmin is dead.'

'It's for you to discover these things for yourself. Spend a night in the sanctum.'

A quiver shook the Zamindar. 'Just to look on Shesha in stone fills me with fear.' He leaned further out of the howdah and the boy with him held onto his robe. The howdah creaked and Kim took a step back. He didn't want to be killed by a falling zamindar.

'Does he live? Does Shesha return to life at the blackest hour?'

'How can a god return to life? And why should another god reveal such deep ignorance?'

Parvati wouldn't permit Kim to leave her and the baby in the village. The last time they'd been torn apart by fate, it had taken years for them to find each other. It was her constant nightmare, that this could happen again. Kim met her halfway. She could come but, if he were sentenced to prison, then she should return to the safety of the village and await his return. Parvati accepted this too docilely for his liking.

For Kim, the clang of a cell door closing on him was a familiar sound. For Kumar, this new ordeal was terrifying. He stared at the walls, the ceiling, the iron bars, in bewilderment. The cell wasn't dank and depressing but airy and full of sunlight.

'This isn't as bad as Tihar Gaol,' Kim said. 'That's an old and terrible prison in Delhi.'

'You've been in such places before? I never suspected you were a criminal.'

'Am I one now?'

'I don't know. I don't know anything. What have we done that is so bad?'

'Nibbled,' Kim said, and knew it made no sense to Kumar. 'What we have done by making saris is to cause the company to lose money.'

'But we only made eleven.'

'Eleven or eleven thousand are the same for the company.' And even though he tried, Kim couldn't make Kumar understand the economics of the company which were inextricably bound to the economics of the empire. Even to him it sounded a mysterious connection and if he were to believe what the Colonel sahib had told him of the vastness of this empire, how even eleven thousand saris could affect it was beyond his imaginings!

Kim expected the Colonel sahib every day. The Zamindar would certainly have reported his presence. Kim hadn't even told Parvati that their hiding place had been revealed. She would only have lived in dread that the Colonel would inform her husband and that he would send his servants to take her back. He had to persuade her to return to the village. She would be protected there, and cared for. In Madurai, alone with a child and with Kim in prison, she could be kidnapped. And Kim feared for his daughter. He prayed the Colonel sahib wouldn't mention anything to Lal Bahadhur but it depended not so much on his discretion but on what use he could make of that lever against Kim. He could use it as a threat to force Kim's return to his service, but then, how would he trust Kim again?

Instead of the Colonel sahib, a stranger waited for him in the visiting room. He was a man of average height and athletic build. There was something scrupulously clean and neat about him, as though he'd bathed and changed just the moment before he'd entered. He wore a long silk jiba, a cotton dhoti and highly polished gold-rimmed spectacles. His left hand clutched a tin of Gold Flake cigarettes. The man offered him one and Kim allowed the man to light it, and study him.

'You are an Englishman,' he said finally. It wasn't a question, but a discovery. 'I wasn't certain. I thought you might have been Eurasian.'

'Does it make a difference?'

'Yes. It makes you more important. I am T. V. Naidu, General Secretary of the Congress Party in Madras. As you might guess, Ravi Srinivasan informed me the moment he heard of your arrest. I have spoken to your wife, a very intelligent woman, and she furnished me with the details. Thomas, Wilson and Whitehead is a very powerful company and their lawyers always seek the maximum punishment against their enemies.' He smiled wryly. 'Lawyers are the modern equivalent of rampaging armies. They wreak havoc, destruction and death. I too am a lawyer.'

'And you propose to defend us?'

T. V. Naidu smiled, a chill and steely smile. 'That is not possible, Mr Kim. I'm sorry, I don't know your surname.' He fell silent, and continued when Kim didn't help him, 'You haven't committed any criminal or civil offence. You are a political prisoner. You are a seditionist according to Mr Farson, who has sworn an affidavit.'

'I spoke nothing against the Crown.'

'But you acted against its interests, Mr Kim. Unwittingly you have joined our ranks. Your act was a political one. It was swadesh, the rejection of foreign-made goods for Indian-made ones. Certainly your motives were pure and innocent: to help a village earn a living. But the whole problem is that you deprived your countrymen in England of a living, Mr Kim. Which people do you care for more, those in England or those here? You will have to decide soon, Mr Kim. The time approaches when men must commit their lives to a principle.'

'And who will rule once the British leave, Mr Naidu?'

'You speak like an Englishman. You avoid the question by asking another. Does it matter? We're not children; we can guide our own destinies.'

'If you have not come to represent me, then what do you want from me?'

T. V. Naidu delicately turned over his cigarette tin even as his mind tried delicately to phrase his request as obliquely as possible. Now that he'd met Kim and understood his innocence he saw it as a barrier. Had Kim been a cynical and venal man, it would have been an easy matter. He decided finally to be direct.

'Names. I know you are an Imperial agent, Mr Kim. It's possible that you work for Colonel Sir John Creighton. The names we want, Mr Kim, are not those of criminal types. Those hold no interest for us. But we are a complex people, in customs, in social attitudes, in our selfish interests. We can pinpoint the European enemy, Mr Kim. He's visible to us all. But we do not know which one among our own people is our enemy. I believe it's possible that you would know.'

'I'm sorry,' Kim rose. 'I cannot help you.'

'Don't be so impetuous, Mr Kim,' Mr Naidu called after him. 'Think about it. How else can we guide our destinies without knowing who is betraying us into the European hand?'

The window behind the district magistrate, Mr G. K. Parthasathy, framed a clear blue sky and palm trees. The high-ceilinged room was hot and still, a punkah stirred the air bringing no relief. Kim heard the rustle of papers, the scratch of a pen, the patient waiting of men. Men and women filled the doorways, awaiting their turn. Kim glimpsed Parvati and Kumar's wife. The baby slept peacefully and he wished he could cradle her. Parvati tried to smile when she caught his eye but the effort only deepened the crease of concern on her face.

Mr Parthasathy read Mr Farson's affidavit, then the Zamindar's affidavit, then Constable Doraiswami's charge sheet, and Kim and Kumar's statements. He looked across to Kim and Kumar standing in the pen. He thought Kim startlingly European in his features and placed him as either Eurasian or north Indian. His small, dark companion, on the other hand, was very local. He looked down at the file. Attached to it was a telegram. 'Maximum sentence should be imposed on these two men stop. Creighton, Political and Secret Department.'

Mr Parthasathy didn't like Colonel Sir John Creighton. Nor did he like political pressure. He was a tall, well-built young man, prematurely bald. The top of his head was very bare but he carefully cultivated the luxuriant fringe surrounding the pate, which grew long and curly. He patted his head dry and once more studied the affidavits. He had met Farson once and distrusted him, a box-wallah who would commit perjury for his company. The Zamindar, of course, would follow Farson's dictates. 'Maximum sentence.' For making saris and uttering 'seditious language'? Six years of these two men's lives? Nonsense, he said to himself and breathed hard in indignation. He would have liked to let the defendants off free but he knew he would be hauled over the coals for dereliction of duty.

'Nine months' imprisonment for both defendants,' he pronounced, and the clerk rose, made a notation and dropped it back on the pile of files in front of him.

In the corridor where there was at least some semblance of a breeze, pushed and jostled by the comings and goings, Kim kissed his daughter and then embraced Parvati. He breathed in her perfume, knowing it would be a long time before he would smell it again.

'You promised to return to the village. You must.'

She was weeping and holding him as the police patiently pushed Kim and Kumar along.

'I'll come and visit you.'

'Always travel with companions. It is dangerous for you alone. Anyway, I'll be here for nine months and you'll always know where to find me. This time we each know where the other is, so don't be afraid.'

'But I am. Without you I'm lost and alone.'

Kim kissed her and felt as though he were about to take a long journey, though it was only a short walk down the road to the Central Prison. Parvati and Kumar's wife trailed behind, silently weeping and holding each other for comfort. The small door set into the gate opened to admit Kim and Kumar, and Kim took a last long look at Parvati.

He was so intent on looking at her that he failed to notice Madan who stood on the far side of the narrow dirt road. When the prison door closed on Kim, Madan limped the few remaining yards to stare up at the high walls. He couldn't help smiling. In his pocket was the Colonel sahib's telegram: 'Proceed immediately Madurai stop keep watch on Kim and note all contacts stop report names immediately stop Cottonseed'.

Madan had lost Kim and the woman in Bhopal after crossing the Narbada river. They'd vanished into the vastness of India and he'd returned reluctantly to his village in the United Provinces, to await further instructions. Now he had Kim trapped in prison, and he would avenge his brother's death. It would be simple to hire a hardened criminal inside the prison to cut Kim's throat one night.

# 16

## April 1913–January 1914

At the end of a love affair we enter into a landscape of despair, Alice thought. If I could draw this place it would be bleak and desolate, silent and still. The sky would be permanently grey without even a hint of rain, and the earth would be carpeted with thorns and rocks. I would be fixed somewhere in the very centre of it chained in a lake of tears. But imperceptibly, a change comes, so gradually that you dare not notice in case it should revert. The stillness remains but the clouds lighten. I feel in this new place a sense of calm, of living in a dream in which I expect nothing to occur. The habits of waking, working, sleeping carry me on and on. And this will be the land that I inhabit until I fall in love again, if ever. Otherwise, I remain becalmed in a shroud, though far from dying.

The land through which she was passing was ominously still and hot, and because of it she had thought of her own feelings in terms of her surroundings. Low hills covered with scrub and thorn stretched out to the horizon. The narrow road rutted by the passing of bullock carts was a thin dusty line separating one group of hills from another. Villages were a rare sight and they'd passed through one the day before where she'd been the most awesome sight in all their small, poor life. A European woman, in trousers, perched atop an elephant, followed by a bullock cart and four men armed with muskets! Alice always carried sweets for the children who crowded around her, silent and wide-eyed. Once she could coax a smile from one, the others would giggle, and then the elders would edge forward.

In one more day, according to her guide, she would reach Porbander and meet Mr Mohandas Karamchand Gandhi. He was visiting his ancestral home briefly before returning to South Africa. Of course she could have arranged the meeting in the comfort of Bombay, but Alice distrusted meeting active men in such artificial surroundings. She wanted to meet Mr Gandhi in the place of his birth, and make her judgements in a natural atmosphere. She had sent a telegram requesting the interview in Porbander and he had promptly invited her – if she wished to undertake the arduous journey.

The Gujerat and Baroda line took her as far as the princely state of Junagadh. She had met the Rajah once in Bombay, a young man with a spoilt handsome face. The corruption now spilled down over his body, rendering it gross. She hadn't liked him then, nor did she again as his guest. He entertained lavishly, squandering money on such extravagances as royal weddings for his dogs, and spent nothing on his people. The government regarded such things with indulgence. Alice understood the importance of these 600 princely states scattered throughout the country. They were kept loyal to the British, tolerated, flattered, and were the secure fortresses from which the British could control the countryside should ever another rebellion arise. The princes would, as many had done in 1857, turn against their own people, as long as their gadis were protected by British troops. His Highness of Junagadh, therefore, was someone she disliked and from whom she very reluctantly accepted the provision of a conveyance to Porbander. He'd never heard of Mr Gandhi and when Alice explained his importance, dismissed him as quite insignificant.

Porbander was a small, glaring white-and-red-tiled town on the coast. It was the capital of a tiny princely state, and the town was dominated by a single large palace. It faced a sea torpid and lifeless in the noon heat. The town was barely alive, awaiting the cooling breezes before people stirred. Alice's arrival was an event that drew the citizens out into the heat and glare to stare up at her as she passed through the narrow winding streets. A small crowd guided her to Mr Gandhi's house, a low, spreading building set in the shade of a tamarind tree. Even as the mahout made her elephant kneel, Mr Gandhi came out to greet her.

'You English are a most intrepid people which I suppose is why I admire you,' Mr Gandhi said. 'I'm deeply flattered that you should make such a journey, Miss Soames, when it would have been easy and most convenient for you to wait in Bombay, when I would have passed through to catch the steamer.'

'Mr Gandhi, we might be intrepid but I admit there is no more uncomfortable beast to ride than an elephant. Thank you for allowing me to visit you here.'

Alice walked stiffly beside him into the cool shade of his home. The room was simply furnished with divans and she began to sink down onto one when she found that Mr Gandhi continued on through the house and expected her to follow. They ended up in the kitchen and she watched in amazement as he began preparing her a cup of tea. A servant hovered in the outer doorway but Mr Gandhi ignored him.

'I've never seen an Indian man even boil water.'

'Boiling water is the most I can manage, Miss Soames,' Mr Gandhi said. 'But I cannot permit my wife to perform such servile tasks for me when I'm just as capable as she in the preparation of tea. It might not be as good as hers, but it will quench your thirst.'

They both watched as though it were a chemical experiment. He sighed in pleasure and relief when the water boiled and he poured it into a tea pot. He took delight in such a simple task, and when he handed her the cup watched her with attention.

'It's very good.'

'Thank you. I would cook you dinner tonight but my

wife feels that on such an occasion I should be banned from the kitchen.'

They returned to the sitting-room and she gratefully sank down onto a divan. Gandhi lowered himself and neatly tucked his legs beneath him. Alice wished she could be as supple, and not big-boned and awkward in front of this small man. He had a kind and mischievous smile and she immediately felt herself at ease in his company.

'I've arranged for you to stay in the dak bungalow. It's simple, but I think you'll be comfortable there, Miss Soames. Once you've had your bath and rested, we'll talk.' He smiled. 'I doubt whether you've come all this way to discuss South Africa.'

'No, I haven't.'

'In which case yours could have been a wasted journey.'

'Is India a waste?'

'Certainly not, Miss Soames, but I admit an embarrassing ignorance of my own country. Maybe over the next few days you would help with my education.'

The dak bungalow was musty and neglected. An ancient chowkidar watched her inspect the grey sheets and the discoloured bathroom. The furniture was barely adequate: a bed with a mosquito net, a dining table, two chairs and an easy chair. She removed the bed sheets, shook them vigorously in the chowkidar's face, hoped she had rid them of bugs and other vermin, and remade the bed.

She joined Mr Gandhi on the beach and they sat on the sand, looking out to sea. It was cool and quiet, gulls swooped and called. They were not allowed much privacy as Alice still drew children and adults to stare at her. Mr Gandhi ignored them. He played with the sand, pouring a fistful from one hand to the other as though it were water. Alice, studying the gentle face behind the gold-rimmed spectacles, wondered whether this small, lean man had the steel. She saw not so much the steel which had been revealed in South Africa, as the doubts. Mr Gandhi wore his native clothes although she expected him to wear the suit in which he'd been photographed in South Africa.

'My work there is still not finished, Miss Soames,' Gandhi said. 'Those people still need me and – this might sound egotistical – someone has to battle for their rights. I cannot leave something unfinished.'

'But once you have completed your work there, Mr Gandhi, will you return to India and take up her cause?'

'You journalists always want answers in black and white. I haven't yet decided as to my future plans, or even whether I am needed in India. There are fine men like Mr Gokhale, Mr Patel, Mr Nehru and others leading the Indian cause. Why should I be so important in the Indian movement?'

'Humility, Mr Gandhi, won't win India her freedom.'

'Nor will arrogance, Miss Soames. The British will always surpass us in that. India isn't South Africa. It isn't a simple matter of asking for freedom when we have not, as yet, any idea as to how to win it. The British will not hand it to us on a plate just because we request it. It must be fought for, Miss Soames, but how one must fight is the problem. This is a vast and complex country. The Congress Party is an elitist party, consisting of lawyers and landowners. We must involve the whole of India in this movement, but such a massive task is at the moment beyond my abilities. How can we draw the villager, the poor, the untouchable into this movement? It's only when we can combine, when we can prove to the British that they can no longer rule, only then, that we can succeed in winning freedom.'

Alice was disappointed. She had travelled all these miles to hear a speech full of force and anger. She'd wanted Mr Gandhi to be as fiery an orator as Mr Tilak, to reveal a magic formula which would win India her freedom. But he was so quiet, so unsure of himself.

He doesn't have the steel, she thought that night as she lay in bed, encased in mildewed netting. He is bankrupt of ideas, of the will to move against the British. But I mustn't judge him from my own disappointment. He has defied South Africa and could possibly change the destiny of this country.

Alice slept badly and woke early. She discovered an angry rash on her leg and dismissed it as bedbug bites. She anointed the rash with calamine lotion.

'I disappoint you, Miss Soames,' Gandhi said first thing the next morning. She felt he was laughing at her.

'No, no.'

'But yes. You expected a big man full of fire and brimstone, exhorting the people to freedom. I disappoint most people. I am small and thin, skinny I'd say, and I am filled with doubts.'

'But you are stubborn.'

'I've been told that often. But it's not stubbornness, Miss Soames. It's a belief that cannot be shaken. Before a man can move against injustice, he must first arm himself with the moral authority to strike down this justice. You must believe, to the exclusion of all else. That is the reason that I cannot at this point in time answer all your questions as to what will be my role in India, if any. I am sorry that you have travelled such a vast distance for me to reply negatively. I see you as a good woman, Miss Soames. A person like you gives us poor natives confidence in ourselves. Your encouragement helps us gird ourselves for the fight. But we must choose our weapons carefully. We cannot choose arms.'

'Then what, Mr Gandhi?'

'Then, Miss Soames . . .' He opened a hand candidly, flat and empty.

Alice knew she was being watched. She saw the men, who never made any effort to hide themselves, from her window. They worked in shifts and followed her almost apologetically around Bombay. No doubt her visit to Porbander had been reported and her article scanned for any sedition. She realised then that Mr Gandhi had made no comment derogatory of the British. Instead he'd been diplomatically evasive, causing no offence, no reason for his arrest in India.

Alice grew adept at eluding her watchers when she needed to. It was never done for long periods, which would arouse suspicion, but for short ones which could be explained easily. She used the advantage of her race to escape them. If she entered a club or hotel barred to Indians, the Indian policemen had to remain outside while she slipped out of a side entrance.

On this late afternoon, listless from the heat, she watched the man across the street by the paan wallah. He was small and lithe, with a waxed moustache. The Peacock. She'd given each an identity. This one's moustache preoccupied him. His face was narrow, ferret-like and two teeth protruded. She would take pleasure in eluding him soon. But not just yet. She hadn't the energy to rise and dress and the minutes ticked by. She felt her face and forehead. They were hot.

She yearned suddenly for England. It came unexpectedly, sickeningly, a wanting for the cold, for the comfort of log fires. She knew the feeling would pass and waited for her resolve to return. It always weakened when such thoughts flooded her mind. Sometimes she wanted to escape India for ever. Yet she knew she would always be drawn back and would one day die here.

With a great effort, Alice rose. Her skin felt prickly, tender and almost painful to touch. The rash had spread and deepened in colour. Resolutely she dressed and walked out of her house, crossed the road and climbed into a gharri. When she looked back through the window, she saw her Peacock sauntering after her. She told the driver to take her to the Willingdon Club and once through the portals, she entered a make-believe land of England with green lawns and the sound of English voices. The Peacock remained at the gate, lighting a beedi, to wait for her.

She strolled unhurriedly through the high, cool rooms, greeting those she knew, acquaintances who'd not seen her for some time and enquired whether she'd been out-of-station. Alice had been something of a recluse since the ending of her affair and gratefully said yes, I have been away. They pressed her for dinner and luncheon and she promised to call.

The glare hurt her and she retreated a moment, as though it were a wave driving her back. Shielding her face, she crossed the deserted tennis courts and went out of the side gate.

'You do not look well, Miss Soames,' Arvind Joshi said. The union leader studied her in concern and drew her quickly into the building.

'A touch of sun,' Alice said.

She was grateful for the gloom. The room was off a side-street near Crawford Market. The walls were of mud, whitewashed, and cooler than brick. There was a rattan chair, specially for her, and a stool on which were two bananas and a cup of tea. They were Joshi's gesture of hospitality and she knew even something so humble was barely affordable. Once her eyes adjusted, she saw the other two men who immediately rose from the floor and namasted. Joshi introduced them as his organisers. He was much older than they, strong and stocky, with a thrusting jaw. Alice thought him more imposing than Mr Gandhi. Joshi emanated physical strength, the strength to fight. There was in him a hint of coiled violence.

'I requested our meeting because tomorrow morning we will call a strike and we have organised ourselves to march peacefully to the offices of Thomas, Wilson, Whitehead & Company. I have drawn up our requests and I wished you to read them, Miss Soames.'

She took the paper and read it carefully, making notes as she went along. It was written in English and the language and writing were ornate and flowery. Indians loved elaborate language and flourishes, and it took an effort at times to make sense of the document. They were, she supposed, the demands of men everywhere. More pay, better working conditions, shorter hours, a grievance committee, health care, pensions.

'How many people know of this?'

'Why, everyone who will participate.'

'Have you informed the company?'

'We have informed them, Miss Soames. This is a one-day strike only. If we cannot get them to agree to at least some of our demands we will go on indefinite strike. My men will suffer. We're poor but they're determined to win better pay, if nothing else is conceded. You will attend, will you not?' Joshi looked hopeful.

'Of course I will.'

'You will see how we Indians can organise ourselves and respectfully request our rights. This is the first strike ever in Bombay, Miss Soames. As a newspaper lady, you will be witnessing history.' Joshi paused and she saw his strength falter and ebb.

'Are we doing the right thing, Miss Soames?'

'Of course you are, Arvind. How else will you be able to win your rights? Men all over the world have gone on strike, and they've been attacked. You must expect that, you know.'

'Yes, we know. But it's the knowing that frightens us, Miss Soames. We are brave here in these dark conspiratorial corners but out in the sunlight, where men see us, will we still have our courage?'

'I know you will. You have worked hard to organise your men. It's been two years since we first met and your efforts have welded these men together.'

'With your encouragement and guidance.'

'It's been a small contribution, Arvind, minute. I have only advised. I wish I could do more.'

Even as she said 'I wish I could', she knew it sounded weak and ineffectual. She was patting them on the back, guiding them like children, but from afar, remaining uninvolved.

'I want to walk beside you tomorrow,' she said.

Arvind Joshi's eyes widened. His two friends sat up straighter and she knew even something so simple had infused them with confidence. Arvind laughed and clapped.

'We will be proud,' he said. 'But, Miss Soames, your

people will not approve of such an action. You will become an outcast to them, an untouchable.'

'I am anyway.' She rose unsteadily, and lightly held on to the chair. 'What time do we meet, and where?'

'I will come personally to fetch you.'

'No, you have too much to do. I'll come.'

In the mirror early next morning, Alice thought her face matched the pallor of a dawn sky. It looked puffy and cloudy. She swallowed quinine tablets and when she tried to eat her omelette and toast she found the taste nauseating. With a liberal application of powder and rouge she restored a healthy colour to her face though she felt the weakness inside spreading down her stomach and into her legs. Determinedly she set out in the gharri, followed this time by the Mouse watcher. He was thin and nervous, and he held his arms in front of him like paws. She made no effort to lose him and he followed her on foot all the way to the outskirts of the city and to the slums outside the mills.

Arvind Joshi, as he hurried to help her down from the gharri, thought Miss Soames looked like a ghost. Her face was too white and her body trembled. He barely touched her but felt the intense heat in her skin and knew she was ill.

'You shouldn't have come,' he said.

'I couldn't let you down,' Alice said and walked with him to the gathering. There were fifty or sixty men. She'd hoped for several hundred. 'Are these all?'

'Yes, with daylight men lose their courage. But we will march on the mill together.'

He ordered the men to form orderly lines and placed himself in front. Alice took her place next to him. They'd made a banner and unfurled it. 'From each according to his ability, to each according to his need'. It was twenty feet across and carried by two men at either end of the front line. Other men carried placards. 'Mill workers starve'. 'Mill workers request more pay'.

Alice worried about the banner most. In its simplicity

lay the threat of revolution and whoever read it would be provoked.

'Why did you choose that message?'

'Because it's a just message,' Arvind said. 'I heard someone speak it and I thought to myself, that is how the world should be and not one of such inequality.' He stepped out of line and squinted at it in pride. 'I copied it myself. It is correct?'

'Yes, it is.'

A large and curious crowd had gathered. Women, children, pi-dogs, a few men. Most of the men were at work. The crowd was silent and stared in some surprise at Alice in the centre of the front line. Slowly the demonstration moved off along the dirt road towards the mills half a mile away.

In front of the gates, Alice saw a long, thin khaki line of policemen carrying lathis. Two British inspectors stood a couple of feet in front of them with drawn revolvers. Though there was no sign of interest beyond the gates she heard the thunder of machinery vibrating through the earth as they approached. It travelled up her legs, shaking her, making her dizzy. She put out her arm and took a grip of Arvind's elbow to steady herself. The sun had risen and burned her eyes, sweat trickled down her face and her body. The line of policemen gently wavered. She wasn't sure what to expect.

'What will they do?'

'Nothing, Miss Soames, unless we provoke them, and I have instructed the men to do nothing. We will present our petition and disband peacefully.'

Alice sensed the silence, the stillness. Not even a bird crossed the air between them and the police line. On either side she glimpsed men and women, waiting and watching. She didn't turn her head but fixed her stare on the head constable, a tall and well-muscled man, with a beard shading his features. He tapped his lathi patiently on the earth. When they were twenty yards away, she looked at the Europeans. They were both staring at her in surprise and in embarrassment. Her presence meant they had to be very careful in their handling of the demonstration, and she felt they hated her for letting the side down. Two cricket elevens meeting on a dirty and dusty road, she thought, and tried to smile, but the muscles hurt.

Arvind stepped forward, turned and held up his arms. The procession stopped moving. He took out his petition and holding it in both hands respectfully stepped forward to the police line. There was no company official in sight to receive it and Alice thought "Now what can we do?" Arvind hesitated, then moved down the line, intending to work his way round it and thrust his petition through the bars of the locked gate.

As he moved down the line a lathi rose slowly and descended swiftly on Arvind's back. Another snaked out lower down and struck him across the legs, driving him back. Two more policemen joined in the attack, using their lathis as prods and Alice screamed.

'Leave him alone! Leave him alone!'

But in the growl behind and around her, her voice went unheard. She knew what would happen next, even as it began to unfold. By beating Arvind, the police knew they would provoke his followers. Four of them now rushed forward to rescue Arvind from the blows raining down on him and in so doing they released the flood behind them. Men angrily ran at the policemen beating Arvind. One was struck down, his lathi seized. In the dust and confusion, in the wild dance of men struggling and heaving against each other, Alice saw the petition, the beautifully written petition, fall from Arvind's hand. Men trampled it, and it turned as brown as the road.

'Get them back, Arvind. Get them back.'

Even though she doubted he heard, he understood. He managed to half-stagger to his feet, shouting orders lost in the uproar. One or two near him heard and retreated. Alice saw him fall to one knee, pushed from behind and in the haze of dust and legs, she saw a man approaching him. It seemed as though he bent down to help Arvind but instead she saw the revolver suddenly appear in his helping hand.

'Arvind . . . Arvind . . .'

She fell to her knees, pushed from behind. The shot jerked her as if it passed through her own head. The echo continued exploding as Arvind fell and dust swiftly muted the bloody wound in his head. She looked up along the hand and arm into a bland, round face liberally scarred with pock marks. The eyes were hidden, the glare on the spectacles turning them to mirrored discs.

Alice shut her eyes tight to stop the spinning, to silence the flow of her own roaring blood that drove out all other noise. She fell forward onto her face as the men retreated and ran, frightened by the shot and the bodies of Arvind and Alice lying a few feet from each other in the dirt.

Alice looked muddy white and drained of life. I could be dead for all the blood there is in my face, she thought. Her hand was skeletal, heavily veined, almost scaly, and she wanted to cry for her lost beauty. But tears only further weakened her; draining her low reserve of strength. She had shrunk to just over half her normal weight, and had only managed to put back a few pounds.

How easily illness destroys vanity, Alice thought as she carefully applied powder and rouge, to soften the muddy colouring. She was careful too in her dressing on this special occasion. The cotton dress hung loosely on her and she slipped on a heavy cardigan to disguise its bad fit.

It was cold on the verandah and she took a chair facing the distant peaks. In the wintry sunlight they looked near and accessible. The verandah plunged down the slope of the hill abruptly and she could watch the winding road that led up to the boarding house on the edge of Kufri. She'd come to the Himalayan foothills to recuperate on Dr Malcolm's orders, though she had at first protested. But now she was glad. The heat of Bombay would only have drained her further. Here she felt her strength slowly returning, like a tide which had receded beyond the horizon. The chill air cleansed her lungs. She ate heartily and took long walks through the deodars and pine forests surrounding Kufri. The sense of dying gradually left her.

What she'd thought was a rash caught from those grey sheets in the Porbander dak bungalow were the eggs of a parasite. They'd infected her blood and eventually would have killed her. The doctors in the Bombay hospital had treated her for sunstroke. It was fortunate that Dr Malcolm had come on duty later and noticed the angry weal on her leg. He'd cut it open, scraped it clean and disinfected the wound. But even so she had been delirious for weeks.

Alice shuddered at the memory of her nightmares. They must lurk on our underside, she thought, like worms and slugs beneath rocks, and in our illness they rise up to strike at us. I hadn't thought monsters and demons existed even in nightmares but these were real and frightening.

She was glad to see the tonga straining up the steep hill and called out to the bearer to prepare tea and cake for Dr Malcolm. He had written a week earlier, enquiring about her health and making an appointment to see her. He was on his way to the foothills to look into the sexual habits of a hill tribe he'd heard about. They would figure prominently in his next volume.

He didn't walk but strode across the verandah, hands behind his back, shoulders sloped forward, a cigarette jammed into a corner of his mouth. He only ever touched it to throw it away.

'You'll kill yourself one day with those cigarettes.'

'I'm sure I shall, my dear girl, but at least I don't allow myself to be bitten by strange and exotic insects.'

'I thought it was a bed bug.'

'Even the bed bugs out here are strange and exotic where a fair English skin is concerned.' He stared at her unwinkingly. 'You look a bit better than when I last saw you, but you still look pretty terrible, even apart from that ghastly rouge. I just don't understand why you women paint yourselves up like kathak dancers.'

'Certainly not for the benefit of rude men like you.'

'I like 'em young and buxom, my dear. Let's have a look. Stick out your tongue.' He leaned over her and examined her tongue and eyes and checked her pulse. 'You'll live.'

'For a man who's perennially decrepit you have ambitious ideas!'

'It's the decrepitude that attracts the fillies, woman. And keeps 'em from proposing marriage.' He tossed his cigarette over his shoulder, barely missing the bearer. 'Ah, if I were twenty years younger . . . !'

'You certainly do give confidence to your female patients.'

'I'd give 'em something else but their husbands would probably have me horsewhipped. I am surprised you haven't found yourself another handsome young husband, m'dear. Once you've got your health back you should think about it.'

'You forget, I'm not yet divorced.'

'Ah, the Colonel. A powerful man. It must have been a strange marriage. He's quite single-minded in what he does – serving India and that queer business he's in.'

She was glad Dr Malcolm showed no further curiosity about her personal life. Alice poured tea and they idled away an hour in banter. Alice found herself roaring with laughter. She enjoyed his company, knowing none of his insults was meant. He was an eccentric man, who cared nothing for convention and she wished she'd met him earlier in her life. Eventually they fell into a companionable silence. Alice hastily dismissed such notions. They were the romantic longings of a schoolgirl, or a lonely, ageing spinster. He was lost in his thoughts, and she waited awhile.

'War,' he said. 'I hate war.'

'Will there be war? I'm sure we'll try to avoid it.'

'Empires, my dear woman, never avoid wars. Wars feed their sense of invincibility. It seems inevitable with the situation building up in Europe. If only doctors were the ones who had to declare war, not the politicians who never see the blood and entrails.'

'But it won't affect us here, surely.'

'It will when England gets involved in the fighting. War affects everyone, no matter how distant they are from the battlefield. Dead men leave behind widows and children, and grieving mothers and fathers. I'm glad I'm no longer a young man. Otherwise, I'd have to volunteer, and I'd have to tell men they were going to die and see the sheer terror in their faces. Poor bastards. I had enough of that on the frontier.'

'I lost my son Richard up there,' Alice said. 'I never met him as a man, and I'll never ever forgive myself.'

'I'm sure you will eventually. You must, because there's no one else to do it for you. We can't live with guilt. It destroys our lives.' He rose and his sense of frivolity returned. 'Erotic indulgence, m'dear! The balm for all our wounds. If all those dried-up old women who govern us were sent off to the hill tribes for a while, they'd learn a thing or two. I'd shock you silly if I told you, m'dear, but believe me, they'd abandon all thoughts of war and killings in sheer ecstasy. Now, if I don't see you on my way down be sure to call on me in Bombay. I must examine you more thoroughly when you're healthy and lively.'

She watched him stride back to the tonga, tossing a cigarette over his shoulder as he went.

Alice was glad to return to Bombay at the end of the month. The rest had strengthened her but work was her main solace and escape from thoughts and loneliness.

The shadow of the coming war in Europe had reached out to touch India. The rumours and whispers among the men who ruled India were tense with the excitement of the adventure, while those of the Indians themselves, she found to her dismay, were all in favour of the war. They were muting their demands for a greater share in government and vying to prove their support of the British. Alice heard of princes bravely volunteering their small armies for the war. But the government was uninterested in these offers of support and Alice wrote, in her first article since her return, that they would rue the day when they squandered such an amount of goodwill.

Now that she had the strength, she went to call on Arvind Joshi's widow and children. She'd never met them and only knew of their existence from the little he'd told her. But in the slum where Arvind had lived, none knew of their whereabouts. She stood in the narrow muddy lane, helpless. She'd brought money and gifts for the family and clutched them like dead waifs in her arms. But the word quickly spread that Soames memsahib had returned and one of Arvind's assistants, one of those who had marched with her on the day of the strike, came hurrying up the lane. He insisted she come into his hut and take tea.

'They went back to their village,' he told her and waved to the shimmering horizon and the thin road, which led into the infinity of India. 'Without a man a woman and children are lost. But we have a new leader now, memsahib. You must meet Mr Bandari.'

'Has Mr Bandari achieved much with the company?'

'No. He cautions us to be careful. He says a time will come for the strike, but that Arvind was too impatient. We must grow in numbers.'

'Is he a good man?' she asked, and read in the young man's evasive eyes that he wasn't.

She strode along beside him to the far end of the slum, to a large brick, tile-roofed house. It was the only one in the neighbourhood and bustled with prosperity. It was the union headquarters, she was told, and also the residence of their union leader. She ducked her head and entered. Men sat around, whispering to each other, and stared at her without any friendliness. Her companion beckoned a man, and when he stepped into the muted lights she saw that Mr Bandari wore glasses and that his face was heavily scarred with pockmarks.

Alice turned and walked out. She felt helpless and

angry. He followed her out into the sunlight and she faced her own reflection in his glasses. The other men would have also joined him but he gestured them back into the house.

'I saw you shoot Arvind.'

'Memsahib, you must have imagined such a thing,' he said. 'I was very distant from here and only came after poor Arvind was murdered.'

'Well, I intend to report this to the police. I gave them a description of you.'

'But the police will have to prove such a thing, and it's your word against mine. And there are many witnesses who will attest to the fact I wasn't present here. Did you see me march?'

'No. But there were many faces.'

'But you recognised me in these so many faces? Arvind was a good man but too impetuous.'

'He was a good man. An honest one. He wouldn't have built such a house for himself.'

'This is only to prove my authority, memsahib. People respect you only if you take one step above them. Memsahib, I know you mean well. I don't know about these unions; they are foreign. I am a jobber. Do you understand that?'

'No.'

'I came to this city years ago from a small village. I worked in the mills too. And then others came too from my village and because they knew me, they asked me for help. I helped. I got them work, found them shelter, took care of them when they were ill . . .'

'For money, no doubt?'

'And this union you bring from foreign parts doesn't ask for money too? But a union won't help the people from my village. I am the only one who will. There are many like me in this place, helping the people from their villages. We are a union in our own way and you should have learned more about us. Next time you interfere in our lives, we might have to kill the memsahib.'

He smiled but she saw no humour in his eyes, only

a dark and dreadful hatred for her. He turned and returned to his house. Alice felt near to tears. The sun grew blurred as she walked. She knew, helplessly, that she didn't understand anything.

'Damn you all,' she whispered.

# 17

# April–September 1914

There were thin lines of pain, barely visible, on Lord Hardinge's face. Like the quick shadings of a fine pencil they brushed his mouth and the corners of his eyes. The Colonel added them to the sketch on his blotter. The drawing wasn't a good likeness of the Viceroy. It made him look far older and tireder even than he was. The office was taking its toll of his spirit. The bomb attack hadn't caused pain so much as inconvenience. He'd had to spend two months lying on his stomach while the superficial wounds caused by the nails healed. The real damage was done deeper down. There seemed to be a permanent flinch in his face, as though he expected another attack at any moment.

But a yet far deeper wound dealt him by fate was the sudden death of Winifred. She had returned to London for a rest and had then fallen seriously ill. She had been rushed to hospital for a major operation and had died there. Looking at his face, the Colonel saw a deep melancholy in the Viceroy. He depended heavily on fourteen-year-old Diamond now.

Only three of them sat in the Viceroy's office in the Delhi Circuit bungalow. The third, General Sir Beauchamp Duff, had journeyed down specially from military headquarters in Simla for the discussion. He was the tallest of them, an erect straight-shouldered man with tiny broken veins in his cheeks, which gave him a strange terracotta hue. As Commander-in-Chief of the Indian Army, he was also the Military Member on the Viceroy's Council and spent more time shuttling back and forth to Delhi for meetings than inspecting his troops. His membership was the inheritance of General Kitchener's battle for power with Lord Curzon of nine years ago.

This wasn't simply another routine meeting of the Viceroy's Council. Lord Hardinge needed the advice of only these two men to begin with. The Viceroy was concerned with war. The one rumbling in Europe was but faintly heard in Delhi. They read of it in three-week-old newspapers and scarcely gave it much thought. If England did enter into a war with Germany, they were all confident that it would be over in weeks, if not days. The empire, after all, stretched from one corner of the world to the other and they had no reason to doubt its great power.

There was, however, the possibility of an engagement much nearer India. For the last few months, reports had been reaching Whitehall that the Germans were making definite diplomatic and political advances in Turkey. The Colonel had the reports and was equally disturbed. The Germans were attempting to woo the Sheikh of Kuwait out of British influence. They had also encouraged the Turks to lay claim to the Qatar peninsula. And they were protesting that Britain enjoyed an unfair trade advantage in Baghdad. The British government couldn't ignore these threats. Apart from trade, there were the huge oil fields in Arabistan but fortunately the Sheikh of Muhammorah was a good friend to the British. The added threat to the oilfields and to the pipeline carrying the crude oil from Arabistan down to the island of Abadan at the mouth of Shat-el-Arab had stirred up a hornet's nest in London.

'I gather the ball's in our court,' Lord Hardinge said. 'The Military Secretary, Sir Edmund Barrow, has suggested that as Arabia is within the government of India's sphere of influence, it is we who should take some action to discourage the Germans. They've already influenced

Enver Pasha, the Turkish war minister, to replace British officers serving in the Turkish Army with German ones. And our friend the Kaiser has gone so far as to declare himself a Haji after his visit to Mecca. He now calls himself, in Turkey at least, the Haji Mohammed Guilliano.'

'It's not going to be an easy matter,' the Colonel said, and stopped his drawing. He drew lines through it, destroying it, obscuring the Viceroy's face. 'If we do send a military expedition to Turkey, we're going to have the Indian Muslims up in arms against us for attacking their brothers in Turkey.'

'But if, somehow, that problem were dealt with, would a small military expedition be possible?' the Viceroy asked.

'We have the manpower, certainly,' General Duff said stiffly. 'The Indian Army is one of the finest fighting forces in the world. I'm sure we'll be able to teach the Turks and their German officers a lesson or two.'

'Can you give me some idea as to how long we'd need for such an expedition?'

'The whole thing shouldn't last more than a couple of weeks. My men have fought the Afghans, and I doubt whether the Turks match up to them in bravery and toughness. I would think we could be in and out of Turkey in a fortnight, a month at the most. I'll talk to my officers and send in a more detailed report. When will this expedition take place?'

'I'll pass on your comments to Sir Edmund. He'll have to write a proposal for Whitehall. I wouldn't think before September. Possibly a winter campaign would suit our men better.' The Viceroy turned to the Colonel. 'Colonel, what can we do about our Muslims? We must keep them in order, somehow.'

'I've given that some thought. The Turkish Muslims are Sunnis and believe the Sultan is the rightful spiritual heir of the prophet. The Indian Muslims are Shia and believe the Agha Khan to be the spiritual successor. We must somehow persuade the Agha Khan to support our cause and get him to persuade the Indian Muslims not to protest. But that initiative should come from London, not from us.'

'I'll pass on your suggestions too. Then we'll wait and see.'

The Colonel didn't return to his office. He no longer worked in a tent but in a small and overcrowded brick building. It was as temporary a structure as the tent and once the Secretariat was completed, whenever that was, it would be demolished. The air all around was a permanent dusty yellow but, despite the activity and the thousands of labourers milling around, nothing seemed to have risen out of the hard earth. He summoned his gharri and instructed his driver to take him out to the tomb of the Mughal emperor Humayun. They passed elephants and bullock carts, and endless lines of men and women and children carrying earth and stones and bricks on their heads in wicker baskets. At the centre of all this activity, and barely visible through the dust, was a large tent. It was the headquarters of Edwin Lutyens and Herbert Baker, the joint architects of New Delhi. He was surprised that they were still sharing the tent, as they were already not on speaking terms. The Viceroy also had ceased to communicate with Lutyens, and messages were carried between him and Lutyens by an ADC.

It was a relief to escape the dust and stroll in the large, silent garden. The domed tomb towered above him and he thought of the waste and extravagance of shrouding a man's body in marble and sandstone and brick. He didn't deny its beauty or magnificence. "But of what use is such grandeur," the Colonel thought. "It's only an ornament of the Mughal Empire and of no earthly use at all. It offers no shelter, no purpose. We at least will leave behind a monument, this new Delhi, which will be of some use." The Colonel walked for a while in the neglected garden and sat on a bench by the fountain, shaded by a gold mohur. The murmur of water was musical but he didn't hear it; nor did he notice the langurs pause in their play to watch him before strolling along the parapet.

He felt bleak. His heart, like the interior of that tomb, was cavernous and deserted. He missed Sushila and knew he always would. The passage of time hadn't decreased the longing nor erased the memory of her. At unexpected moments, in his exhaustion, he yearned to rest his head on her pillow and seek comfort in the warmth of her embrace. Even her perfume still lingered on in his memory like a stain.

He had experienced a tremendous pain as he'd walked out of her house that last time. It was his pride, his stern belief in his Englishness, that had kept him walking on without looking back, knowing he had been dismissed from paradise. He cursed his own upbringing, his inability to bend, to sway. "We're English and damned proud but what is this pride worth if I am to suffer such longing for the rest of my days? I never felt any regret for Alice, only rage, a chilling anger at her betrayal. If I had not put her in a tonga and had her taken away, I could have killed her. But Sushila wasn't the betrayer. I was. Our bodies created that child, but I can never claim it as my own, nor grant it the legitimacy of my name."

He still didn't know whether he was the father of a boy or a girl. He'd waited a few months, wanting her to write one of her sweet love letters, forgiving him. But she'd remained silent. He'd made arrangements for his bank to start making payments to her, but it was only when the money was returned that he'd instituted an enquiry. It had been a shock for him to learn that Sushila had literally vanished off the face of the earth. She'd walked out of the house on that very same evening, she and the unborn child, and none had seen her since. Her father had been distraught too, but equally ignorant. He believed that with the death of her husband, Sushila had committed suicide, preferring that to brutal widowhood. There was no trace found of her body either. But the Colonel didn't believe Sushila would have committed suicide, not with her child yet unborn. And she was also too strong a woman to take her own life. "I know she's alive, I know she's out there, hiding in the vastness of

India. I may never see her again, and it's all my own fault."

He remembered the poem they'd recited to each other after the dinner party at her father's house, a poem by Nishani, an engraver serving in the court of the Mughal emperor Akbar. Sushila had recited the first few lines, and he'd completed it. Now the poem haunted him with its prophecy.

*The old Enchanter, in his patchwork cloak,*
*Sits weaving spells to bind us to his throne,*
*While, seeing nothing in the turquoise vault,*
*We dwell in fear, uncertain and alone –*
*Forgetting that one night he made the moon*
*(By magic from a fish with silver scales),*
*Which in his blue glass bottle, flecked with stars,*
*Unerring on her course serenely sails;*
*He closed the stopper with a thousand seals*
*Of wax the candle of the moon supplied,*
*Since when no mortal has evaded Fate,*
*However long, however hard, he tried.*

He whispered out aloud and fell silent, remembering her fading laughter and seeming to hear it again, though he knew it was only the waters murmuring in the fountain.

The Jat Sikh who came to pawn his wife's gold bangle was an elderly man. His beard was unkempt and greying, and Isaac Newton noted the deep creases of despair around his eyes. For the last half an hour he'd listened to his complaints – the poor rains, the bad crops, the starving buffaloes. Newton had been patient but now, having paid him some money, he wanted the man to go. Then the Sikh told him he had a cousin in Vancouver and wanted to emigrate.

'Then you should,' Newton said. He tossed the bangle on a pile of other bangles and the Sikh winced at such a casual gesture.

'That is what I wrote, saying I will come there. But he now says they're all returning.'

'And why would they return to such misery?'

'To free India, of course. My cousin tells me it's only because India is in chains that they are treated so badly in this Canada. So by returning and freeing India, they will then be free and proud men in their own right.'

Newton took a pinch of snuff and sneezed politely to one side. He shouted for his chokra to bring tea for his friend and also some samosas. There was the possibility of an interesting tale.

'And how will they free India? By just coming here and shouting at the British?'

'With guns. Are you such a fool?' The Sikh chuckled. 'Only with guns can we be freed. He tells me they've gathered enough donations for such a cause and purchased guns and bullets and other things from the Americans.'

'But an army must use those guns,' Newton said and directed the chokra to serve the tea. He was a small, bright boy and reminded him of his nephew Narain when he was a child. He had a good memory and even as he passed between Newton and the Sikh, Newton signalled that he should go out and wait for the Sikh. Then he was to follow him.

'They are bringing an army of men. Thousands upon thousands will return soon.'

'How soon?'

'Soon. They have booked passage on a boat.'

Newton thought deeply about this information and with a sigh concluded that he had to discover whether it was correct. The old Sikh could have been merely entertaining him with tall tales, as a means to pass the time and enjoy Newton's hospitality. The thousands could be two, the guns and bullets bows, arrows and spears. So, with another sigh of regret for his disrupted life, he rose.

Before he reported to the Sir Colonel sahib, he had to be certain of this story. He had an unsuspecting informer in a Sikh cloth merchant. Balbir Singh travelled from the mountains in the north to as far south as Benares and was more dependable and accurate than any poor farmer.

Newton hoped he would find Balbir Singh in his shop on the west side of the Golden Temple. Though the man was getting on, he never ceased his travelling, and most of the time was never in Amritsar. He had so many sons by so many wives, each kept in a separate town, that Newton was constantly confused as to which son ran the shop. Also Balbir had brought up the boys alternately as Hindus and Sikhs. Newton enjoyed the old rogue's company. His stories had always amused him. He liked best the story of the Turki wrestling woman who had wanted to marry Balbir when, as a young man, he had visited Samarkand with his father.

Isaac Newton was ignorant of the fact that Kim too knew Balbir Singh and had heard the same story. Nearly eight years ago, Kim had travelled with Balbir's caravan from Benares to Rae Bareli with the prostitute Lakshmi whom he'd saved from a Bombay brothel and was taking back to her ancestral village. Balbir Singh had parted company with Kim with regret and often wondered what had happened to the young man. He'd vaguely heard the rumour that Kim had been arrested in Rae Bareli and sent to Tihar Gaol in Delhi. But apart from that rumour, Kim had completely vanished from the face of the earth.

Newton locked his pawn shop with three huge padlocks and threaded his way through the narrow, crowded streets. There are too many people in this world, he thought. We make too many babies only because God created such exquisite pleasure in a strange part of our bodies. If there were no pleasure, we wouldn't suffer the pain for our children.

To his relief, Balbir Singh was in his shop. He was as spare and tall as Isaac Newton with a face burned dark by his years of travelling. His beard was ashen and covered half his chest. He sat cross-legged at a low desk in which he kept the money, while two of his sons served the customers who ebbed in and out of the shop. Harish Chand was a slim, wiry young man with a quick smile. He was Hindu. His elder brother, Grehwal, a Sikh, was stocky and strong and usually managed the shop when his father was travelling. There were still three more sons but they weren't there at the moment. Balbir was pleased to see his new-found friend Isaac Newton. He thought it a strange name but it seemed appropriate for the man. Newton sat beside him while Harish brought him tea and a biscuit. He sipped while they talked about inconsequential matters. Balbir Singh was planning another journey up to Rawalpindi and was gathering his energies. Soon, he promised, he would settle down – in Amritsar, near his beloved Golden Temple. But until then he had to placate the wives and children scattered along his route. They expected him at certain times and he had to show himself.

'And why didn't you marry, my friend?' Balbir Singh asked. 'A wife may be a problem but she has her uses in the home and in the bed.'

'When I was very young, only a child, I was betrothed to my cousin. She was a pretty girl, shy and sweet. And even after our marriage while we were too young to consummate this nuptial, I would play with her as a close friend. We lived in a small village near Arcot. One day, when she went to fetch water from the well, some distance from the house, she fell in and drowned. It was very sad as I loved her without knowing the reasons. My parents made efforts to arrange another marriage but I could see myself with none other than my childhood friend. I think of her often and wonder how different my life might have been. Probably I would never have left my village. Probably . . .' He fell silent and Balbir Singh respected the silence at this sad tale. He wasn't to know that Newton had nearly told him that 'probably I wouldn't have started to work for the Colonel sahib and become an agent'.

'You are lucky then, my friend, not to have married. As I grow older, I'm easily confused about which son came from which mother. These two badmashes at least have the same mother and remain here. But it's when I travel and my other sons join me, that the confusion arises.'

'Other men only have one wife. It's entirely your greed that is now causing you these problems. And how far north will you go this time?'

'To Kabul, where I have an Afghani wife and two sons. I spend a month in the spring there, because it's most pleasant.'

'I had a sardar villager in my shop today and I suggested he should travel not to Kabul but to Canada. He told me that his cousin who is there, is now planning to return and free India from British rule.'

'I've heard that too,' Balbir said. 'The Gadhar party in San Fran . . . cisco has organised this thing. They will carry guns and bombs and drive the British out. We Sikhs always like a good fight. Why else would we be fighting throughout our history and losing every time? This will be another we will lose.'

'But this one is to be soon.'

'Yes.' Balbir called to Grehwal. 'That woman yesterday, the one whose brother's wife's uncle lives in Canada. What did she say about his returning?'

'She said he was coming on a ship with a strange name. A Jopon ship, and there will be many of them.'

The Colonel heard Newton's report only in July, for Newton was a thorough man and had no wish to convey a bazaar rumour to the Sir Colonel sahib. He had managed to obtain two letters written by the Sikhs planning this invasion. They had been boastful and angry letters, naming friends who would be on this expedition with them. The letters had been written to a carpenter in Ludhiana from his cousin. It was the village of the Jat Sikh who had first told him casually about the expedition. The boy had followed him and reported back to Newton that he'd heard of this second letter; the whole village knew, as both letters had been read out by the local gurudwar. Newton had paid generously for these letters on the pretext that he wished to aid the expedition against the British.

Newton heard the Sir Colonel sahib sigh at this act of futility. Even a thousand, or 10,000, men with guns wouldn't overthrow British rule.

'But why the Sikhs?' the Colonel asked. The question wasn't addressed to Newton but past his shoulder to the distant mountains framed by the window. At least here in Simla, where the capital moved during the summers to escape the dreadful heat of Delhi, the Colonel's office was permanent as it had always been. It was a high-ceilinged, comfortable room, worn and familiar. His books lived on their shelves and not locked in trunks; his paintings hung on the walls and a small glass cupboard displayed his mementoes. 'They have been loyal to us for nearly a century. They fought on our side during the Mutiny and we've rewarded their loyalty a hundredfold.'

It was this betrayal that hurt the Colonel and drew out a long sigh of bewilderment. If they couldn't trust the Sikhs any longer, who else was there?

He dismissed Newton with instructions to keep gathering information. It was time now to act swiftly, even cruelly, to dissuade others from making another such attempt. Even a small skirmish with these returning Sikhs would inflame the Punjab and the flames would spread across India like wildfire. This time, instead of sepoys, the rebels were Sikhs and they could infect the other Sikhs serving in the army. And the Hindus in the Punjab would join them too in this uprising.

The Colonel immediately sent a telegram to Washington requesting the Embassy to find out the name of the Japanese ship that was carrying the Sikhs from San Francisco to India. He also asked them to request the American immigration authorities to discover as much as they could about these Sikhs. The Colonel waited impatiently for a week to receive a reply from Washington. Then he dropped into the office of the Home Member, and passed on the report, exaggerating the numbers to lend it a sense of urgency. He too sighed, and they both stared out at the mountains. Simla was a delight after the dust and heat of Delhi and they'd both hoped for some peace and quiet. He had planned a holiday in Kashmir and knew he wasn't going to make it. He'd have to send his wife and children alone. Both men then requested an appointment with the Viceroy.

'It's the last thing we need now,' Lord Hardinge said. 'We have this affair in Turkey demanding our attention. Whitehall is asking us to prepare an expedition and once they've chosen the date, the army will sail for Mesopotamia.'

'I suggest we stop these Sikhs at the border,' the Colonel said, quite indifferent to Mesopotamia. It wasn't within his sphere of influence, only India concerned him. 'Arrest them, and try and either hang or gaol them.'

'How are we to stop them at the border? The Foreigners Ordinance Act only allows us to stop aliens entering India. These men are Indian and have every right of entry.'

'I think we should draft a new bill,' the Home Member said. 'This one will deal specifically with Indians intent on returning to India to cause discontent or advocating armed rebellion.'

'That's your department then. Once the Ingress into India Ordinance is drafted, I'll sign it into law. Any idea when this shipload is going to land?'

'Some time in September, I gather. The passages have been booked. There are in fact two ships. One is the *Kamagata Maru*, the other the *Taro Maru*. The Gadhar party is pretty well organised. I heard from Washington that they've even bought an aeroplane and are training some pilots. Apart from those two Japanese ships, there are also two American ships, the *Annie Larsen* and the *Maverick*. They're supposed to be carrying the arms and ammunition.'

The Colonel didn't command the security force that awaited the *Kamagata Maru* as it docked in Calcutta in early September. He watched from some distance, allowing his binoculars to play along the docks stretching out in the dull haze along the banks of the Hoogli river. The day was hot and moist, and as he watched the ship drop anchor he imagined another one in Bombay pulling up its anchor in another week or two to set sail for the Persian Gulf. The government of India had received instructions from Whitehall just the week before to assemble a force and dispatch it to the Gulf. The 6th Poona Division, under the command of Major General Charles Vere Ferrers Townshend, was instructed to show the flag. It was presumed that, once the force arrived, the Turks would withdraw.

The Colonel wished he were young enough to join in such adventures. Two or three weeks in Mesopotamia would make a pleasant change for a young officer. He'd fight a skirmish or two, see a little action and win himself some glory. He remembered his younger days on the North West Frontier. They'd been exciting and heady and he'd been full of zest and energy then. Increasingly these days he felt listless, and knew the burden of his occupation was getting too much for him.

He had not wanted to return to Calcutta. The city brought back too many memories, too many feelings of loss. Richard had been with him here, and they'd had their last New Year's Eve together at the club. He clearly recalled that Kim too had been with them, though he had spent most of the time with Dr Malcolm and only joined them for a drink. And Elizabeth had been quiet and brooding, as though she had some premonition that it was the last time the family would ever be gathered together. No, he no longer liked Calcutta and was glad the capital had been moved to Delhi. It was a fresh lease, a break with the past, especially his own.

He watched the ship dock and Punjabi policemen commanded by British and Indian officers move up the gangplank and onto the deck. Though this was Bengal Province, the Colonel had suggested that Punjab should be responsible for this action, since the Sikhs were planning to launch their attacks from the Punjab. He waited; half an hour passed, then an hour. Then the first group of Sikhs, chained together, slowly trickled down the gangplank, flanked by the policemen. They'd been arrested under the Ingress Ordinance. They were prodded and pushed towards the waiting cart. He was pleased they had surrendered quietly. He had dreaded the prospect of any shooting and for this reason had suggested that the docks should be cordoned off. Even a small skirmish would be enough to stir this city into violence.

By dusk it was over. The Colonel climbed into the gharri and on the way back to the government guest house, on an impulse, went out of his way to go past Sushila's house. He told the driver to stop at the gate and stepped into the garden. It was deserted and the house was shuttered and quiet. It had an air of mourning, a sense of the uselessness of its own existence. A lovely and lonely woman had inhabited this place and the Colonel reflected that he had only immeasurably increased her sadness by his behaviour. He lingered a moment longer. The air was filled with the perfume of flowers, reminding him painfully of Sushila. He knew he hoped to see a familiar light in the window to the far side. If it did come on, he wasn't sure whether he would knock on the shutter and call out her name. But no light came on and he climbed back into the gharri.

The Colonel didn't tell Isaac Newton of his visit to Amritsar. It was meant to be secret and he passed through the crowded city to the central prison in a closed gharri as it grew dark. The gharri entered the prison and the Colonel slipped into the brooding granite building and was met by the Superintendent of the prison in the privacy of his office. The Superintendent immediately rang his bell and two of the Sikhs arrested on the ship were led in, still chained to each other.

One was a portly man with a neatly trimmed beard. The Colonel suspected his hair would be trimmed too under his turban, maybe even cut short in the American fashion. He had pale brown eyes, almost yellow and a hook of a nose. The other was tall and would have been slim except for the round rise of his paunch, not yet reduced by prison fare. He too wore a neatly trimmed beard but his eyes were hidden by thick, steel-rimmed glasses. They both wore western dress and waited quietly, almost stoically.

The Colonel studied them both carefully in the lamplight. Shadows filled the crevices of their faces. He saw no swellings or abrasions; nor did they move as if in pain. It didn't bother him that they could have been beaten up in the lock-up by the police. Beatings were an accepted punishment; they instilled discipline. But he didn't want beatings used as a coercion.

'I gather you don't wish to be hanged.'

'No,' the one with glasses, Kirpal Singh, said. He noted the tightening around the Colonel's mouth and added softly, as if as a deliberate afterthought: 'sahib.'

'And the same applies to you,' the Colonel looked down at the file. 'Vancouver Singh.'

'Yes, sahib. We were threatened with beatings if we didn't join this ship. We were both happy in Canada and had no wish to engage in a fight against the British.'

'But you're here and I can still have you both hanged, or else transported for life.'

'Yes, sahib,' they both said.

'But I can also arrange to have you released with no charges against either of you. I'm told by the Superintendent you are both willing to co-operate with the British authorities. Is that correct?'

'Yes, sahib. We have always been loyal to the Crown. Both our fathers were military men . . .'

'I hope you're not lying.'

'We're not, sahib. We will prove our loyalty if we are given the chance.'

'We'll see,' the Colonel stared unblinkingly at the two men. His eyes made them flinch and they knew he was a ruthless man. 'If you should fail me I will reach out for you both, wherever you are hiding, and hang you within the hour. You understand?'

'Yes, sahib.'

'I'm going to release you both, separately. You will continue to behave as you always have. You will continue to be members of the Gadhar party in your respective villages. But you will constantly keep me informed of all their activities. From time to time you will receive instructions from me and you will execute these instructions promptly. Depending on your service, I will see that you are well rewarded. If you should fail in this, or lie to me, you will both die.' They nodded vigorously. 'You'll communicate with me by letter. You can both write?'

'Only Punjabi, sahib.'

'That's fine. I don't expect the reports in English. We will never meet again unless you attempt to deceive me. Then it will be on the gallows, and mine will be the last face you will see on this earth.'

# 18

## March 1914–January 1915

Even as the glittering sword blade descended on his right shoulder and tapped him once, Lal Bahadhur Ram Shanker felt his power seeping away. It was a sensation so strange and contrary to what he had expected of this all-important event, that momentarily his confidence faltered. It seemed his right knee was pinioned to the ground and his strength was draining out of him. He peered swiftly, almost shyly, around the gathering to reassure himself that he was not the only one present at this ceremony and that there were indeed others who witnessed his elevation to the knighthood. It could have been a dream; longings created their own reality. Yes, they were all present. To Lord Hardinge's right were the Members of his Council and their wives, and to the left princes and prominent Indians, a few of them knights too. All were familiar, yet he couldn't recognise clearly any individual face. They were a blur. Behind him, he knew, were many other witnesses, European and Indian. They were so still, he heard only a discreet cough, the rustle of a dress. Though the knighting took place in Delhi it didn't lessen the honour bestowed upon him. The Viceroy was the King in India. Only a handful of those knighthoods granted in India were actually conferred in London. Most, European and Indian, were knighted by the Viceroy. Naturally Lal Bahadhur would have preferred the sword to be wielded by His Majesty. It was in the nature of such an honour that the King's presence granted it an additional prestige. Lal Bahadhur knew that Colonel Creighton had been knighted by the King-Emperor himself.

Lal Bahadhur looked past the Viceroy and caught the kindly smile of Lady Diamond Hardinge sitting to one side in an elaborately wrought chair with a high back. Above her head was the large portrait of His Imperial Majesty King George V looking down on Lal Bahadhur Ram Shanker, his face benign and approving. The wintry Delhi sunshine, clear and hard, fell across the painting giving it an ethereal shine.

He intended to have a painting done of himself now, wearing his decoration. He was still uncertain whether to wear court dress or merely a suit. A suit seemed common. He had seen a photograph of Motilal Nehru in court dress and could not help admiring the lordly air it lent the man. And he was not even a knight. The sword came down on his left shoulder and rose, cutting through sunlight and turning yellow in the blaze.

'Arise, Sir Ram Shanker,' the Viceroy said, loudly and, passing the sword to his equerry, lent a kindly hand to help Sir Ram Shanker to regain his feet. 'And let me be the first to congratulate you, Sir Ram.'

Lady Diamond Hardinge extended her hand too and he touched it delicately as though it were glass. Once the Viceroy stepped away, leaving him alone to bask in the glory of his knighthood, Sir Ram once more felt this sense of loss. He could not understand it. Here he stood, surrounded by well-wishers, his hand being crushed in congratulation and his back patted by admirers, basking in the envy of lesser men, now, than he. It came to him with startling clarity – his time was past. He was surrounded by the past. There were men outside this select gathering who would soon be moving into the circle but men quite different from him, not merely youthful but more ambitious. They wouldn't be satisfied with a knighthood, the entrée into empty power. He knew that despite his title he was still only a figurehead. The real power lay in those hands which had gripped his, yet which would move just as swiftly to exclude him. The new men would want that power, to rule India alone and not share it with the British. There were names he dimly felt resounded with possibilities – Jawaharlal Nehru, Vallabhai Patel, C. Rajagopalachari. They were the rising stars in the Congress Party, already displacing Gokhale and his moderation, finding Tilak's anger futile. And he could think of others, a rising force which would eventually overtake him. His life would always remain empty except for the pretence, like this title.

Such thoughts frightened him. His whole life had been spent carefully plotting for such a reward, a recognition of his achievements. Yet the men, not his own countrymen, who had bestowed it upon him, would one day vanish, and all his glory would go with them.

He felt a hand on his elbow and turned, already smiling, to receive yet another well-wisher. Motilal Nehru and his son Jawaharlal stood beside him. The elder Nehru smiled; the younger looked disapproving. Sir Ram ignored him. He intended to savour this moment of triumph. The new generation would have theirs later, much later.

'Congratulations, Sir Ram,' Motilal said. He had a loud voice which lifted above the murmur of conversation. 'It has a pleasant sound, like a freshly minted gold sovereign dropping on marble.'

'No doubt your turn will come soon, Motilal,' Sir Ram spoke modestly, as he'd heard the British speak, but deep within he fervently prayed this honour wouldn't fall on Nehru. It would make him an insufferable equal.

'I should hope not,' Jawaharlal said. For a man with such a poet's face, he had a snappish temper. 'These scraps the British throw us shouldn't be wolfed down as if we were hyenas. You should have refused the knighthood.'

'Jawaharlal,' Motilal said in shock. 'You should show more courtesy to Sir Ram. You must apologise.'

'Why? Because he's a knight? The sooner we stop

kneeling to the British, crawling for their approval, the sooner we can stand upright like men. How can we ever throw them out, if they corrupt us with such rewards?'

'I am sure you have a masterful plan to rid us of them,' Sir Ram said. 'Do tell me about it.'

'We could, if the Congress Party made stronger demands. The party should unite the country behind it. Instead it's still a landlord's party, full of lawyers and . . '

'Like you and your father,' Sir Ram said. 'And, of course, myself.'

'We have had this argument before,' Motilal said. 'I'm afraid my son and I no longer see eye to eye as to how we should deal with our rulers. He's a dreamer and dreams of freedom. You and I are pragmatists. We know we have to share the rule with the British.'

'Not for ever,' Jawaharlal said sharply. He turned on his heel and stalked away.

'I must apologise for my son's rudeness.'

'I would prefer he did it himself,' Sir Ram said. 'He has a tongue in his head.' He too moved away, knowing Motilal stared at his back, angry at his refusal to accept the apology and aware that he had made an enemy of the man. At the next Congress Party convention, he would not have the support of the Nehrus.

Jawaharlal stood stiffly, hands clasped tightly behind his back. He resented this splendid hall with its portraits of the King and Queen and past Viceroys staring down on him imperiously. They had no right to be on Indian soil. He disliked the sound of the English voices softly flowing through the room and the regimental band playing waltzes on the lawn. "And we Indians fawn on them for favours, for even a kindly smile," he thought. "As if our own presence here is in question, not theirs." He glanced idly back into the room and saw the Englishman watching him. He was an elderly man, straightbacked, with thick white eyebrows and a sunburned face with hollowed eyes. When Nehru met his stare, he didn't look away but instead smiled almost conspiratorially.

The Colonel studied young Nehru. He noted the stiffness, the flash of those eyes. He had a slim file on him. Harrow and Cambridge. The Inner Temple. But he had made little effort to practise law in Allahabad. He mooned around, a bit uselessly, living off his father's money. He had joined the Congress Party and given one or two speeches, but lacked the gift for inflated oratory of some of the other Congressmen. He and his father didn't quite see eye to eye on the question of British rule. No doubt, once he married and settled, he would meekly obey his father's dictates. Motilal was a great admirer of the British and would keep his son in check. The Colonel couldn't imagine Jawaharlal as a wild-eyed revolutionary. He looked, well, too weak. Still, he could be of use one day.

'I'm Colonel Creighton,' he said.

Nehru shook his hand. 'It's Colonel Sir John, now, isn't it?'

'A mouthful. I know your father and thought I should introduce myself. After all you are a rising force in the Congress Party. I hope, one day, I can be of some help to you.'

'I doubt it, Colonel.'

'Never underestimate the sincerity of your enemies, Mr Nehru. We will be here for many, many more years and I could, let's say, influence your career. I'd like you to keep my card, just in case we may need each other.'

As he walked away, the Colonel glimpsed Nehru's reflection in the mirror. He studied the card and slipped it into his coat pocket.

'Sir Ram Shanker,' Lal Bahadur said aloud to himself, sitting primly in the back seat of the motor car. He wished to say it now aloud in the open air of Delhi. The ancient city would hear him; it would stir proudly for him, his voice reverberating with the past titles granted by other emperors to common men. The Mughals gifted jagirs as a reward for those who served them loyally as well as a title. The British wisely considered a title adequate reward. Sir Lal Bahadhur Ram Shanker. It had a grand sound. He wanted to share it with someone and wasn't surprised that Mohini should come to mind. He grimaced at the sudden thought: the very moment the sword had touched his shoulders she had become Lady Shanker. She waited always on the edge of his thoughts, and he wished he could as easily summon her physically. She would not have shown any pride in his achievement, only a chill disdain but it would have satisfied him, given him pleasure, to show off his new importance to the icy woman. He would have like to imprint the decoration into the flesh between her breasts, as though he could burn it into her very soul.

If his father were alive there wouldn't be such a feeling of loneliness in his achievement. He would have proved to someone he respected that he could rise from his inheritance to this position of eminence. Only he'd never known his father. It was a regret that haunted him and the strangeness of his passing still made him shiver. The cruelty of nature's ills was unimaginable at times.

Lal Bahadhur was glad to be home. He crossed the marble floors of his mansion, walking down the corridors to his mother's quarters. The few servants he saw pressed themselves into the shadows to allow him passage. Strangely, though he had returned eager to show his mother the decoration, he felt she already knew every detail of the events. She never failed to surprise him with her power to pierce the veils of space and time. And how news ever reached her here, where she lived as a recluse absorbed with her occult practices, he never knew. He felt a winter chill as he passed through the inner courtyard. An old crone sat on guard outside Gitabhai's quarters. As far back as Lal Bahadhur could remember she'd guarded his mother's chambers. She was weak, and frail and bent and would be of no use if someone attacked. Still, she was faithful to his mother.

'Tell her I have returned,' he said.

'She knows,' the crone replied. 'You must bathe and

change first, she said. You carry the unclean air of the foreigners. She will see you later.'

Her mumblings continued and faded as Lal Bahadhur returned to his rooms. He felt crestfallen. He could never disobey his mother's commands.

His wife Durga awaited him. She was nubile, young and subservient, yet the subservience was sly, calculated. She had been, as had Mohini, his mother's choice. And like Mohini she had no immediate family, only relatives. That was always an ideal wife. They had no one to run to. Mohini, of course, had run away. That had been brave, and he held her in reluctant admiration. Durga would never do such a thing. Her life was too comfortable, as long as she obeyed his mother. Now, she prostrated herself on the floor and placed her forehead on his dusty Peal shoes. She clutched his ankles in supplication, nearly upsetting him, and he moved away in irritation, leaving her stretched out. She had a supple body which he occasionally enjoyed.

It was decidedly chilly in January and a brazier burned on the verandah next to his chair. Lal Bahadhur picked up the *Pioneer*. The headline in dark, bold print an inch high read: 'ENGLAND WINS MAJOR VICTORY IN NEUVE CHAPELLE. GERMANS SUFFER HEAVY LOSSES'

He sighed with satisfaction and, neatly refolding the paper, placed it aside. India was also in the war and her men were fighting on two fronts. The Mesopotamia expedition, however, was a disaster. Reports were filtering back of heavy losses, inadequate supplies and stupid military strategy. He would say nothing, yet. His role was merely to appear at the Viceroy's Council and agree with much of what was said. To criticise would jeopardise his position. He and many other Indians were determined to prove their allegiance to the empire. The princes of India were all offering their private armies, while in the Congress Party he had managed to steer through a resolution of support and loyalty for the British government and an agreement not to press for any legislative demands until this crisis had passed. They had all, including Jawaharlal Nehru, been surprisingly amenable. He suspected that many of them, especially the younger members, believed that compliance and encouragement now would be rewarded later by a loosening of the reins, even the handing over of them totally. But in this expectation, they were dreamers. Lal Bahadhur knew the British too well. They wouldn't meekly hand over their power. It would have to be wrested from them by force.

He had swayed Congress for his own ends. He was profiting from war. A murmur in the Military Secretary's ear had ensured that one of his friends would supply the Indian Army with some of their requirements – clothes, boots, webbing, blankets. Naturally, he had received his dastur for such a favour.

He saw Mahender approach. His servant came quickly, almost furtively, glancing around to see if he were observed. He bowed to his master and squatted beside his chair. Lal Bahadhur felt some regret that the man's brother, Rajender, was dead. He had been bitten by a cobra and Lal Bahadhur found his death inconvenient. He was more intelligent than this fool but at least Mahender was a useful, violent tool. It had been more than a year since Mahender had returned from his pursuit of Mohini and the man who had rescued her. Lal Bahadhur had had him thrashed for his incompetence and had considered garrotting him, but in a spasm of compassion had permitted him to live. Mahender had crossed the Narbada river and gone as far south as Bangalore, but had been unable to find Mohini. She and the man had apparently vanished.

Mahender listened silently to Lal Bahadhur's account of the war in Europe. He had no idea where this place lay and no interest in it. He only understood that it somehow benefited his master.

With the encroaching darkness, Lal Bahadhur fell silent. There was a clear sky with a crescent moon. He enjoyed hearing the familiar sounds of his garden, the cicadas, crickets and lizards filled the air with their constant murmur which soothed him. It was time for his chota peg and Mahender fetched the whisky bottle, glass and soda. The evening drink was a delightful British habit which he practised discreetly. He sensed Mahender stir beside him and waited. The man spoke only when necessary. It made him exceptional in this talkative land.

'As you instructed, I went to Bombay to visit the Soames memsahib's bearer and paid him the money.' Mahender groped in his pocket and drew out some folded sheets of paper. 'He took this from the memsahib's desk. It's what he says you instructed him to look for. I cannot read, so it is possible he's cheating you. I can return and cut his throat.'

'You like cutting throats,' Lal Bahadhur said and accepted the papers. He'd almost forgotten his arrangement, had even considered cancelling it. When he'd learned that Alice Soames had befriended Mohini and encouraged her to write for the now-defunct magazine *Sher*, he'd arranged with Alice's bearer to watch for any communication from Mohini. Once a month, Mahender travelled to Bombay and each time returned empty handed. Each time too he offered to cut the bearer's throat for his uselessness. But Lal Bahadhur had stayed that murderous hand, counselled patience. 'Not yet,' he said. 'She may write to Soames memsahib, she may not. But we must wait. One day, she'll communicate with her old friend.' Wait, wait, wait.

Now his patience and investment were rewarded. He didn't read the letter immediately. He teased himself. The bearer could have made a mistake and handed over the wrong letter. It could be from Mohini but would bear no information as to her whereabouts. She had grown cautious and he knew that was the influence of her lover, the Colonel's agent. He also had an informant in the Colonel's household, the bearer Abdul who watched and listened, not only for word from that agent but for other scraps of information, political and secretive. Lal

Bahadhur had nearly betrayed Abdul's deceit, in a fit of boasting some years before at the Calcutta Race Club, when he had let slip his knowledge that Alice Soames was the Colonel's wife. He still remembered his own answer when the Colonel had sharply asked him how he'd known. 'Servants,' he'd replied, foolishly pleased to have surprised the Colonel sahib and beaten him at his own game. Since then, the Colonel had been extremely cautious and suspected all the servants and peons and clerks, especially his daughter's ayah Mary, all except his favourite Abdul. Knowing the venal souls of servants, Lal Bahadhur paid Abdul twice the wages the Colonel paid him.

A lantern was placed at his elbow and Lal Bahadhur carefully unfolded the letter. He glanced and was satisfied. Yes, it was Mohini's writing. She had a reasonable hand for a woman. It was dated November 2nd 1914.

'Dear Alice, it has been many, many months since I last wrote

(*And why did I not receive that last letter? I will instruct Mahender to cut that bearer's throat.*)

and the only way I could measure time here was by counting the days until Kim's release from prison, but this time, which once passed so swiftly in his company dragged itself like a wounded creature towards its death.

(*Kim. That must be her lover's name, but it is most unusual and doesn't sound Indian. Possibly it's his nickname. We Indians are prone to giving ourselves British-sounding names to escape the onerous burden of our Indianness. But what is an Imperial agent doing in prison? Which one?*)

On his imprisonment I returned to this village, almost bereaved as a widow at having lost my love, and treasuring the last glimpse of his face as the prison doors closed upon him as if he slipped into a dark and dank grave. I dare not even imagine how real death would affect me as I was only a child when my parents died and children are more resilient and, though it wounds, the pain gradually subsides though it is never forgotten. I would have remained outside the walls of the prison like a spirit trapped in its shadow, moaning and mourning, but Kim made me promise to return here to live among these poor and gentle people, instead of remaining in Madurai

(*Ahh, I have her.*)

where he judged all manner of terrible things would befall me and Saraswati who

(*Saraswati?*)

is my constant reminder of dear Kim and grows by inches every day. I had wanted a son for that is how our female minds have been warped by this male society and we believe daughters, and therefore our own selves, to be worthless people, but Kim who has no such misgivings loves her dearly and kindled my own love and drove out the guilt and I now adore her

(*My heart cannot beat. She has borne his child. His child! How can I not hate her now for this terrible betrayal? Her evil deed must be punished before I kill the adulteress. Yes, and kill the child who stains my honour.*)

and lived only for her while I waited for Kim's release. Our life in this village was quiet and dull but I was contented as much as one can be under such circumstances. Once every two months I travelled to Madurai to look upon Kim's face and to touch his hand in the interview room watched over by the guards. As the journey each way takes three days,

(*On a map I could trace the length of the journey but that will be arduous work and consume too much time. I can feel the terrible sulphur of hate already consuming me. I must find her soon before I am destroyed by this hatred.*)

it wasn't possible to see him more often as I didn't wish to leave Saraswati for such long periods of time though I knew she was loved and cared for by the whole village. It was in the second month of his imprisonment that a ghastly incident occurred. As you have never met Kim, I cannot fully convey his character. He is a man who draws others to him because of his humour and kindness and for the resolute strength of his character, and within those two months he had won himself many friends within the prison, among the convicts as well as among the prison staff. Due to the fact that he was an 'A' class prisoner because of his political activities

(*The Colonel sahib will have a record then of his agent's political actions, which obviously run counter to his employment as an Imperial agent.*)

and not a criminal, he, Kumar and many others slept in a large hall where it was cooler though less private. As you may know, the criminal prisoners are desperate men, cut-throats, thieves, dacoits, rapists. In prison, especially for those condemned for many years, their treatment is heinous and they live worse than animals. Kim told me they're often beaten, tortured, humiliated and forced to perform vile acts for the enjoyment of the prison warders and so for a few rupees, they will commit any crime, knowing that they are already in hell and nothing worse can befall them. Such a man is Venkat. He is small and slim, no larger than a boy in size but he is far older than Kim and is extremely dark in complexion and the darkness is emphasised by his long matted beard while his eyes too are black and fierce, and to look upon him is to recoil in fright. He reminded me of those demons who tormented me during my imprisonment in my husband's palace on the lake.

(*What demons? I had no inkling of such terrible things happening to her. My mother in her jealousy no doubt planted them in her mind, and will continue to hate Mohini because of my obsession for her.*)

Venkat was approached by a limping man called Madan who was in the employ of Colonel Creighton your husband but I do not mean to make this accusatory or hold you to blame for the Colonel's actions and only wish to mention this in passing. The Colonel had heard through one of his informers, the Zamindar of Puducheri, that Kim was in prison and despatched this Madan to murder Kim. I've no doubt about this, though Kim believes Madan was sent to watch over him and not lose him again and I feel this belief of Kim's is more in the Colonel as a man of honour, a sort of 'father'. To believe he would send an executioner is beyond Kim's imagining, but can a man of the Colonel's power and sense of duty to the empire allow him even an iota of emotion to love my Kim who has deserted him? However, Madan did plan murder as revenge for, apart from being responsible for making this man limp, Kim had also killed his only brother when he rescued me from the island palace but this was only out of rage and grief as this brother had killed Kim's dear companion Narain. Madan approached Venkat and paid him fifty rupees to kill Kim. One night, as my Kim slept, Venkat crept upon him with a dagger given to him by Madan. There was a full moon and the light was bright and clear in the hall. Venkat rose to plunge the dagger into Kim's heart but by chance, Kumar awoke, disturbed by the hiss of breath and saw this demon poised over Kim and threw himself at Venkat even as the blade plunged downwards and Kim who sleeps so lightly immediately twisted away but not fast enough for the knife plunged into his side. Despite his wound Kim grappled with Venkat and managed to wrest the blade from him and at once Venkat lay still as a defeated animal and offered his throat for Kim to cut for he knew he would receive a terrible punishment when the attempted crime was reported to the warders. I thank God Kim's wound wasn't deep although it bled copiously and he managed to staunch the blood and at once forgave Venkat and released him and such was Venkat's amazement at this kindness that from that night on, like a faithful dog, he serves Kim with total and embarrassing loyalty.

*(The fool. If he had succeeded how much easier my task would be. But still, Kim is in prison and if I move swiftly I can kidnap her and carry her back to the palace. But I'll have that child's throat cut first. Mahender would do it with pleasure.)*

Unbeknown to Kim Venkat planned his revenge for him. Venkat, I should add here, had slaughtered a whole landlord family for he was a bonded labourer on their estates

(*Horror, cry horror! We must destroy such evil men who defy their karma which is to serve us dumbly. Why does he continue to live when he should have been torn to pieces? I will mention this to the Home Member tomorrow, suggesting the death penalty for crimes against landowners.*)

and being bonded is merely a hairsbreadth above a state of slavery for the men and women and children can never repay their debts and serve out their lives in fear and abject penury. Venkat was married to a girl from his own caste who lived in the same village and in the same state of poverty. However, she was a pretty girl and caught the landlord's eye. Naturally, he demanded his drot de siggnur, I am unsure of the spelling of this foreign word but I am sure you understand its meaning,

(*Naturally. We bless the poor with our carnal attention.*)

and when she refused his advances he had her stripped and beaten in front of the whole village but, tragically, she died from the beating. Of course, there was no recourse to justice for someone so poor except to take revenge, and so one night Venkat slipped into their bungalow and cut the landlord's throat and then stabbed to death his wife and three children and therefore the art of revenge was not unknown to him. He plotted this revenge for Kim with the other convicts and they pooled together their meagre money and bribed one of the warders to look the other way while Venkat slipped out of the prison one night. He knew where Madan lived and that night, while Madan slept, he separated Madan's head from his body and threw the head on to the rubbish heap where it was found the next morning by a servant girl. Kim knew nothing of this until much later and was deeply distressed.

(*A soft man. A weak one. First forgiveness and now distress. He will be easy to deal with. Mahender will have no qualms at separating his head from his body.*)

Kim and Kumar were released in March, no worse for their imprisonment and Kumar struts around proudly, as he had suffered for his actions against the British. In prison, there were other such men who had spoken against them to Kumar and Kim imbibed their thoughts and without even a day's rest now began once more to organise the making of the saris but in a place hidden and remote from the village. But such things are not enough for Kim for he is a restless man used to wandering and adventure and cannot remain passive for long. News of what happens in the world outside seeps only slowly into this village and very faintly we heard that Britain was entering a war with Germany. Strangely this war has had the opposite effect on India here and although Kim's friends such as Srinivasan and T.V. Naidu are ardent nationalists, they are now urging Indians to fight in this war for the British.

(*T.V. Naidu! The Congress Secretary in Madras a friend of this Kim's? What conspiracy lies here? Does the Colonel know of this? And what favour could I extract for this morsel of information?*)

Kim and Srinivasan and Kumar volunteered to fight in this war. I wept and pleaded with him to remain but to no avail for having committed himself to India, it is this commitment now that urges him to fight in this distant war for he reasons that he will be fighting for the future of India and not for the future of the British Empire and I have to believe in this reasoning for I can do nothing else. But where is Europe, and where am I? My Kim joined the Indian Army as a jawan and as I once followed him to the gates of the prison I now followed the train which carried him away to the very end of the platform and down on to the track until it moved out of sight and my tears blurred the sky and the earth. I mourn him and pray God will bring him back safely to me and Saraswati. He believes it will be a splendid adventure and that the reward for such efforts by him and every Indian will be that the British will leave India. I don't believe freedom can be achieved so freely, nor that it can be bought on foreign soil because we Indians have to die here for India and not in France or Germany. You will no doubt be far better informed than this woman stuck away in a remote village for whom news and opinions are scarce. How long will this war last? Will it be over in a month, possibly two? For it to last even a day longer will break my heart for I am missing Kim terribly. Please reassure me it will be over soon and Kim will be returned to my side. I am quite distraught dear Alice and now find this solitude has been transformed into loneliness. The peace and contentment are now dullness and boredom and I do not have the patience to waste away in this village while I await Kim's return and I feel I would like to come and live with you if that is possible for it will bring me a few miles closer to Kim and I will receive news quickly of what is occurring in those distant lands. Also I can occupy myself with writing again. I will come in a month or two, as Kumar's wife is about to bear another child and clings to me pathetically as if I can salve her sadness at Kumar's absence. As this village is quite nameless please write to me c/o the Puducheri Post Office and the letter will wend its way to me.'

'She's found,' Lal Bahadhur said. 'But we must grab her quickly as she plans to move to live with Miss Soames. It will be very hard then. We must go immediately to Madurai.'

Mahender rose, bitterly disappointed that his master would also be present at the capture. The words 'she's found' had filled him with expectation and longing. He yearned to hold her, to squeeze her breasts, see her writhe in pain, and take his pleasure. The memory of seeing her naked with drops of water shivering on her skin as she stepped out of the river in front of his disbelieving eyes had never been erased from his mind. She'd walked past him unashamed, treating him like a lump of stone or a dumb animal which could experience no longing, no carnal desire for such beauty. For that indifference alone he wanted to punish Mohini and spend himself in her body. Now he would have to curb his own passions while his master possessed her.

For the first time, Mahender felt a great resentment at the good fortune of Lal Bahadhur.

'Wait,' Lal Bahadhur said as Mahender stepped out of lamplight into the darkness. 'Come closer.' Mahender leaned over and Lal Bahadhur whispered in his ear. 'Tell no one. You understand? Tell no one.'

Mahender knew his meaning. Gitabhai, whose ears were the walls and the insects, would want Mohini first. She had her own revenge to take on Mohini and the thought of such revenge made even Mahender shiver. Like his master, he feared Gitabhai and suspected she was somehow responsible for his brother's death.

Gitabhai watched her son sleeping through the large mirror hanging opposite his bed. The glass was cloudy but not only through age. The pot of perfumed coal burning in his room to ward off mosquitoes misted her vision. She had always enjoyed watching Ram at rest. His tranquil presence comforted her. In sleep he reminded her dimly of his father. They had married when she was twelve and he had died of a mysterious ailment after she'd conceived Ram. The doctors couldn't diagnose the cause of the illness that spun him out thinner and thinner, no matter how much food he consumed, like a thread drawn from a fistful of cotton. They fed him ghee and rice and milk and meat, but he continued to dwindle and disappear in front of their eyes.

Gitabhai was satisfied with the experiment on her husband. Even as a child she'd been precocious in the use of magic which she'd learned from her mother, and her mother from her mother. The line of knowledge stretched back eight generations, probably longer. It was an intuitive gift, the knowledge passing through the souls of the women. Gitabhai imagined it went back to the beginning of the world when Brahma carelessly granted the boon of this terrible knowledge to a female ancestor.

The girl, Durga, who slept beside her son was slim and lovely with a heart-shaped face, and in repose she seemed at peace for a while. But now and then she would break into a sweat, and toss and turn as though struggling to escape an unseen force grappling with her. No sound escaped her lips. Then she would subside and lie still. Gitabhai was jealous of the girl's good fortune in sleeping with her son. It was her rightful place and she yielded it only on Ram's insistence. He was, despite his greed for power, a prudish man, not understanding totally her power and her needs. He was the only man she loved, not in a motherly fashion but with a greedy sensual longing. This girl merely satisfied his lust. His heart was still trapped by Mohini and she knew that in his brooding solitude his mind would often turn to Mohini, wondering and wanting her. Gitabhai had to destroy Mohini soon before her son discovered her whereabouts. He was bending all his will and political power to trace her and if he should find her before Gitabhai, she knew she would lose her hold over him for ever.

She closed and locked the door to the small hiding place which led to the rear of the mirror, and moved softly down the deserted corridors. She enjoyed the cool of night, the blackness of shadows. She had cat's eyes and saw into the darkest corners, and nothing in the world could frighten her, except the demons who waited to consume Mohini.

She noted a sly movement in the shadow and glimpsed the whites of eyes. She stared at them, willing them forward from the darkness in the recess of the door, and a man reluctantly stepped out of hiding. Gitabhai needed no lamplight to recognise Mahender. She had sent him and his brother Rajender in pursuit of Mohini when the man had rescued her from the island palace. Rajender had returned many months later, emptyhanded, and in her rage she had thrown a cobra at him and watched him grovel for life and die at her feet. And now the brother had returned just as emptyhanded, and she hissed in anger at his incompetence. Stupid man. It was a simple task to find Mohini and he had failed.

She planned his death even as he came to stand in front of her. His beard was matted and his face dark and sullen. He was evil and Gitabhai appreciated this quality, which his brother lacked. But Mahender's evil was simple and human – murder was his only weapon against the world – while she could summon so many more powers to do her bidding. He stood before her, eyes avoiding her malignant stare, but she sensed he had a secret.

'Where do you go, fool?'

'I only answer to your Lal Bahadhur,' Mahender said. Though afraid of Gitabhai, he had a stubborn sense of loyalty to her son.

'Answer me, you fool. Otherwise, you will never set eyes on the rising sun.'

'I'm going to my village,' Mahender said and flinched at her stare, frightened for a moment that she would kill him. This woman surely had the power to make even the dead talk.

'Even I cannot make the dead talk,' Gitabhai read his mind easily, and now roamed the simple labyrinth to discover his secret. She saw Mohini there suddenly, arising out of water naked, and knew the servant lusted after her. But why think such a thought now, unless he did hold a secret? 'What have you discovered about Mohini?'

'Nothing, memsahib. I swear.' And then against his will he heard himself answer truthfully. It seemed as though another person spoke in his voice and he was a helpless witness. 'My master has discovered her living in a small village near Madurai. We are going there now.'

'Which village?'

'It is in Puducheri district. Three days from Madurai.'

'I see. Go now, but no word to my son. If you betray me you will die a death such as even the gods can't imagine. But if you should obey, your reward will be one long night with Mohini and you will be able to do anything with her that your heart desires. Now go.'

She crossed to her granite room. Swiftly, she slid into

the room and slammed the door shut but not before the demon's screams escaped for a second into the still night and once more set the pi-dogs in the chowk howling in fright. The air was hot and foul, flickering with yellow lights from countless eyes and purple sparks from serpents' tongues. She was engulfed by the swirling demons who screamed their demands, deafening her. It wasn't the passage of time that enraged them for in the universe time did not exist and the very second of their creation had not advanced. Their impatience arose from being trapped here, unable to fulfil their duty; they saw that their evil powers were wasted and wished to escape in order to do the bidding of other more competent sorcerers or sorceresses.

'You are useless,' they howled. 'You cannot even find this woman in such a small place as this India.'

'Will you all shut up?' Gitabhai screamed, and then as an afterthought added: 'Please,' though aware that demons had no comprehension of modesty or manners.

One of the demons, a yali whose face was partly goatlike but instead of a muzzle had the great hooked beak of an eagle and the body of a serpent, had been elected as their spokesman.

'We have decided that you must be incompetent and that we must return to the other world. You will enter a trance to give us passage and we will take you with us.'

'Shut up and listen, you fools. When I have been granted the greatest boon from Brahma himself and shown the art of creation, do you expect me to listen to your petty problems? You will now remain until the task is completed.'

They muttered and hissed in consultation. It was true. By destroying her, they could call down Brahma's vengeance. He could condemn them to spend time as a living creature, a water buffalo or worse, a female.

'But the clay model is complete,' the yali said. 'We have laboured long and hard with you, but for what good? She is lifeless. We are trapped here and you haven't found Mohini for us to consume.'

'But I have.'

The demons gleefully hissed their pleasure, and all hovered around her as she moved to the far end of the room. Carefully she removed the sheet, revealing the life-sized form of Mohini. Gitabhai studied it critically, starting from the toes. They were slim and long and wore silver rings. The ankles were well-turned and the calves were, correctly, somewhat thin. The thighs were more muscular and the pubic hair sparse. She had used real hair, silken and soft, cut from a virgin. The belly flattened and rose up to round, firm breasts with large nipples. Gitabhai's face flickered with malignant satisfaction until she reached the face. That beauty stabbed her with jealousy. The mouth was sensual, the cheekbones delicately prominent and the eyes, closed now, would be amber when they opened. The real hair, carefully and painstakingly pricked into the skull, fanned out as if the woman were afloat in water.

Gitabhai was pleased at her artistry. The clay woman was the exact image of Mohini.

'Is she perfectly like Mohini?'

'Yes, yes, perfect,' the demons and serpents hissed.

The face, above all, had to be perfect for otherwise Siva or Vishnu would detect the imperfection and destroy the woman who would emerge from this room. Gitabhai had been labouring over the clay figure for thirteen months, thirteen days, and thirteen hours and it was now time to rouse the clay to life by the performance of pujas and tapas. It would breathe and walk and eat and defecate but it would contain no emotion. Its space for emotions would be filled by the demons who would escape the granite room hidden from the eyes of the gods, who would believe this to be the real Mohini. She would carry the demons to Madurai and there, once they'd entered the real Mohini and completed their dreadful task, they could leave the earth.

But Gitabhai was so loathing of Mohini that she couldn't resist the impulse to disfigure in some way this clay replica before it came to life. She couldn't mar the beauty of its face or those perfectly rounded breasts, for such sensuality was appreciated by god. Instead, unknown to her co-conspirators, she had inserted small, sharp blades into the vagina. They were placed in such a manner that a man could enter the delightful passage but should he try to withdraw, the blades would spring up like teeth and slice his member off. This device was meant for the man who'd stolen Mohini from her; she knew she couldn't kill him because of his protection.

'We are ready now,' Gitabhai said and bustled around gathering all the necessary ingredients for the homam which would bring the figure to life. She had sandalwood logs for the fire, camphor, incense, ghee, rice, saffron, milk. And there were other mysterious herbs which had been described in the ancient manuscript. Beside this heap, she carefully placed a clay pot filled with the menstrual blood of her husband's young wife who had not known the purpose of such a strange request but had been too frightened to refuse.

The firewood was arranged around the naked clay figure, so that its heat would be even. Gitabhai lit the wood and began chanting the mantras in the manuscript while she sprinkled the ghee and milk and blood and rice over the flames. All night she laboured, drenched with sweat from the heat and the exertion of prayer, and the purity of her purpose. It was an hour before dawn, when the sky was a delicate shade of pink, that the eyes of the clay woman flickered an instant, as if she were waking from a deep, deep sleep and hadn't the will to open them fully. Gitabhai's chants grew into a frenzy, and she willed the figure to life, breathing her breath into its face so that the life, like a flame, would catch. Suddenly, the eyes snapped open and the firelight danced in those amber eyes and over the swelling breasts that rose and fell, first hesitantly, but soon steadily. 'Sit up,' Gitabhai commanded.

The woman propped herself up on her elbows and looked down in amazement at the light shining on her belly and thighs. She pushed herself upright and her first gesture was delightfully human for she tossed her head and tied her hair into a knot. She crossed her legs and remained placidly awaiting Gitabhai's further commands. Gitabhai clapped and laughed in delight and circled the woman, examining her, pinching her, caressing her breasts and face to feel the smooth, silken flesh which she had created.

'Open your mouth,' Gitabhai whispered and the mouth opened wide. Carefully she tilted the head back as though the mouth was to receive water but instead Gitabhai commanded the demons and serpents to enter and watched with satisfaction as they poured down the open throat and into their hiding place.

# 19

## March 1915–May 1916

'You are an arrogant man, sepoy,' Captain Edlecliff-Johnstone said to his orderly.

'Sir, I am not a prince to be arrogant. I stand before you now as only a petitioner pleading our cause,' Kim said. 'We came here to fight, but instead we're forced to commit these menial duties.'

He stood to attention and stared down at the heavily lathered face in the small mirror. The daily morning ritual, with Edlecliff-Johnstone sitting on a low canvas stool and Kim at attention, holding a shaving mug took place outside Edlecliff-Johnstone's tent in a grimy light which hadn't changed for months. Kim yearned to glimpse the sun at dawn but even at midday the light never changed and he felt as though he were imprisoned in a large, opaque chamber. He yearned too for a burst of bright colour but the landscape was like a photograph: grey sky, blackened trees, brown roads. The grass surprised him. It was green, a luxuriant lush green, the only promise that the land held a secret existence.

'Surely you don't think British High Command is depending on you people to win this war. You Indians were brought here to serve the fighting British soldier.' Edlecliff-Johnstone glanced at his orderly's face. It was bearded and swarthy but the grey eyes stared at him steadily with a hint of dislike which the man made no effort to disguise. Edlecliff-Johnstone felt uncertain of this sepoy.

Kim now bitterly regretted volunteering for this war. They had left their villages and towns, their womenfolk and their children, and eagerly signed up to serve the empire. He wasn't afraid of the cold or the battles. He understood the nature of war as they all did. Men would die.

No, their angry disillusionment had arisen from their treatment by the British. They had come to fight in a war but instead they were expected to act as servants for the British soldiers and officers. Fetch this, carry that, clean the latrines, iron our clothes. Kim had been reduced to a bearer, expected to wake his Captain Edlecliff-Johnstone with morning chai, bring his shaving water, clean his quarters, polish his shoes. He had never been a servant to any man and now in this distant land called France he was forced into the role, as were his friends too. Each was proud, each had his dignity. Kumar had his land, Srinivasan his degree (nearly), Grehwal was the son of the Amritsar cloth merchant and caravan owner Balbir Singh. They were all part of the Hindustan Division of the First Army. The British treated them all as if they were unworthy to fight, only fit to be servants. Kim ducked his head to hide the blush of shame for these people to whom he had once belonged. How could he ever say he was British when his people were treated so badly? He would far prefer now to die an Indian than live as an Englishman or even admit to the blood that poisoned his veins.

'We were told we came as soldiers. Not servants. I have never served a man in such capacity.'

'Well, you'd better get over your damn caste feelings here. And address me as "sir" each time you open your mouth.'

'Yes, sir.'

'Are you a trouble-maker, sepoy?'

'Sir, I only mention the injustice.'

'First of all, any complaints should be first reported to your Jemedar and not to me. Secondly, I don't see it as an injustice. Don't forget I'm stuck commanding here as well, instead of in a decent British regiment. I signed up too to fight in this war and though I do have a King's Commission I couldn't join a British regiment. So we're all stuck in this together and we may as well make the best of it.'

All the Englishmen who had been serving in India and signed up were tarred with the same brush. All were servants, if not as menial as this jawan, then still running and fetching for the 'real' British regiments. Edlecliff-Johnstone recognised many familiar faces here, men he'd drunk with in the Bombay Club, shot with in Kashmir or played polo with in Cal. The best of the young ICS and IPS and the box-wallahs had all signed up to fight the Germans. Edlecliff-Johnstone wondered who was running India in their absence. The old men he supposed, holding on until it was over so that they could retire to Nainital or Gulmarg and write their memoirs. That was, of course, if any of the young men ever came back to India. To some extent, he sympathised with this sepoy's complaint but there was little he could do about it. And he didn't want a revolt on his hands.

'Do you understand that?'

'No, sir. Aren't we all soldiers of His Majesty the King?'

'Yes, yes,' Edlecliff-Johnstone said impatiently. This man seemed stupid in his stubbornness, but Edlecliff-Johnstone suspected it was an act. Those grey eyes were filled with questioning intelligence. Doubtless he'd been chosen as spokesman by the Indian troops in the regiment. 'It's Kimathchand, isn't it?'

'Yes, sir.'

'Punjabi?'

'Yes, sir.'

'Which part?'

'Lahore.'

'There's something familiar about you,' Edlecliff-Johnstone said. 'As if I've seen you somewhere before. Have I?'

'No, sir.'

Edlecliff-Johnstone turned from the mirror and stared up. The swarthy face was expressionless. No, he didn't know the man and yet something nagged. Possibly the name. Was it in a file in the Political and Secret Department? He wished he could summon a peon to fetch those files. He bet Colonel Creighton would know immediately. The whole department was filed away in his mind, every agent, every devious plot, every secret.

'But you were recruited in south India. What were you doing there?'

'Living,' Kim said patiently, aware of the line of the questioning and the nagging reminder in this officer's head. He knew that Edlecliff-Johnstone had worked in the Indian government. He was an IPS man who had been seconded to the Political and Secret Department in Bombay. His superior would be Colonel Creighton. Kim, shivering in the grey miserable weather, wondered where his old friend Newton was – retired possibly, transferred, even dead. He wished now that he had visited Bombay to see his old friend, or at least discovered his whereabouts. It would be easy to ask the man staring up at him, but that would reveal his own identity.

'You're too damn clever for my liking. Now get out and tell the others to stop their whining.'

Edlecliff-Johnstone watched Kim wash out his shaving things, pack them neatly in the kitbag hanging by the entrance and walk up the road. Kimathchand. The more he thought, the more the name and the man worried at him. Yes, it would give him something to do. He would write to his head clerk, Muthu, and ask him to look through the files for the name and reply immediately.

Kim, huddled in an overcoat too thin for this country and meant for a Delhi winter at most, trudged up the hard dirt road to the tents pitched in a farmer's field. He had never experienced such cold in his life. It was bitter and hard and cruel. He felt his bones turning brittle with ice, and his blood running as chill as the Ganges flowing through the glaciers. Even the time he had been trapped in a snow drift for three days with a caravan on the route from Leh down to Srinagar he had never felt so cold though the snow had been piled like sand dunes above his head. Then at least, he'd had the warmth of a pack pony to huddle against and his companions had been traders and merchants who willingly opened their merchandise of blankets and skins and lent them to the travellers.

They were bivouacked a mile from the front near a small village called Neuve Chapelle – a name Kim could never pronounce. He couldn't imagine this village or the surrounding countryside ever having known peace and quiet. The air and earth were constantly churned by the noisy presence of war. Heavy artillery, trucks, men, pack horses, Lewis guns, ambulances, soldiers milled and muddled everywhere. The road to the front was clogged with the continual passage of men and machines. The men went towards the front full of cheer, singing British songs about Piccadilly but they returned ominously quiet and horribly depleted in numbers. Day and night there was a constant din of artillery.

Kim turned off the main road, dodging dispatch riders and gun carriages and a shuffling line of British soldiers barely able to march. The narrow lane between hedgerows led past a farm owned by a family called Junot. The French farmer lived no differently from the Indian farmer and Kim imagined that so too had the Indian farmer stayed put on his land while huge armies manoeuvred and fought battles in the past.

The biggest revelation for the Indian soldiers had been that not every European lived like a burra sahib. In the months he'd spent in France, Kim had seen the ordinary people – the labourers, the farmers, the shop keepers – and was amazed that they existed. In India he only saw the sahibs and memsahibs, who all lived princely lives, and he naturally believed they lived such lives in their own country as well. Indians only had this one vision of England and Europe, that every man and woman was wealthy. This war had opened their eyes to the millions who lived in humble circumstances, small houses, penury, working at menial tasks. Many even worked as servants to the others, and this was something that shocked him. Englishmen and Europeans mere khanasamas and malis! Among their women there were even prostitutes and many of his companions had slept with them for the sheer novelty as well as the need. "If only we had known of all this years ago we wouldn't still be in awe of the British. They made us believe they all lived splendid lives in their homeland and we poor Indians swallowed such tales because we never saw them differently. Maybe the richer ones of us who went away saw that these were lies but they couldn't tell us of such things. But now we, the village people, the farmers and shop keepers, the clerks and the cooks, have seen for ourselves that it is all myth. Their own people live no better than us and in a far worse climate."

The only livestock the Junots owned was a cow. Once they'd had six hens and two ducks but despite their efforts, the birds had been stolen by soldiers. And the cow lived, like any Indian farmer's, in their own home. The farm house was built of granite with a low sloping tile roof. There was only one room in which the family ate and slept and they too were depleted. Jean Junot's two sons had died at the start of the war and only their daughter, Claudine, remained. Junot was a thin, stooped man with a fine moustache, watery blue eyes, and a face creased and crinkled by the harsh weather.

As usual at this time in the morning, Kim found his companions in the farm house. Today, because of his petition, he'd been the last to complete his duties. Kumar, Grehwal, Srinivasan and a couple of others were watching Madame Junot bustle around a large metal pot. She was only fractionally plumper than her husband and her face was permanently red as though sunburnt like the British faces in India and none of them could understand why this should be so as they hadn't seen this European sun for months.

It was a relief to escape the cold and slip into the

warmth of the farm house. Like the others, Kim noticed how respectful the French were towards them. They treated the Indian soldiers as equals and were painfully grateful that they had come such a vast distance to fight on their side against the dreaded Boche. Not that any Indian had seen this Boche, only the boots and plates of the British officers.

Kim dug into his cavernous pockets and pulled out a piece of ham covered with fluff. From another came three eggs, then a can of beef, and half a loaf of bread and a hunk of cheese. It was a tidy little haul and they all crowded around to exclaim at it.

'Have you not heard of the great Kim of the bazaars of Lahore and Delhi and Bombay? He can slip in and out of the kitchens and the jewellers' shops like a ghost and things miraculously disappear,' Grehwal joked. He was a triangular-shaped man, broad-shouldered and well-muscled, but this tapered to a narrow waist and slim legs. His build would have been more appropriate to a taller man. He had a thin nose and alert, humorous brown eyes and always tried to look for fun in the dull life they led.

'Oh, lazy Sikh, Kim learnt his trade of survival while you grew fat in your father's cloth shop and if it weren't for the fact that I met your father once when travelling from Benares, you would not now be permitted to share in such a feast.'

Madame Junot understood not a word, but beamed and sliced the ham and cut it small to go into the pot.

It was their habit, when they could, to gather here for this simple family's companionship and the warmth of their house. Kim thought his friends looked drawn and thin; the cold had whitened their brown skins so that it looked as if frost had entered their flesh permanently. Kim sat on the stone floor beside Jean's chair. The farmer said little and only listened to these healthy young men joking and chattering in their strange tongue. He would listen with his head cocked as if he was wanting to hear a different sound and Kim noticed his eyes often strayed to the door as if he heard the approach of his sons.

'You too are like us Indians,' said Kim softly. 'Sons are important for us too and to lose them is a terrible blow to the family.'

Kim still missed Parvati, Saraswati, and above all India, with an almost physical pain. He was more acutely aware of his love for his country here in this grey and ugly landscape than ever before. It had all happened so swiftly that he still thought he would awake and find himself in the village, lying next to Parvati, watching Saraswati slowly stir from her sleep and smelling the sweet smoke of wood fires and listening to the crows and squirrels scolding each other in the trees. There was a rush of such sights and smells and he nearly choked as though there were a physical lump in his throat. His last glimpse of Parvati had been stumbling along the cinder track with the other women waving as though her arm would fall off. The men had de-trained at Madras and lodged in tents on Island Ground, a large maidan behind Fort St George. In the dust and humidity of Madras, they had exercised and drilled from dawn to dusk. He'd never been so exhausted and each night gratefully rolled up and fell asleep on the ground. At the end of the training, they had a week of rifle practice and bayonet drill. When their rifles were taken away from them before they boarded the troop ship in Madras he should have suspected the intent of the British. The British officers had assured them that they would receive the newest arms when they reached Europe, a place which he'd never dreamt could be so distant from India. Their misery had started on board ship. They were locked below deck, and the smell of paint and the sea and the press of bodies made them all seasick. They were allowed out for an hour or two at dusk, then herded back in as if they were slaves.

'What did Captain Edlecliff-Johnstone sahib say?' Grehwal asked.

'That we must continue to serve as servants for the sahibs.'

'If they treat us so badly now in this war, how much worse will be our treatment at the end of it?' said Srinivasan.

'That is because we are already their servants in India,' Kim said. 'The only way we can be their equals is to throw them off our backs, like a horse does a cruel rider. We must organise ourselves to fight them, even if we have to take up arms in this cause to free ourselves. But while we are here in this country, we must learn as much about them as we can.'

'They are dirty,' Kumar said. 'They never bathe.'

'Who wants to bathe in this cold?' Grehwal said. 'A quick wash is all I need.'

'That's because you're a sardar,' Kumar said. 'In the south we bathe twice daily.'

'Because you get twice as dirty,' Grehwal said and giggled at his quick wit, ducking the potato Kumar threw across the room. He did this without removing his hands from his pockets. They were always thrust inside, as though they clutched secrets, and he even smoked without touching his cigarette.

'Not such unimportant things,' Kim said. 'I mean their thoughts and feelings towards India. And how can we get them to help us in gaining our freedom. Those who are sympathetic can organise funds for us, talk to others, vote in their elections.'

'You are many men in one,' Grehwal said. 'Wanderer, ascetic, thief, and now politician.'

'If I were not so clever,' admitted Kim modestly, 'how else would I have survived all these years? As I will the few weeks more of this war.'

Those words mocked Kim a year later as he stood in a deep trench next to his friends. They were ankle-deep in muddy water, still cold, still miserable but no longer the servants of the British. The toll on the British soldiers had been extremely heavy and older men were now being called up. Apart from the War Minister Lord Kitchener and Winston Churchill, everyone in England still believed the war would soon be over. The soldiers on the front wanted to believe this too. It was a dream, an illusion, but it sustained them in the senseless carnage. And now Indians were dying on foreign soil in a war that none of them comprehended.

A cold wind swept down from the north and swirled into the trench. It carried the whispers of men on duty and the stench of the dead. The cold air preserved such odours and like an epicurean delighting in their differences Kim could by a twitch of his nostrils distinguish death, urine, excrement, sweat, gangrene, gunpowder. There were no natural odours, as if nature had long been defeated and had abandoned man to his own inventions. Kim remembered now Shesha's last warning: 'You will be entering a hell that no god created. Only men can create such terrible things.' And instinctively Kim groped under his greatcoat with stiff fingers to touch the pebble given to him as protection by Vamana and wondered whether it would save him from bullets and bombs. Kim couldn't help believing that with the disappearance of nature so had God abandoned them.

The light threw their hunched shadows up along the mud walls, silvery with frozen streams of water. He thought how hollow and sad all these men looked.

All along the line men stood and waited. He saw Edlecliff-Johnstone moving in a crouch, whispering to each as he passed. As he passed Kim he said 'We're going over the top in ten minutes. Wait for the signal.' Then he suddenly stopped, recognising Kim in the ghastly light.

'You are Kim, aren't you?'

'Yes, sir.'

'I've heard of you. You're quite a legend in the Department. You're British, aren't you?'

'No, sir. I am Indian.'

'But I thought you were British.' Edlecliff-Johnstone sounded petulant. 'The report said . . .'

'It was a mistake by the Colonel sahib.'

'He wouldn't make that kind of mistake. You're very important to him. I don't blame you not wanting to be an Englishman. Look at the mess we've brought India into. I wanted to read your file but the Colonel never lets it leave his safe. He's a wily old man. But he's old and believes in the past, Kim. He will cling on to power as long as possible. I was going to make changes when I took over but it will never happen now. Report to me tomorrow morning.' He seemed to want to add more but the press of time made him hurry on.

Kim gripped his rifle tighter. His lips were dry from the cold and he couldn't contain his fear. This was the fourth time he'd gone over the top and each time, as he dragged himself and a wounded or dying companion back, fewer and fewer of them remained. It was a deliberate and stupid waste of men's lives, for this land they fought for was barren and worthless. Hill 73 was pitted with rocks and pebbles and scarred by shell craters and trenches that snaked through it like the coils of a huge serpent.

The first time he'd gone over the top, his bravery was too apparent. The Indians had thought it a grand adventure and were wanting to prove their bravery in front of these Europeans who for so long had treated them as worthy only to be servants. He had stood tall and the other soldiers, seeing his example, had also stood up and at the order advanced on the German lines. Kim still remembered the silence, eerie and deathly. They could hear only the tramp of their own feet as they moved in a straight brown line. He saw the faces of Sikhs, Jats, Muslims, Hindus, Bengalis and Madrassis, Gurkhas and Gujeratis, all fixed on the barbed wire and the hidden enemy. He thought then that their very presence had frightened the Germans and that they would return to their trenches unscathed. Then suddenly the air had exploded in rifle fire, the dreaded roll of Lewis guns, shells, screams of men wounded and dying. Men had fallen to the left and right of him and he'd kept going until he reached the first trench of the enemy and looked down at the face of a young German soldier. Kim, blackly bearded, appearing out of the smoke alone, must have startled him. For a long moment they had stared at each other, then the youth had tried to jerk his rifle up and Kim fired down at him, the bullet catching him in his throat and hurtling him backwards. And that dying was as painful to Kim as for the youth and he stood there a long time in shock, thinking how the lama would have wept at his cruelty.

"But how can I escape this duty to kill men?" Kim thought. "I am a soldier now and this is a war. If I had not fired I would now be dead and though there is no such act as dying – for it's illusion, I'm told – I would still leave behind a grieving woman and child and companions. As ugly and as evil as it is to kill fellow men, I must do it to the best of my ability for I believe my actions will be justified. And even as I say this to myself I hear Shesha mock my words of how men can justify every action, no matter how evil, in their own eyes. Strangely, I do not believe it is my karma to die in this foreign land, in this cold mud, thousands of miles from India. I have been granted a boon to live my allotted time, and the pebble of Lord Vamana protects me. When I steal my hand beneath my coat I can feel it almost alive with its own spiritual warmth and power. But is this the vision I experienced in Benares when I meditated on god and saw the warrior shoot three arrows into the air? The first was the magical flower of love, the second a terrible sight of blood and carnage, the third the bliss of eternity. If I am to die here in this vision, it is my karma and god will forgive my killing."

He had fired blindly then down into the trenches and retreated with the others. Again men fell on either side of him and he only stopped when he heard the guttural whisper: 'Kim' rise out from the earth and the crumpled man. He looked down on Srinivasan holding his belly and even in such darkness he saw the pale glow of intestines flowing out between the fingers. He didn't check his stride but scooped Srinivasan up into his arms and carried him back to their lines, knowing Vamana protected his back from the bullets and shrapnel that filled the air with their venom. 'You will live,' Kim whispered to his friend, thinking how once he had carried Narain too and spoken with such false confidence. But the dying know there is no hope.

'When you return to Madurai, go to my father and tell him I died bravely. I'm not a coward, am I?'

'You're as brave as the tiger himself,' Kim said and shouted for the medical orderly. The man came quickly and injected Srinivasan with morphine, and shook his head to Kim before rushing on to another who could be saved. 'I will see your father and carry your love back to him.' He kissed Srinivasan's forehead. His lips touched chilled flesh and even as he held his friend, he saw him die. He embraced his companion and whispered: 'Ram, Ram, receive the soul of my friend and grant him eternal bliss.'

A whisper ran down the line and Kim heaved himself up over the sandbags and rolled onto the cold hard ground. Kumar lost his helmet and Kim grabbed it and clamped it back on his friend's head. Grehwal hissed and shivered as they began the long crawl towards the enemy lines. Kim was glad it was pitch dark and cloudy, so the enemy wouldn't see their approach until too late. A foot ahead of him he saw Captain Edlecliff-Johnstone clutching his revolver and motioning them onwards in silent pantomime. Charred remains littered the battlefield, German, British, French, Indian. Bits and pieces rotted as in an alley behind a butcher's shop, legs and arms and fingers, skeletons picked clean by ants and rats who feasted and gorged on the corpses. Kim crawled past the rotting corpse of a Rajput, his fine handsome face half consumed, yet the moustache still curled jauntily like a pennant on a ruin. He wanted to be ill and, though he had seen so much evil in his life, Kim had never experienced such an evil nor felt such despair for all men.

Ahead of him Captain Edlecliff-Johnstone half rose to his knees and turned to signal the attack. Suddenly they heard the distant 'whump' of a weapon and the whisper of a climbing shell. It burst high above them and the strange silvery glare blinded him. Captain Edlecliff-Johnstone was trapped in the glare and frozen against the dark landscape of barbed wire and sandbags. The Germans opened fire and Captain Edlecliff-Johnstone somersaulted backwards and nearly into Kim's arms. Kim dragged him back, firing over his body. But the German fire was ferocious and he saw that the advancing line had halted.

'Tell them to retreat, Kim,' Edlecliff-Johnstone whispered.

Kim passed the message to Kumar and saw it inching along the shattered line of men. Only when they began the painful crawl back to their lines did Kim begin his own retreat, pulling Captain Edlecliff-Johnstone along by his armpits.

The murderous fire didn't abate and it seemed to take twice as long to make the remaining few yards. When he reached the wall of sandbags, Kim cautiously rolled over and tried to tug Edlecliff-Johnstone after him but he seemed to be stuck. He sweated with his efforts and turned to shout for help but there was no one near by. He rolled back over and saw that Edlecliff-Johnstone's shoulder was jammed under a sandbag and pulled him loose. As he pushed him over the top, Kim suddenly sensed a deafening explosion and felt himself lifted into the air and slammed back to earth in agonising pain.

He heard himself scream and through a thick red veil saw an orderly lean over him. He felt himself handled kindly and moments later as he began to slip into a warm, welcoming sleep, heard a distant murmur: 'He's good as dead . . .' Kim was very alone then and fought the sleep, struggling to catch a last glimpse of the sky. For once it was a clear night but then his vision began to cloud.

Suddenly he couldn't see the stars any longer. Instead a head blocked his vision. It was child sized, with long hair tied neatly in a bun on top. Vamana, Vishnu's avatar, stared down at him in irritation. He wrinkled his delicate nose at the odours.

'You are always in trouble. Each time I find you, you are dying. Can't you stay alive for even a second without my having to save you?'

'This is but the second time,' Kim protested.

'Twice is more than a test of my patience,' he said and placed his small palm on Kim's chest. 'I won't come a third time, I warn you. Men constantly expect us to perform miracles after they've got themselves into a fine mess. I have other things to do.'

Kim tried to smile as Vamana's healing warmth began to spread through his body. An artillery shell exploded a few feet away and showered them with dirt. Vamana paused and fastidiously brushed the dirt off his hair and naked chest.

'Why don't you stop the war? You have the power.'

'We gave men free will and they have chosen to destroy the earth and finally themselves. That is all your destinies. Now try to stay out of trouble and give me some peace.'

Vamana began to waver and faded away even as Kim closed his eyes.

Kim was puzzled as to why Parvati was on the battle front and tried to push her to safety. But she remained, surrounded by light, above his head and held his arms and he imagined they were in their hut making love and tried to embrace her. He wanted the comfort of her body, the sanctuary of normality, the perfume of her innocent fresh sweetness.

'Here you are nearly dead and the first thing you do is try to heave me into bed!' a woman chuckled.

The glare of the Indian noonday sun hurt, and he shielded his eyes. He saw the woman more clearly. She was round-faced, cheerful, her yellow hair crowned by a white cap.

When he looked beyond her his jaw nearly dropped. He was lying in an Indian palace. High above was a domed ceiling, brightly decorated, reminding him of the one in Akbar's tomb. It was supported by a gallery of arches and slender pillars, inset with flower motifs as in Shah Jahan's palace in Agra. And hanging from the ceiling was a huge glass chandelier. The hall in which he lay was circular too and filled with beds set in precise straight lines. Another gallery encircled the floor and through a high archway he looked down a long corridor leading into a garden.

He smelt medicine and blood and soap and the sweeter perfume of the woman.

'Acha hai?' she asked.

'Yes. Am I at home?'

'No. England. A place called Brighton Pavilion. We're using it as a hospital.' She spoke slowly in English as though this would make it easy to understand, then realised he'd spoken in English.

'Well at least it will be easier to talk with you. How are you feeling?'

'Stiff. I don't feel pain.'

'You will soon. But the worst is over. You took the blast on your back. Knocked you clean out. How you survived it is still a miracle. The orderly said your whole back was blown apart and he just gave you a morphine injection and left you for later. But when he came back he found your back nearly perfect, except for some shrapnel. Most probably he confused you with someone else. But it was a bad concussion.'

'What has happened to Kumar and Grehwal?'

'I don't know who they are. If they're your friends, I expect they're still out there.' She saw the shadow of grief cloud his handsome face and thought how they always asked about their friends. She presumed they grew intensely close in the war.

'And Captain Edlecliff-Johnstone?'

'I've never heard of him.' She picked up a small box from the bedside table, opened it and took out a medal. 'You're very brave. You've been given the Indian Order of Merit.'

Kim took it and stared at the face of the King and then placed it carefully back in the box. The feel of this new talisman reminded him of the other and he groped around his neck. It had gone. He sat up in fright, nearly crying out in pain. The nurse saw his panic.

'Is it the stone? It's in the drawer.' She took it out, amused that such a little thing should get him into such a state. 'You people are so superstitious.'

Kim took it silently and slipped it over his head. He couldn't explain to this nice English nurse that Vamana, the dwarf reincarnation of Vishnu, had given it to him and that many years ago, when he was dying from a bullet wound, Vamana had appeared in person and withdrawn the bullet. The medical orderly had reported the truth the first time and it was Vamana who had healed his back and saved his life once more. Looking at the placid homely features, he knew she would never believe such a thing.

There was pain; there was stiffness. His back felt stitched and tight, as if he were wrapped in shrunken buffalo hide. The nurse helped him to hobble slowly between the rows of beds. The ward was full of Indian soldiers only. Some lay still and silent, others were sitting up and he cheerfully greeted each as he passed. 'Namasthe ji, and how are you?' 'You look strong as one of your buffaloes.' 'We will soon be home in the sun.'

She sat him in weak sunlight out in the garden and though the English summer was still cool, he was grateful for the light. He looked up at the sun almost in worship and then around him, not quite believing he was now in England; especially with the Indian palace behind him. 'Ing-land,' he said out loud, and thought it sounded strange. It was still and calm; nurses and doctors moved quietly and he could barely feel the pulse of the country. The walls blocked his view of this place called Brighton but he smelt the sea nearby. An Englishman swept the pathway in the gardens and he watched in curiosity, having never seen one do such a menial task. Another carried a tea tray for a patient, another sat on guard duty, as lazy as any chowkidar. How amazing. He watched them for over an hour, as he had as a child squatted and watched ants scurrying to and fro. He finally called the bearer and asked for a cup of tea and the man politely withdrew and returned with the cup. Kim held it like a prize.

Kim saw his nurse again at the end of the second week. He had asked after her and been told she was off duty. Today she wasn't dressed in a uniform but mufti. She sat and talked to an Indian soldier for a while and then namasted to him and moved to another one. Kim watched her work her way down the ward until she finally reached his side. He sat by a window, wrapped in a blanket. This English summer was as bleak and miserable as a French winter.

'How are you, sepoy?' she asked in faltering Hindustani. 'If there is anything we can do for you please tell me. I am willing to write home to your family too if you wish. But it will be in English.'

She was poised politely over him like a young bamboo bent by a breeze and he realised she didn't remember him. But when he grinned, she smiled back in recognition.

'It's you, the miracle man,' she said in English. 'You are looking well.'

'I am well, memsahib . . .'

'I'm not a memsahib. My name is Victoria.' She sat and he felt her close scrutiny. 'And you're not a native, are you? I gave you a bed bath when you were unconscious. You're an Englishman.'

'Miss Victoria, I am indeed flattered to be considered as such. But I am a native of India. We can be as fair as yourself or dark as teak. It depends on which is our ancestral home.'

'I know nothing about your country but I would have sworn you were English.'

'But you should know everything about India,' Kim said in amazement. 'Your people have ruled there for over a hundred years. Are you not taught in school and the problems of India discussed in daily life?'

'I learnt about the Mutiny in school and what terrible things Indian people did to us . . .'

'And your people to us,' Kim said.

'We did nothing to deserve that barbaric cruelty. If we hadn't gone to India all you people would have been still living like savages.' She flushed, calmed and touched his arm. 'I'm sorry. I want you to know how grateful we are that you people are fighting beside us.'

'You're not sorry,' Kim said. 'I am. You have been taught lies and if a person, as educated as you – not one poor and struggling – should so easily believe them, what chance have we to be understood? Maybe I am wrong in this judgement and that you are only one of the millions in this country.'

She stood abruptly. 'You're not like the others. They're humble and grateful for us. You're not.'

'I'm not. But before you go, memsahib, could I have paper to write a letter?'

It was a long time since he'd received a letter from Parvati. She'd written twice since their parting and then a worrying silence had descended. He was certain the war had affected the mail. A German battleship cruising the Indian Ocean had disrupted shipping between India and England for well over a year. He'd heard it had even attacked Madras and panicked the citizens. That was another myth shattered – that Britain ruled the waves. One enemy destroyer had spread chaos. Kim wrote as fully as he could to Parvati telling her of his experiences. He wasn't as fluent with the pen as with his tongue, and despite great effort managed only to fill a page. But it was proof he lived and it would console her. He addressed the letter care of the Puducheri Post Office.

Kim thought he looked very English in the reflection of the carriage window. He wore a borrowed grey tweed suit, a size too large, a patterned pullover, a flannel cricket shirt and a flat cap. He cautiously studied this stranger who wore these clothes so easily, as if born to them. In the crowded compartment he certainly was indistinguishable. He didn't even exist. He had been the first to board and had carefully greeted the others, only to be met by a chilly silence. The silence of his fellow travellers was oppressive. They either read or stared stonily ahead. In an Indian train within the first half-hour he would have discovered the intimate details of everyone.

He wiped the mist and peered out. England's green reminded him of rice fields, except in India that rich, fertile brilliance lay only in patches. The villages were neat, dainty, quiet. He strained to glimpse the people who inhabited them. They were 'his' people and yet their way of life was unfamiliar. The sky remained gloomy and he ached for the glare and swirling colours that always held his eye. Each time the train stopped, the platforms looked deserted. In India, they teemed with people and noise and smells and . . .

He stopped, feeling almost physically sick. It was such a peculiar sensation that he thought at first it was the effect of his wounds. Then, gradually, he realised it rose not from the body but the heart. It had turned burnt and black. He was suffering an agonising loneliness. Never before in his whole life had he felt this frightening emotion. He was suffocating in a shroud and afloat in an alien universe. He, the friend of all the world, was lost here.

But this feeling didn't last long when he reached London. The city awed and excited him. He just couldn't imagine its size as he hurried down one street and up another, as if in search of its very centre. He stared into shop-windows, stared at the cars and the people and up at the buildings and monuments. They were exactly like the picture books he'd seen as a boy. It was all familiar and yet he felt as if he'd stepped into the book and wanted to escape back into reality. He came to rest finally on a bench in Hyde Park.

"Home!" He savoured the word but it tasted flat. "This is my home. My mind calls it that, not my heart or soul. Somewhere in this land is my ancestral home, the village of my father and mother. But I don't know where. There will be people there who knew them, brothers, sisters, aunts, uncles, cousins, friends. I will be a stranger to them all; they wouldn't even know such a person as me exists. But I should make some effort . . ."

Two well-dressed Englishmen joined him on the bench. He smiled at them as they sat but received only a cold stare and saw them deliberately distance themselves. He felt himself unwelcome and was about to rise when he saw a group of Indians strolling up the path. There were two English girls with them. The men were obviously sepoys on leave and were enjoying themselves. They were laughing and talking and the girls, who didn't understand a word, were giggling to each other. He was about to hail them when one of the men next to him spoke.

'Damned wogs. They shouldn't be allowed into the country. Just look at the way they're behaving.'

'Dreadful people,' the other said. 'They'll think no end of themselves now just because they've met a couple of tarts. Someone should tell those dirty girls they're letting the side down.'

'A good whipping is what they need. Those girls and the bloody wogs. It'll teach 'em a lesson and they'll go back howling. Visited India once. Full of filthy people worshipping ghastly idols.'

'So I've heard. If it weren't for us they'd still be up trees.'

'You two are the most stupid, ignorant, ugly white monkeys I've ever met,' Kim said, barely controlling his rage. 'Those men whom you revile are fighting and dying for dirty people like you.' He rose and stared down at their pink, surprised faces. 'And as an Indian, here is what I feel about you.'

Kim gathered his saliva and being much practised with the art of spitting paan, spat between the feet of the two men, and then turned and hurried after the soldiers.

The Indian Servicemen's Organisation occupied a three-storey building in the Strand behind India House. Indian soldiers milled at the entrance. Inside the front door a formidable European lady, flustered and weary, took down his details. She spoke in a strange accent which Kim suspected wasn't English – he later discovered she was Polish – but despite the chaos she remained continually cheerful. She barely spoke a word of Hindustani but every soldier greeted her with affection and she was apparently something of an institution. The odour of Indian food, the dark faces, the sound of a familiar language made Kim intensely homesick. The canteen was in the basement, simply furnished as a roadside dubba, and he ate greedily. He kept an eye on the entrance, looking for any men from his regiment and at last spotted a familiar face.

'Have you seen Grehwal or Kumar? Are they alive?'

'Yes. They are upstairs in the bar,' the jawan said. 'They will be delighted to see you, Kimathchand, for they have been searching everywhere for you. And we only have a few days' leave left. Will you be returning with us?'

'Yes.'

Kim ran up the stairs. The two were sitting slouched at a table with mugs of beer between them and Grehwal looked the drunker of the two. He had the blurred look of a man trying to stop the liquid motion of his surroundings. They both looked wearier, older; their eyes contained the secret knowledge of death. He felt a surge of relief and affection for his two friends; they had survived that terrible carnage, though it wasn't over yet. They both burst into tears when they saw Kim and embraced him from both sides, crushing him between them.

'We tried to find you but none would tell us correctly. They said you were in this hospital and then that one, and we ran from one to another and finally gave you up for dead as you seemed to have vanished from the earth.'

'And what happened to Captain Edlecliff-Johnstone?'

'He died from his wounds. Many British officers from India have died.'

'And so have thousands of our own people,' Kumar added.

Kim was saddened by all the deaths. Edlecliff-Johnstone had been young and full of energy and maybe if he'd lived he and other young men would have returned to India and responded more readily to the changes that had to occur. Now only the old men with their memories of the Mutiny, and accustomed to the isolation of their power, would continue to rule. He couldn't see someone like Colonel sahib ever bending and swaying to the changes. He would remain rigid, firm, necessarily cruel, for that was the manner of his rule.

They talked and drank until it grew dark outside and then, supporting each other, staggered up two flights to fall on the mattresses in the dormitory. Kim, as he fell into a deep and drunken sleep, felt he had returned 'home' to his people.

'When we go back to our villages and our land, to our towns and our womenfolk and children, we must spread the word of what we have seen in this country and tell our people how we have suffered in this war.'

Kim paused. The soldiers stared up at him and nodded in agreement. The dormitory was lamp-lit and the flame flickered over the faces of the men. He had paused also to note the entrance of two men obviously not soldiers. The one within the glow was a slim, handsome man with a hooked nose and glaring dark eyes. He wore an ill-fitting three-piece suit and carried a cane. His thick wavy black hair perched on his head like a cap. The other remained in the shadow and Kim caught only the gleam of a heavy gold ring on the third finger of the hand which also held a cane.

'We are dying here on their battlefields, not for Mother India but in order for the British people to continue their subjugation of our bodies and souls. For a century and more we have believed them to be a superior people and they have encouraged us to believe their own stories about themselves and that we, the Indians, are an inferior race who know no better than to fight and kill each other. I ask you now, who are we seeing fighting and killing each other in terrible ways?'

'The Europeans,' the soldiers responded.

'Yes, the Europeans. And even the British people, whom they have long suppressed and who lead lives no better than we do in our villages and towns, are asking why they must continue to die for the empire. Then why should we, who have no quarrel with their enemy, suffer the cruelty of dying and suffering for their sakes? We should be free to decide our destiny for ourselves; we should be free to rule our own lives; we should be free to make our own mistakes; we should be free to be equal to the British.'

He sat down, to applause. This was the third meeting Kim had organised. He had done it first so that the soldiers could meet to talk about whatever they wished for he sensed their isolation here, and their need to understand each other more. Apart from talking, the men would sometimes sing or dance as they would have done in their villages. We Indians are a diverse and disparate people and unless we understand each other first, how can we unite to fight our exploitation, was Kim's reasoning. The British had cleverly separated them into community regiments – Sikhs, Rajput, Jat, Madrassi, Mahratti, Gurkha – to keep them from knowing about each other.

Another soldier rose from the ranks and took his place in front of them. He was a Rajput, who spoke about what he had seen in England and France, the condition of the people. For all of them, the war had changed their vision of the European and with this change came a questioning of their own subjugation, the imposed inferiority. The

Rajput spoke briefly, then a Mahratti talked of his family, of his homesickness, of the death of his friends. Kumar talked about his dead friend Srinivasan, and how he had survived so far but knew he would soon return to the front, and confessed his fear. He yearned to go home to his wife and children and live quietly in his village.

As the men filed out at the end of the meeting, Kim was stopped by the civilian. He gestured to Grehwal and Kumar to go on without him. Close at hand, the man had an extremely dark skin and even white teeth. His suit was not only ill-fitting but also shabby. Kim noted the shine and the neat darning. His companion was a complete contrast. He shone with wealth, like the ring on his finger. His suit was expensive and well-cut and he wore it well. He looked athletic and had the fine sharp features of a Brahmin. Mahratti possibly or a Punjabi. The poor one looked as if he came from Travancore or Cochin.

'I'm Krishna Menon,' he quickly gripped Kim's hand and confirmed Kim's guess by his name. 'You will be a great acquisition for us.'

'I am not a water buffalo to be purchased.'

The other man laughed. 'He has a quick wit too, Krishna. What Krishna means is that you can bridge the gulf between us and the common man.'

'You may call them common. They are soldiers dying for India while people like you wear expensive suits and lean on silver-topped canes.'

'Touché,' Menon said. He stared fiercely as if trying to imprint his words in Kim's mind. 'We are members of the Indian National Congress here and we try to meet as many of our people as we can, to talk to them, to persuade them in the cause of Indian freedom. My friend is Romesh Sahni. He's Vice President of the Oxford Student Congress.'

Sahni hesitated only fractionally but long enough for both Kim and Menon to notice, and then his hand was thrust forward. It was soft and quite lifeless, reluctant to touch. But he met Kim's stare with the hint of a smile.

'We're the new blood in the National Congress,' Menon said. 'We're the ones who will change India. People like you and me, who have seen what it's like here, can carry the message back. We have fierce ideals, not wishy-washy compromises.'

'We would be honoured if you worked with us,' Sahni said quickly, not wishing Menon to have all the glory of this new convert. 'We would help you to organise the movement in the countryside. Two years ago we met Mr Mohandas Gandhi here. He was an inspiration to us all when he addressed us at the Students' Union and he told us how important it was for the organisation to obtain the support of the com . . . ordinary man in India.'

'I will work only for India. Not for the Congress.'

'But it is one and the same.'

'We will see,' Kim said and made to move on.

'Where can we contact you in India?' Sahni asked.

'I have no place. But you could write to me care of Balbir Singh, the cloth merchant in Amritsar.' He had no wish to reveal his home to these strangers. 'There is no need for haste. I have yet to finish with this war.'

They passed him visiting cards, Sahni's stiff and ivory with embossed lettering, the other crumpled and worn.

'Splendid chap,' Sahni remarked as he and Menon strolled away. 'A man like him will be an asset for the National Congress. He could reach the peasants in a way we can't. He has the ability to talk and attracts men to him.'

'I like his sentiments,' Menon said. 'He distrusts us politicians.'

'But we're the ones who will win India's freedom.'

'But not without the support of men like him.'

'And they're so ignorant,' Sahni said and pulled out his gold hunter. 'Well, I'll have to run to catch the train to Oxford.'

They parted at the door. Sahni lingered on the edge of the pavement watching his companion trudge eastwards. A Sikh soldier strolled slowly past, gawping at the sights around him. Another jungley, Sahni smiled.

Kim waited until after midnight for Kumar and Grehwal. They came in together and flopped down tiredly beside him, as though returning from a route march.

'I followed the dark one,' Kumar spoke first. 'He is poor. He ate in a dubba which I wouldn't have spat in, and could only afford a morsel of food. He then went to buy books and I followed him for miles until he reached his dwelling. It was in a poor neighbourhood called East End. He has a room below the house and I saw him through the window reading his books. I got lost returning here and if it hadn't been for a British soldier I would be wandering for ever.'

'You owe me money for mine,' Grehwal said. 'He went straight to India House. It was shut but they opened the door for him. He spent half an hour there and then took a hansom cab to a restaurant where he ate a good meal, alone. It cost my month's earnings at home . . . or at least what my father gave me. Then he went again by cab to Paddington Station and caught a train to Oxford Town.'

'You were right,' Kumar said.

'It is only suspicion,' Kim said. 'I knew if we organised such meetings someone would come to listen and carry the report back to their masters. It could be Sahni. Even now, I imagine the question: "Who is this Kimathchand? Send a message to Delhi and warn them about his sedition."' He lay back quietly, and imagined further that in the inevitability of Indian bureaucracy, the message would eventually reach the Colonel sahib's desk.

The landscape hadn't changed. If anything, it was more bleak, more inhospitable. The trenches were deeper, a never-ending maze of mud walls crowned with sandbags. Those on duty looked at the men returning from leave with tired pitiful smiles. Poor sods, their eyes said, you've enjoyed yourselves and now you've come back to die. They lined up for inspection, pressed against the wall, and their new commanding officer slowly walked down the line. He had a ginger moustache and his face looked misshapen. And even as Lieutenant Colonel Richard Goode walked down the line, he heard the whispers race ahead of him. Even here, thousands of miles away, he was recognised. You'll never shake off your rotten past, not until you're dead and even then you'll be remembered and pitied in the bar-rooms of the clubs, he told himself.

Kim heard the whisper, 'Anil Ray', and looked anew at Lieutenant Colonel Goode. The subadar major, a Lucknow Muslim, had recognised the police officer. So this was the man Anil Ray had thrashed. The pale, almost watery blue eyes studied him from a foot away and Kim recoiled at their virulence. He hates us all but above all he hates life itself. Rumour has it that he isn't afraid of the enemy and challenges them to kill him. And we'll be killed because of this madness. It's memory he wishes to kill, to wipe out his whole life as though he never existed and was never humiliated by a native.

'Kimathchand,' Goode whispered.

'Yes, sir,' Kim said and glanced to the subadar major. He shrugged in reply to the silent question. He had no idea why Goode had singled Kim out.

'See me after inspection. On the double.'

Lieutenant Colonel Goode sat at a low table in a dark cellar with mud walls, holding a handkerchief to his mouth. Only a curtain separated him from the trench. Though it was still day, a lamp lit the room, the flame steady and unwavering. He had removed his hat to reveal thinning red hair, the bald patch glowing as he bent his head, studying orders. Kim remained at attention, staring at the mud walls shining with damp. The cold once more seeped into his bones. Even if he should survive he would always remember the feeling of it embedded inside, deep inside, radiating out.

'I read Captain Edlecliff-Johnstone's dispatches,' Lieutenant Colonel Goode said. 'He mentions you twice for bravery. And you were awarded the IOM for trying to save his life.' He looked up. 'Naturally one wouldn't expect any less from an Englishman.' And he gave a wolfish smile of triumph. 'He had a letter from Bombay, identifying you.'

'I'm no different from any Indian soldier, sir. They too have been brave; they have received even the Victoria Cross.'

'One or two.' Goode said. 'I don't like the idea of an Englishman serving in the ranks with the natives. You'll be transferred to a British regiment.'

'I don't wish that. I am Indian. I am not an Englishman, sir.'

'Are you trying to tell me you want to be treated as a native? Are you mad? A damned native? It's a bloody disgrace.'

'I see no disgrace in being who I am.'

'There's nothing but disgrace in being a native.' Two red spots appeared on Goode's cheeks. 'You should be damned proud of being an Englishman.'

'Sir, I was never an Englishman. I was born in Lahore and grew up in the bazaars, like any of my people. I take no pride in wanting to be someone I am not.'

'Get out of here, and don't expect me to mention you in any damned dispatches.'

Once more Kim found himself no longer a soldier but a servant, but a servant not for the British officers but for his own comrades. He was forced to fetch their food, clean the latrines, sweep their quarters and was given extra guard duty. He accepted these tasks cheerfully though his companions were angry about his treatment. Goode would make every effort to humiliate him, hoping Kim would appeal then to be transferred as an Englishman to another regiment to serve with British soldiers. But Kim couldn't imagine himself living or dying among such strangers and the thought never even entered his mind. And yet once again his life had entangled with Anil Ray's, though they were thousands of miles apart. He doubted Ray would have enlisted, he hated the British too fiercely to kill for the empire. He would do his killings on Indian soil.

And when the time came to fight, Kim was forced to take the most dangerous positions, as a point, entering no-man's-land ahead of the men. Goode wasn't to know that here on this battlefield was not Kim's time to die. For Vamana had used his magical powers to save him from certain death. Kim's continued survival, his continued bravery and his comradeship with the other jawans, enraged Goode no end.

It was four months after his return to the front line that the soldiers received their mail. Kim hoped for a letter from Parvati but instead was handed one written to him in a strange hand. It was a thick envelope and weighing it up he felt a dread that it contained bad tidings. He felt its threat and waited half a day before he opened it. There were many sheets and he turned to the last first to discover who had sent it. Alice Soames. Parvati's friend and the Colonel sahib's wife. With great care he turned to the first page 'Dear Kim' . . . and as he read he felt his hair start to stand on end.

# 20

## July 1917

As Kim thought of Anil Ray, his name was spoken in a loving whisper to Anil Ray by a sensual looking woman nursing a naked male child. If it had been possible for their thoughts to leap the thousands of miles that separated them and touched, they would have recoiled in shock at this coincidence. Anil too thought he would never escape the intertwining of their lives. "Like serpents we coil and wind around each other, touching occasionally, weaving patterns beyond our understanding, knowing our beginning but not our ending."

He was spending the night in a village called Rae Bareli with four companions before continuing on a journey which would dramatically alter his life. Their pack pony grazed on the spare grass, its load decorated with innocent pots and pans, but beneath the canvas lay five rifles, sixty rounds of live ammunition and forty sticks of dynamite. It was the child that had brought about the conversation. It had crawled across the ground to him and he'd picked it up and held it on his knee. The firelight gleamed on its healthy, plump body. 'And what is his name?' he'd asked innocently. 'Kim,' the woman had replied and in the shadow didn't notice Anil's start. 'But it is a strange name,' he'd managed to say and waited for her reply. 'The prohit says it's not a Hindu name and that I'm foolish to give my baby such a strange name, but who cares for the prohit?' Anil did not mention that he knew of a man called Kim, and instead encouraged the woman to talk about him. She had an audience not only of Anil and his companions but of half the village which had gathered around under the peepul tree. It was a common place, like a square, where they met in the evenings to gossip.

'It was here that the collector sahib, one Angrezi called Webb, tied Kim to a tree and had him beaten in front of us all,' Lakshmi said. The villagers nodded and sighed dramatically at the cruel memory. 'And this was only because he had picked up the dead body of Rambaj and not let it lie in the dust like a corpse of a pi-dog. He was a man of great compassion and very brave.' She glanced with unconcealed contempt at the village men who avoided her accusing eyes. 'All our men ran in fear when they heard the guns.'

'Was he one of us, this Kim?' Anil enquired.

'Yes, yes,' Lakshmi's husband said, taking up the story. 'He was a true son of Mother India. After beating him, the policemen then placed him in manacles and took him away and we heard later he was imprisoned in Tihar Gaol. We do not know what happened to him after that.'

'He is probably dead,' Lakshmi said and her eyes glistened with tears, as they did each time she thought of Kim, the only man she truly loved. He had rescued her from the brothel in Bombay only because one night while visiting it with the smuggler, whose name she now forgot, and the other man Narain, his friend, Kim had promised to help her escape the life of prostitution into which she'd been forced. He had kept his word and accompanied her all the way across India and arranged her marriage to the Jat ex-serviceman who was now her husband. No one in the village, especially her husband, knew she had been a prostitute.

Kim was woven into this village's history and the villagers told his story to every passer-by who might be interested in the gossip of their small lives. As Kim had claimed to be Lakshmi's cousin she was considered the authority on him. Naturally, she only spoke when invited to, for as a woman she was supposed to remain silent when strangers visited. But submission was not to her liking and she was subtly trying to change the ways of the village women, encouraging them to nibble away at their restrictions. Lakshmi had no awe of men. In the brothel she'd learnt their ways. They were venal, weakened by their lust, making fools of themselves to lie between the legs of a woman. This was the power she taught the other women.

Anil could have added a further episode to the legend of Kim, up to the point he and Kim had parted company in the Chambal ravines when Kim and the woman disappeared into those narrow canyons. He wished now he'd not heard this story. It diluted his passion, his hatred of Kim. He knew Kim as an Imperial agent and grudgingly admitted it was possible he could have resigned the service. In the Chambal ravines he had seemed to be on the verge of rebellion. The narrow beam of hate, which had ruled Anil's life for so many years was already weakening, the edges smoothed and softened by the child he loved now as his own.

On the night he had found Sushila weeping uncontrollably, they had clung to each other, like children trying to hide from the threatening dark. He was weary and bitter. His attempt to assassinate the Viceroy had failed and he'd just escaped Goode's net. He'd virtually walked all the way from Delhi to Calcutta, begging food from villages and sleeping in gulleys. They hadn't spoken a word in those two hours that they held each other, but their mere proximity and touch gradually comforted and renewed them. Then Sushila had collected what money she had, eighty gold sovereigns and a bag of silver rupees, and left her house, never once looking back.

Once, in what seemed another incarnation, Anil's mother had owned some property in Sitakutchi, a tiny village on the banks of a tributary of the Ganges. He'd visited it once as a boy before he'd left for Eton, and the village had remained a vivid memory. A small temple stood by the river, gleaming white, the stripped ochre steps washed by the waters. Beyond was the village, a few thatched mud homes, and the brick bungalow in a grove of mango trees. It had four cool rooms, a slate roof and a verandah. He thought now, with the responsibility of Sushila and the coming child, he would go there. They couldn't follow his nomadic and dangerous life.

The village lay in the princely state of Cooch Behar and could now offer him some sanctuary from the British, since every state was supposedly independent. Each ruler, whether maharajah, nawab or rajah, ran his state with the advice of his own ministers as he pleased. Some princes ruled wisely and well, most not. But this independence was no more than illusion. If one of them should pass a law against the interests of the British, he was promptly removed from the throne. Cooch Behar, like other princely states, had a permanent British Resident who kept watch over all their affairs.

Anil wasn't sure whether the bungalow would still belong to his family. On his father's death, the government had confiscated all their properties for, as a terrorist, he was not permitted to own or inherit property. The one in Sitakutchi had been in his mother's name and he prayed that possibly it had escaped confiscation.

They hired a small boat to carry them north along the river and it took them a week to reach Cooch Behar. He stopped the boat a few miles downstream of Sitakutchi and paid off the boatman. Sushila went ahead to make enquiries about the house and returned delighted. It still remained in his mother's name, shuttered and neglected, looked after by the ancient village chowkidar who was owed many years' wages.

The baby had been born in the village and Sushila called her Yamuna, after the river goddess. The baby was extremely fair and good natured and would grow into such a beauty that she would devastate the hearts of men. As she had already done Anil's. Sushila still had never mentioned the father's name. Nor had Anil asked, though he knew it was the Englishman who'd walked out of the bungalow on the night he'd waited in the shadows.

'But we have talked enough of ourselves,' Lakshmi's husband said, and the village men shuffled closer. 'What is happening in the war? We have heard it's being fought far away but already our people have died. Where is this place?'

'France,' Anil said. 'It is not even a British territory. We will lose many, many more of our fathers and brothers and sons before this war is ended. For what? For the British Empire to bask in glory while we're crushed under their rule. Do you know who pays for this war in which we spill our blood? You and you and you.' He jabbed a finger at each man. 'India has already paid 138 million pounds for the privilege of participating in this madness. Like fools we have rushed forward eagerly, not only laying down our lives but emptying our pockets.'

'And who is winning?'

'No one. They are killing each other even as you harvest your wheat. Thousands die daily for an inch of land which is worthless. They have long accused us Indians of being a savage and barbaric people. They remind us constantly of how we have fought with each other and killed each other by the hundred. Now look at them. They are more barbaric than any other race. The Europeans kill each other in thousands and race to invent new ways of killing yet faster.'

The villagers shifted uneasily. Three of their men had gone to this war. The recruiters had ridden through the village over a year ago, beating drums and looking splendid in their uniforms. They promised all things for those who fought for the King, especially the bharti, a gift of free land, and the landless had joined up and followed the soldiers out of the village. Lakshmi had warned them not to leave, but would they listen to a woman? No. They had not been heard of since.

Anil and his men left at dawn quietly. Two of the men, Vancouver Singh and Mohan Choudary, hurried ahead until a good half-mile separated them from Anil, Satish, Bhai and the pack pony. On the road it was wise not to be seen together, strong, healthy men selling pots and pans. They arranged to meet at midday the following day at a crossroad.

Anil remained contemplatively silent. He had grown content in Sitakutchi and for the first time since beating Inspector Goode in Simla experienced peace and contentment. Sushila's constant affection and her humour drew out the poisonous hatred. Yamuna soothed his rage. He was no longer lonely nor alone and he missed them terribly now as he walked in the great summer heat. The air was dry and lifeless and their feet scuffed up small puffs of fine dust that remained hanging long after they'd passed. The constant brownish yellow landscape was broken by wheat fields and clumps of trees like decorations on a drab piece of cloth. The sky was a heartless blue. Rae Bareli was already lost to sight.

His thoughts turned to Kim and he wondered where he was at this precise instant. Kim had gained immortality in Rae Bareli village, not through violence, but by an act of goodness. He had defied his own people for the sake of a dead Indian boy and had accepted his punishment mutely. He hadn't believed this story when Kim told it to him in Tihar Gaol. Anil hazarded a guess Kim could be in the war. It would be an adventure he would revel in and Anil reluctantly permitted himself the tiny hope that Kim wouldn't die in the war. The hope surprised him; it reflected the change in his feelings, and he wished he had not embarked on this mission. He felt heavy, filling slowly with foreboding like a dry well seeping water. The faces of his companions appeared set and determined while his own, he thought, must reflect his reluctance. I feel like the heat ahead of me, shimmering and illusory, ready to vanish.

He had no one to blame but himself. It was the momentum of his past that carried him forward. Though he was content in Sitakutchi, Anil was driven by his passion, his promise to drive out the British, as if the vow had been made in the temple and could not now be broken. He alone couldn't achieve his goal. He had to organise men, gather weapons, pinpoint targets. And with this war, the only way he could hurt the British was to disrupt the supply of men to the war in Europe. As Englishmen had died at Ypres and Gallipoli, more British troops were being drawn from India, depleting their numbers. It was the right time to strike as swiftly and frequently as possible. The army was thin on the ground and the government wouldn't have the men or the time to retaliate effectively. Other Indians, especially the Indian National Congress, checked their hand, as though they were playing cricket and agitation would be unsporting. Anil Ray hated cricket now, and the memory of playing for Eton at Lord's filled him with shame and a sense of betrayal.

Now that he had a family, Anil was even more cautious. No one knew he hid in Sitakutchi and he planned his attacks as far from his sanctuary as possible. Although Sushila feared for him, she made no attempt to dissuade him from these dangerous activities. It was his duty.

A month ago he'd left Sitakutchi to meet Mr Sen in Calcutta. Sen was one of the names Peter Bayley had given him. Sen had examined Anil suspiciously at first through thick spectacles. He was small and spry and grey-haired. He had received his degree in English Literature from Calcutta University and loved to air his almost obscure knowledge of the origins of English drama, quoting Euripides in Greek as proof of his theory. Opinions were hurled at random like tiny bombs and, having baffled his listener, he would sit back with a contented smile on his thin face. At other times he would quote passages from the writer Karl Marx, but in English and not German. He'd been arrested and goaled for five years for shooting and wounding a British tea planter in Chittagong. Once he realised he was meeting *the* Anil Ray, Sen melted into smiles and bountiful hospitality. He promised to help Anil in every way to drive the damned British out of India.

They conspired, and agreed to attack troop trains. But only those carrying British soldiers. Not Indians, only the British. The first problem was to find out when they would move and from where. Anil remembered that Satish's father worked for an army engineer and sent Sen to Delhi to make contact with Satish. Satish was only too eager to help, wanting to revenge himself for the beating given by the policeman, Inspector Goode, during his interrogation before Anil's attempt on King George's life at the Delhi Durbar. It had taken him time but eventually, through the network of Indian clerks working for the army, he had found a nationalist in military headquarters willing to pass on the information they required: the Royal Sussex Regiment was to be rotated from Lucknow to Calcutta to relieve a regiment being sent to the European front. Anil and Sen studied a detailed Ordnance Survey map of the area between the two cities. The railway line passed through plain and jungle, uninhabited for many stretches. They were looking for an ambush point nearer to Lucknow as they wanted to distance themselves from Calcutta. They found an ideal spot. It was distant from the nearest village, Rae Bareli, and in an area of jungle. The track crossed a tributary of the Gomati river, passing over a single-span iron bridge. On paper it looked fragile and vulnerable. Anil thought it ironic that he should be planning this piece of sabotage when so many years ago he had been arrested and his uncle killed on the mistaken assumption that they were responsible for attempting then to blow up the Viceroy's train. That miscarriage of justice had sown the hatred that had changed his life.

Anil's conspirators made dull company. Satish was silent, staring down at the road, furtively glancing around, while Bhai still spoke not a word, as blank and as simple as a face sketched on paper. Anil hadn't wanted them to come but Satish had begged and pleaded, desperate to be involved in the action rather than sit and think up hare-brained schemes. Anil had reluctantly given permission. He had chosen to travel with these two and sent Sen with Vancouver Singh. Anil trusted Sen and wanted him to keep a watch on Vancouver. One of Bayley's men, the fat Marwari in Delhi, had sent Vancouver Singh with the rifles and the dynamite. The man claimed to have worked as a powder man for a logging company in British Columbia. Vancouver Singh was a jovial man, a better companion than these two, rotund and perpetually hungry as a small child. He also spoke English as well as any Sikh could master another tongue. He had returned as a member of the Gadhar party and had been arrested by the government in Calcutta as his ship, the *Komagata Maru*, had docked. He had been detained for six months and then released.

As arranged, they met precisely at midday, not in a village but beneath a banyan tree. On either side of the dirt road was dense jungle and the bridge was a mile or two to the north. They cut off the road and cautiously moved through the undergrowth, sending peacocks flapping in panic, filling the air with their brilliant colours, while langurs scolded them from the tree tops and boomed out warnings. By four o'clock, they had reached the railway and followed it from deep within the jungle, out of sight of the narrow cleared corridor in case their presence should be noted and reported.

The bridge was indeed fragile-looking. It was fifty feet across, straight iron girders supported by iron pillars. The drop looked about seventy feet and the dried bed, with only a thin sluggish stream trickling through sand, was strewn with boulders. Before the bridge, the track passed through two steep slopes, matted with lantana bushes. Anil scrambled up to the ridge and surveyed the jungle. There was no sign of life nearby and the jungle faded into the horizon. And looking down to the river bed, they would have a clear line of fire on the survivors of the accident. Anil unloaded the pack pony and distributed the rifles. He and Vancouver Singh carefully made their way down to the bridge and Anil watched as Vancouver went over it, foot by foot, muttering into his beard, knowledgeably poking and prodding the joints.

He then went down to the river bed and studied the iron pillars embedded in brickwork. 'Here,' he called up, and Anil carried the dynamite down to him carefully. He squatted and watched Vancouver pack twenty sticks around one pillar, then another twenty around the second. He bound them with coir rope and inserted charges, each the size of a cigarette, into six sticks of dynamite on each pillar. He bared the wires, twisted them together efficiently, and then unwound the reel and backed up the steep slope. At the top of the slope, protected by a boulder, Vancouver connected the wires to a detonator and lifted the plunger.

'Ready.'

'Are you sure?'

'I am expert,' Vancouver Singh said. 'I can blow up a tree-stump and not one stone will move.'

'This isn't a stump. It's a bridge. I want it to fall.'

'You will see. The bridge will fall, boom, down into the river.'

Anil made them check their rifles and then positioned them twenty-five yards apart on either side of the bridge so that they all had a good clear shot. He took up a position a hundred yards up the track. This would give him time to identify the train and signal to Vancouver Singh with the small lantern. Anil settled himself behind a boulder with the rifle cradled in his arms. The twilight was soothingly quiet; the jungle seemed to stir gently as if it stretched and yawned for the long night ahead. The heat hadn't lessened; the sky changed its colour to pink and gold and then a velvety grey.

He heard a faint rustle to his left some distance away and fancifully imagined a tiger slipping through the jungle, smelling him and steering clear. He tightened his grip on the rifle. The humming silence returned, drowsy now and he realised how tired he felt. It had been a long day and it would be many hours before he could sleep. Once the sabotage was done, they would scatter to the four winds. Ahead of him, now, he heard the crack of a twig. Then another. It wasn't quite dark, the sky was faint with stars. Anil rose warily from behind the boulder and peered into the twilight. He saw nothing, the jungle was uniformly grey, a dark misty tangle of branches and vines and bushes.

He thought he saw movement and ducked down. When he peered out again he faintly saw the outline of a head. It took a moment longer for him to identify the man. He wore a peaked cap and even in the gloom he seemed strikingly fair. A Eurasian police officer! He was signalling to his men and didn't look in Anil's direction. Anil knew they'd been betrayed. But by whom? Sen? Satish? Bhai? Vancouver Singh? He didn't have time to curse his ill luck. Carefully he lifted the rifle, aimed and fired at the head. It vanished as would a puppet from a stage. The shot echoed in his ears, and birds screamed and flapped, filling the sky with the panicky beating of their wings. Gun fire opened up on all sides now and Anil knew he'd walked into a trap. He had to escape the net and started to back away.

A bullet exploded into his side, hurling him back against the boulder. His arm snapped as he struck the boulder and the rifle bounced off the stone and fell into the darkness. Flashes of light, twinkling like stars, so close, so loud, accompanied the gun fire. He had to escape but the pain in his side was a living fire, eating into his strength. He clamped his good hand against the wound and felt the hot gush of blood. He had to escape. The guns were firing at random at every rock and bush. Darkness hid the attacking party and him from them. He sat up and painfully rose to a crouch. He couldn't straighten and like a monkey, half bent, he pushed aside the undergrowth and stumbled blindly into the jungle. He wasn't certain of his direction, wasn't certain where an attacker was hidden. He fell again and again, collided with trees, ripped his clothes, tripped over roots. The guns roared continuously around him, coming closer and closer. He tried to hurry, hurry, but his legs moved sluggishly. They obeyed another's commands; they wouldn't listen to the panic in his brain. Then, fatally, they stopped altogether, bringing him crashing to rest against a tree.

"I am dying. I can feel my life slipping through my fingers, like water seeking escape. It is for the best. Why should I hold on to such a body as this, such a mind and heart that have long been poisoned by hatred and violence. I've done little good in this world except sow destruction. I can blame others for my downfall but now in the clarity of dying I only blame myself for turning so bitter. I could have been a different man if I had contained my hate, turned it aside with kindness and gentleness. I squandered the promise of my youth and manhood. I dreamt once of living a just life; instead my name strikes fear into all those who hear it. The very air cringes as I pass, it flies from the sight of me, from the glitter of venom in my eyes. They're dimming now, but not due to death. Sushila. I can only sigh her name in my mind. I wish I could speak it aloud and hear its music but my lips and tongue don't have the strength to part, to curl around her name. I am filled with despair at the thought of her because soon she will be gone from my life. I will not be able to seek her comfort, shelter in her love. Once more too she will be alone, my presence but a brief interlude between the lengthy silences in her life. Yam . . . Yam . . . Yamuna. She will be there always. In my selfish thoughts of dying, I had cruelly forgotten my child. I cannot think of her as anyone else's but my own. Oh God, I've not been worshipful of you; take care of them."

Anil's sigh was heard. He suddenly realised the jungle was still, silent, watchful. The guns had stopped. He was alone and imagined the jungle waiting to consume him. He would be food for the creatures here, jackals and vultures, wild pigs and rats and then the ants. Only bones would remain as evidence of Anil Ray. He felt freezing cold and his teeth chattered the way they always had at Eton. The school dormitory had been like a dark and icy cave when he woke in the mornings and the air crawled with goose bumps as he dressed hurriedly.

There had never been any escape from that cold and he felt it enveloping him now. Strangely, it soothed him, made him drowsy as if he basked in a wintry sunlight that was slowly turning to dusk. The pain had receded, hurting another person.

In his sleep, on the precipice of death, he thought he heard voices. He concentrated terribly hard, forcing his addled mind to focus on those voices. They were flowing, meandering like a stream, coming towards him. No, they weren't speaking; they were singing in a strange tongue and he couldn't understand the words. He had never heard such an enchanting sound. It seemed as if the singing were a physical force, sensitively entering his body and travelling through his nerves and veins. Yes, the voices were in his bones, they tingled in his blood, they warmed it and drove out the chill. The voices dammed the flood of blood and then he felt the strength flowing back into his body. The chill receded from the warmth. The warmth wasn't fire but a glow of gentle light. It was a yellowish blue, faint yet full of flame. He thought he was imagining that it closed the bloody wound in his side and repaired the shredded flesh and healed the splintered bones. But he knew that it couldn't be happening and that these dreams were to be the last conscious memory of his life.

Anil cringed at the red glare, turning away to avoid the ache. His cheek scraped bark and he checked his breath. He could feel, he could hear. He heard the singing still. It was soft, whispery. It enchanted and soothed him and he couldn't help but listen appreciatively, not wishing to disturb the singers. He couldn't tell whether it was men or women who sang. Above their voices came the caws of noisy crows, the shriek of parrots, and he welcomed the ugly sound. Surely, they hadn't followed him into an afterlife.

Anil snapped his eyes open. He wanted to catch everything in an instant, in case it should dissolve and turn to illusion. He was startled to see two young men sitting in front of him a few feet away. The one on the left held a ravanhatta, the one on the right cymbals. He looked for their eyes and found them closed and sunken and knew they were blind. He also saw no difference in their thin faces, the shape of their noses or the tilt of their heads. Their voices were silvery now, crystal, gold, and he couldn't tell which one sang for their voices were in such perfect harmony. All around them the jungle was alive with birds and beasts. Crows, parrots, vultures, kites and peacocks crowded the tree tops and hopped on the ground. Jackals and hyenas, blackbucks and tigers stood or sat within killing distance of each other but made no move. The young men gently fell silent and with a great and reluctant sigh, the birds flew up into the sky and the noise was deafening. The blackbucks started and edged backwards, the hyenas slunk into the undergrowth. The tigers yawned and stretched and slipped through the patches of sunlight and shadow and became one with them. Within moments, they were alone and Anil thought he had only imagined such a wonder.

'You are well?' the young men enquired in a strange chant and Anil thought it a reassuringly simple question to answer. Yet it took time, for he couldn't understand what had happened. He felt his side and it was sore and tender but there was no wound. He looked down and saw the great spread of crusted brown and flies buzzing around it. His broken arm hurt, but it was whole again.

'Yes,' he said, unable to disguise his awe. 'I prayed to God but not for my own sake. Who are you?'

'We are Bala,' they said. 'We felt your agony from afar and found you dying. Lord Krishna granted us the boon of our singing. We sang his praises all night and he came to discover why we were summoning him. He saw you and, taking pity, took it upon himself to heal you and save your life. He has given you a new destiny which only he knows how you will fulfil.'

Anil blinked, partially in disbelief, but he couldn't deny he was alive. He looked around. The jungle remained grey but in a perfect circle around him grass had sprung up, green and fresh. But even as he watched, he saw the patch of bright green fading and crumbling.

'We must go,' they said and rose.

'Wait, wait. You cannot leave without telling me of your miraculous powers and why Lord Krishna saved my life.'

'We are Bala,' they repeated patiently and explained the boon granted them by the Lord Krishna, and the protection of Brahma. Fourteen years ago they had left their village in south India so that people all over the country could hear them sing, and there were still many more years of travelling to be done before they lost their voices. They hoped by then to have reached the Himalayas.

'But why the Lord Krishna saved your life, that we do not know.'

'I will come with you and worship you,' Anil said.

'No. We do not want worshippers. We are only human.'

'I will become a bhakta of the Lord Krishna then,' Anil said.

'If that is to be your destiny, then so be it.'

Anil Ray, who had paid homage to no one in his life, immediately prostrated himself on the ground and touched the dusty feet of the two young men. He felt them touch his head and heard them move away. He sat up and watched them picking their way carefully through the jungle and wished he'd asked how they saw so clearly when they were blind. He noticed too that they walked in a very straight line. Soon they were lost to sight and Anil began to weep.

# 21

## January 1915

The exact likeness of Mohini sat next to Gitabhai in the private railway carriage. Her beautiful but impassive face remained constantly in profile against the window, indifferent to the plains and jungles, the fields and rivers and villages and hills, that slowly glided past.

'Chamunda,' Gitabhai addressed the likeness, having given her the second name of Kali, the goddess of death and destruction. Chamunda turned at the sound and stared at Gitabhai and Gitabhai, looking into those pale amber eyes, saw the demons swirling like bubbles in water, seeking escape. 'It is a pity I could not have invested you with intelligence. But I did not think we would be making such a long journey together and that I would find you such dull company. I am proud of you though. With my own hands and my own breath, I created living flesh. I can see the pulse in your throat, feel your breath on my palm.'

She leant across and pinched Chamunda's cheek, catching the flesh between thumb and forefinger and squeezing hard. She gave the flesh a cruel twist. Chamunda didn't flinch though the skin remained stained with the imprint. Gitabhai wished Chamunda was Mohini. When she had pinched Mohini's cheek with greater cruelty, Mohini would cry out and tears would spring in her eyes. Such small pleasures were denied her by this creation which had neither emotional nor physical feelings. What intelligence existed in that beautiful but empty head was under the guidance of the demons within. They heard and saw and smelt through their human conveyance. Once their duty on earth was fulfilled by Mohini's death they would return to their netherworld and leave her in peace and quiet. The next time she summoned rakshashas, she would make sure they were more flexible and servile. These ones behaved like the Indian bureaucracy: arrogant, unimaginative and pedantic. She would add a verse to her tapas asking for the power to dismiss them, if she was dissatisfied.

She lay back in the leather armchair, rocked by the movement of the train. The private carriage gave her the privacy she needed for Chamunda and her own staff. It was a small house on wheels, comfortable and fairly ornate. The walls were teak-panelled and chandeliers hung from the ceiling. The whole carriage was carpeted and apart from this living-room, it had two bedrooms, a dining-room, a kitchen and bathroom. Her cook and bearer slept in the kitchen while the crone who guarded her quarters at home squatted in the vestibule, permitting no one to enter. She looked weak and frail but her eyes frightened away the chai vendors and chokras and ticket collectors and sweepers.

Gitabhai had planned carefully, not wanting any mishaps in the execution of her plan. She knew Ram had planned to journey south to get his wife back. Men were such fools. They lusted over women who had no desire for them. It's the conquest, Gitabhai thought, and the self-inflicted punishment that they enjoy. Mohini treats him like dirt and my son, though blustering with threats, accepts her disdain as if it were worship. Well, he will never see his Mohini again. With her death I will free him from his obsession. He will still be asleep in Delhi and will only waken in another five days, by which time I will have found her. And ended her life.

The rakshashas were already impatient to consume Mohini and then vanish. Once they had returned to the netherworld, Chamunda would crumble back into dust. But not before Gitabhai had extracted her revenge on the man who had stolen Mohini away from under her sleeping nose. No, for the lover there would be pain and humiliation. She giggled in delight. What a terrible punishment for a man! He would insert his organ between Chamunda's legs and as he withdrew it to plunge back into that delightful passage, his pleasurable weapon would be cut to pieces. His pain would unfortunately be too brief, she thought regretfully. The demons would roar out of Chamunda and consume him then for having violated their sanctuary. She spent a sleepless night wondering how she could position herself to watch such delightful destruction.

Sir Ram Shanker, using his title and his enormous influence as a Member of the Viceroy's Council, had demanded that the authorities place an aeroplane at his disposal to make a swift and secret journey south. Cost was no object. He paid a lakh of rupees for the hire of the aeroplane and the pilot, a young Scotsman called Hetherington who had unruly hair and a cheerful disregard for Lal Bahadhur's importance. The aeroplane was a two-seater and Hetherington at first refused to allow Mahender on board. But for an additional fifty thousand rupees, Lal Bahadhur's servant was permitted to crouch at his master's feet.

Lal Bahadhur sat stiff and upright in the bucket seat, hands gripping his gold-topped cane, indifferent to this first experience of skimming over India. He scarcely glanced down and ignored Hetherington's commentary on the scenery below. Mahender, squeezed next to his master's feet, kept his eyes tightly closed and prayed constantly. Each time he peeped out, he caught a glimpse of a serene blue sky and nothing else.

He was secretly pleased that he had outwitted the witch Gitabhai. Having told her the contents of Mohini's letter, through sheer fright at what she threatened to do with him, he had kept a close watch on Gitabhai without telling his master. She had moved quickly, almost running to that locked windowless cell in the garden. When the door opened he had heard a strange roar which set sleeping birds flapping and screeching in fear and his hair had stood on end. He wanted to bolt then but his hatred for Gitabhai forced him to creep up to the door. He could not see or hear anything but when he rested his hand against the granite wall the heat seared his palm and he experienced such a sense of dread that he sprinted for the bushes, turban flying. He hid behind a bougainvillea and kept watch. Mahender was a simple evil man, earthy in his violent deeds and fearing no one on earth, except Gitabhai. He had never been able to comprehend the forces that Gitabhai could summon. They were not from his nightmares, as he slept dreamless and innocent, but from mythology. They writhed, ugly, frightening and misshapen, under the tridents of Siva or Vishnu, danced in the company of Kali. He wished he too could summon such power, and during his long hours of vigil imagined the women he could control, especially Mohini for whom he devised special and painful pleasures.

Gitabhai emerged at dawn, and he barely recognised her. She was bedraggled and exhausted, and for once that youthful beauty which had never changed resembled a slipped mask. Her features seemed askew, dark holes for eyes, her mouth pinched and drawn, and her skin was creased like crumpled paper. He followed her back to her rooms and an hour later she appeared youthful, supple and alert, her eyes and skin glowing in the early morning light. This transformation, in a strange way, was even more frightening than the locked cell. It revealed her power to control age and death. He followed her gharri to Delhi Station and heard her make the travel arrangements, and give the chi-chi station superintendent two leather bags of coins. The man had peeped in and nearly prostrated himself full length at her feet. With such wealth he could retire immediately and return 'home' to an England he had never seen.

On her return home, Gitabhai went immediately to her kitchen. Mother and son maintained separate kitchens and cooks. Lal Bahadhur, now a knight and a Member of the Viceroy's Council, entertained frequently and his guests were meat eaters. Gitabhai was a pious vegetarian and would not permit meat to contaminate her kitchen. At noon Mahender saw what he had waited for. A dish from her kitchen was passed across to Lal Bahadhur's and he followed the food up to the threshold of his master's dining-room. He scuttled to a window and peeped in. The dish was carefully placed in front of Lal Bahadhur. His new young wife was standing behind his chair and waiting to serve the food. Mahender wanted to burst in but was too frightened of Gitabhai to reveal her secret in front of the wife. She was a tale carrier. Helplessly he watched the food served onto the silver thali. Mahender didn't believe for an instant that the dish contained poison. Gitabhai loved her son too excessively to kill him. No, it contained something else which would prevent him travelling to Madurai. He saw Lal Bahadhur scoop up the food and begin to eat. Mahender writhed in indecision. He had to stop his master eating the food but couldn't tell him the truth. On the verandah stood a glazed blue vase, delicately painted with dragons and women in strange costumes. He was not to know it was a priceless Ming vase, and without hesitation picked it up and smashed it down. It didn't take long. Lal Bahadhur's wife, sent by her husband, came out to investigate. Mahender quickly slipped into the dining-room.

'Master,' Mahender said urgently. 'As your food was brought to the table, I noticed the bearer dip his left hand into that particular dish and remove some food which he then ate. It is now unclean and you should not eat from it.'

Lal Bahadhur, despite his air of sophistication, cringed at the thought of his bearer's left hand dipping into the dish. He pushed the food away quickly and regretfully to the side of his plate. The dish was his favourite, a speciality cooked only by his mother. It was marrow, delicately spiced with coriander, green chilli, mustard and an ingredient only she knew. It was then soaked in curd and cooked slowly in a tandoor oven. He looked at it longingly.

'Why were you watching the kitchen, Mahender?'

'Master, I was just passing by,' Mahender said but Lal Bahadhur caught the fear in his tone and saw his servant shiver and stare at his mother's dish. Lal Bahadhur pushed it slightly further away. He feared his mother somehow could have discovered he knew where Mohini was hiding and would prevent him from finding her and bringing her back.

'Dispose of it, quickly.' He too glanced at the door for his wife's return.

Mahender carried the dish as if it contained a live krait and emptied the food out of the window. He had just replaced it when Lal Bahadhur's wife returned to take her place submissively behind his chair. She seemed surprised at Mahender's sudden presence. Lal Bahadhur abruptly pushed away from the table.

'But you have not finished, my husband.'

'I have eaten enough. I must tell my mother her food is still the best I have ever eaten.' He noticed her pleasure at seeing the empty dish by his plate. She too conspired with Gitabhai then.

'What happened outside?'

'Nothing. The vase fell over and broke.'

At another time Lal Bahadhur, who prized such rare possessions, would have flown into a rage at such a careless mishap but now he nodded and, followed by Mahender, left the dining-room. He was halfway to his study when he sensed an enormous feeling of lassitude creep over him. It was pleasurable, such an aura of calm and serenity, that he wanted to sink into it. He swayed and stumbled and Mahender caught him. He half carried Lal Bahadhur into his study and laid him out on the couch.

'Master, master.' He shook him first gently, almost fearfully, for he could be beaten for laying a hand on his master. But when he saw Lal Bahadhur slip deeper into this sleep which summoned him such pleasures that a smile spread over his face, Mahender shook him harder. He rushed to the bar and snatched a bottle of cognac, and sprinkled the brandy over Lal Bahadhur's face. It was to no avail, Lal Bahadhur had slipped into a deep sleep and his breathing was gentle and steady.

Mahender kept his vigil all that day. It was briefly interrupted by Gitabhai who, ignoring the servant squatting by the couch, checked her son's pulse and then, in a swirl of perfume and a rustle of silk, hurried away to Delhi Station.

Lal Bahadhur slept for three nights and four days and suddenly came awake, refreshed. He blinked at the ceiling. His last memory was of walking along the corridor after rising from the dining table. He smelt strongly of brandy and couldn't remember having a drink. He didn't suffer a hangover but on the contrary felt as if he was a youth again. His blood and body seemed cleansed by the sleep. It was only when he turned and saw the dark and concerned visage of Mahender that he remembered the dish he had consumed.

'She came to see if you slept, and left for Madurai five days ago,' Mahender answered the unspoken question.

Gitabhai chose the finest and strongest looking jutka horse among those standing in the ranks outside Madurai Railway Station. The pony was coal-black with powerful hind quarters and shone with good health and loving care. The owner, a slim arrogant youth in his twenties, claimed it was the finest racing pony in the whole district and had won him more money in bets than Gitabhai could offer. She threw a bag of gold sovereigns at his feet and when he opened it, his greed overcame his pride.

'I will pay you another bag, if you can get me to the village by the lake in Puducheri district by dawn tomorrw.'

'But it is two days' jutka ride. My horse will die in such a race.'

'It is only a beast. You can buy two others. If not, return the money.'

He looked at his proud pony. He had lavished love and care on it and knew this race without rest would surely kill it – if it should ever manage that distance in such time. The leather bag outweighed his compassion. The pony would have to die for this strange woman's request.

'I will only carry you then.'

'No. Three of us. And don't think we're helpless women and try to rob us. I can destroy you without lifting a hand.

The jutka owner, looking into Gitabhai's ink-black eyes, saw the evil there and knew it wasn't an idle threat; they had a hypnotic power that made him break into sweat and he gladly looked away to her two companions. One was an old crone, bent almost double and toothless. But her eyes too blinked malignantly at him and he worried now for his own safety. The third was obviously a woman but she was draped in a black burka. From the turn of her ankles she looked young, and her silence he misread as shyness. But when he touched her arm to help her up into the jutka he pulled back in terror. He felt such an evil power that his mind was for a moment crowded with monsters and serpents, yalis and demons. He nearly fainted from the shock and fervently prayed that these three strange travellers would vanish. He thought of returning the gold then, but the woman's eyes willed him to climb up on the shafts and whip his pony into motion.

He crouched as far from the women as possible, keeping the pony at a brisk trot which gradually covered the miles. Its coat was soon soaked with sweat and foaming lather formed around the collar and on its flanks. By midday its tongue lolled out, and its body began to heave in exhaustion. He felt pity and pride in its bravery, and took courage from it. He pulled up in the shade of a banyan tree.

'Who told you to halt?'

'If the horse should die so soon, you will be stranded here all day. It must rest for a while.'

Gitabhai looked out. The sun was blazing white and the landscape was parched and dusty. Nothing moved. There was no choice. She clucked in malignant frustration, thinking that in another two days the effects of her sleeping potion would wear off and Ram would begin his pursuit of Mohini. She had to deliver the rakshashas soon, very soon; she sensed their growing impatience under the burka. They whined and whimpered and the pony skittled in fear while the jutka owner felt his hair standing on end.

'Hurry, hurry,' Gitabhai ordered and reluctantly he backed his pony back into its shafts. He had given it some stagnant water to drink and wiped the sweat from its hide. Its eyes already bulged from fatigue and his own welled with tears at the sight. He would have howled in fright had he known that Gitabhai had no intention of paying him any more gold but planned to kill him at the end of the journey.

They travelled more slowly now, the pony being rested every hour. At nightfall, when the jutka owner wanted to sleep and rest his pony, Gitabhai urged him on. It seemed none of the women required sleep; every time he glanced back he caught the gleam of their malignant eyes. By dawn the pony was staggering and heaving. It could barely walk and despite his whipping it couldn't manage to walk more than five feet before stopping. He got down to lead it, whispering and cajoling it. They only had a few miles left to go, but he saw death in its eyes and the bewildered hurt of an animal once loved and now being driven to its death.

'The village is but a kos now,' the jutka owner said when his pony finally stopped. No whipping or tugging could get it to move, and only the shafts held it upright. 'You must get out and walk.'

'No. Let it rest,' Gitabhai suddenly said with kindness.

If she revealed herself suddenly in the village, Mohini would take fright and flee. Of course she could easily be caught. What worried Gitabhai was her protector, the man who held even greater powers than hers. He had defeated the rakshashas once and could do it again. She wasn't to know that Kim had sailed for France with the army. Gitabhai needed the jutka to hide in until she could find Mohini alone and trap her. Once Chamunda was placed in position, the rakshashas would rush out and consume Mohini and then it would be too late for her lover to save her.

'Go into the village,' she ordered the old crone, 'and discreetly discover the whereabouts of Mohini. Hide your face so she won't recognise you. And make sure her lover is out of the way. We must find her alone. All alone. Then we will place Chamunda in her place and her lover will have his manhood sliced off. Even Lord Siva will not be able to save that piece of his flesh. Go.'

Even as the crone, supporting herself with a cane, and taking on the guise of a beggar woman with her sunken breasts revealed for all men to see but none to desire, Sir Lal Bahadhur Ram Shanker reined his horse to a walk. They were a few miles from the village and he still cursed Hetherington who had refused to fly further than Madurai, though Lal Bahadhur had offered him more money. 'No petrol there, old chap. We'd have to push the old girl back here.'

Lal Bahadhur rode the finest racehorse owned by the Zamindar of Puducheri, but it was trained only to race eight furlongs. It shivered now and shook with exhaustion. There was no doubt it was ruined for ever. It limped and hung its head almost to the ground. Behind him, Mahender slid off his horse and walked alongside his master. Fatigue was etched deep in their faces. Lal Bahadhur felt his age acutely. His body ached and he felt his bones rattle as though he were already a skeleton. His eyes were reddened with dust and the glare, and he could barely see for his exhaustion. Mahender helped him to dismount and for the first time ever master and servant lay beside each other on the hard earth. Lal Bahadhur no longer looked elegant and urbane, but dusty and dirty. His face was grizzled with white stubble and his thinness was exaggerated by the loss of his arrogance. He finally pushed himself upright and Mahender supported him.

'My mother is ahead of us still. She will kill the only woman I have ever loved, and I must save her. Mohini is mine, mine to do with as I want. Only I have the right to punish her, to destroy her.' He pushed Mahender away. 'Go to the village and find her. Don't show yourself or she will bolt in fright. Have no fear of Kim. He is at the war.'

Mahender regretted being cheated of killing Kim. But if he should find Mohini, he knew his master would reward him with her, and he could inflict his own punishment. After his master had used her, she would be tossed to him like a bone to a cur. And this was one scrap he would relish.

Through the shimmering haze, Parvati looked up from her work in the rice fields and saw an old beggar woman slowly making her way to the village. The distance was too great but by now Parvati recognised the gait of all the villagers and knew the woman was a stranger. She felt sorry for the woman and hoped someone in the village would give her food. She bent her back once more to her toil, planting seedlings of rice in ankle-deep water in the company of the other village women. When she had first worked, her back and arms ached for days and her ankles swelled. The task was no less arduous but came more naturally. In the shade of a coconut grove Saraswati played with other children, crawling in the dust quite naked.

The old crone barely glanced across the fields. She entered the village and wailed for alms but the few elders too old to labour in the field had none to give her. However, one of the men, moved to compassion, gave her a handful of rice and dhal. The crone ate, for in the urgency of the mission Gitabhai had forgotten the need for food. For Gitabhai and Chamunda food was unnecessary but the crone was famished. She profusely thanked the man and settling in the shade listened to the gossip. She asked about the village, the people who lived there, and then casually mentioned that at the market months ago she had met a fine young woman. And she described Mohini in minute detail, adding that the woman's kindness had to be repaid. 'Ah,' the old man replied, 'that is Parvati and she is truly kind and generous. She is working in the fields and if you wish you may go out to her.'

'No, no, I don't wish to disturb her. I will wait by her hut and if you would show me I will sleep in its shade.'

She was grateful that the hut was some distance from the village, and once the man had seen her settle down and gone, the crone scurried back to Gitabhai to report what she had discovered.

'And her lover?' Gitabhai asked eagerly. 'Where is he?'

The crone had forgotten to enquire and being afraid of Gitabhai's wrath at this forgetfulness, lied that the man too laboured in the fields and would be returning at dusk with the other villagers.

'Good, good,' Gitabhai chortled. 'You must take Chamunda and place her in the hut.' She turned to the silent black-draped figure. 'Go, Chamunda. Do you duty. You will not live out this night and I will mourn your loss. But at least I will be rid once and for all of the wretched and useless rakshashas.'

She lifted the burka and the jutka driver sucked in his breath at the sheer beauty of the woman who emerged. But he noted a deadness in the eyes and an immobility in her expression and thought perhaps she'd been cast in wax. He didn't know what was happening and wisely turned away to attend to his dying pony. It lay panting, with blood and foam dribbling from its mouth; its eyes had taken on the glaze of death.

Chamunda walked boldly beside the old crone and they only passed one villager, Tambi, on their way to Mohini's hut. Tambi greeted Chamunda with affection and stopped to talk, but when Chamunda passed by without recognition the villager turned to stare after her in surprise. He thought it strange too that Parvati should be so clean and neatly dressed when she had been labouring in the rice fields. He considered following her home to discover why she had ignored him but remembered he was due to purchase a goat in the next village and as it was a bargain he couldn't afford to waste any time.

'Go in there and wait,' the old crone ordered Chamunda and pushed her into Parvati's hut. She peered in after her and saw Chamunda meekly settle down in the shadowy far corner, quite indifferent. But even as she stuck her head in, the old crone was overcome with a sense of unease. There was an indefinable force for good in the humble room. She saw the small idol of Lord Ganesh in a corner. The rakshashas in Chamunda too trembled and a shivering fit passed through her as if she were cold.

'It is only a statue of Ganesh,' the crone soothed the rakshashas. 'Surely you cannot be afraid of something so harmless.'

'No,' Chamunda answered for them bravely, though her voice quavered gutturally. 'But remove it.'

The old crone did so. She took the idol and hid it behind some bushes and returned to report to Gitabhai who commended her foresight. The rakshashas were frightened even of their own shadows, and she thought their cowardice disgusting. Evil should fear nothing but strike fear even into gods, but these ones were incapable of such bravery.

'Mohini will return from the fields only at dusk. We will hide and wait until then. I have to see what will happen and the rakshashas will thank me for what I have done to release them from their duty on earth.' She sniffed. 'Next time I will summon braver ones.'

They left the jutka and made their way to the cane field that bordered one side of the village. It was the nearest vantage point for Parvati's hut, not more than twenty-five yards separated the edge of the field from her door. It was an uncomfortable hiding place, and the old crone was poked and scratched by the young cane, but she was too exhausted to care and promptly fell asleep in the stifling heat. Gitabhai watched the entrance unblinkingly but gradually even she grew weary and nodded off. The sun had begun to slide down and the shadow of the trees crept over the edge of the cane fields, hiding them even more effectively.

Sir Lal Bahadhur Ram Shanker moved in the darkening shadows towards Mohini's hut. Mahender had discovered her hiding place, also that she worked in the fields like a peasant woman. If she had stayed with her husband, she would still be draped in silks and jewellery and not have to do back-breaking labour. He shivered in distaste at the thought of mud and sweat on his Mohini. She should smell of attar and sandalwood and the skin he delighted to caress be as smooth as silk.

He hesitated at the entrance and looked around. He saw Mahender in the shadow, watching protectively. This servant was a loyal and faithful man. When he had finished with Mohini he would give her to him as a reward. It would be her punishment. Yet even as such a malicious thought entered his mind, he longed to keep her only for himself. He was shaken by the obsession he had for her and knew he loved her, in his own strange and twisted way.

In the distance, he saw the line of women begin to return from their day's labour. Their shadow rippled alongside them in the still waters of the rice fields and he strained to recognise Mohini among them but they all looked alike at such a distance. He could hear their voices and laughter. The air was cool and quiet and carried the tang of freshly turned earth and the lazy hum of insects preparing to end their day.

He slipped quickly into the hut, his eyes slowly adjusting to the gloom. Then he saw her, sitting silently in the far corner. He caught the glint of her eyes and the familiar perfume and didn't hesitate for even a moment to wonder why she sat so quietly, as though awaiting him.

'Mohini,' he whispered, and she turned to him as if puzzled at his presence and didn't appear to be afraid of him. 'My Mohini at last. So long I have waited for this moment, savoured it, anticipated your body with delight.'

He moved closer to her, and in the shadows thought her stare to be the fright of a trapped animal. She delighted him with her hatred. He touched her ankle, smooth and firm, and slid his hand up her calf. He felt her tense as if expecting him to release her, but she was too frightened to fight him, he thought.

'Thank God I found you before my mother did. Stand up.'

She stood and Lal Bahadhur took the end of her sari and lifted it from her shoulder. Her breasts were firm and round in the blouse and he felt her erect nipples as he fumbled to undo the buttons. The cloth fell away and he cupped her breasts, his palms remembering the feel and texture of the flesh anew. Slowly he began to unwrap the rest of her sari and in his lust paid no attention to her stillness.

Parvati reached the village in the company of the other women. She held Saraswati on her hip and balanced firewood on top of her head. They were all weary from their labour but the great pleasure was the ending of the day. Tambi, who was returning with his new goat kid, stopped in surprise in front of her.

'What is it?' Parvati asked. 'Have you not seen me before?'

'That is it. I have. An hour ago. You were dressed in a new sari and looked as if you had never worked in the fields.'

'Ah, Tambi must not only have bought a new goat but also drunk enough toddy to imagine such things,' a woman chuckled. 'I will have to tell your wife what you get up to. Parvati has been with us in the fields all day.'

'I swear, I saw you walking home in the company of an ancient woman who was almost bent double with age. I greeted you but you ignored me.'

'Too much toddy,' Parvati laughed. 'How could I be in the fields and at the same time walking along the road?'

Tambi scratched his head and watched Parvati move gracefully towards her hut. He knew he had not imagined her, but couldn't explain it. He bore the laughter of the other women patiently and trudged back to his hut, pulling the goat kid after him.

It was the sound of the laughter that woke Gitabhai from her doze and she nudged the crone awake. They saw the returning men and women and stared hard for a first glimpse of Mohini. The moment she entered her hut, Gitabhai planned to follow swiftly to witness the rakshashas emerge from Chamunda and gorge themselves on Mohini. It would be bloody and delightful, and her only disappointment was that Mohini's lover would not be able to experience the pleasure of entering Chamunda and seeing his manhood sliced off. Gitabhai wondered whether she could persuade the rakshashas to remain in Chamunda a while longer after killing Mohini, with the promise of getting a little revenge against the man who had defeated them earlier. She would negotiate with them on this matter. Revenge was enough for them to remain on earth another hour and though they would not be able to kill Mohini's lover because of Siva's protection, they could at least scar him for life.

'She comes,' the crone whispered.

Parvati came slowly, at the pace of the child clutching her hand. Gitabhai had no regret that the child too would die. The rakshashas had to kill it. Gitabhai crept closer to the edge of the cane field, ready to rush in after Mohini. Parvati dropped her bundle of firewood. She lit a small clay lamp and entered the hut with her child.

'Quickly,' Gitabhai said and moved as fast as she could across the open space so she was only a step or two behind Mohini. She anticipated the shock and surprise in Mohini's face when she saw her twin in Chamunda.

Parvati stood in shock. She couldn't understand what she was seeing in the dim lamplight. Shadows flickered over the mud walls and on a woman, herself, on her back, naked, with her legs in the air and wide apart.

Poised between her legs, ready to make the first thrust with his manhood was her naked husband. She stared at the woman and felt confused. It was her, there was no difference between the naked woman and herself. Vaguely she remembered Tambi telling her he had seen her on the road. But how could this twin exist? How could she be in her hut? How could her husband now be penetrating this woman who was herself?

Suddenly Parvati glimpsed Gitabhai and her mouth opened in fear to scream at the woman who frightened her more even than the sight of her husband but instead it was Gitabhai who screamed.

'Ram, Ram, no! No! No!'

Gitabhai rushed to her son. Lal Bahadhur, startled by the sight of Mohini and his mother, vulnerable in his lust, had already thrust into the sweet heat and wetness of his delightful Mohini. And yet she stood agape with a lamp in her hand staring down at him and at this woman beneath him. He thrust in to the hilt of his manhood and as his mother rushed to him, he jerked to withdraw and experienced such an incredible pain that he shrieked like a wounded beast. He was free of the woman and stared uncomprehendingly at the blood pumping from between his legs. His manhood had vanished. Pleasure had become agony. He tried to staunch the wound but the blood pumped between his fingers onto the smooth belly of Chamunda who lay still and unmoving. He fell back against Gitabhai screaming, and felt his mother's strong comforting arms and vaguely felt her try to staunch the blood with the edge of her sari.

But even such pain was erased by the sight of the woman's mouth opening and a beautiful yellow light emerging like a flame from a cannon. Through the haze of pain and tears he saw the most ugly and evil demons and serpents rise into the air and descend upon him.

'No, no. Stay back!' Gitabhai screamed at the rakshashas. 'This is my son, you fools, you idiots. Leave him alone.'

'He violated Chamunda and us. Your orders were to destroy the violator,' they sang out.

Gitabhai struck out at them and shrieked curses, invoking all the powers of the netherworld to aid her, but the rakshashas attacked Sir Lal Bahadhur Ram Shanker. They tore at his feet and hands, stung his face with their poisoned fangs, ripped at his belly and sucked on his blood. Gitabhai threw herself over her dying son to protect him but the rakshashas paid her no heed and chewed on his flesh like hyenas on a living cheetal, wriggling and ripping at him.

'Amah, save me; amah, save me,' his screams filled the hut, and filled the village too with fear. Small silver-headed serpents entered his open mouth, choking him, and slithered into his ears and his nostrils. His brains were consumed even while he thrashed and writhed, and Gitabhai flayed out at them with her fists and used all her magical powers. But nothing could stop them.

Parvati couldn't run. Blood flew and sprayed all over the hut. She was rooted to the spot in sheer horror and terror, recognising the rakshashas from her dreams and knowing she too was now doomed. She screamed in fear but her husband's dying shrieks drowned out her voice. Her child howled and hid her face against her legs.

Gitabhai felt her son heave once in a convulsion of dreadful agony as the silver-headed serpents pierced his heart and burst out of his chest like tiny geysers. He died then in her arms. But the frenzy didn't stop. They stripped him of all his flesh and within moments she held only the raw and shiny skeleton of her son, Sir Lal Bahadhur Ram Shanker.

She rose, a dreadful and frightening sight, her face contorted with her own pain and fury, spattered with the blood of her son, and surrounded by the evil yellow aura of the rakshashas who hovered around like hunting creatures on a leash. They quivered and shrieked in delight at their destruction, unheedful of Gitabhai's curses on them.

'Her, her, her,' Gitabhai pointed her finger at Mohini.

Her face was foul and frightening in its hatred of Mohini and the youthful mask had slipped to reveal a woman as old and ugly as the crone who cackled in delight beside her.

Parvati clung to Saraswati and cried out: 'God, God, save me.'

She didn't expect God to answer. She was all alone. Kim wasn't beside her with the special talisman granted by Vamana which had protected her before. The rakshashas swirled closer and closer, and Gitabhai wore them like a cloak of evil light. Parvati backed and then, waking from her trance, turned Saraswati to the door and pushed her hard.

'Run, run!' she screamed to the child.

Saraswati ran, stumbled, fell and cried in fright. Parvati scooped her up and pushed her out again, and Saraswati ran into the open. The villagers huddled together outside the hut and a woman reached out and grabbed the child. The hut looked as if it were on fire; yellow light seeped through the dry palm leaves of the roof and spilled out of the low doorway. Yet the hut wasn't on fire. They all felt a terrible sense of evil emanating from the hut and they all prayed. None was brave enough to enter to save Parvati. Some distance away, Mahender too cowered. He had seen Gitabhai rush in after Mohini and had heard his master's screams. But he was too frightened to enter the same room as Gitabhai.

'God help me,' Parvati wept and sank to her knees.

Unseen by her, in a corner of the hut, the earth cracked. A small circle heaved and fell away. The five heads of Shesha rose out of the hole, small and graceful at first, swaying to shake off the dust and dirt piled on top of him by Kim. As Shesha drew himself out, he grew in size. His body grew longer and the great hood expanded. The lamplight threw his swaying shadow over the advancing figures of Gitabhai and her awful host.

They sensed Shesha's presence and on seeing Vishnu's huge serpent slowly filling the hut, they screamed in fear and rage and rushed to escape. The five mouths opened wide, the tongues flickered out and sucked in the rakshashas. Even as they entered the mouth, they turned into puffs of harmless dust which Shesha spat out. His heads turned this way and that, swaying and hissing, and the demons and yalis and silver-headed serpents disappeared into those gaping mouths to become dust.

In rage, knowing they could not defeat Vishnu's serpent, the remaining rakshashas turned in revenge on Gitabhai. They believed she had lured them into this hut deliberately, having planned their murder by Shesha.

'You betrayed us,' they screamed at her. 'You must die too.'

'Fools, fools. How can I command Shesha? I do not have such powers. It's your own stupid fault.'

She screamed out her protests, for she too was fearful of Shesha. She tried to escape but the rakshashas descended on her and dragged her down. Within minutes, even as Shesha consumed them from one end, they attacked and tore Gitabhai to shreds as they had done her son. The stench of blood and evil was such that Parvati fell down in a faint. She didn't see Shesha consume the last of the rakshashas even as Gitabhai was stripped down to a skeleton. In the far corner lay a mound of dust shaped like a woman. Razors gleamed in the dust between her legs and among them lay a piece of shrivelled flesh.

When Parvati opened her eyes the hut was quiet, except for a strange, soothing hum which filled her. It seemed to soak through her skin and into her head and heart, and a great calm descended on her, as if she'd consumed the poppy and felt no fear. She noticed Shesha's shadows swaying in a mesmeric dance. But when she lifted her head she couldn't see him, only the shadows weaving hypnotic patterns on the walls. And though the serpent didn't speak, she felt him urging her to rise and leave the hut. The whole village was crowded outside, silent and frightened, and they were relieved to see her emerge alive. They weren't sure what to do next.

The hut contained the ghastly remains of Lal Bahadhur and Gitabhai, and none of them had the courage to enter. Then, without warning, the hut burst into fire. The light was pale blue and though there was nothing inflammable except the roof the hut burned all night. Even the mud burned and at dawn there was nothing, not even the charred remains of bamboo. The earth was clean and dry as though nothing had ever stood there.

# 22

## October 1917–December 1918

Mohandas K. Gandhi, bundled up against the London chill, studied the Indian soldiers sitting in rows, patient and still. His small fame had touched their lives and aroused their curiosity. He noted the dark hollows under their eyes, the cold which frosted their brown skins. Some carried their wounds openly, displaying bandages and crutches and scars. All carried wounds no surgery or salves or bandages would ever heal. And through their eyes he saw the exhaustion and the muddy battlefields of France and Flanders. Battle-hardened soldiers had a secretiveness about them, a veil which none who had never experienced war could penetrate. They radiated a contempt, an anger against those who had not suffered as they had.

He steeled himself in the glare of their eyes. There was barely any warmth in this meeting hall, and he remembered his own days as a student in London and how much he had hated the cold. He had left England the day after he'd been admitted to the bar, expecting never to return. But his life was now leading him to another battle front, and he had returned to meet the government as a representative of the Indian National Congress.

'I am proud of you all,' he spoke softly and they swayed like corn to hear him. 'You have left your villages, your people, your fields and families, to come here to fight for the British Empire. Three years ago, when war was declared, I urged that we Indians should be part of it. I believed then, as I still do now, that it was important, as part of the family of this empire, that her wars should be ours.'

A hand rose from the audience.

'Gandhi sahib,' Kim said. 'You advised us to fight for the empire. Now that we have done this thing, what is our reward? I do not mean mine or his or his, but India's. What have we gained by our deaths for India?'

'The British have promised us greater freedom in ruling our own lives,' Gandhi said. The sepoy acted as spokesman for the others. He was a finely honed man, with angry eyes. They pierced Gandhi as if trying to fix him to the wall behind. Gandhi fleetingly thought he might have been Eurasian but a Eurasian wouldn't have mixed so freely and been accepted so easily by the other sepoys. 'I have come here to discuss these things with the British government. And the Secretary of State for India, Mr Edwin Montagu, intends to come to India next month to discover for himself what legislative changes must be made.'

'And you believe their promises, Gandhi sahib?'

Gandhi chuckled. 'We must believe those who hold power, until the time comes for us to suspend this belief. Mr Montagu has promised me that the government has every intention of introducing legislative reforms which will see us in larger numbers in the Governor's Council as well as the Viceroy's Council. He has further assured me that eventually we will be granted self-rule. But this will happen only in stages.' Gandhi noted the flicker of a smile on his questioner's face. 'And you don't believe this?'

'Why should they give us freedom when they have benefited so much from us? We have died in France and Belgium and Mesopotamia for them. It will not be easy for them now just to turn around and say: "you are free".'

'I didn't say it would be easy. But this will be the beginning of the changes. We had to fight in this war in order to win their respect. To have remained distant from the battle would have proved to them that we are not worthy of ruling our own lives.'

'So if they respect our fighting, will they not respect us more if we fight them too?' Kim said, and waited for the growl of approval around him to fade. 'Why should we wait for Mr Montagu to dole out crumbs?'

'You're not much older than I, but quite impatient. And you obviously distrust the British.'

'I have learned well from them, Gandhi sahib. Their promises are meant only for convenience.'

'We will see their convenience. If they renege, then we will protest and resist but through peaceful and non-violent methods.'

Kim saw a small man, not more than five feet tall, frail, blinking rapidly behind his spectacles. He could have even been called ugly. Gandhi's square face was dominated by thick lips, a beak of a nose and ears that stuck out like handles. Kim had to admit to disappointment. Having heard so much of his defiance against the South African government, he had expected more of Mr Gandhi. Since his return to India in 1914, Mr Gandhi had also led a successful satyagraha against the European planters in the Champaram district. He had organised the peasantry in a protest against being forced to grow indigo. Kim remembered his own dismal failure to help in that same area. He didn't have the skill to organise.

Kim hesitated. The first appearance was deceptive. Gandhi's face was, finally, compelling. It was full of expression and an underlying strength, also humour. The eyes smiled suddenly and he found himself warming to this Gandhi, though not to his way of thinking. Having experienced war, Kim understood the power of weapons. He knew their destructiveness, knew how they frightened men, tyrannised them into submission and death. How could this non-violence, this absorption of pain – and here he was remembering his conversation with Anand, the old priest in the Benares temple – achieve freedom? Pain was not mathematical, Anand had said. There is no infinity. Mr Gandhi believes there is infinity to the pain he and a people can suffer under a tyrant.

'But that will take years,' Kim said. 'In Russia it has only taken days. We have seen an emperor toppled, vanish from the earth. And he was the tsar of his own people. His own people condemned him to death. The British are not our people and we are vast in numbers, millions to their thousands. Do we have time to wait so many years for a foreign ruler to give us back what is rightly our own?'

'You are a true patriot but too headstrong,' Gandhi said. 'I cannot believe that violence will not generate even more violence in Russia. It must. It will. And besides, in India, do we have the unity to challenge the British? Not yet, I think, and to achieve this unity we need time. It's only when we can combine, when we become a moral force and not a violent one, that we will be able to escape our yoke.'

He rose. The sepoys rose too and Gandhi stepped down from the podium. For a moment, he stood a foot away from Kim, a quizzical look in his eye.

'I understand your impatience, my friend,' he spoke only for Kim's ear. Behind him, at a respectful distance stood Krishna Menon and his companion Romesh Sahni. They had barely glanced at Kim during the meeting and even now hovered possessively behind Gandhi. Kim sensed the power of Gandhi, the intensity and the persuasiveness. 'But remember that once we release the violence in India, there will be no containing it. It will turn on ourselves. We are a people easily divided, easily aroused to passions. And when we lose control of this anger it will fly off in a thousand directions and the British will easily subdue it.' He put his hand on Kim's shoulder. 'We have yet to learn what lessons the Russian Revolution will teach us. When you return to India, I would like you to join me in my ashram. I would prefer to work with someone like you than against you.'

'I will come,' Kim said.

Gandhi took a step away and paused. 'Where are you from?'

'Lahore.'

'Ahh,' he said as though this explained the puzzle. 'And your good name?'

'Kim.'

He expected Gandhi to make some comment. Instead he bobbed his head as though committing it to memory and moved, quick and sprightly, through the crowd.

Kim felt a tug at his elbow. Sahni's smile was extremely friendly. Kim thought him now too handsome, too perfect. The smile was too exact, too charming. Kim allowed himself to be tugged to a corner.

'That was a very forthright debate you had with Mr Gandhi,' Sahni said. 'It's absolutely right that we question our political leaders. What do you intend to do?'

'In what way?'

'You spoke of our need to organise and overthrow the British.' He looked at the milling soldiers. 'These are trained men. They will be more than a match for the British once they're back in India.'

'And who will provide the arms?'

'I'm sure we'll find someone. There are many rich and powerful men in India who would like to be rid of the British. And a bold man like you would benefit from meeting these men.'

'But Mr Gandhi advocates the use of non-violence only,' Kim said. 'I thought you were a follower of his.'

'I am, I am,' Sahni said. 'But we must be ready for alternative methods. You have my card. I want us to meet when we return to India.'

He pushed through the soldiers brusquely, a busy man, full of schemes and plans. Kim wondered whom he truly worked for. India? Our rulers? He knew then that he would be watched, that what he had spoken this evening would be reported at some length to the authorities, and finally to the Colonel sahib, who would now know Kim had totally rejected his Englishness. To the Colonel sahib this would mean betrayal and Kim would now be his enemy.

The heat was welcome. On the open sea, reflected off the waters and the ship, it burned his skin almost black. He stood on deck with the other sepoys, indifferent to the discomfort, watching for India. Each man wanted to be the first to see their homeland. They had suffered four years of cold and wretchedness, fear and exhaustion, and were depleted in numbers. They pressed together as if to fill the gaps left by dead friends and comrades.

When the ship sailed from Tilbury, Kim had not looked back once. He had been a stranger in that land and had felt no longing to belong, to remain in the chill with its perpetually green fields. England! England! He had thought his blood would stir, his soul recognise his ties with the land which his parents had left thirty years ago. But there had been no stirring. Instead his bond with India, through his longing to return, had only been strengthened. He was Indian.

Kim suddenly pointed. They all stared and for a while couldn't see what he had seen. Then it appeared, an indistinct break in the horizon, a blur, a bump. It grew larger gradually, as though they were approaching another island. The ship hummed with their sighting and those below decks raced up to stand at the bows and stare eagerly through the glare at the brown lump that turned into a line that slowly grew and grew until it stretched from horizon to horizon. But it was dusk; then night fell swiftly, not teasingly as it had done in the European summers, and India vanished. None of the men left the decks. When the sky was full of stars, they imagined they saw the twinkle of lights on the land that was coming closer without their seeing. They imagined villages and huts, cooking fires, fires for warmth, the sacred fires in the temples and those in the prayer rooms of houses, the twinkle of oil lamps flickering beside doors.

At dawn the sun banished imagination, revealed India.

They saw white beaches in the first pink rays of dawn, they saw fishing villages and palm trees. Tiny figures threaded the groves and fishermen on catamarans, their skins glistening black, rode the wake of the ship. The men waved and shouted, and the fishermen lifted their paddles in salute. The land slid nearer, the sea carried the debris of coconuts, rotting wood, bottles. At first Bombay seemed only one building, a white mound rising out of the coast. Then it grew and grew until it hid their whole view of India and Bombay became India. They smelt the city in the hot breeze; dust, food, spice and the sweet odour of wood smoke.

A rose garland fell on the deck at Kim's feet. He picked it up and held it to his face, inhaling the delicate fragrance and allowing the soft petals to caress his skin. The men crowded around, touching it as though a piece of India had leapt the distance to welcome them. Kim looked up and saw Jatayu circling above him. The eagle rose higher and higher and vanished into the blue haze.

There were throngs of people on the docks, a blur of brown faces, a blur of white clothing, sprinkled here and there with the vivid colours of a sari. Kim strained to glimpse Parvati, wanting to catch her upturned face. But there was too large a crowd and, as the ship docked, he was pushed and jostled in the excitement. A regimental band struck up as the gangplank was lowered. The officers, European and Indian, were the first to set foot on Indian soil. It took half the morning before the sepoys were finally disembarked. Kim stood on deck, patiently scanning the crowds and to his disappointment saw no sign of Parvati. He had written hastily once he knew they were being sent home and the letter had possibly travelled on the same ship. He had Alice Soames's address and would find his way there. He would also see his friend Isaac Newton soon. He paused. Would it be safe to see his old friend? It would reveal his presence to the Colonel sahib too soon. He needed time, a space to recover from the war.

When their feet touched Indian soil, nearly every

soldier prostrated himself to kiss the earth. They were marched to the lorries waiting to take them to the Victoria Terminus. From there, they would scatter across India to their homes and villages. Kim didn't board the truck. He too had a travel warrant and his discharge papers in his pocket. He embraced each of his companions until only Kumar and Grehwal remained.

'Won't you be returning with me?' Kumar asked.

'No. Parvati and Saraswati are here in Bombay. They're staying with a European memsahib.'

'And then?'

'I wish to go to Mr Gandhi's ashram and see what further things he has to say.' Kim shrugged. 'I don't have land like you, an ancestral home to which I truly belong, except all of India. We will see what God ordains for me.'

'You know if you should return, my home is yours,' Kumar said.

Kim embraced Narain's brother and helped him into the lorry. He turned to Grehwal.

'And sardar, when you see your father Balbir remember me to him. Tell him I was the traveller who joined him in Benares.'

'You have a home too in Amritsar,' Grehwal said. 'A lamp will be lit nightly and placed in the window so you will find your way to my home, Kim. Anyway, it's a lot nearer for you than living in the jungles of south India with Kumar. God alone knows where he comes from.'

'And that is why he doesn't tell you sardars. Otherwise you would all be sitting there.'

The tailgate was slammed shut and Kim watched four years of comradeship and shared suffering and hardship disappear in dust. For a moment, he felt leaden and unable to move, as though he sensed he would never see these companions again and the dust would be his only memory.

Once past the dock gates, he was immersed in India. He walked slowly, savouring the people, the colours, the smells, the noise. How heightened his perception was now. He saw the brilliant blue of the sky, the painful whiteness of the buildings, the blood red of a canna flower, the odour of channa masala. He was jostled and absorbed by the people, flowing with them, indistinct from them. He remembered in London how separate he had felt, standing in Piccadilly. Now he was united again, one with the people to whom he belonged.

A temple elephant, its forehead decorated in saffron and white, a brass bell around its neck clanging with each step, ambled towards him. Its trunk reached out through the crowd to descend gently and rest a moment on his head. Kim accepted its blessing and dug into his pocket for a coin to place in its trunk but the mahout waved away his offering.

'Ahre sepoy, you have fought for Mother India and God blesses you.'

'I am indeed blessed. He brought me home safe.' Kim said and brushed the beast's coarse hide as it passed. He sensed a feeling of calm, of permanence.

He remembered his way to Church Gate and noticed the changes already. How swiftly things happened when you were away! The streets had electric lights now and telephone wires connected some of the buildings. The Europeans moved sedately, still withdrawn, still aloof, passing by as if India didn't exist around them. Once he had stared at the sahibs and memsahibs; he now saw them as ordinary men and women who came from small, cold homes. He had seen with his own eyes that they too suffered poverty, they too worked as servants, they too could be inferiors in their own land. The illusion of superiority they had created here had been shattered by the war, and Kim knew that every soldier from every village who saw them now would remember his days in Europe, and would lose his awe. The knowledge would spread and eventually there would be a change in the deference the Indian paid to the European.

He prepared himself for Parvati, combing his hair and curling his moustache, trying to smooth away the wrinkles in his uniform, though he knew it mattered little. They would fall into each other's arms and, he hoped, their life together would continue calmly. She too had been in a battle but the scars would remain hidden. One of the few letters of hers which had reached him had sketched the ghastly scene. He still shivered at the thought of what might have happened had he ignored Shesha's command to make that small idol and bury it in the hut. Parvati would now be dead. And even in the war he had not witnessed such a horrible death.

The door was opened first by a bearer, old, white-haired, and rheumy-eyed, who peered at him suspiciously before asking him his name and then shutting the door. Kim heard a European woman's voice scolding him, then the door was flung open. Alice Soames was a commanding figure. She stood straight-backed, open-faced and forthright, and her smile was full of delight. The Colonel sahib's wife was not one who could have played the great game. She didn't have the guile or the deception in her face.

'I am Kim.'

'I know. Come in. I know everything about you, my dear.' She didn't add that she had expected a younger man, for that was the image fixed in her mind. Parvati had described an adventurer, cocky, cheerful, possessed of perpetual youth, constant optimism. War had affected him. On the surface he smiled, and she glimpsed the Kim she had imagined, but beneath she felt a change. He'd aged swiftly but not peacefully. There was a hint of anger when his face settled in repose. She wasn't sure against whom it was directed.

The room was large, comfortably and casually furnished. After the sunlight, it felt cool and gloomy. There were no portraits of the Imperial family on the walls, no English landscapes, only books everywhere. He waited expectantly, looking for Parvati. A small girl, dressed in a long skirt and blouse, came to clutch at Alice's dress. Instinctively he knew she was his daughter.

'Saraswati, this is your father. Don't you remember him?'

She gently pushed the child to Kim but Saraswati clung tightly to Alice's dress. Kim knelt with open arms and the child still hesitated, and then crossed to allow him to embrace her briefly before struggling free to run back to Alice.

'Where is Parvati?'

'In gaol, I'm afraid,' Alice said.

For the first time in four years, Kim felt at ease. He had shed his uniform for a simple white kurta and pi-jama, his habitual dress. Saraswati clung to his hand. She was almost a replica of Parvati, with fine cheekbones and an oval face, but her eyes were grey. And this heightened her beauty. She had started by being very shy but gradually her curiosity and Alice's urgings overcame the shyness and by the end of an hour, she was ensconced in Kim's lap. The baby had awed him, and now the child, soft, fragile and vulnerable, did too and he felt protective.

Kim and Saraswati waited in the press of people at the entrance to Bombay Central Gaol. He held a basket of fruit and sweetmeats in his other hand. The sight of the newly whitewashed walls and forbidding gates brought back a flood of his own experiences. Saraswati grew impatient in the heat and fretted and Kim tried his best to soothe her. But he was unfamiliar with children and bribed his daughter by feeding her another sweetmeat.

A door swung open and the prison guards allowed a narrow file to enter, examining each package. They removed two oranges from Kim's before waving him through to the women's section.

He saw her immediately he entered the interior courtyard. Parvati was sitting with a group of women in the verandah. He knew she wasn't expecting him. His letter hadn't yet reached her. He allowed the people to push past him, wanting to watch her. There were some changes. She seemed more confident and her figure had filled out. Her laughter was the same and there was still the same proud way she held her head. She was beautiful still but no longer the girl he had rescued in Delhi Station so many years ago. It was strange how, at so many years' distance, he could only remember that lovely girl disguised as a boy. Change didn't move in step with memory. For a moment he felt a stranger, and awkward. Saraswati wriggled from his hold and ran across the courtyard to her mother. Parvati opened her arms and the child flew into the embrace. She looked up expecting Alice and saw Kim standing alone. There wasn't even a second's hesitation. She freed herself of Saraswati and ran across the courtyard and flung her arms around him.

'Kim, Kim. My darling, my dearest.' She kissed his eyes and mouth and cheek and forehead frantically, as though he would vanish.

'Parvati. Even when I just say your name my heart seems to stop beating. And now to hold you, I feel fulfilled again. An emptiness has been filled. I love you.'

'Oh god, I can't believe you have returned.' She touched him tenderly, caressing his face, pinching him playfully then. 'You are real. You are holding me. You are here.' She stood back. 'I want to just look and look and never ever stop. But I can't stand back. I have to hold you again.'

'When I inhale your perfume, I feel cleansed of the smell of guns and blood and mud that I have lived with all these years.' He breathed her, wanting to hold that odour, to let it wash him clean, though he knew nothing ever would. He felt tears for his good fortune in holding Parvati again.

'I want you.'

'And I you.' She shyly stepped away, flustered and blushing. 'But we will have to wait another three weeks. Now how was I to know you would be returning?'

'And how was I to know I would find you in gaol.' He kissed her longingly and felt her respond and then pull away. They had an appreciative audience. Saraswati was playing with the women and Kim took Parvati's hand and they moved into the shade of a mango tree.

'When I was wounded, my last conscious thought was of you.'

'God looked after you,' she said and felt around his neck for the pebble given him by Vamana. 'He protected you and brought you back safe to me.'

'I had thought . . .' Kim hesitated before continuing. 'In my vision I imagined myself in a terrible place. I had seen smoke and bodies all around me. It wasn't the war. The vision, my nightmare still awaits me.'

'How do you know?'

'I continue to have those dreams. The scene grows clearer. I see the backs of houses, high walls and uniformed men kneeling. If that dream was the war, it should have stopped now. The war is past.'

He took her hand and pressed it against his cheek. 'Vamana will protect you again,' Parvati said and silently prayed, fervently, for Kim's continued protection. She didn't want to be afraid but his dreams chilled her. She shook herself free of foreboding. 'But let's not talk of such things. You have returned to me.' She turned to watch Saraswati. 'See how your daughter has grown.'

'And she will be as great a beauty as her mother. And with your influence, as headstrong. I hope a prison doesn't lie in her future too.'

'It runs in the family obviously. What chances has she?'

'Does Saraswati remember the horror?'

'At times, she cries out in her sleep. I cradle and hold her and tell her it was a nightmare. She's forgetting slowly. I never will. It was your power of goodness that aroused Shesha's compassion to help. Even from so far away, you saved me once again from that man.'

For a moment, the horror returned and made her shiver. But Kim held her close and his presence calmed her.

'Were there no questions?'

'Many, especially in the newspapers. But Sir Lal Bahadhur Ram Shanker's disappearance remains a perpetual mystery. I think he loved me in his own way, though I hated him. But I only thank god Gitabhai was destroyed too. Life repeats itself for me. I turn to the same people for succour. I began writing again with Alice's encouragement and I've now had some of my poems published.' Parvati tightened her grip on his arm and her voice grew breathless. 'Through Alice I met Annie Besant and Lokamanya Tilak. You must meet them Kim. She is an Englishwoman who came out to India and with Tilak began the Home Rule League. She believes in swaraj, like Tilak, like Alice, like us. She believes India should be free from British rule. In England she led a strike against the mill owners in Manchester. She is also a deeply spiritual person. Miss Besant and Tilak organised a march to demand Home Rule. We all marched on Government House by her side demanding Home Rule. And they arrested us. Do you blame me?'

'No. I am proud of you.'

'You have changed then?'

'Yes. We must be free. We have given our blood to the empire and now they must repay us with our freedom.'

Kim looked around. Parvati's companions were all Indian women and all smiled at him kindly. They knew who he was.

'Then where is this Besant?'

'The government didn't arrest her. They were frightened that if they did there would be riots.'

'Yet they're not afraid to arrest Mr Tilak again, and you. It's because she's an Englishwoman that they don't arrest her. It will be their disgrace. One day we won't need people like Miss Besant to lead us to the cliff edge.'

'But she is sincere.'

'I have no doubt she is, if Mr Tilak accepted her. But for how much longer must we follow the British? Either they rule us or lead us against our rulers. It's a great game for them. But we are the ones arrested, we are the ones flogged, we are the ones hanged. They will never ever die for us. On the day an Englishman dies for India's freedom, the empire will end.'

Kim was fierce now in his passion for this cause, Parvati thought. It was difficult to remember that he had ever been against it. He was born Indian and would have remained one all his life, if Colonel Creighton had not found him wandering with Teshoo the lama and discovered he was English. Kim had been deliberately used by the Colonel, who didn't remind him of his Englishness for Kim didn't know he was English but trained and inculcated him with this false identity to make him useful in serving the Crown. At that moment, she felt a passionate hatred for the man who could take a boy and convert him for his own ends. And out of that conversion had risen the years of confusion. But Kim's life had turned full circle. He was Indian once more, unquestioning in his allegiance to India.

'I thought that when you went to England and saw it, you would never ever want to return to me, to India. I thought it would claim you. It was a dread I couldn't confide in you for I felt you had to make your own decisions without any cry of fear from me.'

'I was a stranger there, like every Indian.' He looked at their severe surroundings and laughed. 'I am more at ease here than in a London street. But while I was in London I met Mr Gandhi. And he invited me to his ashram. Will you come?'

'Gandhi,' she whispered the name almost reverently. 'Yes, we must both work for him. He will guide us all.'

Gandhi's ashram was a day's walk from Ahmadabad. There was no other means of transport and the narrow, dusty road should have been deserted in the midday heat. But Kim and Parvati were part of a small stream of people moving doggedly in the same direction. They joined the others, and walked in silence to their common destination. The great heat was as much a barrier, Kim thought, as the mud and cold of France. It took an effort of will to keep moving through this shimmering landscape. There was some cultivation along the banks of the Sabramati river but for the most part the land was harsh and barren. A sudden hot, dry wind would funnel up dust, spinning it like a very thin, tall top, and whip the travellers with dirt and dead leaves. Saraswati huddled against Kim for protection but wasn't afraid. The passing of each funnel left them dustier and when they slapped at their clothes, the dust rose in small puffs.

They reached the ashram at dusk, as the lamps were being lit. The main building was a simple, low bungalow with two or three rooms. It had a tiled roof and a verandah. The other two buildings were merely thatch-covered shelters for visitors. Nearer the river was a small fenced-in enclosure holding goats. A few cows were tethered to pegs driven into the hard earth. Kim realised the ashram was a subtle blend of sanctity and practicality. The air was fragrant with the odour of wood smoke and cattle and cooking food. People sat in groups or eddied through the lengthening shadows as if in search of direction. They spoke in low whispers and in many languages. There were even a few motor cars drawn up at a discreet distance.

'What should we do?' Parvati asked.

'First find food and then a place to sleep. It will be too late to see Mr Gandhi this evening. Take Saraswati. I'll join you later.'

He wanted to discover more about the people who came to wait so patiently to see Mr Gandhi. The main building, growing brighter as the evening darkened, was filled with activity. Men waited on the verandah and hurriedly entered and departed. It seemed incongruous that such a small and humble place should attract such attention. He talked to men squatting in the shadows and by the end of an hour discovered that, like him, they all came to serve Gandhi. There were young men and old, Hindus, Sikhs, Muslims, Christians, poor and rich. Since Gandhi's successes with the peasants of Champaram and his latest victory for the mill workers of Ahmadabad against the mill owners, the majority of those who came were the poor. They came for justice, and believed he would redress all their grievances by calling for a satyagraha in their cause. And the causes of the poor in India were numberless. Kim sighed in sympathy as he listened to them and wondered how Gandhi would deal with all these demands. Yet strangely, standing apart, also made to wait, the rich remained as patiently as the poor to see Gandhi. Gandhi had fashioned an economic and religious philosophy called sarvodya. In his sarvodya he emphasised a man's belief in god, whether he was Muslim or Hindu or Sikh. And, using the faith of the people, he wanted them to believe that it was a moral obligation that the rich should place their wealth in a pool in order to benefit all society. He didn't advocate the expropriation of this wealth and in this way kept the rich satisfied, while at the same time they donated a small amount to this pool to help the poor. Kim wasn't sure how sarvodya would be embraced by those outside the ashram.

Men were summoned for audiences and Kim noticed that the messengers were mostly young women. They looked like the daughters of wealthy families and Kim found their presence somewhat unsettling, although those who were habitual visitors greeted the women familiarly. The discussions took hours and he wandered off in search of Parvati and Saraswati. He found them with the other women and Parvati brought him food from the kitchen.

'Who are all these young women?' Kim asked as he ate.

'They're his disciples.' She leant over to whisper. 'He practises celibacy by sleeping beside them.'

'How can a man have such control?'

'Gandhi-ji does. The women swear he doesn't touch them.' But there was some doubt in her voice.

Before dawn they were woken by the sound of bhajans sung by the women. Their voices were sweet and clear and Kim felt deep satisfaction in being woken in such a way. It made his sense of belonging even deeper. When he went down to the river to bathe, the morning sun had turned the water a delicate pink. The man bathing beside him moved cautiously in the water, as though unused to such a simple ritual. He was young, balding already, with a handsome yet delicate face. He pinched his thin nostrils and ducked in and rose shaking in the chill.

'Where are you from?' Kim said.

'Allahabad. And you?'

'Lahore.'

'We have come from all over India to be with Gandhi-ji.' He spoke with a distinct English accent and Kim guessed him to be another young man educated in an expensive English school. The young man did, however, make an effort to disguise this accent.

'Maybe we all expect too much from him. But who else do we have to lead us?'

'No one. Tilak is past it, Gokhale a British pet.'

'Those are harsh judgements.'

'We have to be harsh. India is changing and they are our past. I am Jawaharlal Nehru.'

'I am Kim.'

They didn't shake hands, though Kim noted the impulse in the young man.

'I have not seen you before. Are you a member of the National Congress?'

'Not yet. I have just returned from the war. We should never have fought for them.'

'But Gandhi advocated our participation.'

'I do not agree with everything he says and does.' They moved to the bank and dried themselves in the sun.

'Tell me about your own experiences. Why do you feel we did wrong?'

They discussed the war and the changing India Kim had returned to, for over an hour. Then the sun grew too hot and they moved to the shade of the verandah. Nehru was an intellectual. His experiences were derived from books and his knowledge of India, the India Kim knew, was almost non-existent. But he was an attractive man, warm in turn and then falling into brooding silences. A dreamer, Kim thought, a rich man's son seeking a sense of purpose in life. Gandhi was his purpose, but he wondered for how long.

It was only in the afternoon that he and Parvati found themselves finally in Gandhi's presence. Bare-chested, cross-legged, hunched over a writing pad, Gandhi looked even smaller than Kim remembered. He looked frailer too and it was only when he lifted his head and smiled that Kim remembered the spirit and personality of the man. Kim namasted. Parvati reverently bent and touched Gandhi's bare feet. She sensed his lingering and appreciative glance.

'The sepoy Kim. Sit, sit. Wait a moment while I finish my letter.' The silence was broken only by the faint hiss of Gandhi's pencil. He wrote on the back of a used scrap of paper. It was peaceful and calm in the room. People peeped in and a woman brought in tea. She was young and supple and her eyes remained on Gandhi even as she withdrew, backing away as though out of a royal or religious presence.

'Have you lost your anger yet?' Gandhi asked without looking up.

'Does one lose anger? It is contained. It will not be lost until the injustice is over.'

'Good. You must have the discipline to keep your anger in check. To lose that is to give your opponent the advantage.' He put aside his paper and gave Kim and Parvati his full attention. They felt themselves enveloped in a charismatic power. They sensed his will, his unshakeable belief in himself. 'And do you still distrust the British?'

'Gandhi-ji, I worked for them most of my life and my distrust is built on this experience.' He took a deep breath. 'I was an Imperial agent for Colonel Creighton of the Political and Secret Department."

'I have met him. A powerful and secretive man. His loyalty too is to India, his India. So you're trained in secrets, but are no longer in the employ of the Colonel?'

'I left his service before the war.'

'I have never met someone who frankly admitted this

profession before, thought I suspect many of the men around me could be in the employ of Colonel Creighton. Even this meeting will be reported to him by his agents. But it is impossible to tell which one it will be. They all profess fervour but until the time of action, I won't know.' Gandhi laughed. 'At least you have a skill apart from the ability to talk. We have too many men who love talking and talking. You are from the Punjab, if I remember correctly.'

'Yes, Lahore.'

'Freedom can't be won merely by words and actions. We need an organisation like Congress, which you should join. It is the most important foundation for any political movement. Someone like you, used to the discipline of the army, with knowledge of men and of this country, can work for me in distant parts of India. You asked me why we would take so long to overthrow the British when the Russian people took a matter of days. They were a national group of people, Kim. They were but one nation, as was the case with the other revolutions that occurred in Europe in the eighteenth and nineteenth centuries. Empires broke apart to allow people with a tradition and language and culture of their own to form autonomous units. In India, it is the other way around. We are taking different nations, different peoples with different languages and customs and trying to instil in them a sense of a nation called India. It will not be easy. See . . .' He picked up a ball of cotton thread, broke off a length then broke it into still smaller ones. He opened Kim's palm and placed the first piece in his hand.

'That is the Hindu. Now this is the Muslim. This one is a Sikh, this a Christian. This is a poor peasant, this a zamindar, this a mill worker, this the owner. This is a south Indian Brahmin, this an untouchable.' As he spoke he placed the threads side by side. 'The landless come asking me to lead them against the landlords, the urban poor against their exploiters. But in this India we need the support of the landlord and the mill owner too in our freedom movement. All these threads must be twisted together until they become the rope that will pull down British rule. Each and every Indian must feel he has much to gain from freedom, socially, politically and economically. That is the task that lies ahead of us. Are you celibate?'

Kim looked up startled.

'No? You must practise celibacy.' Gandhi took Parvati's hand. 'Your wife will understand that a man loses his intelligence and moral strength when he spends his seed in a woman. The ancient rishis and all the great sadhus practised celibacy to preserve their integrity and to give them the strength to resist all temptations . . .'

Gandhi spoke at some length on celibacy, urging them both to follow his example and he spoke with the same persuasive fervour as he had spoken of India's freedom. Gandhi held Parvati's hand tightly and she was mesmerised by his attention. If another man had held her hand with such passion, Kim would have been enraged. He stilled himself to listen to the lecture. Abruptly, Gandhi returned to the original topic.

'And are you as committed to the freedom movement as your husband, Parvati?'

'Yes. For many years I have been an admirer of Tilak. I wrote for a magazine *Sher*, about how I thought we women should be involved in the movement. The government closed the magazine. And I have just come out of prison. I marched with Miss Besant to demand Home Rule.'

'Ah yes, Miss Besant. A good woman,' Gandhi fell silent a moment, and it wasn't possible to tell exactly what he thought. 'It took me many years to understand the complexity of India. And what men and women like you must do is help me to draw these different people into the freedom movement. That is what will take time, and of course the British will not make it easier. They understand India's diversity and that it is India's inherent weakness. We can be easily divided, like slicing through a chocolate cake. But we must hold together.

They will use greater violence if we use violence. You have heard of the Gadhar party?'

'Yes. They believe in the violent overthrow of British rule but have met with very little success. Most of their members have been arrested and a few of them hanged for their activities.'

'That is exactly what I mean. We must practise satyagraha. We must achieve our end through peaceful means. In the Punjab, they have not yet learnt the lesson. They could achieve more through peaceful protest than with guns and bombs. I want you to go to the Punjab for me, and meet the men and women you once knew, and tell them about the movement. Only non-violence will give us the moral force to drive out the British. Use your skills as an Imperial agent to keep me informed of developments in the Punjab.'

'And if we should be attacked by the authorities?'

'Offer no resistance, Kim. Offer none. Accept their blows . . .'

'And their bullets?'

'Those too.'

'But many will die,' Kim said and realised that he was dealing with a man with the hardened sensibilities of a military general, a man as deceptive as the Colonel, and equally ruthless.

'The British still remember 1857 and they are always fearful that such a thing will occur again. It has haunted them these sixty years. And because they're haunted, they will react exactly as they did then. They will hand us the moral outrage to unite India against them.' He chuckled and picked up his pad. 'Always give men enough rope to hang themselves.'

Kim heard the calculation in Gandhi's voice. He sensed it was deliberate and when he looked into his eyes he saw a stubbornness, a force that wouldn't be deflected by bloodshed. He knew that soon there would be a terrible collision between the forces this man unleashed in India and in the British.

# 23

## January 1919

'There is not a single faction in India which believes in, or is anxious for, democracy,' Sir Reginald Craddock, the Home Member, was heartened to see nearly every head nodding, except one. 'The nearest approach to it is the mob rule liked by the howling proletariat of the towns, which the communist in his malice and the seditionary in his blindness are combining to produce in all the large cities. We must be ready for mob rule and suppress it ruthlessly, once and for all. I believe we must be prepared for another Mutiny.' He tapped the thick, khaki-bound report in front of him. Every Member also had a copy. 'Which is why I would like to introduce Mr Justice Rowlatt's recommendations as to how to fight the anarchy and terrorism that have been stalking this land for the last two years. Mr Justice Rowlatt has made a deep and detailed study of the various terrorist acts which have taken the lives of countless civilians, European and Indian, and caused untold damage to government property. I am sure you have all studied his report, so I will merely sum up his main proposals.

'The police and security forces must be given a free hand to arrest anyone, anywhere, without a warrant and search any home. Those suspected of terrorism will be tried by special tribunal and will not be entitled to engage a counsel. And, if found guilty, they will have no right of appeal.'

He waited for the table-tapping of approval to die

down before continuing. The Colonel knew Reggie was well launched into persuading the Council to vote Mr Justice Rowlatt's proposals into law. He agreed with him: Indians weren't ready for change. They, London, were bringing India to the brink of anarchy and chaos. The Montagu-Chelmsford reforms, recently and reluctantly passed by the Viceroy's Council under pressure from London, allowed Indians to be elected to all the Governor's Councils. They would also be given ministerial posts, not important ones, such as finance, revenue and the police, but minor ones. This system of governing had been dubbed dyarchy. The Colonel thought these elections farcical. They were based solely on territory, and the numerically superior caste or community in each area would win, time and time again. The Indians, of course, led by Gandhi, had shown no gratitude but demanded more important portfolios.

'No, we certainly don't want another '57,' the Colonel said, when Sir Reginald had sat down. 'There are signs of growing unrest now that the war is over. The Indian sepoys are spreading stories about what they saw in Europe and I'm told they're behaving more arrogantly towards us, especially to our women.'

'See, those were the signs before the Mutiny. The sepoys . . .'

'Except they are not now so organised,' the Colonel interrupted quickly, 'and the Indian Army today is too highly disciplined ever to mutiny again. So it will not exactly be another Mutiny. These sepoys have been honourably discharged, but they are highly trained men. It is possible that they can be manipulated by rabble rousers. In the Punjab the Gadhar party has been crushed and destroyed, which is one avenue closed to them. Still, these acts of terrorism have continued unabated. Government officials, European or Indian, cannot perform their tasks with the threat of assassination continually hanging over their heads. To protect them, Mr Justice Rowlatt's proposals must become law. But a minority of Indians have found a new leader in Gandhi. He's had success in Champaram and in Allahabad with his satyagrahas. He claims his movement is not violent, but is astutely ignoring the passions it can arouse. Mobs will take over and we must move swiftly to suppress them and teach them a lesson they won't forget for another sixty years.'

As he leant back, the Colonel deliberately shifted to face the new Viceroy at the top of the table. Lord Chelmsford smiled uncertainly at him, and then at Sir Reginald Craddock. Chelmsford was a thin, tall man with a clean-shaven bony face. He held his head at a tilt as if still listening, though silence had fallen in the room. He reminded the Colonel of one of his school masters, polite, scholarly and shy. He also had a somewhat puzzled smile, as if he suspected his Council was ragging him but wasn't sure why. Edwin Montagu, the Secretary of State for India, who had spent six months the previous year working with Chelmsford on the dyarchy reforms, complained often that Chelmsford was a most unimaginative man. Even the Viceroy's youngest daughter had told a stranger, admittedly repeated by the Viceroy against himself, that 'my name is Margaret St Clair Thesiger. My daddy works very hard and my mummy is the Viceroy.' For all that, the Colonel liked Chelmsford. He was a sympathetic listener. But he also knew India needed a stronger man in these troubled times. Chelmsford lifted a finely shaped hand and gently rested two fingers against his cheek.

'I presume you agree with Sir Reginald Craddock and the Colonel?' The question wasn't addressed to anyone in particular, and hung like a kite in the air.

'I see no alternative,' the Colonel said. 'We do need additional powers of arrest and confiscation of property. I believe, Your Excellency, that you should sign these proposals into law at the earliest possible moment.'

The murmur of approval around the table was interrupted by a firm 'May I?' from opposite the Colonel. Sir Sankaran Nair was their newest Member, one of three Indians personally appointed to the Council by

Mr Montagu. He was handsome and dark with a hooked nose, and considered by everyone quite brilliant. His hair was still untouched with grey and there was almost a touch of cruelty in his unlined features and suppressed energy.

'Yes' Sir Sankaran,' the Viceroy said.

'I feel . . . I think . . . that these measures might be a bit hasty. And too harsh,' he still wasn't used to the eyes watching from across the table. The Colonel was unblinking in his attention and yet Nair read his disapproval. 'We fought for the empire in the war in the expectation of some reward.'

'You have it in these latest reforms,' the Colonel said quietly.

'Yes, we have,' Sir Sankaran said. 'But on the other hand this Council is now going to introduce further repressive legislation. It is planning to transfer the authority of the judiciary to the executive. The Act will be a direct negation of the rule of law which is supposed to be the cornerstone of British rule in India. I know Indians will resent these new measures. You mentioned the returning sepoys, Sir John, as one factor. But the other is that even those Indians who didn't fight now have higher expectations. They have been educated in increasing numbers, many of them have risen high in service and a large number are now financially far better off than before. They expect . . .'

'I'm aware of what they expect,' the Colonel said. 'But they are a very small, law-abiding minority. They will not riot or throw bombs. These measures – repressive, you call them, but I consider them merely a necessity – are meant to be temporary. Once we feel the situation is less threatening to life and property, the law will be rescinded. But I think it is essential we be prepared and armed with the legislation so we can act swiftly.'

'I firmly believe these measures will be provocative,' Nair said, but looking around he saw he was alone in this, and despaired of ever making his rulers understand. In this grand chamber they were too distant from

India, unheedful of her needs. They still believed in their divine right. He was facing centuries of power, which showed in those old faces. They were wrinkled and lined, like laundry crumpled beyond ironing. Younger men should have been seated at this table; they could have understood the changing mood of India, but they lay in graves all over Europe.

'Gentlemen?' the Viceroy said and every head except Sir Sankaran Nair's inclined in the affirmative. 'I will sign the proposals into law today.'

They rose and bowed. Chelmsford drifted almost like a shadow out of the room. The Council still met in the Viceroy's residence. But the old feeling of adventure had faded with daily routine. They all knew that this room would have to serve its purpose for many, many more years. The new Delhi Council Chamber was still a stubble of bricks and stone and scaffolding.

The chill in the weather caused the Colonel pain. He tightly controlled a spasm and stilled his hand. Arthritis was a recent ailment and he raged against it. It was a sign of age and he hated the weakening of his body. The pain showed; it etched deeper marks around his eyes and tightened the creases around his mouth.

'Well!' Craddock hovered behind his shoulder. A small plump man, red faced, with a stubby nose, he resembled a busy gnome. 'Thank you for your support.'

'It wasn't just for you, Reggie. I too think the situation is worsening. But once we're over this hump, the country will calm down.'

They both smiled politely as Sir Sankaran Nair stalked past. He barely inclined his head; the lines around his mouth reflected his anger at their decision.

'He can't have everything his own way. I'm sure he means well, but a firm hand never did anyone a bit of harm. Pity he isn't as amenable as Sir Ram. Ever find him, by the way?'

'No.'

'Most undependable people, most undependable. Probably become a sunyassi or some such thing.' They walked to their motor cars.

'You've met Gandhi, haven't you? Sounds like a religious crank to me.'

'Yes, I did. Last year. I went to his ashram.' The Colonel handed his file to a peon. 'He's a wily politician, not a religious fanatic. But he does understand the importance of religion in appealing to Indians, not only to Hindus but Muslims too, and the Sikh and the Christian. He's trying to bind together politics and religion and in so doing he's broadening his appeal to the masses.'

'He'll go the way of all the others. Only we can lose India. The Indians will never win it from us.'

'Gandhi is a different kettle of fish. He won't fade away. He's a calculating politician beneath his gentle exterior. Cranky at times but we mustn't ever underestimate him.'

'You sound like an admirer.'

'No. I dislike him but I feel . . .' The Colonel didn't want to voice his doubts but he sensed in Gandhi a change in leadership. Hard, pragmatic, wily, deceptively simple on the surface, he would make a worthy adversary. 'Nothing. The others, Tilak and Gokhale, tried to appeal purely on a political level. Gandhi appeals through God. And in India, God is visible everywhere and more potent a weapon than guns.'

His own words sounded prophetic. They weren't meant to be. Those gods had not saved India before. They had made the Indian fatalistic, passive towards her many conquerors. It was the clever use of this passivity by Gandhi that troubled the Colonel. India could become a great lava flow of people inexorably flowing towards another destiny.

India was restless, stirring as if from a deep sleep. Rumours were racing from one end of India to the other. The same spirit, he supposed, was abroad just before '57. Indians were a volatile people beneath the placid surface, and easily misled. A riot could explode without a moment's notice and when it was as suddenly over, it could have been an illusion if not for the carnage left in its wake.

Sir Sakaran Nair was sentimental, and as distant from his people as any European. And he hadn't read the secret reports. Four of the Colonel's agents had been brutally murdered. One had had his throat cut, another had been shot, one burned and the fourth hacked to pieces. The executions were public and dramatic and meant to warn any collaborators. Someone was betraying them, one by one.

The Colonel loved the Punjab capital, Lahore. His first posting as a subaltern had been here and it had been too many years since he had visited the city. The train slid slowly past the tomb of Emperor Jahangir and the Colonel thought of his poems. There, under a magnificent marble dome and minarets set in a lovely garden, was his poet. He felt intensely his connection with the Emperor, with India's past. To think he possessed the very paper on which the Emperor's hand had once rested. Through the opposite window was the smaller, more humble tomb of Jahangir's Empress, Nur Jahan. She had been exiled to Lahore by the Emperor Shah Jahan and had lived out her last days building her husband's magnificent tomb. Nur Jahan had been fortunate to escape so easily. While she was Empress, and virtually ruler of India, she had constantly plotted against Shah Jahan. It was only his wife, Mumtaz Mahal, who had intervened and saved Nur Jahan from an emperor's revenge. How ironic that a railway line should divide these lovers until eternity.

A motor car awaited him at the station. At this time of the year, Lahore was delightful, dry and cool and almost green. The old city, which was the native quarter, its fort walls long broken, was almost totally encircled by a garden. The motor car stopped at the Kashmir serai. It had been years since the Colonel had entered. The old wooden gates were permanently open and would now be impossible to shut. The Colonel picked his way slowly through the narrow, crowded gullis into the mohallas. The gullis were so narrow, the balconies almost touching, that he felt he was passing down long dark tunnels burrowed into the sunshine. Cows and goats and pack ponies and camels jostled and pushed for passage. All the races of north India passed before his eyes: Pathans, Sikhs, Jats, Kashmiris, Rajputs, Dogras. The stalls offered everything from spices to silver, from gold to gulab jamuns, and the din was unceasing. He felt himself deep in the heart of India here.

Years ago, he regularly walked through a bazaar like this to get a sense of the people. He would be respectfully greeted by most and offered food from the stalls. Now he noticed how they fell silent as he passed, how the whispers would race ahead of him. Usually men's eyes lowered in respect when they met his, but now they remained stubbornly fixed, angry, sullen and defiant. He didn't like the feeling, but wasn't for a moment afraid. He was in his India and none could make him feel a stranger here.

After an hour, the Colonel returned to the car and was driven to his quarters in Government House. It was only in the privacy of his suite that he allowed his features to take on the sense of sadness he felt. He couldn't understand the hostility. Another man's hair would have prickled at the stares, the venom in those dark faces. Yet he loved them all, cherished them, and was baffled and angry. "Why?" he wanted to know. "Why? What have we done to incur such silent hatred? This is my land too, they are all my people and I have nothing but respect and deep affection for everyone of them. Have we not been just and kind? Have we not united them, created an India when there was none before. Haven't we nurtured and cared for them? Haven't we raised them up from their poverty, removed the feudal yoke from their shoulders? Now, they show only hatred. Yet I mustn't blind myself. Those were only a few faces, yet those few showed hate and I was shaken by such nakedness."

At precisely eight o'clock, in evening dress and wearing decorations, the Colonel stepped out of the car at the Lieutenant Governor's residence. It was an imposing edifice, with stately neo-classical pillars flanking the entrance. It was ablaze with lights and bearers waited to lead him down the corridors, through reception rooms, to the small informal study. Sir Michael O'Dwyer, the Lieutenant Governor of Punjab, rose to greet him. O'Dwyer was slightly shorter than the Colonel and not much younger. He had a square face which hinted of determination but then his chin receded somewhat, giving the opposite impression. And there was also a hint of the bully in his eyes.

'Sir John, what a pleasure to meet you at last.' His handshake was overly strong and firm. 'Whisky? Soda or pani?'

'Soda, please, Sir Michael.' He accepted the glass from a bearer and sat down. Sir Michael tapped his own glass and the bearer quickly filled it. 'I went for a walk in the old city . . .'

'And?'

'The mood is sullen. They seem to be angry.'

'Don't worry. I'm on top of the situation. Any trouble, and I'll tell the police to crack a few heads. I gather the Council has approved Rowlatt's proposals?'

'Yes. We all thought we should be ready to deal with any further violence.'

'Thank God. We need those powers. The people just don't understand democracy, elections or anything. For God's sake, they're still living five centuries behind, bowing and scraping to the princes. And now they're supposed to vote. Sheer, arrant nonsense. I told Montagu as much, but of course he totally ignored my advice.'

'Have you talked to the community leaders?'

'They're a waste of time. The moment they think I'm depending on them to control the situation, they start acting high and mighty.'

'I wouldn't totally ignore them,' the Colonel said gently. 'Those men could be a great help if the situation should get out of hand. Who are they?'

'There's Fazl-i-Husain, a dissident leader of the Muslim community. Then, for the Hindus, Harkishen Lal the industrialist, Lala Duni Chand, a lawyer and member of the Arya Samaj, Rambhuj Dutt Choudray, another lawyer. One or two more. They're all, by the way, dead set against the Rowlatt Acts. They've made speeches which have been reported back to me. So I'm not sure they will co-operate if there's a crisis. Neither here nor in Amritsar.'

'Still, it's important to remain friendly, I think. But they're not the only ones making speeches. Sankaran Nair has been ranting and raving nearly every day in public, making the people uneasy. If only they'd all shut up for a moment.'

'I'd have them arrested. That Gandhi chap in particular. He's calling them "the black acts".'

'I don't want to arrest anyone at the moment. It could touch off riots.'

'At least that would bring things to a head. What's it like elsewhere?'

'More or less the same in Madras, Bombay, Bengal and U.P. Just be prepared for trouble.'

'Oh, I am,' Sir Michael said with gusto. 'I've told the Police Commissioner to cancel all leave, stockpile extra ammunition, and to have additional patrols in the old city. I've also warned the European community to keep their guns handy.' He looked at his watch. 'I think we'd better join the others, Colonel, or Lady O'Dwyer will have us shot at dawn.'

The moment he boarded the Frontier Mail back to Delhi, the Colonel recognised a familiar face. In himself, General Reginald Dyer wasn't personally to blame for the anguish his presence caused the Colonel. But he did evoke memories of Richard. Richard had died under his command and the Colonel didn't want to be reminded.

'Creighton, how are you?' Dyer spoke heartily, almost with a parade-ground voice. He patted the seat in invitation. The Colonel saw that his face too was creased with pain. Dyer's horse had thrown him while on parade and rolled over him, crushing his hips. But the determination of the man, who could have been an invalid, was quite amazing. He had willed himself to recover and had even taken part in a campaign against the tribesmen on the North West Frontier during the war.

'I'm on my way back to Delhi. You posted there now?'

'No. Worse luck. I'm in Jullunder. Just back from a little holiday up in 'Pindi.' He hesitated awkwardly, unsure whether to stir-up painful memories, then plunged on. 'Richard was such a fine, splendid chap. But we've lost so many more in the war. You know, I just don't have any young officers. Frightfully depleted. Frightfully. Whisky?'

The Colonel politely refused the flask. Dyer took a long swig.

'Helps the pain a bit,' he said.

'What's the situation in the army?'

'In what way? Oh, you mean if they're dependable? Absolutely. Not one sepoy will step out of barracks without permission. They'll fight to the last man if there's any trouble in the streets. I always knew all these reforms would go just a bit too far. It only makes them want more and they're just not ready. Don't you agree?'

'I do. We tried to reason with Montagu but London was quite determined.'

'They haven't the faintest idea what effect these things have. Bloody ignorant lot. You know, I honestly believe that once we teach the bloody wogs a lesson they'll never forget, there won't be a spot of bother for the next century. We've been too damned lenient, I say. We let those babu politicians get away with murder. Shoot a few, especially that Gandhi and a couple of ringleaders, and there won't be a peep of trouble. The wogs only understand discipline, strict discipline. It works wonders with the sepoys. And a good dose for the civilians will soon have them all in pukka order.'

The Colonel listened in silence until General Dyer dozed off. The countryside was rich in wheat, sparkling with the canals they'd built for the Punjabi farmer. It all seemed so worthless now. He couldn't help but agree with Dyer: teach them a short, sharp lesson and peace would return to this beautiful land.

The Colonel still shared a small building with the Home Office. The Secretariat, an impressive pile of red sandstone in the plans, was still only a granite foundation. It would take ten years to finish and he hoped he wouldn't be still in office. He yearned to stop, to rest, to unpack his Urdu poems and spend his time looking out on the mountains as he worked on the translations. He would lead a simple, spare life. He still had the volume of Emperor Jahangir's poems, the gift from Sushila, to work on. His mind wanted to wander to her but he pulled himself together. He couldn't mourn someone so lost to him.

Isaac Newton awaited him in the porch. The Colonel was surprised to notice that Newton looked old too. His face wasn't as lined as the Colonel's but his hair had whitened and the Colonel was sad he'd not noticed his friend ageing. He still wore the same suit and tie, and clutched the same bag.

'Newton, how good to see you.'

'Colonel sahib, it always gives me the profoundest pleasure to be in your august presence,' Newton said and waited deferentially for the Colonel to pass. He was taken aback by the Colonel's warmth, and wondered what caused it.

'How many years now?'

'Over thirty, Colonel sahib,' and Newton saw his superior flinch at the passage of time. "He feels his age," Newton thought. "He is aware of mortality, pain, the burden of his office." He felt sad for the Colonel.

The Colonel, like him, was alone. But Newton never felt lonely.

He closed the door and waited for the Colonel to be seated. 'Kim is in the Punjab.'

He sensed, rather than heard, the Colonel sigh. It was a gust of bewilderment. He hadn't understood Kim at all. He had seen Kim as an Englishman, as an opportunity to slip into India, because he wanted to. That was his self-delusion. He had never realised that the Indian surface was as deep as the soil, that in fact it was the English in Kim that was rootless and shallow.

'I expected that. He met Gandhi a couple of months ago. What is he doing?'

'He is . . . meeting people. He knows many people, old friends, war comrades, and they in turn introduce him to others. He always was a friend of all the world, and people listen to him.'

'And what does he talk about?'

'India's freedom.' The Colonel's eyes narrowed and Newton added quickly. 'He does not advocate violence. He believes in satyagraha too.'

'Yes. That would appeal to him. Have you seen him?'

'Yes, Colonel sahib.'

The Colonel waited. Newton remained silent and uncomfortable under his stare.

Newton had been working on his invention, and the result had been disappointing. A man had entered his shop and Newton had instinctively recognised Kim, although he remained in the shadows. His son had returned. But Kim was closer even than a son, for a son could be disobedient. Wordlessly, Newton had opened his arms and they had embraced. But Kim was not the youth Newton remembered. A man now sat beside him, experienced, changed by war. To celebrate, Newton had ordered the chokra to bring arrack and bhang. They had smoked and drunk all evening and half the night. Kim had told him everything, and Newton had been amazed by his adventures.

'Well, what did he say?'

'Colonel sahib, he talked about his days in the war mostly, and all the things he saw.'

'Did . . . did he mention me?' The Colonel had not wanted to ask, and steeled himself for the answer.

'Yes, Colonel sahib. He wished me to tell you that he has deep regret that he can longer be your agent. "Men change," he said, "and I have returned to what I always was. And having discovered my true self, I can no longer serve the Crown." He hoped you would understand and he asked me to convey his salaams.'

'Please thank him. Tell him I always thought of him as my own son.'

Newton wasn't surprised that an Indian and an Englishman should both consider Kim as their son. He was still the bond between them. But still Newton looked askance. The Colonel sahib seemed agreeable, yet he distrusted such docility. The Colonel never forgave, and Kim had betrayed him. Newton knew he had to protect Kim at all costs.

'Does he know what happened to Sir Ram Shanker at all?'

'He mentioned nothing,' Newton lied. To explain such things to an Englishman would be impossible.

The Colonel was still baffled by Lal Bahadhur's disappearance. They had traced him all the way south to the village where Kim and Lal Bahadhur's wife Mohini had hidden. And then Lal Bahadhur had simply vanished. The police had questioned the villagers thoroughly – he had their report – but none had seen Lal Bahadhur nor, it turned out, his mother who had also gone to the village. She too had vanished. It was as if they'd stepped out of this world the moment they entered the village. The police had searched the countryside for their remains. Nothing was ever found.

'And has he told you the names of the people he has met?'

'No, Colonel sahib. He is aware I am still in your employ and does not wish me to lie.'

'God, how ideal it would be to have Kim working for

me now. He has met all the troublemakers and . . .' He stopped abruptly. There was no point in regretting. 'Where lies your loyalty now, Newton?'

'I have served you all my life, Colonel sahib. I am too old to change.'

'Thank you, old friend. Now, what do you think is happening in Amritsar?'

'I feel impatience in the air, Colonel sahib, a need to hurry. The people want more opportunities, they want to more control their lives, they want . . .'

'We have given them the opportunities; we have given them dyarchy.'

'But that is the whole problem, Colonel sahib. As they take, they see how much more they have not been given. And there is no return now.'

'Of course there isn't. But we can call a halt to all this nonsense. From now on, I want you to keep me informed daily, do you understand?'

'Yes, Colonel sahib.'

'And telegraph your reports. If it's very important, ring me up here.'

Newton looked at the black telephone balefully. He had, many years ago, endeavoured to invent this very instrument. But one Alexander Graham Bell had long beaten him to the invention. And he disliked it.

'Yes, Colonel sahib. And the people are unhappy with these Rowlatt Acts. They are saying they are an unnecessary punishment and a betrayal by the British.'

'I'm aware of that, which is why I want you to report daily. And please be careful. Does anyone know you work for me?'

'None, Colonel sahib. I am only an ordinary jeweller.'

'Except Kim.'

'But Kim will never tell anyone.'

'Well, the terrorists are finding out my agents and killing them. Be very careful. I am only concerned with your own safety. That'll be all Newton,' the Colonel said and waited until he had reached the door. 'Newton. I want to meet Kim.'

'Meet Kim?'

'Yes, see Kim,' the Colonel said patiently. Newton seemed bewildered as though he hadn't understood. 'I told you, and you know well, I have always considered Kim my son. I want to see him again. It has been many years. Not since . . .' He stopped, remembering too clearly the last time he had seen Kim. It had been at the New Year's Eve party at the Calcutta Club. Richard and Elizabeth had also been there. His children were faded memories now. 'Many years. Will you please arrange the meeting?'

'I will tell Kim, Colonel sahib,' Newton said, trying to stare down through the Colonel's mind. What was he thinking? True, he had loved Kim once but the Colonel wasn't a sentimental man, not like the Indians. He was pragmatic, calculating. 'What if he doesn't wish to meet the Colonel sahib?'

'Tell him it's for old time's sake, Newton. Tell him to remember all those years we played the great game together. I am old now and will soon be retiring. I would like to make my farewells to Kim. Persuade him.'

'Yes, Colonel sahib. Where should he meet you? Here?'

'No, not here,' he opened his diary. 'In a month's time. Saturday the twenty-first. Say about nine o'clock in the evening outside the Emperor Humayun's tomb.' He closed his book, caught the mistrust in Newton's eyes and smiled. 'I only wish to be discreet, old friend. I am a government official and Kim is not someone I should meet openly.'

'Yes, Colonel sahib,' Newton said and closed the door quietly.

# 24

## February 1919

Goode wasn't afraid. He wanted to die but knew he wouldn't, ever. His destiny was an immortality filled with bitter memories. The war hadn't killed him; it had preserved him like a unique specimen, killing instead all those who wanted to live. He could swagger and bluff with this certainty in mind. The small crowd of Sikhs barring his entrance to the Golden Temple sensed it too. This sahib's indifference, his rage, were not courage but madness. Otherwise why would one European with only two constables seek to challenge them?

'Let me through.' He didn't raise his voice. His baton remained tucked under his armpit. He stepped brusquely forward and pushed the first man away. He was burly, heavily bearded with a blue turban, and unafraid too, but forced back by Goode he made way. The others, like cards, swayed and broke. Some were nihangs, armed with swords, spears and contempt.

Goode, in deference to the Sikh beliefs, removed his shoes and kept his head covered. The marble floor was wet and cold. He passed under the arch into the main temple complex. This main part of the Golden Temple was a huge square. Along the outer walls was a honeycomb of rooms for pilgrims. In the very centre was the gold-domed shrine. The waters surrounding it were glossy black, sequined with lamplight. A single marble footbridge spanned the water. The shrine was full of light and the shadows of pilgrims listening to the priests reading from the granth. Others bathed in the tank or perambulated along the perimeter engrossed in prayer. If Deputy Commisioner Goode had had any sense of worship he would have felt the sanctity of the place. Even with such a crowd, the temple felt peaceful, almost silent. He turned away and strolled along the water's edge, his reflection wavering. Immediately behind him came his two constables, both Sikhs, and behind them the silent, sullen protectors. The burly one hurried to walk beside him but at a distance.

'What do you look for?'

'Sahib.'

'Sahib?'

'Terrorists.'

'This is a place of worship. No terrorists here.'

'I've been told otherwise. I have warned you people once. If you harbour terrorists in your place of worship I will defile it with my presence. And with guns.' He stopped at a closed room.

'Open them all up and bring the people out.'

'I can't disturb them. They're asleep or resting.'

'Either you do, or I do.'

The Sikh moved to another door and opened it wide. Goode remained waiting at the first door.

'There is no one in there, sahib. It is empty. See, this one has pilgrims for you to harass.'

'I'm at this door, sardar. Open it.' Goode drew his revolver. The constables flicked off their safety catches. 'This door. If the room is empty I will go away.'

The man came reluctantly, looking to the gathering crowd for support. Goode ignored their restless movements, their subdued angry murmurings. He gestured with the revolver and the two constables flung open the door. The room was small and gloomy and apparently empty. Then in the shadows he caught a sly movement and pointed his revolver, drawing back the hammer. The click was too loud and the room magnified it like an echo chamber. The shadows rose and approached the door. Four men filed out of the room. They were all young, not even fully bearded, and their eyes had a common look of hatred.

'Search the room.'

A constable entered and lit the lamp. The room was bare except for rolled mats. He unrolled them: two rifles and a revolver clattered on the floor.

'Who told you?' the burly Sikh asked.

'Why, one of you did, of course,' Goode said.

'That was a dangerous remark, Commissioner sahib,' Vancouver Singh said. They met now in darkness in an open field outside the city. Goode was in mufti, Vancouver Singh heavily muffled and wrapped in a blanket so none would recognise him. Goode sat in his car, and the Sikh bent down to speak through the window.

'It was the only thing to say,' Goode said. 'Now everyone will suspect everyone else, but maybe not you. Be careful.' He handed over the payment, and without counting Vancouver Singh slipped the money into his pocket.

'It is getting too dangerous for me to continue. I need money to return to Canada. I have served you all well.'

He didn't have any regret. He could either choose the noose or turn informer. The Colonel sahib had given him a simple choice. Vancouver Singh hadn't expected to face such reality. In Vancouver, when he had been recruited by the Gadhar party, the liberation of his homeland from the British had seemed an adventure. He imagined the glamour, the excitement of war. He came from a martial race – how often he'd been told that! – although he had never committed a martial act in his life. But even before the adventure, while he was still dreaming of heroism, he had been arrested on the ship and imprisoned. The stark choice had shaken him. Now all he wanted was to return to Canada but he had no money.

'Not yet. The time is coming when I will need your services even more.'

'It's getting very impossible, Commissioner sahib. No one trusts anyone and the terrorists have split into smaller groups. I cannot ask too many questions.'

'Well, you'll just have to. Or else . . .' The threat remained in the dark air. Vancouver hated this Angrezi. He had no compassion, no patience. He demanded constantly. And now, he understood, he could be betrayed if it suited his convenience. Vancouver shivered at the threat. His throat would be cut, if he was lucky.

Goode felt the intensity of Vancouver Singh's feeling. Men gave off violence, as they did love. He let his hand drop from the steering wheel to the revolver on his lap. Informers were double edged; Vancouver could as easily set a trap for him one day. Maybe even now he was sliding a knife from under his blanket.

'I must go.'

'Not yet.'

Goode ignored the vast Indian sky, didn't smell the jasmine in the night air. He cared for nothing here. Yet he had returned to India after the war. On his discharge, he had gone home. Bradford was grey and stark even in the summer. His parents, living in one of the long monotonous rows of houses in a narrow cobbled terrace, depressed him. The house was small and cramped and smelt of cooking and washing soap. He had forgotten this during his years of Indian service, and now it choked him; he wanted to gag on the food, on the beer, on their hard narrow lives. He had no skill to offer except his experience with the Indian Police and that would be worth little to the Bradford police. He could only begin again as a constable. He found himself imagining India with intensity, ferreting the map for a sign of Anil Ray, as though he would materialise as a face on the printed names of provinces or cities, swim out from the pages. And he knew he had to go back. But not to his old province. He requested a transfer to Punjab and was promoted to Deputy Commissioner, Crime Branch. He could never escape his face but at least in Amritsar it could remain a mystery, a speculation as to what might have happened.

Vancouver Singh saw the intense preoccupation and the hand squeezing the wheel as if to snap it. He guessed at Goode's thoughts.

'Anil Ray,' Vancouver Singh said and nearly regretted his boldness. The policeman struck like a snake, catching him full in the mouth.

'What the hell do you know about Anil Ray?' Goode asked, and knew he would never escape. Even here they knew of his encounter, and read his thoughts and feelings even on the darkest night.

'Nothing.'

'You spoke of Anil Ray. Do you know him?'

'Oh yes. We tried to blow up a train together. But I told the authorities. There was a lot of gunfire and Anil Ray was shot.'

'He's dead then? Are you sure he's dead?' Goode was bitterly disappointed, cheated again by fate.

Vancouver Singh stirred uneasily. He squinted at Goode, saw the distortion of his face and felt the intense urgency. Anil Ray was important to him.

'I am not sure.'

'He's still alive?' Goode couldn't hide his relief. There was still the possibility of revenge, of the hunt and the final satisfaction of putting a bullet through Anil Ray's heart.

'I am not sure of that, too.' He was gripped suddenly and jerked close to the car window.

'Tell me everything, then.'

'Apart from myself, two other men were killed. As there was no sign of Anil Ray we presumed he had escaped. The following day the police began to search for him. They found only blood. We presumed we would eventually find him dead. He had lost a lot of blood and left a trail easy for us to follow. Finally we came to a clearing where he had lain down. There was a large patch of blood.'

'And then?'

'Nothing. He disappeared. His wounds couldn't have healed so fast, yet there was no further trail of blood from there. If a tiger had got him there would have been his remains.' Vancouver Singh shrugged free. 'We never found what happened to him from that point on.'

'So he could still be alive?'

'It's possible, but how I do not know. His wounds were very bad and he lost a lot of blood.' Vancouver knew of Goode's obsession. That is his weakness. And when I satisfy that, I can be free. He waited.

'Can you discover his whereabouts?'

'It's possible, but very difficult. I will do it for a lot of money.'

'Naturally.'

'Enough to take me back to Canada.'

'Fair enough. How will you find out?'

'I have my own informers,' Vancouver Singh said. 'And I spent many days with him and learnt some of his habits. Of course it will take time.'

'There is not much time. Find him. Quickly.'

'And the ticket.'

'You'll get it.'

'What if he's dead?'

'Then you won't.'

Vancouver Singh stepped back and watched Goode struggle to turn the heavy motor car around in the narrow road. On either side were ditches and the effort had Goode panting and Vancouver Singh amused. He could have told Goode that a few yards further on the road widened into a field. He began walking back to Amritsar in the dust of the motor car and laughed. He could have also told Goode that Anil Ray was alive and that he knew exactly where he could be found. This was common knowledge among the people but the British were not people. They were sahibs and couldn't hear the whispers that ran through the streets. Such easy knowledge eluded them. He would have to move quickly and carefully, giving Goode morsels and only the whole when he had the money for his ticket. He never trusted a policeman's word: they had no izat.

On the long train journey south, lying on the bunk and watching India drift by, Goode writhed with the pain of his memories. Images, long suppressed, now burst out, flooding his consciousness. He was no longer aware of his surroundings. Instead, he was back in his own sitting-room in Lucknow. He had been alight with love, suffused with the romance of impending marriage. Rebecca's kiss still lingered on his lips and he smelt her fragrance on his skin and clothes. They had clung lovingly. He had been whistling 'Tea for Two' and the melody ran through his head again with clarity, even the bad notes repeating themselves. Then the figure crouched in the chair surprised him. A friend, a colleague, awaiting him? The bald head shining dully alarmed him, and even as he reached for his revolver, the face was trapped in a shaft of lamplight. Anil Ray. He saw the polo mallet swing up towards him and desperately wanted to dodge it. He had felt paralysed, incapable of jumping aside and trying to free his revolver. One shot was needed, only one. And then he had experienced such agony exploding in his arm. He even heard, before his scream, the quiet crack of the bone. And following the scream came a gush of violent, raging hatred for Anil Ray. The humiliation of the blow, not the pain, caused the hate. It stained the sense of his own moral righteousness, shattered his pride. He wanted to hate only, and no longer bother to believe that he was a good man, a kind man, a loving one. An animal had been released in him and he rejoiced in its ferocity. Caged by his pain, tormented and disfigured by Anil Ray, he was filled with a savagery which set him apart for ever from other men. He didn't have to behave with false humility, act lovingly. He could hate and show it to all.

When he reached Madras, he borrowed a friend's car and driver to complete the final leg of his journey.

His head ached and pounded, his mouth was parched with excitement. He tried to appear calm and hoped his damaged face was not twitching. He couldn't reveal anything of his intent now until the moment when he pressed the gun against Anil Ray's head and pulled the trigger.

The motor car stopped at the border post. Two policemen in white uniforms and peaked caps emerged from the low brick hut and studied it admiringly. Few cars passed their post. They touched their caps and held out a hand for Goode's papers. One of them addressed him rapidly in a strange tongue and he shook his head and shrugged.

'The purpose of your visit, sahib?' the driver translated.

'Tell him "sightseeing".'

Goode listened to the flow of another European language. At this border, at this pole across the road, British India ended. Beyond the barrier, though the land didn't change, was Pondicherry French India. Another country. Once past the barrier he had no authority; he was an ordinary civilian. If he told them he was a policeman they would ask endless questions. Now they merely glanced over him and while one lifted the pole, the other waved him through and saluted.

'How far now?'

'Tomorrow morning,' the driver said.

Goode was surprised when he woke. He felt rested, alert, calm. He checked the revolver and dropped it back in the bag. The car was waiting under the porch and Goode adjusted his topi to shield his eyes from the hard glare.

The journey took scarcely an hour. He looked around in surprise. There wasn't a building in sight, only the jungle to his left and in the distance the edge of the sea. It looked flat and still as the land. The driver pointed to a grove of trees between him and the sea and to a narrow path leading through the hard sandy soil.

Goode began walking purposefully towards the trees,

looking neither right nor left. There wasn't another human in sight, not until he was closer to the grove and saw movement. The contrast between the sunlight and sombre shadow was too harsh for him to distinguish anything else. As he drew closer he saw people sitting and standing, facing a low building. They grew into a crowd and Goode wondered how they had managed the journey and why they were drawn here. He entered the grove and a few faces turned towards him and smiled in greeting. He barely saw them. His glare was fixed on the building. It was fairly large and primitive; a low mud wall and evenly-spaced bamboo poles a few feet higher held up the thatched roof. Men and women crowded within and Goode removed his shoes, leaving them with scores of chappals and bent and entered.

It was cooler inside. The people faced a bearded man dressed simply in a saffron robe. He was bare-chested and the beard reached his waist. His hair was long. A lovely woman with an oval face, dressed in a simple sari and no jewellery, rose and greeted Goode. He knew her name from his informer; it was Sushila. Though her expression remained polite he sensed with that policeman's instinct that she had recognised him. She led him to a vacant space on the dhurry. He sat awkwardly, not expecting this kindness and unsure how to behave. Every face was intent and rapt.

Goode too finally turned to listen to Anil Ray's discourse on the Bhagavad Gita. His voice was soft and musical and there was an aura of calm, almost visible, surrounding his face. Goode studied him carefully. The broken nose was the only recognisable feature. Goode had imagined that he would instantly recognise the face branded in his memory. But it had been years since he had set eyes on him, and he was suddenly uncertain. This Sri Ananda didn't look like that Anil Ray. The beard rose just below dark wise eyes and masked even his mouth. His eyes were not fierce and frightening but luminous and kind. This man was at peace and his smile almost lit the room. Goode felt his compassion.

He scarcely listened, instead focusing on that face. He wanted to meet the eyes and finally they settled on him. He thought he would see recognition, even fear; instead Sri Ananda smiled, almost welcoming him and not breaking off his discourse. Goode held the revolver tightly.

The discourse finally finished at noon. The people around him rose and one by one prostrated themselves at Sri Ananda's feet. He blessed each, and listened to them with gentle understanding. Finally only Goode remained, still seated. Sri Ananda looked at him and smiled and beckoned. Goode rose and walked up to him. He took the revolver out of the bag, drew back the safety catch and pressed the barrel against Sri Ananda's temple. The man didn't flinch or move. Goode might as well have placed a stick against him. Sri Ananda's smile seemed to envelop him, and in that silence he hesitated.

'If you have come here to shoot me, then you must shoot. If that is your duty, then fulfil it and press the trigger.'

'You are Anil Ray, aren't you?'

'I am Sri Ananda. But if you wish me to be Anil Ray, I will be him for your sake. It's important that I be this man for you, isn't it?'

'You talk like him. At least you seem to. I was told you had escaped into Pondicherry and become a sunyassi. I came here to kill you.'

'Who is stopping you?' Sri Ananda chuckled. 'Surely I am not. I see your rage, your hatred, and if killing me releases you from such savage passions, I welcome my death. I will have helped at least one person in my life to escape the evils of our emotions. For me, death is an illusion. For you, death will be release from your pain.'

'Are you Anil Ray, damn you?' Goode's arm ached suddenly, and the revolver seemed unnaturally heavy. He didn't receive any reply, merely the seraphic smile. He felt his finger loosen and the revolver slowly swung down to point at the floor. Tears sprang in his eyes at the frustration. God, I want to kill this man; God, give me the purpose to kill him. I know he's Anil Ray and my life will be empty without his death. It is for this point in time and place that you have kept me alive. Goode looked into the man's eyes, twelve inches away. He saw compassion, then tears sliding slowly down into his beard.

'Why the hell are you crying?'

'Because you have even prayed to God to give you strength. You must do it then.' He put out his hand and helped Goode to lift the revolver. His touch was dry and gentle, almost like a child's. 'I am not afraid and dying is of no importance to me.'

'But you must be afraid,' Goode said in relief. 'You escaped from British India and sought sanctuary here in French India. You know damn well I can't arrest you here.'

'Escape? But I have not left India. You may call her your India or their India. But it's my India. I am still on her soil.'

Goode looked down. The man had pressed the gun against his chest calmly. He held it without shaking. Goode gripped the butt. He thought perhaps they were playing a child's game, and that the weapon wasn't dangerous. He felt drained suddenly, confused by the circles of fate and the futility of this killing. He had expected that only the bullet exploding against Anil Ray's face would free him. But he already felt a release.

'You know who I am, don't you?' he said and looked into Sri Ananda's eyes.

'Yes, Mr Goode. I know who you are.'

'So you are Anil Ray.'

'If that is whom you wish me to be, then I am Anil Ray. See, I do not even deny that. And I must help you.' He pushed his thumb against Goode's finger curled on the trigger. The hammer drew back and Goode, staring deep into Anil Ray's eyes, saw his own face reflected. Strangely, his face, in the curves of those eyes, was whole again. The scars vanished, the jaw straightened and he saw the young man of many years ago who had fallen in love and known the importance of living. He touched his face and felt the texture of his unscarred skin.

He wrenched the gun away from Sri Ananda, and looked around to see people peering in. Their faces were etched with worry and concern. He rose and walked out. They parted for him and he kept walking to the edge of the shade, the gun dangling in his hand. The motor car waiting for him on the road seemed very far away. He looked back, not at the people, but at the hard blue plain of the sea. The narrow fringe of sand was dazzling white and hurt his eyes. He wanted to walk on it and found himself on the edge of the colours, like a small boy balancing on a narrow wall. The heat was cruel but he didn't mind it, and he trudged along. When he looked back he saw only his own footprints, and found he was out of sight of the ashram. Ahead was a fishing village. The sea had the stillness of the earth and he thought that if he stood on tiptoe and peeped over the horizon he would see England. The water caressed his ankles and then his calves and he thought it welcomingly cool. He knew that if he kept walking and walking he could escape India.

# 25

## February–March 1919

Kim saw the Colonel pass within a foot of him in Lahore. Only the glow of the midday sun illuminated the gloomy passageway. Their clothes brushed. The Colonel had been too intent, staring straight ahead of him, to notice the familiar face hidden partly by shadow. Kim heard the silence and the whispers ripple ahead, warning of the Angrezi's approach. The stiff back, the high head, the steely eye invited no familiarity and for an instant Kim didn't recognise him. That distinctive face emerging from the crowd was almost a stranger's.

"He has aged swiftly. His hair is white as are his brows and moustache. I remember them brown and glowing. There were no lines in that powerful face. Now I see the loose skin wrinkling cruelly, gathering itself like a shroud. The eyes are the same, watchful and inpenetrable. He carries himself still as though he moves through his own kingdom and expects our homage. I admit I feel pride in his bravery, his confidence that he can move among us and expect no harm. But those days will soon be past. I also feel a deep well of sadness for him, for he's incapable of seeing we no longer want him among us. He is already the past and receding at increasing speed. Yet he dreams of us as he wants us to be."

Kim allowed him to pass without a greeting. He still had a deep affection for the Colonel and would not easily forget his kindness, but it wasn't the time or place for recognition. The old city was filled with hostility. It pulsed with anger. Kim watched the Colonel fade into the crowd and turned back to Humayun Sait. Humayun and he had played as children on zam-zammah, the great cannon outside the Ajabgher. In those days Kim had been the leader of the young pack that roamed the walled city. He knew the gullis and mohallas like the back of his hand and could pick his way unerringly also over the rooftops. Humayun was his age but respectable now. He worked with his father in the grain business. He had been delighted to see Kim again. Since childhood they had met only once, years earlier when Kim had passed through Lahore on his way south from Kabul. He had told Humayun then that he was a trader and that fabrication was still believed. Humayun's face mirrored his origins in the Asian steppes, remaining Mongol even though his ancestors had swept down through the passes over seven centuries ago. He sat crosslegged at the entrance to his stall, a cubicle not more than eight feet by four, packed with sacks of grain. The smell was pungent and dusty. Kim perched beside him.

'They walk like princes but they're only thieves,' Humayun said with bitterness. They had been discussing their rulers when one had brushed past. The great bitterness had been caused by the Lieutenant Governor of Punjab, Sir Michael O'Dwyer. Humayun was full of complaints. This O'Dwyer had deliberately undermined a bank owned by Harkishen Lal whose Punjab National Bank had followed a policy of only financing indigenous businesses and local manufacturers. The British-owned banks, who encouraged the import of British-made goods, had moved in a consortium with O'Dwyer to cause a run on the Indian-owned bank, and thousands of the Punjabi middle class had lost their savings when the Punjab Bank failed. The Lieutenant Governor was held directly to blame. Now, to add fuel to the fire, came the Rowlatt Acts.

'We must all now combine together and protest against these "black acts",' Kim said. 'Muslim, Hindu, Sikh,

Parsi are all one in the eyes of the Rowlatt Acts. We are Indian; these Acts are made by the British against us. But in our protests, we must always behave peacefully and not allow our anger to erupt into violence. That is all they want to see in us, our violence. It will give them an excuse to use their guns to kill us. So when you and Fazl-i-Husain and Rambhuj Dutt Choudray and others lead the people, you must ensure that you control their rage. It is Gandhi's satyagraha which will save our lives and save us from the British.'

'Ahre, Gandhi! He preaches this peacefulness but it will not get us anything. The Angrezi only understand violence.'

'No. They will only kill us. They want to kill us. You must understand their need to impose their will. I know them too well. It's only our silent and calm protest, the massing of millions, which will check their natural reaction. They have ruled us for too long to believe we can rule ourselves.'

Kim had repeated his message time and again and used all his powers of persuasion now to convince Humayun. As a merchant he was an influential man and close to the Lahore political leadership. Kim had already spoken to the others. He knew it was only his own belief which could sway Humayun's thinking. They talked for a long time, interrupted often by clients and acquaintances who also joined the debate. He noted the heated manner in which everyone spoke. The Rowlatt Acts were taken as a personal insult to each and every one, the reward for many having given their lives in the Great War. They were bitter and felt betrayed.

While Kim addressed the men, Parvati spoke to their women. She did not expect them to become involved in politics overnight. The centuries of suppression were too heavy for them to shrug off. But one day they would have to play a role in the movement. Some did respond to her words. The younger women's eyes lit up with hope and excitement as she spoke to them about freedom, not only for India but for themselves too. An escape from habit, from tradition, from their passive role in life. They too wanted to escape their imposed ignorance. Their minds flickered like candles with the force of her words, leaping to burn brightly then sinking back into apathy. Saraswati learned much about politics even though she was still too young to comprehend. She understood the feeling of excitement in the land they passed through and sensed the anger too in the loud argumentative voices.

They travelled east from Lahore on the Grand Trunk Road. Kim clearly remembered as a boy starting out his adventures on this famous silk route, guiding the old lama Teshoo in search of his sacred river. The road had changed little over the years. When he squinted through the glare he imagined the boy and the lama just ahead, the boy chattering away, filled with excitement and curiosity, the lama listening patiently. He told Saraswati how he had passed this way and the many adventures which had befallen him. She would have to wait some years before he told her of his recruitment as an Imperial agent.

On reaching Amritsar, they went straight to Isaac Newton's shop. His old friend was delighted to see him and scooped Saraswati into his arms. He considered her his granddaughter and spoilt her with sweets and presents. Kim sat quietly, watching Newton playing with Saraswati and Parvati, and caught the frequent glances. Newton had a message for him in private. They waited until Parvati took Saraswati into the back room to put her down to sleep.

'I have a message for you from the Colonel sahib,' Newton said. 'He wishes to meet you.'

'He passed by me in Lahore but was too preoccupied to notice.'

'The Colonel sent his salaams, Kim, and called you his son. And he wants to see you as his son.'

'But . . .?' Kim said. 'I know you too well, old friend. I sense the caution in your voice. There is a "but", isn't there?'

'Yes. The "but" is: be very careful. The Colonel is old

and tired, but there is still danger left in him. He has yet to sheath his claws. I fear for you. I say this against my old master only because my love for you is greater than my duty. May God forgive me. I don't wish to be responsible for your death.'

'But he will not kill me,' Kim said. 'We have known each other for too long.'

'And more's the reason then. You know too much and you have left his service. He will never forgive that disloyalty.'

'But I have not revealed his secrets.'

'Someone has. Four of his agents have been murdered. And like a fool, not knowing this until too late, I told him you were in the Punjab. He suspects you have betrayed him. You do know his agents as you have worked with them in the past.'

'Yes. Now I avoid them. But I have kept a watch on them to see what they do. They will cause trouble, I suspect. For the Colonel knows that by causing the trouble he can control it. He has done that before, in Bombay when I first met you, with Tilak at the Surat Congress, and then in Allahabad when he forced the split. Also in . . .' There were many more instances. When they played the great game together, he would be sent north to infiltrate the tribes and pit one leader against another, a whisper here, a bribe there. He remembered too much. 'Now here in Punjab, I know he waits for the moment to strike. And it must be at his time and place. He wants, like all the Angrezi, to teach us a lesson, as if we were children and should be punished because we won't do what they tell us. He will use his men to bring us to this classroom that he has made for us. He will have spun a trap for us.' Kim leant closer. 'What has he instructed you?'

'To report daily, if necessary by telegram or telephone.'

'Nothing further.'

'No. But there are other of his agents in Amritsar and I don't know them. He no longer confides in me.' He sighed in regret. 'In Bombay I knew everyone. I paid them. Now, I work alone and only out of my loyalty to him personally. When he retires, I too will do the same and turn to my inventions.'

'Can you discover who his agents are here?'

'No,' Newton said. 'I won't betray the Colonel. I have already told you much, Kim. I cannot change as you have. Your change came through the discovery of your true self. Yes, I too am Indian, but all I have is my loyalty to a man I have served nearly all my life. I cannot now go to him and steal his secrets.'

Kim placed his hand over Newton's. 'I am sorry. I should not have asked such a thing of you. Forgive me.'

'You are forgiven easily. I know your concern.'

Through the window, they saw the lights being lit in the Golden Temple. The black patch of water slowly came alive, looking like a piece of the heavens. Down below, in the brown and dusty square, pilgrims jostled and pushed to enter the temple. Cows settled down in their path and they flowed around them; goats scavenged in the rubbish heaps; lanterns cast small pools of light on the passing people. Opposite the main temple entrance stood the telephone exchange. It was a new building and two armed policemen stood on guard.

On the third side of the square rose the enclosed walls of Jallianwallah Bagh. It wasn't much of a garden but a maidan surrounded by houses. No flowers or grass grew in that large irregular-shaped area. One or two trees gave the hard bare earth some shade during the day. There was only one entrance into Jallianwallah Bagh, a narrow passage between two high walls about twenty feet in length and only a few feet wide. Still the Bagh was quite popular. Families escaped the crowded mohallas through that narrow passage to sit out under the evening sky when sometimes, in the summer, a slight breeze would blow in their faces and bring them some relief. Children would gather in the late afternoons to fly their kites or play gilli and dandoo or marbles. Students would come later, while there was still light, to study in quiet. And when the light faded completely would gather with their hookahs and gossip of the day's events. Occasionally, a politician would call his faithful to address them. That barren little open space was all things to all people in the fort area.

'I'll come with you.' Parvati said that night as she lay in his arms.

'No. Stay here with Saraswati. I'll return.'

'Kim, he means to harm you.'

'Why should he? I have done him no harm.'

'You are still a little boy in your innocence. You will remember him for ever for his acts of kindness and not look beyond to see his manipulation of your life.'

'What he did was meant for my own good. But I am aware also that he saw in me a perfect instrument for his purpose.'

'And he needs you more now than ever before. You are still the perfect instrument. You have the confidence not only of Gandhi but of all the people we have met. You know their names, their faces, their thoughts. That is what he needs to gain control and hold onto power. He will try his best to persuade you and if you are not persuaded, he will kill you. He won't ever let go of you Kim. He loves you, yes, and like a lover he is jealous of India. Jealous and angry that she has wooed and won you from him.'

'I can't refuse him his request. I can't forget my own affection for him. He was the closest I ever had to a father, and for that alone I must see him.'

'Then why does he choose Humayun's tomb as a meeting place? Pah,' he felt her shudder. 'Like the Taj Mahal at night it will be desolate and lonely. He means to harm you, Kim. Otherwise, the meeting would be in the day, in his office.'

'We cannot meet there. It will be equally dangerous if I am seen in his company by others. We always met in secret places when I worked for him.'

Kim left at dawn. Parvati clung to him as long as she could. She had spent a sleepless night and her eyes were swollen from weeping. Her tears brought out the tears in Saraswati and mother and daughter both looked miserable. Newton was worried. Despite his scientific bent, he couldn't suppress the superstitious feeling that this could be the last time he would see Kim. Only Kim was cheerful. He laughed at their concern and looked forward to the journey down the Grand Trunk Road to Delhi. He didn't fear the Colonel but promised to heed their advice and move cautiously.

It was on his second day out of Amritsar that he saw a strange sight ahead of him and instinctively knew what caused it. About a mile away, the sky grew dark with birds as they flew from all directions to circle and alight, while high overhead Jatayu circled endlessly, swooping lower and lower until his shadow rippled across five wheat fields, then rising with one beat of his wings. There was no breeze. The air was stilled and waiting and as Kim drew nearer it seemed to become cooler. The earth vibrated as if an army approached, yet there was no dust cloud. Soon he heard the sweet, clear voices of his old companions, Bala and Bala. He hurried now and saw that a crowd had gathered and sat in a quiet circle around the brothers. Their faces were turned to the sky and it seemed the sun itself settled a gentle glow on their blind faces. They had grown thin and tall, their faces looked firmer despite their blindness. Both had grown soft beards of exactly the same length. Their voices had not lost their magic ability to enter the mind and body. He could feel their songs humming through his blood and beating in tune with his heart. Time was meaningless. Their voices suspended it. Hours passed like seconds and he forgot his own existence. He was enveloped in a pale gold light that sprang from the centre of his mind. Bala and Bala stopped singing at nightfall, and a great sigh rose from the crowd. There was a long stillness and then the birds, remembering their own ways, filled the air with the beating of wings as they rose into the dark. People laughed and wept in wonder at the power of Bala and Bala to purify them.

Kim pushed his way through the crowds and bent to touch their dusty feet. Even without turning their heads in his direction, they knew who it was and laughed in pleasure and embraced him. They spent the night talking, for it had been many years since they had seen each other. They told him of all their adventures and he in turn regaled them with his. They planned to soon pass through Amritsar on their journey to the western edge of India before they turned north and then moved east. Kim left them at dawn, promising to meet them again in Amritsar.

Kim reached the outer wall of Humayun's tomb an hour before the arranged time. The nearest he had ever been before was passing by on the train. He hadn't realised how huge it was. It rose like a carved cliff honeycombed with doors, jalis and windows, dwarfing its surroundings. A half-moon barely silvered the marble dome. It seemed afloat as the red sandstone walls remained in shadow. He scaled the outer wall and landed softly inside the garden and remained crouched for a long while, allowing his eyes to adjust to the peculiar light. Where the tomb's shadow fell, the night was dark and impenetrable. Otherwise, the garden and the tomb seemed deserted. All he could hear was a sly rustle in the undergrowth and the insistent hum of cicadas. They had faltered at his sudden appearance but soon settled back into their constant rhythm. A mongoose slipped swiftly through a patch of moonlight, peering nervously at him; a bandicoot scuttled into a flower bed; and overhead in the trees a monkey gently scolded. Apart from the skirt of trees bordering the wall, the great garden was too open and offered no cover, except for rose bushes and marble benches along the long central fountain. He rose, hesitated, and then moved cautiously along the trees towards the tomb.

"Why do I hesitate? I laughed at Parvati's fear but now I prowl around this open garden, like a tiger round a tied goat. I have met him alone before and in secret places where none saw us. But this time I am not that obedient and loyal Kim he fashioned out of the boy. We meet as possible enemies. He summoned me here to woo me back. If he succeeds, I am once more valuable. My mind is filled with different secrets, ones he needs. If he fails, those same secrets will be dangerous to him. I would see proof that he failed. If he cannot hold me what chance has he to hold India?"

He saw a swaying lantern and heard the tapping of a stick. A chowkidar made his rounds in a desultory fashion and returned to his hut behind the tomb. Kim doubted he would stir again that night. The long narrow channel in front of the tomb was silvered. He settled himself in the tomb's shadow from where he could see the whole garden and the entrance and not be seen. He had no idea of time and only guessed it was nine o'clock when he caught the lights of a car brushing the wall and trees. It stopped outside the main archway and a few moments later the Colonel sahib entered. He walked briskly and confidently to the centre of the garden, caring to look neither left nor right, and sat on a marble bench. It seemed the most natural thing for a man to do in this lost and lonely place. He didn't even glance at the great tomb towering over him and blocking out half the night sky. Once he looked at his watch and then stared straight ahead. Kim wondered what he thought and somehow knew that the Colonel was aware of his presence in the garden. It wouldn't have been intuition. He had trained Kim: always get there first and scout the terrain. And he waited now with patience for Kim to show himself. Kim stood and scanned the garden. It remained empty and silent. He heard only cicadas and lizards, the hum of the night. There was no other movement.

Kim committed himself to the moonlight. He felt vulnerable for a moment, then moved quickly towards the Colonel. Whatever was planned would happen only after their meeting. The Colonel faced away and didn't notice him at first, but when Kim was still some distance away, those sharp ears heard his footsteps and he turned. That was his only movement and Kim felt the sharp, well-trained eyes studying him. They flicked away behind and then returned when he saw Kim was alone. He rose only when Kim stopped a few feet from him and waited.

"I am always surprised by the man," the Colonel thought. "I expect to see the cheeky boy, for he is the one most firmly fixed in my imagination. I wish Kim were still that boy. The boy was unquestioning; the man always questions. He won't accept his fate. I gave him a destiny, his true one as an Englishman, believing his mind, his logic, ruled him. And I was wrong. His heart betrayed me. How can I change, not his mind, but his heart? Like me, he loves India. I must persuade him of our common interest."

'Colonel sahib,' Kim said with respect.

'Kim. You're looking well. Come and sit down.' He sat and patted the marble bench.

'You too look well, Colonel sahib,' Kim sat on the cold stone. 'It has been many years since we have seen each other. We think we don't change but it's only when time has passed that we notice the changes in each other.'

The Colonel suddenly chuckled. 'We're behaving like strangers when we've known each other so many, many years, Kim. I have missed you a great deal. Seeing you always gave me great pleasure.'

'Colonel sahib, I too have missed your guidance and love,' Kim said. 'I will never forget what you have done for me.'

'I only discovered your true identity, that you are an Englishman. Or I should say you were an English boy. You can't ever forget that either. You are English. Your father died for the the Crown, Kim. He was a good and loyal soldier.'

'But he didn't die in battle, Colonel sahib. He died in an opium den and abandoned me to India. I learned of this from the ayah who raised me as her only son. Yes, I am English. And because you wanted my loyalty as an English boy, you made sure I would always be

English. Yet, you never wanted me to escape India, my Indianness. I was too useful to you to be entirely converted to my new identity.'

'Of course you were useful. I won't deny I saw an ideal agent in you. You are clever, a friend of all the world, and can go without fear anywhere in India, as an Indian. I saw all those advantages and observed the affection you stirred in all those who came in contact with you. Ah, Kim how I always envied the way you could move through India unseen. When I walk through a bazaar today, a silence falls like a dark black shadow. You can pass that same way, and never hear that wounding silence.' The Colonel sighed loudly and deliberately. 'But that is all in the past. We enjoyed the great game together, did we not?'

'Yes. We worked well together.' He waited, content to allow the Colonel to talk. Suddenly, the cicadas fell silent and then started again, loud as ever. Kim scanned the perimeter of the garden where the silence had fallen. Still nothing moved. 'But, as I mentioned in my letter of resignation, you have played the great game now within my country and I can no longer be a part of it.'

'Yes, I received your letter with regret. I wish we'd had a talk first. You are impulsive at times, a sentimental person. There are people in India who only work to destroy her. They are the ones who murder innocent men and women with their guns and bombs. I'm aware India is changing and one day, with our help, the people will rule themselves. It is the same India you love that I serve with every fibre of me. It is that India I fight to save. Do you believe in the senseless killings that take place?'

'No.'

'Do you believe, then, in those politicians who stir up trouble between one community and another for their own gain?'

'No,' Kim said. 'Often they are encouraged and abetted by you, Colonel sahib. Many times, when serving you, I helped instigate such discord on the frontier. By keeping men at each other's throats, you made sure they had no time to combine and fight the British. You divide people for your own purpose and not for India's good.'

'India's good and our good are one and the same,' the Colonel said sharply. 'We both love this land.' His eyes fixed on Kim's. He wanted Kim to believe in his sincerity. 'I will never ever ask you to do anything which will harm India's aspirations.'

'It's our beliefs that have diverged. Once I believed as you do, and with the same passion. But no longer can I believe that a foreigner's good and our good are one and the same. Colonel sahib, because of the nature of your office and the power of your people, you will always put your own interests above ours. Men whom you believe are bad for India, I will believe are good. The things we aspire to will be those you will deny. You will never give up India until you are forced to leave, by us.'

'Indians cannot . . .'

'I have heard that said often, by the Angrezi. We cannot rule ourselves. We are useless, we are foolish, we are children. And we believe these lies because we hear them often. One day we will believe in ourselves and rule India without your guidance.'

'And how long will you maintain the illusion, Kim?' the Colonel asked. 'You are not Indian. Once they discover that, you will be distrusted by them. They will always think that one day you will betray them because of your blood. But that day is a very, very long way away. The reality of our lives, Kim, the hard truth, is that we, the British, will rule India for ever. You are one of us and will never be distrusted by us.'

'But I cannot live like an Englishman in India, Colonel sahib. This is only a prison you have fashioned for yourselves. Maybe one day they will distrust me but I will have to give cause for that. I am Indian. I have an Indian wife and child.'

'I heard about the child,' the Colonel said. 'And the woman. I hope one day I'll be able to meet her.'

'Yes, one day,' Kim agreed and fell silent. He heard the chill in the Colonel's voice.

The Colonel sighed again. 'So you won't return to service?'

'It is too late.'

'I suppose it is. I had hoped . . .' And he didn't finish. He was disappointed and regretful. But Kim was no longer any use to him. He rose and put out his hand. 'Goodbye, Kim.'

Kim held the dry, strong hand a moment longer than necessary and released it. The Colonel turned away abruptly and set off along the fountain to the gate.

Kim didn't hesitate. He slid off the bench and dropped to the ground. War had taught him excessive caution and for a moment he thought himself foolish. And yet he had reacted only because he knew he couldn't trust the Colonel any longer. He would not let such a failure live. Kim poked his head above the bench. The Colonel walked easily, not looking back. Kim rolled over, rose to a crouch and sprinted to the next bench. He heard only his own panting breath. He was mistaken. There was no trap. The moon was higher and, apart from the benches, there was no hiding from the baleful glare until the distant trees.

He started, then jumped back. The bullet whined a foot ahead of him and sent marble chips flying. He heard the shot a second later. It came from the trees to the left of the gate. Kim sprinted to the next bench. The rifle sounded like a .303 and it took a couple of seconds to eject the shell and load. He looked back. The Colonel hadn't paused; he hadn't even looked back to see if the bullet had found its mark. He was finished with Kim.

The sniper was good. He would be aiming in between the next benches. To turn back would only fool him for a second and he would know Kim would have to cover open ground. There was too much of it, even to run and dodge. Kim wanted shorter odds. He rolled over and slid down into the channel. The water was lukewarm and wasn't more than a foot deep but gave him cover from the sniper. Another bullet hit the water. He'd been seen. He had to keep his head down as he moved towards the tomb. Two more bullets plopped ahead of him. His back itched and tensed, awaiting the impact. He reached the far end of the channel. The tomb, aloof and chilly, rose above him like a liner. It offered no cover, and Kim calculated he had fifty yards to cover to the trees.

When he moved, he would have to be swift and sudden. He only had two choices, left or right. Which one would the sniper choose to aim for? Left was farther, right was nearer. Even those vital seconds he took to change his mind would save Kim. He gathered himself, rose suddenly, running even before clearing the water. Right. Right. He wove like a snake. He covered ten yards and the bullet plucked at the ground. Another ten feet and it smacked into the plinth. Like a swimmer now, he dived for the shadow, rolling over and over, and slid into a bush.

# 26

## April 1919

The silence and heat were oppressive. They pressed down on Alice like stones on her chest, hurtful and suffocating. The heat especially was magnified by the black burka enclosing her from head to toe and she made a move to lift the veil to gulp in air. Parvati stopped her.

'If they see you are European, they will kill you,' she whispered. 'They have already killed the European bank manager and a lady missionary. You are always in danger now. You shouldn't have come to Amritsar.'

'I had to see what was happening.'

Alice felt afraid, looking down from the rooftop at the vast crowd. It filled Aitchison Park, flowed past the walls of the old fort and spilled into Hall Bazaar. As far as she could see, men were pressed together in an ominous silence. She barely heard a murmur. Like a beast, she thought, that had woken suddenly, frozen for the attack. It was going to attack. She knew that from the very stillness of the multitude. She sensed that this was the beginning of the end. The stubborn defiance of the ordinary man would bring down British rule. Here were not politicians and revolutionaries, but common people gathering themselves. And Kim was somewhere in that crowd. He and Grehwal and Balbir Singh and Isaac Newton had been in front. In the glare the faces were a blur, hypnotic, as if she were staring into every one of those countless eyes. She forced herself to look away. From other rooftops silent women looked down on their menfolk.

'It's the end for us,' she said. 'There's no going back. Things will only get worse. This mass of people will frighten the authorities and they will be looking for an excuse to open fire.'

Kim, too, knew that the thin line of soldiers and police would fire. He saw the fear in their taut faces as they knelt and waited. Even a single shot would provoke violence but for the British it was the only resort. They had set in motion the chain of events that had brought about this confrontation. The only way for a reconciliation, he knew, was for the government to withdraw the Rowlatt Acts. But they wouldn't, couldn't. Retreat would undermine their authority. He wondered whether the Acts, which had become law on March 18th, had been deliberate. Mr Gandhi had dubbed them 'the black acts' and condemned them. He said they were, 'unjust, subversive of the principles of liberty and justice, and destructive of the elementary rights of an individual on which the safety of India as a whole and the state itself is based.. We solemnly affirm that in the event of these Bills becoming law and until they are withdrawn, we shall refuse to obey these laws and such laws as we may think fit, and we affirm that in the struggle we will faithfully follow truth and refrain from violence to life, person and property.'

Gandhi had then called for a campaign of satyagraha against the 'black acts' throughout India. And that call was the signal for the opposing forces to march towards each other. Kim was no longer in the middle, he had committed himself to one side against the other. And, like Arjuna in the Mahabharata, when he looked across he saw men of his own blood in the opposing camp. Having committed himself to India, it was his duty now to fight to the end. Blood would flow; men would die in this battle. He knew, and suspected that the astute Mr Gandhi too was aware, that once the call for satyagraha had gone out, it would be impossible to control the people. A crowd of 100,000 would always be as volatile as gelignite. There would be agents provocateurs among them, ready to ignite the violence and give those soldiers and policemen the excuse to open fire. Already in Delhi and Lahore the police had fired and killed half a dozen people. The mood in the Punjab especially was bitter since the end of the war and the Rowlatt Acts had only increased the distrust of the people for the government. A satyagraha, though meant to be peaceful and non-violent, would only gather the forces together and unleash destruction.

Kim was partially responsible for this huge gathering. He, with two Congress members, Satyapal and Kitchlew, had worked hard to organise this satyagraha. They had gathered in Aitchison Park to lead a peaceful procession to Government House to protest against the Rowlatt Acts. With him were Bala and Bala and Nadir Shah. The brothers had come to attend the Hindu festival of Ram Naumi, and the old magician Nadir Shah and his son Salim to entertain the festival crowd. They had been caught up in the fervour of the protest and were somewhere in the vast crowd.

Suddenly, to his right, he saw an arm raised and a brick flew over their heads and bounced beneath Deputy Commissioner Irving's horse. It skittered aside. The armed men tensed.

'No,' Kim shouted. 'We are to be peaceful. No one must throw any more stones.'

But even as he called out, other stones began to fly through the air and the silence was broken by an inarticulate and enraged growl. Irving retreated; the soldiers and policemen fell back a dozen steps. The officials conferred in a tight group, dodging the missiles which fell far short of them. The crowd began to surge forward, pushing past the leaders trying to control them. And then, out of panic and fear, the English soldiers of the Royal Sussex Regiment suddenly fired, though no warning was given or even the order to fire. The shots sounded puny, Kim thought. Three men fell and the crowd stopped.

'You must disperse,' Irving shouted. 'Please return to your homes. We don't wish to harm any of you, but you are breaking the law.'

'We only wish to protest against the Rowlatt Acts peacefully,' Satyapal shouted back.

'I cannot give you permission to cross the railway line behind me.'

The crowd should have fled with the killings but it remained still and watchful, as if waiting for the moment of weakness. Satyapal turned and appealed to the people to disperse and quietly they began to ebb away, a flood slowly seeping back into the mohallas and gullis of the old city. The policemen moved forward as if it were their doing and Kim glimpsed the three dead men lying in the dusty road as he was pushed back.

He returned to Newton's home and stood on the rooftop with Alice and Parvati watching the dispersion. It seemed now as if nothing had occurred, except that silence prevailed. The bodies had been removed.

'We must get you out of here,' Kim said. 'It will be impossible to protect you any longer. I'll escort you to the European cantonment where you might be safer. But it would be wisest to leave Amritsar.'

'I can't. I am a journalist, Kim,' Alice said. 'I have to stay. Surely you and Kitchlew and Satyapal can control them?'

'Not any more. The firing will have provoked them further. They've dispersed but only for a while. It's not a matter of whether we can control them. There will be men out there who want this violence to discredit Mr Gandhi's call for a peaceful and non-violent protest. And turning a peaceful protest violent will give the British an excuse to punish us. The time is coming soon for the lesson they've been promising us for our disobedience.'

'I'm sure they won't do anything drastic.'

'I don't know what they will do. But since '57, they've been waiting. It has haunted them, poisoned their minds against us and they've never escaped those memories. They want us to get angry, they want us to fight them, because they have been waiting all these years to kill us again. And these Rowlatt Acts are their way of expressing their contempt for us as a people, knowing it will enrage us. We will only have to wait and see. But the first move that will tell us their intention is if they arrest the leaders, Gandhi, Satyapal, Kitchlew, me and the others. If they arrest us, there will be no one to control the people and they will run wild with the goondas and agents provocateurs.' Kim paused. 'I learnt all this from the Colonel sahib. Divide and rule, divide and control events.'

Alice sensed Kim's hostility. It wasn't directed at her but she was enveloped in it, as she was trapped in this burka that hid her so effectively from the crowd. She couldn't blame him and yet she did. She wanted to tell him she wasn't one of them, she was for the Indian, but she knew it was too late. By her very colouring, she belonged to the opposite army. It was at this moment she envied Kim. With such ease he belonged, and she wished she could too. He had chosen; she had been given no choice, but instead had been judged and excluded from this movement. She looked over the city. In the glare it seemed a mirage and she thought first that she imagined fire and smoke. And then she knew it was real. A fire was raging just beyond the walls. Kim saw it too and watched it tiredly, knowing that already the crowds had begun rampaging, burning and looting, that the call for peaceful protest had turned ugly with violence.

It was a bloody dawn. The sky seemed wounded and rent, and the summer heat already made the men flinch. The room turned warm even before dawn had faded and in the silence they heard only the crows and squirrels in the garden. There were five men around the table. Their faces were drawn and their eyes reddened from another sleepless night. Deputy Commissioner Irving was flanked by the military commander for Amritsar, Captain Massey, Police Superintendent Rehill, Deputy

Superintendent Plomer and Colonel Sir John Creighton. Only the Colonel looked refreshed and alert. He sat straight, vigorous, eager to fulfil his duty. A bearer brought in tea and the men slumped back, smoking and staring ahead of them unseeing. Looking out through the verandah at the policemen lined up in the garden, the Colonel thought of a different time and place when men such as he had gathered to deal with a crisis.

'A strange thought has entered my mind,' the Colonel spoke quietly, to no one in particular and the men didn't seem to hear. 'We who sit here, planning to deal with this violence, can't be so very different from those who had to deal with the Mutiny. They were, admittedly, caught by surprise and didn't believe the Indian could turn so savage and violent. But history has warned us and haunted us all these years and we aren't going to be caught unprepared. Unlike '57, when the men who led prevaricated and delayed, we must act swiftly and decisively. Otherwise, what happens here will reverberate right through India. If this crowd can get away with defying us and killing and looting, a thousand crowds in other cities will do the same. And it will be impossible to control India ever again. We might as well leave.'

His voice faded, the silence returned. A cup clattered against a saucer. He wondered whether they had heard him and whether their thoughts too turned back to '57 and the horrors. Rehill's and Irving's would. Irving's china-blue eyes turned to him briefly. He looked unkempt and his blunt face was creased with concern. He was the senior civilian in charge and unless he declared the situation unmanageable, the military commander could not take over. Captain Massey was too young. He may have studied history but India and Indians were unknown to him. The Colonel ignored Plomer, the deputy. A peon carried in a buff-coloured telegram and handed it to the Colonel. He read it and slid it across to Irving.

'GANDHI ARRESTED AT BORDER,' it read, and was signed Sir Michael O'Dwyer, Lieutenant Governor, Punjab.

'Was that wise?' Irving asked. 'He could have calmed the crowd.'

'Irving, it boils down to who is going to control this city and, on a larger scale, the country. Maybe Gandhi could cool down the mobs but that will only give him the power he seeks. It will prove to him and to the people that he is in charge, not us. I think you should also arrest Kitchlew, Satyapal and the other ringleaders.'

'I have summoned them to meet me here at ten o'clock.' He looked expectantly at the Colonel, flinching at the unblinking stare. He turned to Rehill and Plomer. 'Have a truck waiting. And the moment they arrive, place them all under arrest and take them out of the city. Do it quickly and discreetly.'

'But the people are going to riot when they hear we've arrested them,' Rehill said.

'They'll do it anyway.' The Colonel opened his file and drew out a cheaply printed news-sheet. 'My agents found this. It's called the *Danda Akbhar*, and it's distributed all over Amritsar, the district and even as far away as Lahore. I'll read it out: "O Hindu, Mohammedan and Sikh brothers, enlist at once in the Danda army and fight with bravery against the English monkeys. God will grant us victory. Conquer the English monkeys with bravery. Leave off dealing with Englishmen. Close offices and workshops. Fight on. This is the command of Mahatma Gandhi."' The Colonel paused. 'Mahatma means great soul. They have already elevated him to sainthood. My agents also tell me the peasants are responding to this call and are planning to invade the city.'

'But Gandhi called for a satyagraha, not a bloody war.' Rehill found the face opposite him unmoved. Briefly he wondered who could have used this opportunity to call for violence in Mr Gandhi's name, but the thought flitted out as other worries pressed down on him. 'Oh, my God,' Rehill's voice was almost a moan. The Colonel expected him to wring his hands at any moment. He did entwine his fingers tightly and the Colonel felt no sympathy. It was the burden of office and the man was breaking up under the strain. 'Maybe I should call Sir Michael O'Dwyer for advice.'

'He's got enough on his plate up in Lahore. The mob's taken control of the old city.' He stopped and lit a cheroot. 'Besides, the telephone wires have been cut. God knows how long it'll be before the telegraph wires will also be cut. We are alone.'

The 'alone' tightened the faces around him. Rehill looked to Captain Massey. He merely shook his head once. He just didn't have enough troops under his command to control the city. Rehill knew that but he hoped that miraculously the 250 men would have multiplied.

Precisely at ten, much to the Colonel's surprise, Satyapal and Kitchlew strolled through the gates, accompanied by a few of their followers. He peered from the window. There was no sign of Kim or Grehwal or Balbir Singh. Damn Kim, damn him. He had found him and created him and shaped him and loved him. And his reward was Kim's betrayal and treachery. Kim had no right to do what he was doing now. He had to destroy Kim; he couldn't allow him to live. And yet, when he had heard the first rifle shot in the garden, his heart had leapt in agony. He couldn't turn; he didn't want to see a man he loved dead, and he kept walking. At first he had experienced relief and pride that Kim had escaped the sniper. But that was brief. Kim was his shadow, his creation, and he knew Kim was dangerous as long as he lived.

Outside, a truck backed up and the police swarmed around Satyapal and Kitchlew. Irving spoke to them briefly in the mêlée. Even now we obey the law, the Colonel thought; Irving is informing the scoundrels that they are under arrest. The followers protested and shouted slogans but the police drove them out of the compound and the Colonel knew it wouldn't be long before the whole city knew the two leaders had been arrested.

At noon, the quiet didn't unsettle Alice. She walked quickly, and alone, along Hall Bazaar. She no longer wore the burka; it had been too suffocating, too cowardly. Instead she wore the salwar kamiz, the Punjabi women's costume of a loose shirt with pi-jamas and a light scarf over her face and head. Where once there had been a huge throng, the gullis were now deserted, and she thought the crisis was over. The shops were shuttered, though. She reached the zenana hospital and asked an ayah for her friend Miss Easdon, the doctor memsahib. She found Betty on the rooftop looking out across the city. Betty was a thin, worn woman, a spinster who had dedicated her life to the hospital. She was distracted, but relieved to see Alice.

'You shouldn't have come.'

'Oh dear, everybody keeps warning me about the terrible things that will happen to me. A dear friend escorted me to the cantonment and ordered me to stay there. But no one will tell me anything. I had to come and see you and find out what was happening in the city.'

'Everything,' Betty said and gestured hopelessly. Smoke and flames rose now in three other places. 'I don't understand why Irving hasn't ordered all the Europeans out of the city. We aren't safe here. What should we do?'

'Stay put until this tamasha is over. They never last long.'

'No. I think we should leave, Alice. Come on.'

Then they both froze. They heard the distant murmur turn to a hum, then to a roar. 'Angrezi . . . mar . . . Angrezi . . . mar . . .' They peered down and saw the mob coming down the gulli. No one seemed to be leading them and the men in front carried lathis. The men behind struck out at the confining space, tearing at the shutters and looting the shops, throwing food and clothing and pots and pans into the dirt. Neither Alice nor Betty could move. The violence of the mob reverberated through them and they knew that if they should be seen, they would be torn apart.

Alice dragged Betty from the edge. 'We must hide. They'll pass by but just in case they see us . . .'

There was a small cupboard under the stairs, filled with brooms and dusters and the two women squeezed into the narrow space and shut the door behind them. The blackness was suffocating and claustrophobic. Alice clung grimly to the latch to prevent anyone opening it.

'What'll we do?' Betty began crying.

'Sshh, they mustn't hear us. Quiet.'

The silence seemed to stretch on for ever and Alice began to think they were being foolish, when she heard the clatter of chappals on the stone floors. The voices were indistinguishable at first, but then she heard the men talking to one another.

'The ayah said the two European women were here.'

'We've searched but we can't find them.'

'We will. Then we will kill the Europeans. "Butcher them all" is the order. Try the roof.'

Men ran up and then came down again. Alice strained to hold the door. A man tested it and walked away. 'They must have escaped when they saw us coming. Let's go on. We will find other European monkeys.'

Alice slowly released her breath. Her fingers hurt from holding the latch and she let go, flexing them. She began to push the door open, when she heard the ayah: 'They are still in the building, you fools. They haven't gone past me.'

'Help me with the door,' Alice whispered. Betty took a firm grip as well and they pressed back together, squeezed into the black hole and prayed the door wouldn't give way. Someone tugged at it on the other side, stopped and pulled again.

'This is locked,' a man said. 'We're wasting time here. Let's go.'

The silence was unbearable. Alice imagined the men crouched outside, waiting for them to step out. They didn't move hand or foot but held the latch, knowing it was their only salvation. Minutes passed, then hours and they remained locked in, not even whispering. Their throats were parched and the heat grew intense. They could smell the fear on their bodies. Their sweat was rancid and bitter.

To distract her mind, Alice tried composing the story she would send to the *New York Herald Tribune*. 'These events began sixty-two years ago and, trapped in another Black Hole, though of smaller dimensions, I cannot but feel that history is repeating itself. But with a difference, the difference being that this time the British have deliberately provoked the Indians into revolt by introducing the Rowlatt Acts. The Acts are an iniquitous reminder to the Indian that he is ruled by foreigners and that if he should raise his head or voice in protest, he will be gaoled . . .'

Suddenly they heard solitary footsteps climb the stairs, return, fade down the corridor. Just when they began to sigh with relief, the footsteps came back and paused outside the cupboard. There was a gentle tap on the door. They tightened their grip and Alice thought how deceptive such softness could be. They would open the door and find the mob waiting for them. The tap was repeated.

'Alice,' a man whispered. His mouth was against the door. 'It's me. Kim.'

The women released the door handle and stumbled out. Kim crouched in the dusk and placed his fingers to his lips. The air smelt sweet and fresh and they took great gulps. The whole building was silent. Alice felt herself trembling and couldn't control it. She and Betty began to cry in relief, as a release from their fear.

'Put these on quickly.' Kim handed them burkas.

'How did you know we were here?'

'A nurse told me. She persuaded the crowd to leave. Then I heard the crowd was looking for two Angrezi women. At first I didn't know it was you. We mustn't waste time.'

They followed him out into the gulli. Once again they were surprised by the silence. It was even more ghostly when they thought of the murderous chaos of a few hours earlier. The silence lingered like a warning that it could shatter any moment. They flitted through the deepening shadows and Alice was relieved once she stepped through the portals of Hall Gate and out of the old city. She never wanted to return, knowing now she would always be afraid. This fear dismayed her. All these years she'd never been afraid and now she would flinch each time she saw a crowd.

'What's happening elsewhere?'

'The crowd's out of control. They are being led by thugs, men we've never seen before. They murdered the bank manager, Mr Thomson, and have attacked a lady missionary. She's badly wounded. And they also killed Mr Stewart and Mr Scott of the National Bank.' He sounded exhausted. 'By arresting Kitchlew and Satyapal, the government let loose the mobs.'

It was a long walk to the Gobind Garh Fort and they scarcely saw a soul. Whenever a man was seen, Kim pushed them into the deepest shadow and they waited until the man had passed. The fort stood on a slight rise, overlooking Amritsar. It was a dark, foreboding building with massive granite walls. Kim led them up to the gate. A British soldier stared down at them, aiming his rifle. 'Show yourselves quickly.'

Alice and Betty took off their burkas and the soldier lowered his rifle and shouted down for the men to open the gate.

'You will be careful, won't you, Kim?'

'I have little to fear from my own people, Miss Soames,' Kim said. 'I only fear what your people will now do to us.'

In his recurring dream Kim looked beyond his dead companions and saw high brick walls, a well and a narrow passageway. Three trees shaded the dying and the dead, the sky was a blank blue and the silence so complete he thought himself deaf. He could not hear the guns which continued firing, nor the screams, and he knew this was because he dreamt it all.

He woke, sweating, his heart beating as though he had

run a long distance. There was a clear night sky overhead. He swept the heavens, horizon to horizon, and this visual sense of permanence and inevitability calmed him. He knew it changed, shifted, danced, but in men's vision it appeared to remain the same forever. He smiled at this self-delusion, this need to believe in immortality. He glanced down. To his immediate right Parvati and Saraswati shared a charpoi and slept peacefully. And to his left, further away on the roof, Newton snored gently. Kim rose from his charpoi quietly and walked to the edge of the rooftop and looked across Amritsar. Nearly every rooftop was occupied by sleeping people escaping the dreadful indoor heat. The air, even at this time of night, was hot and still.

But this sleep was another illusion. It gave Amritsar a false sense of tranquillity and calm. Kim sensed the mood even in the collective dreams of the people. Their sleep wasn't disturbed by the heat but by their collective anger. He felt the eddies of rage and disillusion, of betrayal and deception, in the night air. They ebbed and flowed, rising with the sleeping murmurs. Below, a police picket moved cautiously down the gulli. The officer had his revolver in hand, the four constables held their rifles at the ready. They passed by, their whispers floating up to him. They were afraid of the city.

'What is it?' Parvati whispered. She had woken with the intuition of a lover, and joined him.

'I dreamed again. It becomes clearer and clearer each time.'

Parvati moved closer to Kim and shivered. She hated his dreams; they filled her with foreboding, returning time and again like a ghost to haunt them. Even though he hadn't told her, she knew she too lived in his dream. He couldn't separate her from him in this illusion and she wondered whether somewhere ahead of them, soon, the reality and illusion would become one, joining together and ending.

They stared out at the city in silence, holding tightly to each other. Parvati knew other thoughts troubled Kim too. He was still shaken by the Colonel's attempt on his life. He had not wanted to believe the Colonel would make such a bold attempt to kill him. He remained bewildered and uncomprehending. The man he loved as his father had deliberately set a trap and walked away, leaving him at the mercy of a sniper, knowing and hoping Kim would be killed. He hadn't even looked back at the first shot and Kim still brooded over what would have happened if he'd not rolled off the bench. If he had died, would the Colonel have returned to his body, or let it lie in the open to be thrown on the rubbish heap? Their relationship had never been a simple one of controller and agent. Their belief, their dependence on each other, had flowed deeper into love. Parvati hated the Colonel even more now for having hurt Kim so deeply. She knew that when he stared in such silence he was going over the events of his life, his intertwining with the Colonel and pondering how love had been destroyed with the sound of a bullet.

'What do you think they'll do now?' Parvati asked.

'They've already done it. I hear Irving has declared the situation unmanageable and has handed the city over to the military commander. The army is now in charge. And they've ordered a General Dyer to administer martial law.'

The Colonel felt as if the waiting would soon be over. He let his breath out in a gust, wanting to sense the tranquillity of an Indian dawn. He could tell from the stillness and the blueness of the sky it would be another white-hot day. Beyond the fort, the city awaited the unfolding of events. It was deceptively quiet and still and yet he sensed that, like a serpent, it was coiling itself in the gullis and mohallas to strike. He looked down into the fort. All the Europeans had been herded into it and, despite the adversity and overcrowding, seemed to be cheerful. He was proud of them. With a start he remembered it was a Sunday. Was it an omen? In '57 the Mutiny had begun on a Sunday when all the Europeans were in church. Since then, it had been compulsory for soldiers to bear arms in church.

General Dyer mounted the stone steps and the Colonel watched him approach. The Colonel had summoned Dyer from Jullunder. He was the most senior army officer within driving distance of Amritsar. He looked a real soldier, stiff and straight, with a strong determined face. It was good to have a man like him in charge, an old India hand who was aware of history as something alive, not as a fairytale in a storybook. They shook hands and both turned to survey the city.

'It's in your hands,' the Colonel said carefully. 'And you must act swiftly, even harshly, to bring law and order.'

'We still haven't got enough men, Colonel,' Dyer said. 'Twelve hundred in all, including cooks. A city eats men and to scatter my forces will be to weaken them. We must remain concentrated in order to strike hard.' He plucked at his lower lip. 'If only they would gather in one place, stay there until we could hit them . . .'

'They won't,' the Colonel said. 'So don't expect a miracle. But I think you should put on a show of strength.'

'I'm going to go out there myself today.' He drew a sheet of paper from his pocket and handed it to the Colonel. 'I'm hoping this will do the trick.'

The Colonel read:

> It is hereby proclaimed to all whom it may concern, that no person residing in the city is permitted or allowed to leave the city in his own private or hired conveyance, or on foot, without a pass from one of the following officers . . . [The Colonel saw his own name and scored it out.]
>
> No person residing in Amritsar city is permitted to leave his house after 8 p.m. Any persons found in the streets after 8 p.m. are liable to be shot. No procession of any kind is permitted to parade the streets in the city or any part of the city or outside of it at any time. Any such processions or gatherings of four men will

be looked upon and treated as an unlawful assembly and dispersed by force of arms if necessary.

'Excellent,' the Colonel said, returning the proclamation. Dyer looked pleased.

'General Beynon, the Divisional Commander, told me to take any action fit to control the situation. We'll see whether this will cool tempers. I'm going to read it personally around the city this morning.'

A small speck appeared in the sky and moved slowly to Amritsar. Soon they heard the roar of the aeroplane and watched it circling the city for fifteen minutes before turning back the way it had come.

'I should get the pilot's report within the hour. And I'll be well prepared.'

They watched the troops assemble below. The men consisted of 125 British soldiers of the 2/6th Royal Sussex and 310 Indians from the 1/9th Gurkhas and the 1/12th Baluchis. Dyer also had two armoured cars. At the head of the small force waited Dyer's horse and a bullock cart carrying a large drum.

'Well, wish me luck.'

They shook hands firmly, as men should at such a moment, saying little else. The Colonel remained on the ramparts while Dyer inspected his troops. Crowded around the edge of the square the other Europeans stood, silent and hopeful. The gates swung open and Dyer rode out at the head of his pathetically small force. The Europeans below crowded up the steps to line the ramparts and watch the procession make its way into the city's maze.

It was getting too hot and the Colonel wished he were still a young man. He would have accompanied Dyer, ridden behind him. But he was too old for such things and he cursed the infirmity of age. He turned away and his face drained of all colour when he saw Alice. She stood not more than a yard from him, watching the procession. The lines of her youthful beauty had been blurred and, in the harsh sunlight, she looked strangely ghostlike. Beneath the layer of age and wrinkles he saw the faint outline of Elizabeth.

Alice felt her husband's startled stare. She had the advantage. She knew he was in the fort, closeted with Dyer and Irving. She remained watching Dyer and his men slowly disappear from view. Finally, she turned away.

'Hello, Jack.'

It was her voice that shook him. It hadn't changed. It was still throaty, with that underlayer of humour as though she were laughing at him. Thirty years ago when he'd first seen her under the banyan tree it was her voice that had attracted him. Now, he felt a hatred. 'Jack'. The last woman who had used that familiarity had been Sushila and he never wanted to be reminded of her again.

'I never knew you to be surprised or tongue-tied, Jack.'

'I'm not. I should have known you'd be here, poking your damned nose into this business. The press aren't supposed to be in this province. How did you get in?'

'By pulling strings. And why don't you want us here? So you can carry out another underhand act which can't be seen by the world.'

'You flatter yourself that the world is interested in this affair.' He felt his anger burst. 'It's people like you who are to blame. You and your support of Indians. You encourage them to commit sedition, to revolt, to burn and loot and murder innocent people. If you people didn't interfere, India wouldn't be at the brink of this bloody revolt and we wouldn't have to call in the army. You put ideas into their heads. They were content and happy before people like you fed them your lies.'

'You believe they're children, and want them to remain like children. You can't hold back change; you can't bring back the past. You've managed to fabricate this crisis through imposing the Rowlatt Acts. Of course they're going to revolt if you suppress them, treat them as if they're backward and helpless. You want to go on ruling here for ever. There won't be a for ever; it's already over.

And you'll be the one responsible for destroying their trust.'

Alice felt like slapping him in front of everyone. She knew he would never see sense, him or the others, old and hardened to their vision of India and Indians. Either they had to have their way or they would wreak havoc on these recalcitrant children. Their imaginations had all been narrowed by power and memories. She stared him in the eyes, knowing few could face their chilling rage. The pouches were deep as wells; she knew he had calculated every move and that there was nothing she could do except watch helplessly. He remained in power.

'Destroying trust?' The Colonel seemed shocked. 'But I love India. My whole life has been dedicated to her. It's just that they don't understand that we know what's best for them. This . . . rioting and revolt . . . will pass and things will be the same again. I know they will. They have to be.'

He turned on his heel and marched down. Alice watched him moving stiffly through the people until he vanished into the inviting shade. She wanted to cry and now that he wasn't here to see her, she allowed some tears to course down her cheeks. He was wrong. Nothing would ever be the same.

# 27

## April 13th 1919

Kim heard the drum beat and General Dyer read out the proclamation in Hindustani. That was followed by a translation into Punjabi, the local language. It was stifling in the small room, and in the silence Dyer's voice was clear and authoritative. Kim rose to peep out at the procession; a crowd had gathered and when Dyer moved on, it followed. A chokra hit a tin can in imitation and a man mockingly repeated the proclamation.

'What shall we do?' Balbir Singh asked.

'Hold our meeting,' Kim said. 'We must continue with our plans. By remaining peaceful and non-violent, we can persuade others that we can achieve our ends without rioting and killing.'

Isaac Newton looked worried. His thin face gathered in a frown and he pushed at his spectacles as if trying to place a finger on his worry.

'But we heard the General sahib just now. They will shoot.'

'Why should we listen to the Angrezi?' Kim said. 'They order us to do this, then do that. We will hold our meeting, but it will be a peaceful one. Women and children too will attend and their presence will confirm our intentions. But it is important we regain control of our people. The goondas and provocateurs have taken over. They are the ones responsible for inciting the crowds to loot and murder. Our intent will be to protest the "black acts". We must continue to speak out against them.'

'To hell with the British,' Vancouver Singh made it sound like a slogan. He basked in a murmur of approval, except for Kim's steady stare which made him uneasy. He didn't like Kim; it seemed Kim had read his secret and knew he was an informer. He didn't like his own position. He yearned to return to Vancouver, to escape this heat, the constant intrigues, the danger of discovery. He would have escaped but that chuthia Goode, having promised him the steamer ticket, then drowned himself in the sea. 'Accidental death', said the newspaper report.

'At what time?' Grehwal asked.

'Four thirty, when it will be cooler,' Durga Das, a Congress man said. 'And we will hold it in Jallianwallah Bagh.'

Newton waited for the others to leave and went to sit beside Kim. He put his hand on Kim's and gripped it tightly.

'You should not be doing this, my dear friend,' Newton said. 'This will enrage the Angrezis, and they will pour damnation down on all our heads.'

'But we cannot retreat now. To bow to their authority is to for ever believe ourselves less than they. Yes, I am afraid too, but I must overcome this fear and do my duty. And you should not be among us.'

Newton sighed. 'I should not be in many places and I should not hear many things. But life has cursed me with such a talent for problems. I am here; I have heard. I will report to the Colonel sahib, but late this evening. That will give you time to hold the meeting and escape.'

'Thank you,' Kim said.

'Naturally, as an agent, I too will have to attend.' And they both laughed.

Half an hour later, the Colonel sahib knew that a gathering would take place in Jallianwallah Bagh at four thirty. Vancouver Singh waited for his reward and accepted the handful of silver rupees grudgingly. It was still not enough to get him out of the country and he was too afraid of this Colonel sahib to bargain as he had with Goode. When he'd left, the Colonel brooded.

He knew it to be true. Another agent had also told him of the meeting and Vancouver Singh had only confirmed it. The Colonel's eyes fixed on the wall, his mouth tightened. The colour of his face deepened. Kim again, defiant and disobedient. He was one of them, taunting the government. Taunting him. They were breaking the law, defying the proclamation. If there was no terrible and frightening retribution, the people all over the country would laugh at the government. They'd know it was helpless, gutless, impotent.

He rose abruptly. His frame trembled with anger and he swayed with the force of it. He paused, and controlled himself. The sandy square was a furnace of dust and sand and he was thankful for the shade of Dyer's room. Dyer lay on the bed, gasping for air. He looked worn and tired. The march through the city in the heat had exhausted him and his men. Dyer had meant to read the proclamation many more times around the city but had had to retreat from the heat.

'They are gathering,' the Colonel said at once. 'I've heard there will be a meeting in Jallianwallah Bagh at four thirty.'

'The Lord hath delivered them into my hands,' Dyer said and sat up. His exhaustion drained off; his eyes were alight. 'I couldn't have devised a better way to trap them. They are where I wish them to be – within reach of my sword.' He lifted his eyes to the mottled ceiling. 'Lord, I thank you for this miracle.'

It wasn't much cooler at four thirty, except that the shade of the buildings and the trees now stretched over the dusty maidan. There was a large festive crowd, men, women and children, pushing and jostling through the narrow entrance into the bagh. Chai-wallahs and metai-wallahs drifted among them, selling tea and sweetmeats, and did a good business, for the shops were all still shut.

Kim and Parvati, holding Saraswati's hands between them, drifted along with the crowd. When they entered the bagh, they looked for familiar faces and found Newton, Bala and Bala, Grehwal, Balbir and Nadir

Shah pressed together in the shade. They made room for them. Kim settled Saraswati on his lap and looked around. Bala and Bala had never attended a political meeting before and listened carefully to the speakers, their blind faces cocked at exactly the same angle. Nadir Shah and Salim had done well at the religious festival the previous day and were resting before continuing north. They planned to travel to Lahore and then to Rawalpindi before returning to Delhi in the autumn. The speakers addressing the crowd repeated themselves and the drone of their voices, although the import of their words contained passion and anger, was lulling. Kim was to be the sixth speaker at the rally.

As he looked around him, he began to tremble. He had seen this place before, many times, although this was the first time he had ever set foot in it. This was the place in his dreams. He recognised the walls and the trees and there, in the far corner, was the low wall of a well. Nearby was the round dome-shaped samadhi, the burial place of a holy man. He felt a shock and then fear, not for himself but for Parvati and Saraswati and his friends.

'You must leave here at once,' Kim whispered to Parvati. Her eyes widened in surprise. 'This is the place of my dreams. There will be killing here. Hurry. Take Saraswati, flee quickly. Tell the others.'

'And you? I can't leave without you.'

'It is my destiny and there will be no escape.'

But even as he spoke, Kim saw movement at the narrow entrance to the bagh. He half-rose to look over the heads of those in front of him and glimpsed the khaki uniforms of soldiers. None was English. They were men of the 1/9th Gurkhas, the 54th Sikhs Frontier Force and the 59th Rifles Frontier Force.

'Please stay calm,' Durga Das motioned the crowd to sit down again. 'We are not threatening them. We will not incite them to violence.'

Kim picked up Saraswati and handed her quickly to Parvati.

'It's too late. Go and hide behind that samadhi. Quickly. Run.'

'No,' Parvati said. 'I won't leave you now.'

'For her sake then,' Kim said and pushed Parvati away. At the entrance he saw Dyer stalk into the bagh and deploy his troops into a thin line to the left and right of the entrance. And behind the general, he saw the Colonel sahib. He stood straight and stiff, clutching his walking stick, watching the scene dispassionately.

Parvati threw her arms around Kim, weeping, and he struggled to disengage them and push her away from him. He wanted to scream out in urgency but couldn't panic the people around. Some were standing now, watching the soldiers, while others had begun to drift to the walls and the samadhi.

'You must come with us,' and she began to drag him with her. Kim couldn't free himself from her fierce grip. Her strength rose from fear and panic.

The soldiers knelt at a command from Dyer and aimed at the crowds. People began to run now but the bagh was a giant box. The walls were too high to scale and the only way out was the narrow passageway behind the General.

Kim saw Bala and Bala stand up. Their faces were turned to the soldiers and they remained calmly watching them, like children seeing a new curiosity. Suddenly, he realised that with the powers granted to them by Lord Krishna they knew what was to happen, and now calmly accepted the inevitability of their fate. He remembered the prophecy of that boon which had protected them on their travels all these years: whoever harmed them would incur the wrath of Brahma and the man who killed them, his family and the kingdom to which he belonged, would all be destroyed.

The first bullet caught Bala of the ravanhatta in the chest and his frail body flew backwards in the air. And as it fell, a piercing and frightening scream rose out of his brother's mouth as he felt the terrible agony. He knelt by his dead brother and began to sing but, alone, he no longer possessed the divine power. His voice broke and changed into a hoarse chant and Kim watched his life drain away even as his brother's blood seeped into the dust. Then, slowly, untouched, he toppled over his brother. They were dead and Kim knew that the prophecy would be fulfilled: this empire would fall.

He scooped up Saraswati and holding Parvati's hand pushed and fought his way through the frightened crowd. He had to hide them behind the samadhi, hide them from the murderous fire. He saw men struggling to climb a wall, and General Dyer directed his troops to fire at the men and women bunched against it. The bullets cut through them like a knife, scattering them.

Newton materialised on the other side of Saraswati and lifted her off her feet, trying to protect her with his thin, frail body. He managed to struggle a few yards before a bullet caught him full in the back of the head. Saraswati screamed as he stumbled, fell and rolled over her. Kim grabbed her up and pressed his palm against Newton's face in farewell. He could barely see for tears and the dust that rose from the milling people. He saw Nadir Shah fall and Salim immediately threw himself down to cradle his father and hold him and protect him against the feet of others.

They were near the samadhi. Not far from it was the old well and people began leaping into it without any thought. It was deep and stagnant, and Kim knew they were jumping in to their certain death.

Kim suddenly felt an excruciating pain in his side. It was as if someone had thrust a live coal against his flesh. He wanted to cry out and clenched his teeth. He had to save Parvati and Saraswati and if he fell, he knew they would stop. He pushed them ahead of him, using his body to shield his daughter.

But then, unbelievably, he saw her hurled forward onto her face. Parvati pulled her, screaming 'get up, get up' but the child limply dragged her feet. He snatched her up and his side blazed and he screamed in pain but in the roar of the gun fire, none heard his scream. Her head lolled uselessly over his arm and he buried his face in that frail, small body.

He felt Parvati tugging at him, calling him to come with her. His feet felt leaden and gave way under him. He freed a hand and stretched out and felt Parvati's grip.

'Ram, Ram, Ram . . .' he whispered and tasted the dust as his face pressed into the earth.

'Kim . . . Kim . . .' were the last words he heard and the last feeling was Parvati's lips against his cheek.

It was night when the Colonel entered the bagh again, accompanied by two soldiers carrying lanterns. The air was putrid with the stench of cordite and blood, one bitter, the other sweet and sickly. The night was noisy with the buzz of greedy flies. The dead lay still; the wounded flopped and twisted and called out to him. They moaned for help, they called for water. He carefully stepped past them, shining the lantern on their faces, and moved on. He stopped when he saw Newton, his spectacles askew on his face. He knew he wouldn't have to look very far now. He stepped over the bodies of two women holding each other, and the pool of pale light fell on Kim's face. His hand was stretched out, holding onto a woman's. His native woman. Between them lay a child. The Colonel knelt and freed the woman's grip. He felt her pulse; there was a faint beat. She would live. Kim was dead. The soldiers carried him out of the bagh. He could not let an Englishman be discovered lying among the natives.

As the sun rose, a soldier carried the flame and lit the crude funeral pyre. The Colonel stood away, watching the wood smoke, the flame crackle and spread. The fire was white and he could barely see the flames in the morning light. The air remained still and hot and he felt the intense heat even at this distance. Tears trickled down the Colonel's cheeks as the flames began to consume the body of the man he had loved more dearly than any other person. His life, his dreams, his love had been invested in that boy. And now he felt a part of himself going up in smoke.

He sensed a shadow pass over his head and looked up, startled at the sight of a huge eagle. It glided effortlessly in circles around the pyre and the Colonel thought he'd never seen so terrifying a sight before. The soldiers ran away from its shadow and even the Colonel stepped back and back as it flew lower and lower. It seemed as if it descended to bid farewell to the body on the pyre. It called once and its keening sent a shiver through his body.

Then, with one beat of its wings it rose, and the wind carried Kim's ashes and mingled them with the dust of India.

# 28

# July 1919

Alice was determined not to look back at India. She chose to stand in the bows and stared down at the hull parting the blue waters. She wept at parting with the land she had loved and knew she could never ever return to it, not without being stained with the guilt and shame of what her people had done at Jallianwallah Bagh. Like the Mutiny, this massacre too would haunt them. But there would be no forever. She knew British rule was over; trust had been shattered, and no Indian could look on an Englishman again without revulsion. The ending would take a few more years, and it would only be bickering and anger; then the flag would be lowered for the last time. This was their last victory in India.

"They will all follow me one day," she thought, "although they believe that Dyer's killings have saved India for them to rule for another hundred years. He is being proclaimed a hero in England and by the British in India. They don't realise he has destroyed love and loyalty, and no king can rule without them. Three hundred and seventy nine men, women and children have been brutally murdered and fifteen hundred wounded. Monstrous, monstrous," Alice cried out. "How can we ask for forgiveness? How can we claim to be just and wise and human with such a stain on our souls? God forgive us."

The Colonel was pleased with his sanctuary. It was exactly as he'd imagined it, a small bungalow, on the rise of a hill. He had a bedroom and a sitting-room and his study. All his books and papers were crammed in the study, and his roll-top desk overflowed with papers except for a single empty space where the Emperor Jahangir's poems lay. He had waited all these years to translate them and knew the work would take the last few years of his life. He would be remembered for this scholarly work of love. And when he raised his head from his task, he could look through the window at the Himalayas. On some days they looked so near that he felt he could stroll down to the bottom of the garden and touch them. They looked serene and magnificent and at night when the wind blew down from those high icy peaks, he felt himself soothed and calmed by the whispers he heard.

Another window opened out on to the valley of flowers and in the distance he could see the nearest village, a clump of whitewashed huts. The air was drowsy and scented and he stared out at the valley, dreaming of the past, when he saw a jutka moving along the narrow dusty road. He idly watched it draw nearer, the pony coming at a walk up the slope. The pony wore a proud black plume and the jutka was gaudily painted, a vibrant scrap of colour in the landscape. He expected it to pass by, but instead it halted at the gate. For a minute no one climbed out and the driver sat waiting placidly.

Finally, a woman stepped down. She was slim and straight and wore a kashmiri shawl over her shoulders. Her sari was pure white, without even a border and he instinctively knew she was a widow. She stood at the gate, staring at the bungalow, then opened the gate and came up the path. The Colonel waited for his bearer, Abdul, to announce her. He was not curious; probably the woman was lost, someone enquiring the way. He bent his head to his work and only looked around when he heard Abdul's bare feet shuffle slowly across the stone floor. The door opened and Abdul stepped aside to allow the woman to enter. Reluctantly, the Colonel carefully put down his pen and rose. He bowed formally. The woman's hands were folded under her shawl. She stared at him with such intensity that he recoiled a step, backing into the desk.

'Can I help you?'

'Colonel Creighton?'

'Yes.'

'I am Parvati,' the woman said.

Her hands emerged from beneath the shawl. They held a revolver. She lifted it very calmly and the Colonel watched mesmerised as it reached the level of his chest. She fired, and he stumbled back onto the desk, spilling his blood on the precious book of poems. Another bullet hit him, even as he tried to save them from such dreadful desecration. His dying eye saw the woman come close and slowly fill his vision. He felt the muzzle pressed against his temple.

Parvati fired again, then turned and walked away.

# Glossary

| | |
|---|---|
| Acha hai? | Are you well? |
| Ahre bhai | a greeting |
| Angrezi | British |
| Arrack | fermented coconut water |
| Arthi | Hindu ritual in worship |
| Ashram | a retreat |
| Avatar | incarnation of a god |
| | |
| Babu | clerk; also British derogatory for Hindus |
| Badmash | scoundrel |
| Bagh | garden |
| Bandh | a political action to shut down a city |
| Beedi | rolled tobacco leaf cigarette |
| Bhajan | congregational religious singing |
| Bhakta | disciple of Lord Krishna |
| Bhang | marijuana |
| Bharti | British land grant for soldiers |
| Burka | shapeless garment covering a Muslim woman |
| | |
| Chaatri | a monument |
| Chai | tea |
| Channa masala | spicy whole peas |
| Chappal | slippers |
| Chaprassi | a servant |
| Cheetal | type of deer |

| | |
|---|---|
| Chettiar | a caste |
| Chokra | an urchin |
| Chota | small |
| Chowk | a market |
| Chowkidar | watchman |
| Chuthia | an obscenity |
| Crore | ten million |
| | |
| Dacoit | bandit |
| Dak bungalow | government resthouse, orig. mail stop |
| Darwaza | door |
| Dastur | percentage kick back |
| Dharma | one's duty |
| Dharshan | to bless |
| Dhoti | kind of sarong worn by men |
| Diwan | a prince's prime minister |
| Dubash | British company's translator |
| Dubba | cheap wayside restaurant |
| Durbar | reception, a court |
| | |
| Fakir | a mendicant |
| | |
| Gadi | throne |
| Gharri | horse drawn carriage |
| Gilli and dandoo | child's game |
| Gold mohur | red flowering tree |
| Goonda | a street tough |
| Gopuram | carved tower over Hindu temple |
| Granth | holy book of the Sikhs |
| Gulli | lane |
| Gurudwar | Sikh temple |
| | |
| Haram | Muslim wives and concubines; women's living quarters |
| Hathphool | elaborate interconnected finger rings |
| Homam | fire in religious rites |
| Howdah | canopied seat on elephant's back |
| | |
| Iyer | term of respect |
| Izat | Honour |

| | |
|---|---|
| Jagir | Mughal land grant |
| Jahaz Mahal | walls of building curved to resemble ship's sides |
| Jali | screen |
| Jat | north Indian community |
| Jawan | Indian army private |
| Jezail | ancient musket |
| Jiba | loose shirt |
| Jutka | covered pony-drawn cart |
| | |
| Kala pani | black water |
| Karma | man's concept of fate |
| Kathak | south Indian dance form |
| Khadi | hand-woven cloth |
| Khanasama | cook |
| Kos | unit of distance |
| Kutcha | shoddy |
| | |
| Lakh | one hundred thousand |
| Langur | sort of monkey |
| Lathi | staff, stick |
| | |
| Mahout | elephant driver |
| Maidan | open space in a town |
| Mali | gardener |
| Mantra | sacred formula addressed to deity |
| Marwari | north Indian community from Marwar |
| Mohallas | community residential areas |
| Moksha | spiritual liberation |
| | |
| Namaskaar | verbal greeting of respect |
| Namaste | pressing of palms together |
| | |
| Paan | betel leaf |
| Panchayat | elected village council |
| Pani | water |
| Peg | drink |
| Pice | small coin |
| Prohit | brahmin priest |

| | |
|---|---|
| Puja | prayers with offerings |
| Pukka | perfect |
| Pundit | a learned man/teacher |
| Punkah | hand pulled fan |
| | |
| Rakshashas | demons |
| Ravanhatta | a stringed instrument |
| | |
| Sadhu | wandering ascetic |
| Salwar kamiz | north Indian women's costume |
| Samadhi | bliss, perfection |
| Samosa | pastry containing spicy meat or vegetable |
| Sarapa | elaborately decorated Mughal cloak |
| Sardar | a Sikh |
| Sar panch | head man of a Panchayat |
| Satyagraha | non-violent political protest |
| Serai | wayside inn |
| Seth | village trader/money lender |
| Shamiyana | a tent |
| Sher | tiger |
| Shikar | hunting |
| Slokas | poems from the Vedas |
| Sunyassi | wandering ascetic |
| Swaraj | freedom |
| Syce | horse groom |
| | |
| Tamasha | a show |
| Tapas | special prayer |
| Tashildar | government revenue collecter |
| Thali | gold chain worn by Hindu married woman |
| Thanedar | sub-inspector of police |
| Tonga | carriage or cart |
| | |
| Yali | demon |
| | |
| Zamindar | large land owner, step below Rajah |
| Zenana | women's quarters |